D1713171

SCAPEGOAT

SCAPEGOAT

A Mystery

POUL ØRUM

Translated from the Danish
by Kenneth Barclay

PANTHEON BOOKS

A DIVISION OF RANDOM HOUSE

NEW YORK

First American Edition

English translation Copyright © 1975 by
Victor Gollancz, Ltd.

Library of Congress Cataloging in Publication Data

Ørum, Poul.
  Scapegoat.
  Translation of *Syndebuk*.
  1. Title.
PZ4.0766Sc3 [PT8176.25.E7] 839.8'1'374 75-4964
ISBN 0-394-49055-X

1

"WHERE ARE YOU going?"

"I'm going to buy an American folding-spade," said Detective-Inspector Jonas Morck, taking off his slippers in the hallway and putting on his shoes. His wife could see him through the kitchen door as she stood at the sink peeling potatoes.

"A what?" she asked.

"A folding-spade."

"What's that? A spade you can fold up, or something?"

"Yes. I've just seen an ad for them in the American surplus stores on Osterbro. Exactly what I want. At only fifteen kroner, it's at least worth having a look at."

"What's it for?"

"For digging gun-positions, I suppose. But I'd be using it for digging up worms. It'd be handy—better than lugging a shovel all the way down to the beach."

"I don't understand how you can do it," said his wife—meaning "put worms on a hook". "I could never bring myself to touch the creatures."

"Why, what have you got against them?"

"Oh, stop it, Jonas."

When they spent holidays at their house by the North Sea—and they would be there some time the following afternoon—he did some small-scale line-fishing. Wading out at low tide, he would stretch a line between two poles and to this single line attach a few hooks. On the hooks he'd put the sandworms he had dug up. Occasionally he caught a flounder or two. Only once had his wife watched him checking his hooks. She had continued on her way after due expressions of disgust. This, of course, didn't stop her eating his catch with gusto.

"I've been used to baiting hooks ever since I was a boy," said Morck.

"Yes, and that's the only excuse you can offer," she said, coming out of the kitchen. She watched him tying his shoelaces.

"We're not going to eat right away, are we?" he asked. "I won't be much more than half an hour."

"I know your 'not-much-more-thans'," she replied. "We'll eat at six-thirty."

"What are we having?"

"Salad and caramelled potatoes, despite what they say in the paper."

"What who says?"

"These culinary people, whatever they call themselves."

"Gourmets?"

"Yes. It's just a load of nonsense. I read it in the paper just after I'd been out for a pound of these small button potatoes. Caramelled potatoes, according to that gourmet, are an abomination, a piece of culinary barbarism. So I'm afraid we're a couple of barbarians."

"Sure we are," said Morck, pulling on his parka. "But presumably the man is an expert; so he ought to know."

"I don't know who they think they are. Not wanting people to exercise their own taste. Anyway, it's your favourite dish. But I couldn't get those smoked sausages you like to go with it. The butcher suggested a piece of cured loin of pork but I was feeling too mean, so I just bought a pound of mince for rissoles. Jonas, you're not listening!"

"Yes, I am. Rissoles, did you say? That'll be fine." Morck zipped up his parka, and patted his back pocket to see if he had his wallet with him. "Well, I'll just go over and———"

"And buy your folding-spade." She dried her hands on her apron, took hold of the front of his parka, and snuggled up to him.

"You're at the seaside already, aren't you? Sometimes I wonder how you manage to get your work done if you pay as little attention there as you do at home."

"I pay even less, sometimes. But that's because I'm thinking about you, Marie."

"Oh, then you're forgiven." She let go of him, and he kissed her.

6

"Looking forward to the sea?" he asked.

"Yes, it'll be nice," she said, "having you all to myself for eight whole days."

He went out; and when she had finished peeling the potatoes and mixing the mince for the rissoles she went up to the bedroom and packed the rest of their things in the suitcase. There couldn't be anything to stop them getting away now—or could there? Surely not at this hour: it must have been almost five-thirty, and it was third time lucky. Twice before their winter holiday had been postponed because of a case cropping up somewhere or other—a case the flying squad could not supply the manpower for, if Jonas and Einarsen were to have the leave they had been entitled to for so long. Each time the cancellation had come at the last minute, and, though it had happened so many times before, the disappointment always made her tired and depressed. If only people would stop killing each other every second day! Things never used to be as bad as this before, did they? Never so many murders and other serious crimes. Or if only they'd make sure more manpower was transferred to the flying squad so that people could lead a more reasonable life. Still, it was always the same story—not just the flying squad, but every department of the force was suffering from a severe shortage of staff. Jonas had dug out his sandals and put them on the floor by the chair on which the open suitcase lay. What was he thinking about? That he was going to the seaside pretending it was summer? Marie packed his thick-soled shoes as well. They were much more sensible for taking long walks along the beach on cold, windy days. Instead of a winter holiday they were having a spring one.

She put the last few things in the case and checked over the contents. What was missing, apart from their toilet things, which would not go in till early next morning? Nothing. She stood up and listened intently.

"No, you will *not* answer it," she said aloud. Downstairs in the living-room the phone was ringing. It would be them, of course. If she didn't pick up the phone, they might think they were already on their way, and so leave it at that. But surely she knew better? She might as well.

She hurried downstairs; but the telephone had stopped ringing before she reached it. Should she disconnect it? Even if she did, they could easily be intercepted by a phone call on the ferry boat, as had happened once before.

7

Of course, it wasn't necessarily them on the phone. In fact, it wasn't necessarily anybody. It could be a wrong number. But if it was them, they would certainly make a point of ringing again; and as she stood in the kitchen frying the rissoles, she waited nervously for the phone to ring.

At six-fifteen she went in to lay the table. There was the sound of footsteps on the pavement outside and she looked out of the window: only the engineer from next door coming home.

The evening sun shone on the red roof of the house next door and, if it hadn't been for the distant background noise of cars revving up in Great King Street, you could have imagined you were in a quiet country retreat. She glanced at the street name fixed to the yellow-washed wall opposite. "You can hardly call that a street," she had said to Jonas when he had come home many years ago and said a miracle had happened. At last he had found them a flat—no, a whole house of their own. But in Crocodile Street. How could any-one have hit upon a name like that?

"Christian the Fourth. He was an inventive man on the whole."

"Do you think . . .?"

"Yes," he'd said. "The street was built for his personal staff."

"Miracle" was no exaggeration. They had lived in a cramped, leaky, two-roomed flat in Norrebro, the only one they could lay hands on when they had moved to Copenhagen from the provinces. It was on the fifth floor and had a solid fuel stove. Fifteen or sixteen years had passed since they had moved from there to this peaceful village in the middle of the capital. Yes, time went by. It was nearly six-thirty.

Might as well get going with my culinary barbarism, she thought. She was just about to put the pan on the burner when she heard him coming in.

"Well, did you manage to buy your——?"

She fell silent in the middle of the question, noticing the expression on his face as he stood in the hallway—the tight-shut mouth a little crooked, and the nose appearing more prominent than usual.

"Jonas? What's wrong?"

He didn't reply immediately, but stood staring as if it wasn't Marie at all he was looking at.

"Swine," he said, and went into the living-room. She followed.

"Jonas. What's wrong?"

"You should have seen them."

8

"Seen who?"

"My worthy colleagues laying about a lot of defenceless people."

"What had they done?"

"They were demonstrating—at least some of them were. The others were chance passers-by who found themselves trapped between two lines of policemen; and that was sufficient reason, of course, for ill-treating them and knocking them unconscious. Most were demonstrators. They had been indulging in the unheard-of impertinence of demonstrating against the Vietnam war in front of the American Embassy on Dag Hammerskolds Allé. That's what they were doing."

He was calmer now, yet spoke with subdued fury.

"What's going on in this country? How can it happen in a country like ours? You should have seen them go at it, both the riot police and the men on the beat. And then there was a bunch of police cadets for good measure. Damn me if they didn't take full advantage of a bit of field experience to show off their talents to the full."

"Jonas, you must be exaggerating."

"Not in the least. I'm seldom one to exaggerate."

"Oh, do calm down," she said. "It won't do any good getting worked up. How about a beer to bring you round?"

"A beer!" he exclaimed, with that sudden, short laugh she was a little frightened of. She felt as if she were the butt of his fury. Going through to the kitchen, she brought them each a beer.

"There was one gold-top left for you."

"A gold-top for a white man," he said, laughing again, but this time happily, in another and gentler way. "Thanks, Marie."

Then he told her all about it.

He had taken their favourite detour to Osterbro, the one they had taken the previous evening, through Oster Park where the flowering shrubs were in bloom, golden-boughed forsythia and red ribes. Silent families of ducks were floating on the dark mirror of the evening water, as the last rays of the sun shot through the trees. He had emerged on Dag Hammerskolds Allé at the height of the commotion. Police in their hundreds had gone into action and were hacking their way into thousands of demonstrators. The police forces had formed a wedge to split the demonstration into two groups in front of the Embassy. They had then split themselves into two chains to drive the demonstrators back towards either end of the Allé. Behind the backs of the two police chains, extra police waded in wielding batons and lashing out with their feet at anyone caught in no-man's land with no chance of escape.

"They beat everyone up as if they had been looking forward to it for a long time. People were lying unconscious in the street. One man was crawling away on all fours, his head bleeding, when a policeman came up and kicked him in the side while a second hit him with his club. When at length he lay still, they hit him a couple of times more. Marie, it's true, damn it. At one point I saw four policemen dangling a man in the air."

"Dangling?"

"Yes, two held his arms, two others his legs, while a fifth battered him with his club."

"But why?"

"Don't ask me. Blood-lust, suppressed aggression—what can one call it? Of course, people knew only too well what to call it. Nazi pigs, they were shouting. Fascists!"

"Did you get mixed up in it, Jonas?"

"No, I'm afraid I kept discreetly in the background and contented myself with being a passive spectator."

"Should you have done anything?"

"No, nothing. They were my colleagues, after all."

"Drink up your beer."

He nodded and took a mouthful of the beer.

"Do you remember Sergeant Olsson?"

"The one you were at police college with in Aalborg? Yes; when you were on patrol together, you used to slip home sometimes for coffee."

"Yes, strictly against the rules but 'not tae worry', as they say up there. Yes, it was him all right. While people were running away from the baton charges, a heavily pregnant woman was trying to protect herself and her unborn child in a bus shelter. Naturally she feared for her safety with all these panic-stricken people about and she said so when approached by the policeman. But he couldn't make allowances like that—that's no business of ours in the police force. So he grabbed her and twisted her arm behind her back . . ."

"No!"

"He did, and said, 'Just get out of it'. 'But can't you see I'm pregnant,' she replied. 'I said, Get out of it', my old pal Olsson insisted. The lady was a journalist into the bargain, and with her one free hand she took a press card out of her pocket, showed him it and said she was entitled to be there anyway. 'Piss off with your bloody press card,' he said, dragging her away still twisting her arm. As they came towards me, I saw who it was—'Olsson,' I said, 'let the lady go; she has a legal right to be here.' 'Clear out; we'll decide for ourselves what's legal around here.' He had already raised his club before he recognized me. The lady was moaning. It's a painful thing to have one's arm twisted up between one's shoulders. 'Oh, it's you, Morck,' he said. 'Haven't seen you for years.' His face was all ablaze with excitement. 'What the hell are you doing here, getting mixed up in all this? You're not a dirty red, are you?' "

"What answer did you give, Jonas?"

"I just told him to let her go, which he did with a violent push from behind which made her stagger across the pavement towards me. She would have fallen if I hadn't caught her."

"So you managed to get her out of the way."

"Yes, and myself as well. It wasn't the kind of thing I wanted to get involved in. I'm not a dirty red after all, am I? So I came home. And they'll still be at it down there at this very moment . . ."

He finished his beer, and she pushed her bottle across to him, untouched. They sat in silence for some minutes, and there was silence too outside in the cobbled street between the low yellow-washed walls. People would be eating their evening meal. There was only a distant growl of traffic from Great King Street and from the junction of Gronningen and Hammerskolds Allé two minutes away—where they would still be at it.

"Almost unbelievable, isn't it?" she said. "And here we are sitting here in comfort."

"When people read about it in the paper tomorrow they'll tell themselves it's a pack of lies. And they'll not believe otherwise. Old pal Olsson certainly knew what he was talking about. His orders about the disposal of the press card will have been carried out to the letter—they bloody well will——"

The telephone was on the window sill between them. They sat watching it as it rang, then looked at each other.

"That's the second time," she said. "I was upstairs and I waited till it stopped before I came down."

"Cunning little schemer—do you think that makes any difference?"

"No, they'll get hold of you—if it is them."

"They certainly will," he said, lifting the receiver. "Morck here . . . yes . . . Oh hullo, Einarsen. You don't mean that . . ."

"Yes, he does mean it," she said, getting up and removing the bottles and her glass. "That's done it."

But they would still have to eat. She went into the kitchen to brown the potatoes.

"In Esbjerg division?" she overheard him asking.

He would be going by himself to that part of the world. She would not go with him. Well, he could just go off to West Jutland alone and hum his silly little tune she'd heard him humming that morning in the bathroom. It had been running through her head ever since, and now she could hear it again in the sizzling of the fat in the frying pan.

"Now you're being unfair," she said to herself. "After all, he can't help it."

The conversation had finished and he appeared at the kitchen door.

"Leave cancelled? Yes, of course it is," she said, noticing how unnecessarily severe she sounded—which was not at all her intention.

"Yes, we'll just have to postpone our holiday."

"As usual."

"I'm sorry, Marie."

"You can't help it," she said, still sounding brusque, though, in fact, he couldn't. Here they were, looking forward to a break and at the last minute . . . He hung around in the kitchen doorway, looking at her in a faintly helpless way. At times like these, a childish, guilty look would come over him.

"They're just taking advantage of you," she said.

"Yes, that's what they are doing. It's the same for all of us. Einarsen is due for a holiday too."

"Sure it's the same. But I'm thinking about *us*."

"Do you know what we could do? Go and buy a bottle of wine."

"To celebrate?"

"To soften the blow, rather. What do you say, Marie?"

"Very well."

He went over and put his arms round her and said, "You're not going to cry are you?"

"No, I'm used to it by now. It's just that I'm never really prepared for the worst at the time."

"Yes," he said. "I'll ring the grocer in Gerners Street about that bottle."

"But it's after closing time. A policeman can't very well break the licensing laws."

"I wouldn't dream of it," he said. "We're not like that in the force. The police don't break the law—all we do is bend it with discretion."

He went through to phone the grocer in Gerners Street.

"You know that bottle of red wine I bought this afternoon and forgot to take with me?" he said.

"You forgot it, did you?" the grocer replied, "Oh, yes, so you did, Mr Morck. A Châteauneuf-du-Pape, if I'm not mistaken."

"You are, unless you mean the magnums at 20 kroner 75."

"I'm sorry, we don't have any of those at the moment. But would the cheap Portuguese be suitable?"

"Would it be suitable if I come round to your back door and collect it?"

"You're welcome any time, Mr Morck," said the grocer. It was not the first time they had had the same conversation, which had become something of a ritual, with more or less the same choice of words each time. Nor was it the first time that Marie had stood at his elbow saying, "How dare you."

"The law isn't designed to be taken literally," said Morck. "From time to time one has to show a little discrimination in applying it."

She was just about to say "Yes, that's exactly what they're taking it upon themselves to do down there at the Embassy," but fortunately she didn't. There would be no point in bringing the subject up again.

He went over to Gerners Street and collected the wine at the back door, while she finished cooking the meal. They ate their salad and sat on at the table a long time as the level of wine in the bottle dropped lower and lower. The pitch of Morck's voice deepened with it, the look in his eyes became more piercing, and their brilliance increased with the wine. They had been talking about other things, but now he reverted to earlier topics.

"I can't stand these Olsson types," he said. "I really ought to get out of an organization that tolerates the excesses I witnessed this afternoon."

"Who says they will be tolerated?"

"The police shield the police. The judiciary does so too as much as possible."

"Rubbish, Jonas," she retorted, referring not to what he'd just said but the previous remark.

"What's rubbish?"

"Well, to begin with, you don't need anyone to shield you in your work, do you?"

"Yes, I need you, Marie."

"Now you're getting a tiny bit drunk," she said. "Secondly, there are a great many right-thinking people in the police force, and it wouldn't be to their advantage to give in to the whims of a load of club-swinging thugs and gorillas."

"You put it all very lucidly, Marie."

"Thanks," she said. "Just as well there isn't much left in the bottle. Anyway, there's always bound to be a few of them around."

"What, club-swingers?"

"Yes, some people with these tendencies are always going to be attracted by the job."

Morck nodded. "And in the third place?"

"In the third place, you're forty-seven and where else could you find work?"

"I could be a labourer."

"Could you really?" she said. "You're just bragging. Have you anything else to say?"

"Not a single word, so help me. I'm completely subdued. So let's have coffee."

"You sound the very opposite of subdued. Why the sudden desire for coffee?"

"Well, I have a little something in my back pocket."

"You're not going to tell me you bought Cognac?"

"No, not at today's prices. I just bought some of that liqueur you're so fond of."

"The one you don't much like yourself," she put in. "You seem to think you have to do penance on my account, don't you? Because of your work . . ."

"Yes, I do," he said. "You get brushed aside because of it, time after time."

"There's nothing we can do to prevent that," she sighed. "So why bother thinking about it? Come on."

They went through to the kitchen together and he made the coffee while she piled up the dishes.

"What's up this time?" she asked.

"A woman."

"Murdered?"

"Yes. Einarsen said she's been strangled and then had her face smashed in."

"Good God—that as well?"

"Yes."

"Do you . . . Jonas, do you have to see her?"

"I don't know. Possibly."

"It must be horrible for you."

"For me? Oh, I put up with it. But for her, at the time . . . and for the murderer, when he saw what he had done . . ."

"Do you think so? For a monster like that? He must have been a monster."

"Maybe he was just overcome by revulsion."

"Maybe. But still. How he must have hated her."

A moment later, as he was standing with his back to her, filtering the coffee, she stopped wiping down the kitchen table and added, "Just to think of it brings tears to your eyes."

2

MORCK HAD A headache, a dull throbbing behind his eyes, as they drove across Sjaelland. It wasn't because of the red wine but the two beers he had drunk beforehand and, particularly, Marie's sweet liqueur. Although he had bought it for her, he had finished by drinking most of it himself.

"You're just the teeniest bit drunk, little Jonas," Marie had said. They had gone to bed late, and it was even later before they fell asleep. "The teeniest bit drunk" was putting it mildly. Drunk and maudlin. "Marie, my darling——" (Had he actually been spouting poetry in bed—at his age?)

> "I kiss thee now. He kissed me then;
> I said him yea, I said him nay;
> I . . ."

"Oh, come on, Jonas," she had said. "If you want me . . ."
"I do."
"Then let's not do it in verse. I don't need that."
"What do you need, then?"
"Just you."
"Do you like it then, with me?"
"I always do."

"What the hell are you sitting there grinning at?" snapped Einarsen, at the wheel.
"Me? Nothing really."

"Well, I can't see anything to laugh at either."

Waking up hadn't been so blissful. The alarm had gone off at seven, and half an hour later Einarsen had drawn up at the door. Fortunately, they had arranged to go in his car. Morck didn't fancy taking the wheel. He tended to go off into a day-dream; and a driver whose thoughts are anywhere but on the road is liable to be a danger to other traffic. But Einarsen liked driving. He was a fast yet safe driver, and the mileage allowance must have been quite a help in paying for the car, the latest Opel Rekord. An expensive car for a detective-inspector's salary, but his wife would no doubt be bringing in a tidy sum as well.

They drove out through Slagelse. The sun was shining, the fields were pale green and a sheen of moisture glistened on the dark earth. A fine mist hung over the south-facing slopes. Spring growth.

The headache throbbed away behind his eyes, but would soon wear off.

"Did you see Real Madrid last night?" asked Einarsen.

"No, we didn't watch television. We just sat down and had a good old farewell drinking party."

"I managed to do that too. It was a draw—zero-zero. And rotten football into the bargain—you could see it was going to be from the word go. You didn't miss anything." Einarsen sounded annoyed. He swung the wheel hard round and more or less kicked the new car forward to overtake a truck. "But I just sat there gaping at the idiot-box till the match ended."

"It's easy to get hooked once the thing's switched on . . ."

"I sat there on my own and I must admit I got modestly plastered."

"What about the wife?"

"Went to bed, of course. Slept like a log. Sometimes I ask myself——"

Einarsen broke off in mid-sentence and merely shook his head, keeping his question to himself. Soon after he glanced at his watch and said, "Right. Just about time for take-off."

"Take-off?"

"We were to have had eight days in Mallorca."

"Infuriating, isn't it? And what a shame for your wife."

"For her? You needn't worry about her. She's taking a girl friend along instead," said Einarsen. "They'll see to it they don't miss out on anything, you can rely on that. Do you know, Morck, sometimes . . . no, forget it, forget it."

He gave a blast on the horn to make the car in front move over to the side of the road. It was lumbering along at a mere forty miles an hour. He overtook it impatiently, the Rekord's speedometer touching sixty-five.

"Take it easy, Einarsen; we're in plenty of time for the ferry."

"So we are. What's up, then?"

Presumably he could answer that best himself. He reduced speed a little.

"I've reached the age when I get hung-over the morning after," Einarsen said, adding, apparently out of context, "and I'm bloody well getting fat besides."

Morck knew that he was thirty-six. Eleven years younger than me, he thought. Yet it was true—Einarsen was getting fat. His neck spilled over his collar. He had just had his hair cut and the skin was pink beneath the pale stubble. Einarsen was of the blond athletic type and, until a few years ago, had been an odds-on winner at police wrestling matches. But now the tough muscles were overlaid with fat. In the morning his light-blue eyes were blood-shot, and the irritable pouting of his mouth was more noticeable than before. He didn't seem to be at peace with himself. That was to say . . . with his wife.

She owned, or managed, a perfumery business. Morck had met her a few times. She was three or four years older than Einarsen without a shadow of a doubt, but she dressed at least fifteen years younger. A smart emancipated piece of work, or whatever the word is nowadays, if the word can be used at all of women around the forty mark. Exuding the suffocating aroma of her stock-in-trade, she displayed a lean, angular femininity in the presence of which Morck felt himself utterly helpless. He had once seen her turn on Einarsen in a fury, lashing out at him with her tongue. It had made him shudder.

"Honestly," said Einarsen after lengthy reflection, "it's a bloody dog's life we lead, isn't it, to be quite frank?"

"I suppose it is," said Morck; "but would you rather have some other job?"

"Sure. One with twice the salary. No, three times. You might as well go the whole hog. Now, that would be quite something."

"You'd be happier with that then?"

18

"She would be, at least," said Einarsen; "you bet she would."

No answer was called for.

"At least the weather's decent," said Einarsen, slowing down. They came to a halt at the ticket office by the ferry. While they were waiting in the departure area they bought the morning papers. On the front page, the bank rate was reported to have fallen by a half per cent which meant that the business world would save 250-million kroner in interest, calculated on an annual basis—if that made sense to anyone. Then, political refugees from the Eastern bloc had found a new means of escape. Two lots of refugees had arrived in Copenhagen by trans-continental train, having concealed themselves, for two and seven days respectively, in the cavity between the carriage roof and the compartment ceiling. After the newspaper report, there could be no further employment of that method.

"I'm damned if I saw that!" exclaimed Einarsen, having turned over to the sports page.

"What?"

"The linesman was hit on the head by a bottle during the European match. Knocked unconscious, 'the dramatic highlight of the game', and I missed it."

"What a pity."

"I wonder if I was asleep or unlucky enough to be in the can at that point," Einarsen ruminated. "It also goes on to say the match was a pitiful display. Just what I said, eh? So they don't always write complete and utter lies in the papers."

They were signalled aboard, and soon they were seated in the restaurant, browsing through the newspapers. Violent demonstrations outside the American Embassy . . . Police take stern measures against demonstrators . . . Whew! Morck didn't read the report. He assumed it would give only a pale, watered-down version of the scene he had witnessed. He wondered whether he should discuss it with Einarsen, but didn't in the end. He knew what Einarsen's reaction would be. "If these long-haired idiots don't get thumped when they stick their necks out and provoke us, they'll end up thinking they're running the country." The waiter came to take their order.

"Shall we have coffee?"

"What? On the Storbelt ferry? No fear; they make it with sea water."

"Mocca, then? Is that good enough for you, Einarsen?"

This part of the conversation was always the same. They had made countless crossings of the Storbelt together.

"I'll have to start off with a medicinal lager," said Einarsen. "Two Carlsbergs, waiter, and two mocca, and two cheese sandwiches."

"It's on page seven in this one," said Einarsen. "One of half a dozen news flashes in the provincial round-up. 'Gruesome murder of woman.' Is it gruesome in your paper too?"

"Yes, but on page three."

"They always call it gruesome."

"Well, that's what it is—'Thirty-three-year-old nurse, Kirsten Bunding, strangled and her face crushed out of recognition'. These papers. 'The body was found on a deserted site on the fringe of a plantation.' What do they mean by site? A place where there has been a house, or one where a house is to be built? Or both? 'The local police have called on reinforcements from the central flying squad.' That's us."

"It was Graumann who rang me up," said Einarsen. Graumann was the Deputy Chief Inspector in charge of the flying squad. The Grey Man they called him sometimes. It was one of his duties to be "candle-snuffer"—the one who told people at the last minute that they would not be having their days off or their holidays after all. "He tried phoning you first but you weren't in."

"Marie was. She had a nasty suspicion what it was about so she turned a deaf ear to it."

"How did she take it when I called you?"

"Oh, very calmly," said Morck; "but, of course, she was disappointed. She's used to it happening by now, as she says, but she's never really prepared when it comes to the crunch."

Einarsen looked up from his paper, stared at him with his light-blue, bloodshot eyes and said, "You're a lucky bastard, aren't you?"

"Yes, I am."

"Graumann knew a bit more about the particulars of the case. But probably you're not interested in them just at present?"

"I'd rather wait till we get to the place."

As a rule that was the way he worked. The particulars wouldn't mean very much to him until he had seen the place which gave them a context. This included not merely the scene of the crime itself, but the milieu in which it had been committed—the streets, the houses and the people. He had to have a general picture of these in his mind before he could make any conjectures about a particular crime. A murder is never—or almost never—haphazard, divorced from its surroundings. It grows out of them. It has special roots, causes and explanation—and the solution lies in where it happens, and in the people amongst whom it takes place.

The waiter came with the bill.

They drove the fifty miles over Funen in fifty minutes. As the day wore on, Einarsen had become more restrained in his driving, though not so much that he forgot to swear under his breath when they had to creep along for several miles behind two lumbering juggernauts, hemmed in by the double yellow line down the middle of the narrow winding road to Kolding. Eventually they slipped past and drove slowly through the town itself. A few miles out of Kolding, Morck made the remark he usually made when he had his wife with him.

"We're in West Jutland now."

"What's that?" said Einarsen at the wheel, turning to look at him.

"That slope there, with the fir trees and the red painted shed. Every time I come this way I say to myself this is where West Jutland begins."

"Gosh, that's something worth waiting for. What goes on here then?"

"Nothing you could ever understand, Einarsen."

"You can say that again. Get the hell out of here, dog!"

A dog came dashing out from a farm, stopped at the roadside and yowled until they had gone by. They rushed through a tall fir plantation, up a hill, and that was the end of East Jutland's beechwoods and fields of rich clay. The landscape spread out, open and flat in front of them. The meagre fields were hedged with spruce. Fir copses reached for the skies and some where beyond the broad horizon was the sea.

"One can really breathe out here," said Morck.

"God in heaven, I don't know how they managed to hit upon the crazy idea of annexing this desert to the realm," said Einarsen.

"Copenhagen snob."

But, nevertheless he cheered up visibly the further they were from the capital and from—— what was his wife's first name?

Cilia. That was what she signed herself. Probably on her baptismal
certificate it was Cecilia. If it were abbreviated another way it
would become "Cecil", the girl in Blicher's *The Hosiery Shop*, who
went insane from unrequited love and sang her melancholy little song,

> To lose the one we hold most dear
> Is the deepest woe the heart can bear.

But that was Cecil. There was nothing of the Jutland lass about
Cilia, either in her name or her person; nor did it ring true that she
might be the least troubled by unrequited love. As for Einarsen——
Morck was roused from his idle musings by Einarsen asking him,
"Have you ever been in Vesterso before?"

"No, I don't know the place at all."

"There's a guide-book in the glove compartment."

Morck took it out and looked up Vesterso.

"Population just over two thousand. Situated snugly in a
sheltered part of Vesterso Bay. Immediately north of the town is a
stretch of dunes one-and-a-quarter miles in width, leading to broad
white sands; to the south lie marshlands and tidal mud-flats, haunt
of thousands of wading birds both in spring and autumn, hence
giving excellent facilities for ornithologists——"

"Never mind the ornithology. Does it say anything about a
drugstore?"

"There is one. Also a post office and a school, if that's of any
interest."

"Not unless I can have my school fees refunded there."

"Do you want some Aspirin?"

"Yes, and seltzer," said Einarsen, shifting uncomfortably. "I
seem to remember a time when I hadn't the faintest idea I even
possessed a stomach."

"It says it's a seafaring and fishing town of distinctive character
with many hundred and two-hundred-year-old houses thatched in
the Frisian style. In former centuries, Vesterso had a fleet of fifty
cargo boats and a considerable fishing fleet. But when the Bladyp
Channel silted up because of changes in tidal conditions, the boom
years came to an end. Fishing is now of minor importance and
tourism has become the chief source of revenue. Marine hotel
north of the town. One inn with eleven rooms and a tap outside——"

22

"With cold water in it," broke in Einarsen. "No, thank you. I'll be staying in Esbjerg. It can't be far away."

"There are also several seasonal guest houses and private houses with rooms to let. Camping site."

"Great. But did we remember to bring the tent?"

"It isn't the camping season yet. It says in the off season the town is almost dormant, an idyllic retreat."

"In other words, a dump," said Einarsen.

Morck replaced the guide-book in the glove compartment. They drove on through the West Jutland landscape. The farms were few and far between and herds of piebald cattle roamed the bare fields where the grass was just beginning to sprout again. Towards the west, the sky was less overcast, and there was a distant sparkle from the sea as they neared the coast. A low-flying airplane was coming in to land to the right of the road.

"That's Esbjerg airport across there. We turn off at the junction near Korskro Inn."

"Korskro Inn, did you say?"

"Yes, let's have a beer there."

"Before we cross some damn parish boundary or other," said Einarsen. "I've heard from a number of people who've managed to escape alive that there are some completely dry areas out here."

"Yes, there are still a couple of places with no licensing."

"As I say, I can't understand why nobody stood up to oppose him."

"Who?"

"That nut who decided to annex the——"

"Ah, yes, him," said Morck pacifically.

Less than an hour later, they were driving along Vesterso Main Street. Its large paving stones were worn thin and, on each side, a strip of asphalt had been added. The old thatched houses were painted red, with white window frames. Through spaces between them one could catch a glimpse of the sea and the steel-blue water of Vesterso Bay. Morck noticed that all the houses had their gable ends facing east to west.

"So what?" asked Einarsen, peering out at the shop signs.

"On account of the prevailing west wind. That way they're sheltered from the weather."

"There isn't a shortage of wind," said Einarsen. "Look, there's the drugstore."

He stopped the car, went in and emerged with a small white cardboard box which he stuck in his jacket pocket.

"Did you ask the way to the policeman's place?"

"Yes, he lives just round the corner."

The green oval police sign was displayed outside a newly constructed villa standing behind a hedge which was about to leaf. The name of the villa was written in cement on the wall—"HOMELEA". Above the name there was a decorative motif, which could have been either a palm leaf or a fern.

"Cozy and peaceful, eh. Just like a graveyard," said Einarsen. "Let's hope for the best—namely that we'll be out of here again in less than two shakes."

3

THE LOCAL POLICEMAN, Petersen, had set up his office in a kind of annex to his living-room. His wife had put in a couple of dining-room chairs for them to sit on. The desk had been cleared, and its contents now lay in small heaps on the book shelves and the bureau. In the chair sat Detective Jessen, who had been in charge of the case so far and was itching to get back to Esbjerg. There was a vital drug-pushing case going on with seven suspects so far under interrogation, and they couldn't really do without him, being under-manned—as they usually were. Morck had known Jessen from previous cases over a period of years. His close-clipped moustache was turning white and yellowing at the edges. He was leafing through some papers, obviously at random.

"You can keep Herting," said Jessen, stubbing out his cigarette in the ashtray and lighting a new one. Doubtless the cigarette smoke was to blame for turning his moustache yellow.

Herting was the young detective whose presence required Mrs Petersen to bring in another chair, though the room was cramped enough already. Herting had moved one of the plants and was leaning on the window sill. He must have been about thirty, and although his features were firmly drawn, there was still a boyish look about them, due perhaps to his serious, observant expression.

"What's more, I don't think the fellow can be far away," Jessen was saying. "We have reason to suspect that——"

"Shouldn't we begin at the beginning?" put in Morck. "But first let's solve the problem of where we are going to operate from. There certainly isn't enough room here. What about the council? Surely the rural district council has a committee room somewhere?"

"They've all been turned into offices," answered Petersen, the local policeman. "This is a development area so naturally the administrative side is expanding. The rural district council meets in the marine room at the inn these days."

"Then maybe we could too."

"Is that where the local yokels get together for their daily beer?" interrupted Einarsen in his haughtiest Copenhagen manner, here curiously out of place and obviously lost on a local cop. Formerly a police sergeant in town, he was a man of at least sixty, whose ashen, furrowed features sometimes seemed as if they were about to register acute pain. He was probably transferred out here for health reasons, thought Morck. A superannuation in effect.

"Or perhaps they don't serve drinks?"

"Oh yes, they do."

"Well, you never can tell." When you are this far out in the sticks, Einarsen meant to imply.

"Shall we get on with the case?" growled Jessen, fixing Einarsen with a look that clearly indicated he didn't think much of either Einarsen or his irrelevant remarks. But Einarsen presumably didn't care. He was hardened to it. He put his hand to his mouth, blew out his cheeks and whistled as he exhaled.

Morck said, "If this marine room isn't next to the public bar——"

"No, it isn't," said Petersen. "I can easily ring up Mehlsen, the landlord . . ."

"Tell him we'd like another room as well."

The policeman took the phone through to the bedroom to ring. No sooner had he gone out at one door than there was a knock at the other.

"What's up now?" muttered Jessen irritably. He was indeed itching to get back to his drugs case. "Come in."

It was Petersen's wife.

"Excuse me, gentlemen, coffee's just ready."

"Thank you, Mrs Petersen," said Jessen, "but really . . ."

"It's already laid out, so it won't take a minute."

"Yes, but even so . . ." Jessen faltered. He was cornered, and there was no escape. "We can always discuss the case while we have coffee, I suppose."

They got up and took their chairs through to the dining-room.

"Could I have a glass of water?" asked Einarsen, putting his hand in his jacket pocket for the package he had bought at the drugstore.

"Surely. I'll get it right away."

"No, don't bother. I'll come through to the kitchen."

He went with her, as Petersen returned with the news that the rooms at the inn had been booked. Steam from the coffee cups hovered over the white tablecloth and a faint aroma rose from the homebaked biscuits, which had just been taken out of the oven. They sat down and Einarsen emerged from the kitchen looking as if his insides were taking a turn for the better.

"Go on now, help yourselves," said Mrs Petersen, disappearing with the empty coffee jug. "I'll make more in a jiffy."

They passed round the plate of biscuits.

All together round the coffee table—an interesting way of solving a murder, thought Morck; a line from the *National Song Book* came to mind, "Oh, Denmark, Thou knowest naught of guile and snare,"—though in this context it didn't seem to have any very obvious relevance.

"May I have the cream?" asked Detective Jessen. "Then perhaps we can get on?"

Her name, as they already knew, was Kirsten Bunding. Age thirty-three, unmarried. District Nurse, living in Barkway, Vesterso, and formerly a nurse at Esbjerg hospital. She had been rung up two nights ago, shortly before 1 a.m., from a telephone booth by the harbour. Soon after that she had driven off in her Volkswagen. The next morning the car was found standing in a curious place on the Beach Road, a couple of hundred yards from Vesterso Marine Hotel.

"There are no buildings out that way," said Jessen, shuffling the papers before him, "and no side roads. Only a footpath leading through a stretch of undulating ground overgrown with pine scrub."

He must be reading from a report he hasn't written himself, thought Morck—you could tell from the enunciation. Herting would probably have written it. Morck leaned forward over the table a little and looked at the page Jessen had in front of him to make sure he wasn't altering words as he went along.

" 'This path leads to the summer houses south of the Marine

Hotel but can hardly be regarded as an access road inasmuch as it must be more difficult at night to negotiate than the other roads that likewise lead to the area . . .' "

Jessen pushed the report another inch across the table, as if tempted to repeat what he had just read. He didn't like long-windedness or, to put it another way, unduly minute descriptions.

"Well, wherever it leads," he said, "it was near that path that the body was found, not far from the Beach Road."

"Fifty yards," put in Herting, and Jessen scowled at his uninvited intrusion.

"Why not leave it at 'not far'?" He glanced at the report again and continued: " 'At this point, the path runs through a hollow, a round grassy clearing, six or seven yards in diameter. Here there used to be a red brick house whose foundations can still be made out, together with some scattered sections of brickwork. With one such section, made of two or three bricks still held together by mortar, the body had been battered on the face after attempted strangulation. It was lying to the right of the path, up against the edge of the scrub'—but we don't have to go into that in detail as you'll be seeing the area for yourselves."

"Who found her?" asked Morck.

"Petersen," said Jessen. They all looked at the policeman, who had been fiddling unawares with his coffee cup for some time. The spoon tinkled on the saucer, as he moved it to one side.

"I was rung up about 7 a.m. by her neighbour, a retired customs official," said Petersen. "He had heard her drive away during the night. Every morning he takes a walk down to the beach, and he became suspicious when he saw her car standing at the roadside. Later that morning, I went out and found the body."

"Thank you," said Jessen. "Petersen has written a detailed report and Herting can give you an account of the inquiries and interrogations we have carried out so far."

"What! Right now?" asked Herting.

"No, later, if you don't mind," said Morck. There wouldn't be much point in going into the details round a coffee table. He would not be able to make them cohere unless he had some direct experience to connect them with—an impression of the murdered woman, her environment and the place the crime was committed.

"Have you had any results at all?" asked Einarsen, putting his hand to his mouth to stifle a yawn.

28

An air of drowsiness had settled on the company, thought Morck. Or was it merely his own preoccupation? Coffee and warm biscuits indeed. Not the sort of thing that sprang to mind as catalyst to an investigation. However, they were only here to relieve Jessen as officer-in-charge.

"So far we've only come up with a young fellow who has a reputation for going about at night peeping in at people's windows," said Jessen. "You've caught him at it a couple of times, haven't you, Petersen?"

"Not exactly. People used to ring up and complain but no one wanted to report him in person. So I just had a little talk with him and said if it happened again, then——"

"Does that imply you didn't catch him red-handed?"

Einarsen had put the question.

"I didn't have to," replied Petersen. "He knows full well that we know what he gets up to——"

"So you have your own special methods in this neck of the woods, then? I see you distinguish between direct and indirect reporting. For example——"

"As far as possible we try to sort things out peaceably," said Petersen curtly.

Morck noticed he was reaching for his teaspoon again. It began to tinkle against the saucer and his fingertips were quivering visibly. The coffee had scarcely been touched. Obviously he was not in the best of health; a duodenal ulcer, maybe? Jessen raised his voice:

"The fellow's name is Otto Bahnsen. Age twenty-two. A clear case of low IQ. He has a job down at the inn, as a kitchen-hand and odd-job man; but he lives at home with his mother. She says he was at home all evening and all night."

"Of course she does; what else would she say?" said Einarsen. Morck tried to catch his eye to restrain him, but Einarsen was utterly intractable. He yawned.

"Nevertheless," went on Jessen irritably, "he was seen by the newsagent down on Main Street after midnight, looking in at the shop window."

"Have you interrogated him?" asked Morck.

"No. We only talked to the kiosk owner this morning. But we have spoken to the mother, as I said—or rather Herting has."

"I was down there before seven this morning," said the younger detective. "He had already left for the inn. The mother realized immediately why I was there, and assured me, without being prompted, that he'd been at home all the time."

"So what? Mother-love to the rescue," yawned Einarsen, as if the whole affair bored him to tears. If Morck had been sitting next to him he would have kicked him in the shins—not that it would have done any good. Einarsen had apparently come to Vesterso with the express intention of making himself thoroughly unpopular, playing the arrogant Copenhagen snob—the blockhead. All because his wife had gone to Mallorca with a girl friend and had given him hell the night before. So Einarsen had to compensate for his annoyance by being annoying himself.

There was a short silence.

Morck said, "Fine, we'll deal with him. Anything else of note?"

"The technical department was here yesterday. They've just sent these pictures," said Jessen, taking them from a yellow envelope and placing the pile in front of Morck, who looked at the top one, if only to disguise his lack of interest. Einarsen had put his foot in it enough already. Moreover, he didn't fancy taking a closer look at the pictures in these highly informal surroundings.

The woman was lying on her back in an awkward position, her torso twisted round at an angle. Her legs were showing, and stood out white against the grass. Had she no stockings on, or was that only the light? Her face was a dark blotch, hidden beneath a sapling.

"Good God!" Mrs Petersen had returned noiselessly with the coffee pot and was in the act of filling Herting's cup, and his saucer as well—the brown liquid spilled over on to the tablecloth. "Is that her? Good God!"

"Put it down," said Petersen, meaning the coffee pot. The spout dipped perilously but she only had eyes for the picture. She put the pot down on the table and burst into tears.

"Marie, go out to the kitchen. We can pour our own," said Petersen.

She hurried out and Morck looked after her thoughtfully. So her name was Marie too. He had scarcely noticed her when she had been in the room before. She was not the sort of person one did notice. Though smaller and thinner than her husband, she resembled him in some other respects: a case of a marriage where one of the partners affected the appearance of the other so that they ended up looking like brother and sister. Morck turned to

30

Petersen, who was glaring after his wife with a tight-lipped expression on his ashen face. He pulled himself together eventually.

"There's more coffee in the pot," he said.

"Thanks all the same," said Jessen, "but I think we should all be getting on our way."

"Yes, we'd better," said Morck. "We ought to see the place before we set up shop at the inn. Thanks for the coffee, Petersen."

"Rooms have already been booked for you there."

"Not for me, thanks," said Einarsen. "I'll be staying in town."

He could scarcely have made it any plainer.

When they were outside, Einarsen put his finger inside his collar and ran it round from one side to the other.

"Phew, it was hot in there."

"Yes, and you obviously got properly het up yourself," said Morck, going over to the car and opening the door. "Here. Take your coat all the same. There's a cold wind."

"You're not suggesting we should walk, are you?"

"Sure. You can't get a proper picture otherwise."

"Proper picture of what?"

"The crime. Besides, it'll do your digestion good; and that's a point worth bearing in mind."

"You're full of consideration."

"I'm only thinking of your well-being."

"Lord Almighty," muttered Einarsen, taking his coat from the car. As he struggled into it, he gave the back wheel of the car a hearty kick. "What on earth persuaded me to buy that crate?"

"It's useful for longer journeys," said Morck, "but it's less than a quarter of a mile to where we're going. So we can see the house on the way."

"Where's Herting?"

"He noticed the doctor driving by on his way home and nipped off to have a word with him. He'll catch us up."

"Full of youthful enthusiasm."

"Just like the young Einarsen in his day," said Morck.

"Like who?" asked Einarsen. "I don't remember him. That must have been a very long time ago, so my old worn-out policeman's feet tell me."

They went down to Main Street, turned left and soon saw the blue street sign with its white lettering.

"So this is Barkway, where she lives, just to prove they didn't make it all up."

"You mean lived."

"Her name's Bunding, and that peeping Tom they were on about is called Bahnsen."

"Yes, that stuck me at the outset. It's a B-case all along the line, if you ask me."

"Everyone knows that already," said Morck. "You made it abundantly clear the case was considerably beneath your usual level. But you'll feel better when you're under way."

"Better," spluttered Einarsen. "What the hell do you mean? There's nothing wrong with me."

"No, of course there's not," said Morck, as they turned down Barkway.

The street consisted of five or six low thatched houses, with white fencing round the front gardens. At the end of the row of houses, the metalled road gave out, and beyond a pale green and yellow stretch of meadow was the bay. The sea glistened brighter now than the overcast sky. Between them was a faint strip of land, almost black, an outcrop on the verge of the horizon.

"This must be it," said Morck; "the last house on the right."

4

THE FENCE NEEDED painting. It divided the front garden in two, each with its wicker gate and front door. The first was hers. On the plate by the green· door were the words, KIRSTEN BUNDING, REGISTERED NURSE. She had planted pale and dark-blue pansies against the red walls of the house. Two neat spruces stood at the street end of the garden, and along the fence the rambling roses were on the point of bursting into leaf, though still more yellow than green.

Herting caught up with them, a little out of breath. He hadn't managed to intercept the doctor.

"He gave me the slip, but I'll get hold of him this evening."

Her Volkswagen stood under a canopy fixed to the side wall of the house. Einarsen took hold of the door·handle on the driver's side, intending only to look through the window. He had no particular end in view. It was only a car, but he was interested in cars . . . the door opened easily.

"Not even locked," said Einarsen. "It's scarcely surprising car thieves prosper when even the police can open car doors."

"The lock's faulty," put in Herting.

"Yes, rusted right through," said Einarsen, "and the upholstery under the seat cover is beginning to split. Let's say a straight 5,000 kroner and call it a deal." Then, turning to Morck, he asked impatiently, "Are we going in?"

"I have the key here," said Herting.

"Who lives in the other half of the house?" asked Morck.

"The retired customs man who rang to tell us about the car standing on the Beach Road."

Morck nodded.

In the customs officer's part of the front garden there were a couple of mountain firs and some stunted junipers. The icy winds from the sea had blackened them, but they still gave some shelter to his neighbour's orderly spruces. Herting was waiting with the key in his hand.

"We might as well go in," said Morck. He was the last to do so.

The carpet in the narrow hallway had a silver stripe, but it looked more like yellow when he closed the door behind him, excluding most of the daylight. Her coat was hanging on the rack, and on a shelf above lay an oval hand mirror and hairbrush in bronze, like those that girls in his day were given as confirmation presents. In the mirror above this shelf he saw Einarsen and Herting and then himself entering the house in procession.

He had never really got used to this part of the proceedings, though he often had to go through it—this rough intrusion into another person's private life, this opening of cupboards and drawers, and poking about among a stranger's personal possessions in order to uncover intimate secrets which the person concerned had believed to be safely hidden behind his own front door. Occasionally, they would even uncover secrets which the individual had been concealing from himself—repressed feelings or forgotten events.

Anyway, they would dig them out and size them up with the cold gaze of strangers, though they were unable to form the vaguest notion of what these things had meant to their owner. Or rather, Einarsen would dig out anything that might turn out to be relevant to the case. Einarsen was good at "vacuum-cleaning" a flat. Tomorrow he would be able to go over the whole place.

Morck went from the hallway into a little double-windowed room. A dining-table with a blue cloth on it stood against the wall between the two windows. There was a shelf with books on it— books bound in black with gold lettering. Next to that, an old writing desk with a telephone on it. In the corner by the window, an easy chair with a floral cretonne cover. This would be where she had sat while making phone calls.

The apples in the bowl on the table had developed brown patches and were going bad. He went on through the open door into the living-room. It had four windows—a well-proportioned, if narrow, room, with a low, beamed ceiling. The floor boards were the old, wide sort with the gleam of many years' varnish upon them. The soft light of the afternoon was streaming in through the four windows. Against the opposite wall was a broad divan, scattered with multi-coloured cushions, a bow-fronted bureau and a few wooden easy chairs.

He only took a brief look round. That evening he would return alone to form a more detailed picture, without the distraction of the others. He could hear their voices in another part of the flat. Cupboard doors were being opened and immediately slammed shut. Einarsen was making his first, rapid survey, prior to coming back tomorrow to "turn the place inside out" as he put it.

On a round table was a vase holding a large bunch of tulips. They had begun to droop, but they hadn't completely withered yet. He counted them. Seventeen in all. As he stood bending over the vase, he detected a faint, sour smell. The water hadn't been changed—of course it hadn't. How old were these flowers? Three or four days, maybe five?

"Herting."

Morck's voice was drowned by Einarsen exclaiming, "Just look at that, she's got a ruddy bidet! Who would have thought it, out here in this rustic paradise? Yet she's advanced enough in that respect. Believe me, we're not at that stage yet back home in Gladsaxe, and I live in a brand-new block of flats."

You bastard, thought Morck, though he knew he was being unjust. It was only Einarsen's rough and ready manner. Yet the thought struck him all the same—you bastard.

"Go and show him that," said Einarsen. Herting came into the living-room and gave him a picture.

"Is that her?"

"Yes," said Herting. "There's a larger photo too, portrait size. But it's five years old, according to the date on the back."

What can one tell from a passport photo? It was certainly no bigger than that, and taken at a slight angle. The nose was ordinary but a little prominent, the eyebrows almost black, the mouth nearly breaking into a smile. The lips were probably soft and ample, but in the photo they merely looked heavy and tense. The cheeks seemed a little swollen. She was not looking at the camera but beyond and to one side of it—at nothing. One could not make out the look in her eyes. The hair appeared to be dark, combed back in a soft wave from the brow. But, in reality, it must have been nearly blonde.

35

Ordinary—yes. She looked quite ordinary, one could scarcely say beautiful; pretty rather. A woman no longer in the first bloom of youth. But what kind of person she had been, what her basic characteristics were—about this the picture was silent.

"There are more of them—in that drawer," said Herting.

"Drawer?"

"Yes, the drawer in the cabinet by the bed."

"Let's take them along with us. We can go through them later. Otherwise nothing has been touched?"

"No, everything is exactly as it was when we came yesterday morning," said Herting.

Einarsen appeared in the opposite doorway of the living-room, the door leading into the bedroom.

"Don't you want to look at the maiden's bower, Morck? I must say my old expert's eyes would be playing me tricks if she always locked the windows to keep the village lads out."

"No, I won't look now. I'll get round to it this evening."

"No doubt you will," said Einarsen, who knew his methods. "You'd rather make it a two-man show, eh?—a rendezvous with the departed in the appropriate setting."

"Herting," said Morck, "is there more than one florist in the town?"

"No, just one."

"Go and ask them who sent these flowers and when."

"Very well," said Herting. "You don't think she could have bought them herself?" he added.

"Do you know anyone who would?"

"Who would what?"

"Buy themselves seventeen tulips?"

"No, now that you mention it, I don't," said Herting.

5

THEY WENT NORTH along the cobbled Main Street. The rows of thatched houses were interspersed with houses of modern design, set at right angles to them. Some incorporated shops—a book store, a hardware shop, several grocers and about three butchers. The iocal population could not possibly have kept them all in business; they would make their profits from visitors in the tourist season. Behind the white fencing, cherry trees and luxuriant yellow forsythia were in blossom. The lawns were just beginning to sprout fresh grass.

The old part of the town petered out and there was not much else besides. One or two villas in the solid master-builder style of the twenties and thirties vaunted their self-importance, while some single detached houses of recent construction bore the blank stamp of democratic dullness, despite their variety of design.

The road here was wider and there was even a sidewalk. They walked three abreast, and where the sidewalk was too narrow, Herting walked in the road, as befitted his rank. He looked rather puzzled when Einarsen said to Morck, "Well, Morck, are you on to anything yet?"

"I never know until I am."

"And as a rule not afterwards either."

"Exactly," said Morck. "Listen. You can hear the sea."

"That won't do anything for my poor feet. Will we be there soon?"

"From that corner we're coming to, it's less than two hundred yards," said Herting.

They passed a tiny spruce plantation on one side of the road. On the other was the inevitable camping-site in a flat field of patchy grass. The Beach Road swung round and cut its way through undulating dunes covered with pine scrub, heading straight out towards the sea, which was hidden by higher dunes, a mixture of green and grey in the distance.

At the end of the road was a three-storey pile of a building, painted yellow, though as they approached it, they could see that the paint was peeling off, revealing patches of grey cement. The windows were painted royal-blue, as were the clumsy Biedermayer cornices and the Greek temple pillars that flanked the main entrance.

"What is that? The chamber of horrors?" said Einarsen.

"Vesterso Marine Hotel," Herting corrected him.

"Good Lord! I thought it was an amalgamation of thirty blue pillar boxes and an outside public lavatory. Most impressive. But I thought only the Germans could attain such heights of splendour."

"It was built by German capital, in fact: some German syndicate about the turn of the century financed it."

"Exactly. As I always say," said Einarsen, "they should never have been allowed to make peace."

"Oh, belt up for a second, Knud," said Morck. He seldom called Einarsen by his first name.

"I hope I'm not preventing you listening to the roar of the sea."

"Yes, you are. And that's not all."

"Pardon me, my Lord," said Einarsen. Herting looked puzzled again.

"This'll be it," said Morck.

"Yes, that's the place," said Herting rapidly, though he was still one step behind Morck. After all, he was the one who ought to have pointed it out to them.

Reality never answers to the picture one forms beforehand. Morck had expected the path to be half a yard wide, winding its way mysteriously through the scrub, and disappearing from view after a yard or two. That was his general idea of a path leading through low pine scrub. He could remember paths like that from his childhood. But this path was over a yard wide and went straight on for thirty or forty yards before dipping down into a hollow.

Einarsen went first, meandering along as if they were only out for a stroll. By this time he had forgotten about his feet and his bad temper. Now and then he stopped and looked round, craning his neck, so that his incipient double chin disappeared. The rolling scrub stretched away for over fifty yards to the right of the path, and on the other side some summer houses were scattered among the dunes. Einarsen's demeanour betrayed his sullen scepticism: he had taken his hands out of his pockets and was swinging his arms in a random fashion.

Herting kept in the background. He had made one attempt at communication:

"Just down there . . ."

But they evidently hadn't heard him. Somehow he felt excluded and faintly humiliated. He might as well not have been there until Einarsen asked him, "Is anyone living in these summer houses?"

"No. Petersen came out to take a look at all the houses in the vicinity," he said, "but they were all locked up for the winter."

"Hm. A well-chosen place."

"That is, if it was chosen," said Morck absently. He kicked at a tuft of moss which gave off a puff of dust. A grey film settled on the toe of his shoe. They both looked down at it, and Herting was struck by a certain similarity between them at that moment despite their basic differences—perhaps not a similarity, but rather a unity of opposites. He felt very much out of it.

"So she was rung up at night, and called out here," said Einarsen.

"Yes," said Morck, wiping his dusty shoe in the bracken that flourished everywhere among the pine saplings, dark green fronds with brown withered tips after the winter.

"It's called Angel-sweet," he said.

"What is?"

"The bracken. Or Polypodium Vulgare. There are two hundred varieties of the family but only this one grows in Europe. Odd, isn't it?"

"You can be mighty odd yourself," answered Einarsen. "Does it grow over at your summer house, or what?"

"Yes, that's how I know the name. I wonder if it has sugar in the root, since it's called that. Angel-sweet?"

"We'd better have that looked into so that it can go in the report. Were you on the way to your summer house this time too?"

"Yes, Marie had even packed our bags."

"And she wasn't annoyed even then? I can't see why for the life of me," said Einarsen, and they went on, Herting following at a respectful distance. Angel-sweet, sugar in the roots, Marie and the summer house? They were talking in code and he didn't have the key.

As the path dipped down, the saplings became taller, almost proper trees. They were so close together that the bracken only grew at the edge of the plantation. Further in, the earth was carpeted with dark, gleaming pine needles.

The circular clearing was scarcely three feet below the level of the surrounding land, but as soon as you went beyond the point where the path led into it, you were invisible from the road. The sound of the sea was almost entirely shut out by the trees. The path weaved across the clearing like an uneven parting in a head of hair, and at the other side it shrank to the width Morck expected of a path through scrub.

"She was lying there," said Herting, pointing at a place to the right of the path, where the scrub began. The fresh green grass, sprouting up through the withered tussocks, had been heavily trampled down here and over most of the clearing.

"Her face is towards the road, isn't it?" asked Morck, unaware that he was using the present tense. He visualized the photograph he had seen briefly at Petersen's.

"Yes, it was," said Herting.

"That doesn't tell us much," said Einarsen impatiently, with a hint of contempt. "And there's helluva little worth looking at anyway," he added.

"Yes," said Morck.

"Half the town must have been out here sightseeing, I should think . . . not that it matters. If there'd been anything worth looking at, the technical department would have found it; and Jessen's to be counted on as well. So I don't see why we should waste our time. Still, I suppose that's up to you."

Morck did not reply. Einarsen turned away and crossed over the path. As Herting had written in his report, the remains of some concrete foundations were just visible. They were overgrown with moss, and sections of brickwork of different sizes lay scattered about. Einarsen turned over a couple of them with his foot, then picked one up and felt its weight.

"Was it about this size?" he asked.

"More or less," said Herting. "Maybe as thick as that but not so long. More compact."

"Compact is a good word," said Einarsen, smiling for some utterly obscure reason, and swinging the cluster of bricks back and forth in his large fist. "So . . . he tries to strangle her and then gives her a smart, compact thump with this lot, and that's the end of that."

He raised the lump to shoulder height and threw it down. It struck the moss-covered foundations with a dull thud and broke apart.

"Yes, I understand that much," said Morck, "but to use that thing . . ." He nodded towards the remains of the cluster of bricks.

That wasn't the one the murderer had used, thought Herting, annoyed by Einarsen's language and behaviour, and surprised that Morck did not seem to be troubled by them. Morck just stood looking at Einarsen, as if he was listening to some totally different conversation.

"You'd have to be bloody furious," said Einarsen, "or stark, raving crazy, wouldn't you say, Jonas?"

"Why not both? After all, he could have drawn the line at . . ."

"At smashing her face in."

"Who knows?" sighed Morck. "He could just as well have panicked. Fear might have made him hit out at her."

"But, if so, he wouldn't have had that lump of masonry ready beforehand."

"True."

"And wouldn't he have run off instead of groping about in the dark for it?" said Einarsen.

"Yes, probably," said Morck. "But we're none the wiser. Herting, could the doctor say how many blows had been struck, from his examination?"

"One or two, he said, but wasn't quite sure. Perhaps the autopsy will reveal . . ."

"Yes, perhaps."

"Are we any the wiser, then?" said Einarsen. "Not a bit of it. Shall we be going?"

"All right," said Morck, hesitating, though there really was no reason to remain. "What was the building here used for, by the way?"

"There are traces of tar on several of the bricks," said Herting. "I suppose the fishermen tarred their nets and stored their gear in it. But it was demolished years ago, and I must confess I haven't gone into the matter in detail."

"At last, a confession," said Einarsen. "That cheers me up so much I think we should let him go free."

Obviously he was in a better mood. But Herting wasn't sure whether he should interpret the remark as a piece of bonhomie or as infuriating condescension. They went back to the road.

"Where was the car found?" Morck asked.

"Eight or nine yards further on," replied Herting, pointing in the direction of the Marine Hotel.

"The originator wasn't necessarily a German of course," said Einarsen. "One can't overlook the possibility that it was a bankrupt confectioner, presumably schizophrenic as well."

"Pay no attention to him," said Morck reassuringly. "He hasn't the faintest idea what schizophrenic means."

"Suffering from a split personality," Einarsen put in informatively. "Those whose consciousness is divided into two parts. For example, those poor devils from the flying squad who tear about from one end of the country to the other with half their attention focused on a murder and the other half . . . well, that's their own affair."

"So it is," interrupted Morck. "Where did you say the car was parked, Herting?"

"Over there," said Herting, leading the way. "The front wheel was just off the edge of the road."

"Anything else of note?"

"I don't think so. The car was searched. No, there was nothing one could immediately latch on to."

"Was it windy during the night?"

"Windy? I don't know. When we came out here in the morning there was a slight breeze."

"From the north?"

"Well . . ." Herting hesitated. He wasn't sure which quarter the wind had been in, yet he didn't want to be caught napping.

Morck was looking down at the thin film of blown sand about two yards wide that covered the tarmac by the edges of the road. Back home in Crocodile Street the wind had been northerly because the bedroom window had been rattling. He had got up in the middle of the night to wedge it in, taking care not to wake Marie. Once she was asleep, it took a lot to wake her, especially if they had . . . He brushed the thought of Marie aside, but in some far corner of his consciousness, she was still telling him she always liked it. He put his hand in his trouser pocket and pulled out a handkerchief. It was freshly ironed and beautifully folded, so he put it back again and found a crumpled one in his jacket pocket.

"You didn't check the wheel marks to see where the brake was applied, did you, Herting?"

"No, I must confess, I didn't."

"You'd better be careful with all these confessions," said Einarsen. "If you want to make a career in the police, you have to be good at saying no with conviction. What if there *are* skid-marks, Jonas?"

"Let's see now," said Morck. "The road has recently been re-surfaced."

"Yes, they were in the process of laying it when I came here a few days ago," said Herting.

"Why were you out here?"

"A couple of summer houses had been broken into. You know the sort of thing: a pane of glass smashed and the odd bottle of wine and some of last summer's beer stolen."

"Did you find out who did it?" asked Morck, using his handkerchief as a whisk to brush the fine white sand from the tarmac.

"No. Probably it was the same bunch of lads from Vesterso that Petersen's been having trouble with. But I haven't had time to question them, and they wouldn't own up unless I did."

"So you see, crime pays," Einarsen broke in. Then turning to Morck he said, "Are you on to something down there?"

"Yes, she braked fairly sharply."

Morck stood up, shook the handkerchief and put it back in his jacket pocket. The skid-marks stood out clearly on the tarmac, slanting in towards the pavement.

"And what does that tell us?" asked Einarsen. "That she didn't see the path until she was almost past it—or past the man, assuming they'd arranged to meet here."

"So he couldn't have been on the sidewalk."

"No, he was in there on the path, hidden by the bushes."

"Only his lower half would be hidden, but the background is dark, of course."

"And if he didn't want her to realize who he was, he must have waited with one foot poised on the sidewalk until the car was actually driving by."

"You're just spinning a yarn."

"I'm not."

"Shall we go?" said Einarsen. "We're about as much use here as . . . what's it called . . .?"

"A snowball in hell? I hope not," said Morck.

They turned back towards Vesterso.

6

PICKING UP THE car from Petersen's house, they drove down to
the inn by the harbour. It was a red brick building, about 200 years
old, with a neat row of white-painted windows with small window
panes. Set in the dark-green double doors in the middle of this
façade were two round, greenish panes, reminiscent of the base of a
bottle. The wide doors in the entrance hall, ornamented with brass,
were pleasing, but the walls . . .! They were mist-blue and marma-
lade. A fleet of ships, each at least fifteen inches long, was splashed
across them.

"Either we've got mixed up in the Spanish Armada," said
Einarsen, "or these frigates are the latest discovery of the mad
confectioner."

"They're caravelles," said Morck.

"A caravelle's an airplane," declared Einarsen.

"The *Santa Maria* was a caravelle."

"Don't listen to him, Herting. From time to time he's apt to have
a fit of Catholicism, but it soon passes. Santa Maria indeed."

They hung their coats on the rack but Morck left his case outside
for the time being.

"That's the ship Columbus was sailing in when he discovered
America. A caravelle."

"Pity he's not with us now. We could do with discovering a
thing or two."

The atmosphere in the dining-room was pleasantly subdued, the
colours warm and brown despite the bright sunlight streaming in
through the windows, and reflected from the steely-blue water of the
bay. There were dark beams on the ceiling, the spaces between them

sometimes white, sometimes light fawn; dark pine panelling covered the walls and the tablecloths were bottle-green.

It was four-thirty and there were no customers. The young waitress was sitting with her knitting behind the bar: her face was pale, immature and somewhat puffy. The light colour of her skin contrasted with the dark bottles and sparkling glasses on the shelves behind her. She laid aside her knitting as they sat down at the nearest of the three tables by the window and came over to take their order.

She did not speak dialect but the accent was there. There is often a kind of underlying whine in the West Jutland accent, among the women at least, thought Morck. Einarsen was thinking about smørrebrød, and he ordered two with his beer.

"What's on the menu for dinner?"

"Rib roast and red cabbage. But we only begin serving that at six o'clock."

"Until when?"

"Until half past seven."

"Good. What's your name, by the way?"

"Eline."

"What a nice name," said Einarsen with approval. " 'Hear Eline's artless song . . .'."

Sometimes Einarsen went too far. The girl had turned very red and was looking at him suspiciously; but there was no doubt that he had made an ally.

They ordered beer. She cast a sidelong glance over her shoulder at Einarsen; so when she came back with his plate of smørrebrød, he nodded reassuringly at her, saying: "Splendid. That looks great."

The girl seemed to take his remark as a compliment to her own efforts. As so often before, Morck envied him his gift of making immediate contact with people.

Einarsen gobbled down one piece, pushed the other to the side of his plate, then put down his knife and fork and said: "Well then it's a natural temptation to assume he was standing out there on the Beach Road when he met her—but we don't need to pin him down to one place."

"No," said Morck.

"And we're already talking of *him*."

"You don't imagine it might have been a woman, surely?"

"I don't imagine anything; that's your department. But of course

46

I don't think . . . well, Lord protect us from the species if it was."

"Surely it must have been a man," said Morck.

Herting broke into the conversation, almost apologetically, "There was that telephone call, if you remember."

"That's the first sensible thing I've heard today," said Einarsen. "Here we are both talking a load of rubbish."

"Yes, let's listen to what Herting has to say," said Morck.

"I went down to the telephone exchange," Herting continued. "The lady in charge is a Mrs Bergquist. She runs the exchange with her daughter, and it was her—the daughter—who put the call through."

"What did the man say?"

"He just asked for the number."

"And she didn't notice anything particular?"

"Nothing, except that the call came from the phone box down at the harbour."

Herting had asked her if she thought she would recognize the voice.

"From a number alone? No, I shouldn't think so."

The mother and her unmarried daughter lived together. The house had old-fashioned furniture of a stiff and upright design. The sideboard had curtains behind the panes of its glass doors, and on the wall hung a framed piece of embroidery with the message "God is Love". They had motioned Herting to an easy chair, seating themselves each on an upright dining-room chair, as much as to say they wouldn't let him get on their soft-side. A door leading to the exchange in the neighbouring room stood open, and in it a young girl sat with her back to them repeating numbers, sticking plugs in the board, and taking them out again.

Herting asked whether it was unusual for Kirsten Bunding to be rung up so late at night. The answer came from Mrs Bergquist, whose superior rank was beyond question.

"People can be taken ill at night, you know."

"But in a phone box?"

"Everyone doesn't have their own phone," the lady pointed out, adding: "But we're still kept busy here, I'm glad to say. Are there any further questions?"

They were two distinctly severe types, Herting said, or rather they were birds of a feather, and equally tight-lipped. He didn't trouble to conceal his impression that every time he had opened his mouth they shouted him down. Especially when he was so bold as to ask the daughter if she hadn't accidentally overheard a few words of the conversation when she put the call through. The mother replied on behalf of both,

"What on earth do you take us for? Do you think we spend our time here listening to other people's conversations?"

"It is just possible that——"

"It is nothing of the kind."

So they left it at that. On his way out, Herting had noticed another piece of embroidery, hung on the wall in the hallway. It read:

> The Lord shall preserve thy going out and thy coming in from this time forth, and even for evermore.

He was much relieved at his going out.

Einarsen had finished his smørresbrød. He peeled a bit of pickle with his fork, and lit a cigarette, taking a long draw at it before going on.

"For God's sake, they must know very well what goes on in the town . . . what else is there for them to do at night in that accursed wasteland of a telephone exchange? Of course they won't let on. Or will they? Now, if it was our friend Otto Bahnsen and she recognized the voice . . ?"

Nobody commented on this.

"As a rule, people of that sort are quite harmless. They generally are content just to spy on women, because they're afraid to make a pass at them. But in certain situations, under pressure——"

"Yes, but that's very unusual," Morck put in.

"What are we discussing if not an unusual situation? As I was saying, if you'll let me finish, a situation can arise where the little timid fellow who's always ready to take to his heels, suddenly makes an about-face in the opposite direction."

"The opposite to what?" asked Herting.

"The opposite to running away," explained Einarsen patiently; "namely, he attacks. Even a frightened hare is capable of pouncing on its pursuer and biting him, if it finds itself hopelessly cornered."

"That's a lot of moonshine," said Morck. "There's no justification for conclusions of that kind, so far."

"Well, it's at least a possibility. You're the one who always says we should take account of every possibility . . . but anyway, time will tell. I suppose it's my job to give Bahnsen a grilling?"

"Let's get a few more of the details first," said Morck.

But Einarsen saw that as his job too. He was the right man for that kind of interrogation.

7

THE WASH-HAND BASIN had two taps, one with an "H" on it. Morck turned it on and felt the water temperature. Of course there was hot water. The guide-book Einarsen had in his glove compartment must have been out of date. He washed his hands and ran them through his hair, then dried them. A glance round the room convinced him it was the best in the inn. Three dormer windows looked out seaward over Vesterso Bay, stretching towards the horizon between sky and ocean. In the window alcove there was a cheap pinewood desk with a telephone on it. Two worn easy chairs and an old-fashioned round mahogany table completed the furnishings. The table—bought at an auction possibly—had maybe seen better days in the landlord's own living-room. Cigarette burns had ruined its surface, and the edges had evidently been used by previous guests as a bottle-opener. Funny how some people behave like animals with other people's property. On the floor was an imitation oriental carpet, more or less worn through in the corner nearest the door. The bed had a yellowish crochet cover, home-made; and on the wall hung a picture, discoloured by damp, of a five-masted barquentine, the *Copenhagen*. Five thousand square feet of sail, he remembered suddenly—from what? The oddest things tended to come crowding unbidden into his memory. Anyway, it wasn't a barquentine but a barque, because the mizzenmast was schooner-rigged. And she lived in Barkway—or rather, had lived. The murdered woman.

At present, all he knew about her was that her name was Kirsten and she was a nurse—if one could call that knowledge. He had seen a picture of her, though not of the living person—a picture that revealed nothing about her nature as a living being.

He hung up his shirts and other clothes. Before putting the empty suitcase in the bottom of the wardrobe, he felt in the pocket. Yes, he had brought it with him—the little meerschaum pipe with the amber mouthpiece. He cradled it in his hand for a moment. The bowl was faintly yellowed by smoke. There were times when he smoked it a lot, but so far he had not managed to bring the true colour out. Marie had given it to him for Christmas—or was it last Christmas? He found it a pleasure to look at. Its short, firm profile reminded him of . . . he smiled secretly, and thought he would be as well not to tell his wife what it reminded him of.

Petersen's wife was called Marie too. But she didn't remind him of that in the least. Rather the opposite. And Petersen didn't look as if he was in the best of health. Was he really sick? Or was he fully recovered, now that the dust had settled after the recent invasion of foreign police, and his house was restored to its usual tranquillity?

Morck debated whether to light the pipe before going downstairs. That was what Marie had meant it for—"to take the place of all these cigarettes, Jonas!" She worried a great deal about the dry cough he had first thing in the morning. But there was too much on his mind at the moment, so he lit a cigarette and left the pipe behind in the ashtray. On his return, it would signify that he lived there. He was happy with the room: exactly what he wanted.

When he came down, the landlord, Mehlsen, was at the foot of the stairs, pressing a thumbtack into the door marked MARINE ROOM. He was a short fat man with a rotund body and plump hands; a round nose protruded from the moon-shaped face that was turned towards Morck after the pinning up of the notice had been accomplished. On it were printed the words DO NOT DISTURB.

"Just to make sure all and sundry don't come bursting in on you," he explained.

"I'm not sure that's a very good idea," said Morck. "Somebody or other might want to give us information."

"They can surely ask me first whether you're busy," said Mehlsen.

"That would be bound to deter some people."

"Well then, as you wish . . . I could always make a placard. What should I write on it? 'Police Criminal Division' would be a bit long. What about just 'Police' in big letters? Will that do?"

"Yes, why not? That should do very well," said Morck. "It's what we are, after all."

"Yes, you are," said the landlord, with a laugh which he immediately stifled. "I'll have that done right away. How awful this should have happened to her, eh? I simply can't understand why——"

"No."

"And who could have done it?" Mehlsen persisted. "I don't suppose you will have anything to go on yet . . . no, you've only just arrived."

Morck looked severely at him and the little man shuffled aside.

"The room should be ready now, Inspector . . . if there's anything you want, you just have to ask."

"Thank you," said Morck, entering the marine room. He was aware of the landlord's disappointed gaze following him in, his desire to gossip thwarted. No doubt he was keen to figure in the investigation. How astounding it was, the way people wormed their way into appearing as witnesses in murder cases—often people who had nothing of significance to report. As if by this means they could become one of an exclusive circle of initiates—those in the know.

Fortunately, the marine room was not too spacious. There was hardly room for more than five tables. Three of these had been stacked up against the back wall, and the two to be used as desks had been moved over next to separate windows. Their surfaces were grey and worn, covered with scratches, and the edges were raised to stop the glasses sliding off. Einarsen had set his typewriter up on one table and was taking a thin dossier from his briefcase, containing reports and other material Jessen had passed on to them.

In the background, the boy was folding the superfluous table-cloths. From the first moment, Morck thought of him as a boy. Otto Bahnsen, twenty-two years of age. Yet the face was that of a fifteen-year-old, only out of proportion, as it were. The unpleasant word "flabby" sprang to mind. He was fairly tall, about five foot ten. A faded blue jerkin clung tightly to his large body and drooping shoulders.

"Well, I see you've got us settled in," Morck said to Einarsen, noticing the sudden awkwardness in the boy's movements at the sound of his voice.

"I'm not sure whether we mayn't need seasickness tablets," said Einarsen with a glance at the nautical pictures in a double row round the walls: brigs and schooners and schooner-brigs, barques and double-riggers, either sailing in a heavy swell, or with their bows ploughing through the crests of the waves. "But I reckon we should pull through safely. Do you have ships on the wall in your room too?"

"Just one, over the bed."

"A genuine maritime locality," said Einarsen. "Before long we'll be able to feel the deck heaving underfoot. Maybe we should send the boy for these tablets right away."

"The boy." He naturally called him that too. Turning to him, Einarsen said sharply, "Here, you!"

The boy stared vacantly at him in trepidation, opening his mouth without uttering any sound.

"You're the one by the name of Otto Bahnsen, aren't you?"

"Yes."

"I've heard about you," said Einarsen, letting the words sink in for several seconds before continuing. "That tablets business—it's just my idea of a joke get it?"

"Yes," whispered the boy, moistening his lips. Einarsen liked that sort of thing, given certain opportunities, thought Morck. Was he aware that his need to retaliate was what made this particular demon take hold of him? A demon which also cropped up in his interrogation technique: "Take care that they don't know which way you're leading them," he was wont to say, "and that way you can have them where you want."

"What about a telephone?" said Morck, going off at a tangent.

"There's one in a box as far away as possible at the other end of the passageway," said Einarsen without turning round. He was still looking fixedly at the boy. "Not much bloody use there, is it?"

"It'll do," said Morck to the empty air. He was sorry for the boy, who put the pile of tablecloths over his arm and blinked one way then the other, as if vainly trying to find some escape route. When at last he did speak, he tripped over his words.

"Will that . . . will that be all?"

"Yes, for the time being," drawled Einarsen. "There will be other things for you to see to, but they can wait. You might as well go."

The boy made for the door, crouching down awkwardly, as if he didn't dare to leave in a hurry.

"Just a minute," said Morck; "maybe you could go out to the shops and get me something?" In detaining the boy, was he making a gesture of opposition to Einarsen? To calm him down a little, proffer friendship and acceptance? Yes, Morck had meant precisely that, and Einarsen stood by uneasily, fully aware of the connection. "If you have time, that is?"

"Yes, I have," said the boy, reacting to his intervention in the opposite way to what he had intended. He lingered in the doorway, trapped at the very moment he thought he had escaped.

"Go down to the newsagent's and get three large sheets of green blotting paper for us to use as writing pads. Here's ten kroner, that should be enough."

Morck went over and handed him the money, adding, "Keep the change."

The boy darted a shy glance at him, and immediately withdrew his eyes, then hurried out.

"Timorous as a hare and scared as a mouse," said Einarsen. Morck sat down, trying the table for height.

"These table-tops are something of a strain to look at," he said in explanation. Unintentionally he had used the familiar "you" to young Bahnsen, because Einarsen had done so—or was it because he thought of him as a mere boy?

"I'm not that fussy," said Einarsen casually; adding shortly after with the same degree of detachment, and without so much as looking up from his paper work, "As we were saying, shouldn't I be left to deal with him when we get to that stage? Not that there's any harm in letting him soften up a bit first."

"Soften up." Morck didn't like the expression. It was too near the truth for comfort. "Where's Herting?"

"He's gone to have a word with the doctor. He should be back soon. There's a cubicle next door where he can install himself. It would be useful too for more private interrogation."

The door was open, and Morck went to take a look. The room was used as a store; blue painted linen cupboards and shelves for china lined the walls from floor to ceiling. It was not much more than nine feet across. In the far wall was a single window, fitted with a creased and discoloured blind on a spring roller. A single bulb in a white kitchen lampshade dangled from the ceiling and shone on the table. There was just room enough for one chair on either side.

"Where does that door lead to?"

"To a passageway which in turn leads to the kitchens and then out to the stairway."

Morck turned the handle. The door was locked.

54

"Highly suitable for a meditation chamber, eh?" said Einarsen. Morck had to turn the expression over in his mind a little before he remembered what it referred to. Meditation chamber was a euphemism in reform school for the cells where children used to be put into solitary confinement following a breach of discipline. Did they still exist? The idea was that they should meditate on what they had done . . . to soften them up under lock and key.

Just then Herting returned, having spoken to the doctor.

"He really had nothing to say—this was lying outside the door."

The wrapping-paper had owls on it. Morck unpacked three sheets of rolled-up blotting paper.

"Carrying all these birds of prey around must have given him the willies," said Einarsen.

"Quite," said Morck. "So the doctor didn't know of any sudden illnesses that night?"

"No, neither in the summer house area nor in town," said Herting. "He was called out to deliver a baby about midnight and didn't get back till nearly three in the morning. Nobody had rung him between these hours."

"Could his wife corroborate that?"

"No, she was away for a few days visiting relatives. But when he goes out, he turns on the telephone answering-machine which gives his whereabouts, and messages can be left for him on it. You can tell if the phone has rung even if no message is left."

"And there was nothing on the tape when he came home?"

"No, nothing," said Herting. "I didn't get much joy out of him."

"Joy or no joy, it's still information," said Einarsen. "What do you say, Morck?"

Morck didn't reply immediately, but crumpled up the wrapping-paper and looked under the table for a wastepaper basket. There wasn't one. Laying it down on the window sill, he hesitated a moment then put one piece of blotting paper at the end of his own table, saying to Herting: "You might as well sit here. We can use the small room in there as a writing-room for the time being."

He went over and laid another piece of blotting paper on Einarsen's table. Einarsen regarded him quizzically, "Well . . ?"

"Our unidentified patient maybe didn't need the doctor, but did need a nurse . . ."

"If so, the doctor would know about it. He's in charge of the nursing service, isn't he?"

55

"It might have been a former patient, whose case she was familiar with."

"And who suddenly recovered sufficiently to murder her in gratitude for her care and attention," added Einarsen sarcastically.

"Cut the chatter," said Morck. "We're weighing the possibility that she was called out there on some pretext by a patient."

"Out where?" queried Herting. "We found out next day that the summer houses in the area had been unoccupied."

"Yes, the next day," said Morck. "But even if the patient wasn't in any of the summer houses, how was she to know that?"

"Maybe she didn't know."

"It's at least a strong possibility that she was called out in a professional capacity whether or not that was a mere pretext."

"Actually, there are two possibilities," said Einarsen.

"Yes. If it was a pretext, we can assume that the murderer made the telephone call," said Morck. "But if the call was genuine . . . in other words, if she was really called out to see a patient, we can readily imagine that——"

"We can readily imagine all manner of things," said Einarsen. He looked bored, as if these were no more than utter trivialities being dragged up for the hundredth time.

"That the murderer was a different person to the one who made the call," Morck concluded. "If this is so, the murderer must have accosted her on her way to visit the patient."

"How could he know she was on her way there?"

"I don't know."

"Surely you don't think he took up his position on that path miles out along the beach road by chance; then stood there killing time till one in the morning when he saw her driving along, stopped her, and asked her to come for a walk in the bushes?"

"No, that's not what I think," said Morck. "Have you any other objections?"

"None, except that I can see us mounting a search for a patient who possibly doesn't exist, together with your mad telephoner, who presumably doesn't exist either."

"You've got the picture exactly."

"Then that's given us something to do at least," said Einarsen. "But having some dirt to scratch about in doesn't mean we've got a case. If we do find we have a spare minute or two after all, we could always consider using them to look for the murderer."

"Yes, we could do that," said Morck impassively.

Was he even listening? It occurred to Herting that their conversation was less of an exchange of views than a sparring match, where each needled the other about the ideas they supposed each had formed.

"Can you take in these summer houses tomorrow when you've gone through the flat?"

"Sure I can," said Einarsen with a shrug; "but it means I'd have to break in unless we want to waste a few days getting permission from the owners."

"Most of the houses are let when the owners aren't using them, I take it?"

"The tourist office sees to the lettings," said Herting, "or rather, the bookseller does; he keeps the keys."

"Thank you," acknowledged Einarsen with a slight inclination of the head. One could never be sure when he was being sarcastic, thought Herting, or rather one couldn't be sure where his sarcasm was aimed. "I can always send the boy to fetch them," Einarsen went on. "Stage two of the softening-up process, you realize." Morck didn't rise to the bait, and Einarsen went on, "Then I'll work on him afterwards, OK? Of course, it'd be useful if we could force his mother to admit at the outset he'd been absent from home on that particular night."

"It would indeed," said Morck.

"Will you see to that?"

Einarsen turned to Herting and explained, "You see, we've adopted a division of labour, based on our experience, that Morck makes most headway with the more elderly ladies, while I, in all modesty, do best with the younger ones. You'd agree, eh, Jonas?"

"Of course," said Morck. "What else had the doctor to say, Herting?"

"Nothing of much importance," said Herting, consulting his notebook, but he put it away again as if there was nothing to be gained from his notes. "She has been a district nurse here in Vesterso for five years; we knew that already. The patients liked her. She was skilful and friendly. The doctor and his wife thought highly of her; they used to meet socially from time to time——"

"And so on," interrupted Einarsen. "Your doctor friend tends to rabbit on, doesn't he?"

"Yes. Frankly, he didn't have anything but commonplaces to offer."

"Let's hear them all the same," said Morck.

But Einarsen had been right. Jessen and Herting had had similar reports about her from the neighbours. Skilled, popular, engaging. She had several acquaintances whom she visited, but evidently no close friends.

"What about relations?"

"No immediate family, but some more distant relatives dotted about. There's an aunt in Grenaa where she spent the occasional holiday." Herting put the notebook back in his pocket and then added apologetically; "That's all we've managed to discover."

"And nobody hinted at any skeletons in the cupboard?" asked Einarsen.

"Skeletons? No, nobody."

"Hm . . . shall we drop this case? For today, at least. It's nearly seven and the rib roast will be getting cold."

Herting said, "If there's nothing else to do tonight, I have a date, actually."

"Off you go, then," said Morck.

And Einarsen added, "But if she starts talking about other people's happy marriages, don't let yourself be taken in. That's just an elementary tactical manoeuvre. It's only a decoy to lure you into marriage—her marriage, since that's the only one she can think of."

"I'm afraid your advice comes just a bit too late," said Herting; "we're getting married in three weeks."

"Well, why shouldn't you make as big an idiot of yourself as the rest of the present company," said Einarsen, "except Morck, of course. I'll go and order dinner."

8

THE DEAD AND the living. If Morck had not known they were pictures of the same woman, he would never have guessed. She was smiling at him from a large portrait photograph. Had she thought of making some man a present of it? And the affair had never come to anything? It was hardly the kind of picture anyone would take to keep. A sweet girl, would one say? Or a good-looking woman? Quite a handsome woman? Her smile wasn't cheerful, but rather serious, with a hint of affection . . . a hint of affection for the person taking the photograph?

Pictures can't be trusted, or rather, our impressions of a picture can't be. How much do we really see and how much do we colour what we see?

Herting had recalled that he had noticed her a number of times in Vesterso Main Street, and he had once stood next to her in a shop.

"What was your impression of her?"

"No real impression at all. She was just a very ordinary person. I didn't pay particular attention to her."

She was several years older than Herting, and he was head over heels in love, hence for that reason if no other. . .

"But what was she like? What effect did she have? Inviting, or . . ."

Herting thought that a rather strange question. Yet everyone's character radiates from them, and can be sensed immediately, whether it be cold and forbidding or warm and inviting, or whatever. The patients liked her; they were fond of her and had nothing but praise for her.

"She wasn't fat, if that's what you mean," Herting replied.

"No, I didn't mean that."

Morck sighed. He had laid out the photographs on the mahogany table in his room. He rose to switch on the lamp, sat down again and took out the pictures from the technical department. There were footsteps on the stairs, and Einarsen came in to take a look round.

"Not a bad room."

"You could easily have a room here as well."

"No, I'll be off to Esbjerg soon."

"You could drive back here tonight."

"What! In my condition? No, that would be quite inexcusable—especially for a policeman. No sense in jeopardizing your driving licence."

"Well, you'll just have to keep out of the pubs."

"A thoughtless piece of advice," said Einarsen. "Would you have me sever the connection between me and my dear wife?"

"Connection?"

"Well, both us of will be sitting in the pub at the same time although she's in the deep south and I'm bloody well . . . Apart from that, you might well ask what connection there was."

"The wind's getting up again."

"Yes, so it is," said Einarsen, with his hands deep in his trouser pockets, looking down at the pictures on the table. "Have you solved your crossword puzzle yet?"

"Hardly looked at them yet," said Morck, as more footsteps were heard on the stairs. He gathered the pictures together and covered them with a newspaper. "That'll be our tea arriving."

"Tea?"

"Yes."

"What an unlucky mishap."

"Not necessarily. Use your imagination."

"What do I have you here for?"

The girl knocked on the door and Einarsen sat down. She came in and set a tray down on the table.

"I've brought you some home-baked biscuits with your tea in case you wanted something."

"Thank you. That's very nice of you," said Morck. But though he had ordered the tea, it was Einarsen she was talking to.

"Eline, my dear," said Einarsen, "close the door a minute. There's something I want to ask you."

When Morck had left the dining-room and come upstairs, Einarsen had hung about at the bar chatting to her, which explained the familiar manner he was adopting.

"About that fellow Otto, you remember," said Einarsen.

The girl closed the door, and came back to him with a fixed stare on her face. Probably without being conscious of it, she was rubbing the back of her hand on one hip in an attempt to loosen some over-tight garment.

"Do you think he did it, then?" she asked.

"Surely you realize we can't begin by thinking anything . . . not for a while at least. We have to make step-by-step inquiries, don't we?"

"Yes."

"And you've had a lot to do with him, haven't you?"

"I suppose so," answered the girl, her stare becoming more suspicious. "If he said so——"

"He didn't. We haven't asked him yet."

"Then who——?"

"You get me wrong. I meant you both work here at the inn."

"Oh, is that all?"

"Yes, so far. Here, have a cigarette and relax a bit," said Einarsen, passing her a pack. She was blushing.

Morck wondered whether Einarsen had deliberately created this situation in order to make her give herself away—if she really had anything to give away. She lit the cigarette nervously.

"What do you want to know?" she asked.

"Anything you can tell us about him," said Einarsen. "You probably know something from working at the inn, eh? Did you say you started work here a year ago?"

"Last summer."

"And he was here at the time?"

The girl nodded and inhaled deeply. Einarsen allowed her to do this again, then went on confidentially, "Tell me, didn't you two have a bit of a flirtation to start with?"

"If anyone said that——"

"What if they did?"

She looked at him uneasily and glanced at Morck, not sure how much she could safely deny.

Einarsen said, "Damn it all, you didn't know anything about him at the time, did you?"

"No. If I'd known he kind of went round and . . . but anyway, there wasn't anything between us."

"Or at least, nothing came of it?" said Einarsen.

"No, as soon as I heard what sort he was, I didn't fancy him at all."

"Of course not. But before that?"

"There wasn't anything before that. Well, nothing much."

"Nothing much?" Einarsen raised his eyebrows with an insinuating smile.

"But that's the way it is here usually." She went on, "If you so much as walk along the street with a chap, they immediately say . . . well you know . . . and with one of his sort. . . . Do you really believe he . . ?"

Einarsen shook his head and she fell silent.

"At the moment, we're only talking things over," he said. "We have to take care not to say too much, don't we?"

"But still, it's difficult to imagine how he . . . someone you meet day in, day out——"

"Didn't he date you a lot then, during your first few weeks here?"

"Goodness, no. There was just a couple of times he came and asked me to come for a walk."

"Where to?"

"Out of the hotel and along the beach and back through the dunes and the summer houses."

"Through the plantation and the pine scrub?"

She replied, "Yes. When I think about her being murdered there . . . though I don't know if that was the exact place we came to . . . sometimes we sat down and talked."

At this point, Morck would have asked if the boy, no, if Otto Bahnsen, had made advances to her. But Einarsen was doing the talking. He smiled at her in a sceptical, knowing way.

"Did you go any further?" he asked.

"No fear. I didn't want to have anything to do with him in that way."

"Yes, but that was after you got to know about his little ways."

"But I didn't want to before that either. I suppose I must have thought there was something odd about him even then."

She sounded full of righteous astonishment as this idea dawned on her.

"What about him though?" said Einarsen. "You're not going to tell me he wasn't after a bit more, eh?"

"No, I wouldn't say that he wasn't."

"So he did try to get his way with you?"

"Yes. He tried sure enough, but I've never come across anyone who went about it as ham-fistedly as him."

"That's not hard to believe," said Einarsen.

You fool, thought Morck.

Einarsen grinned at her, "When did it happen?"

"I think it must have been one evening in late summer, we were sitting somewhere out there——" The girl stopped talking, suddenly scenting danger. "Will this get into the papers?"

"What an idea. That wouldn't do us much good. But you understand we do have to make inquiries about him?"

"Yes, I suppose you do."

"You said it happened one evening in late summer?"

"Yes, before it began to get dark early. We'd gone on one of these walks, you see, and we were sitting there and we were supposed to be having a chat. But you could hardly get a single word out of him, just mumbles of 'yes' and 'no' and 'oh', mumbles and fumbling—he's a proper clod, he is."

"What do you mean by fumbling, Eline?"

"I don't know what else you could call it—just as we were going to leave. Well, he hadn't made the faintest suggestion that's what he was thinking. No, not a hint. He was really quite stand-offish. So I just said to myself, I can't be doing with this much longer; then suddenly, just as we were about to go, he flared up."

"Flared up?"

"Yes, he did an' all, but in a funny way—he just grabbed hold of me without as much as a by your leave and squeezed himself against me. Oh, what you must be thinking."

The last remark had been addressed to Morck. She had just remembered his presence and seemed to suppose that if anyone was going to be scandalized, it would be him, not Einarsen.

"Don't worry about him," said Einarsen, "he's used to a lot worse, even if he doesn't look as if he is."

"It wasn't me that put him up to it," she said, again to Morck.

"Yes, I accept that," said Morck. "You say he grabbed hold of you. So that he could put his arms around you?"

"Yes, or something of the sort, I don't know what though," said the girl.

She was so absorbed in her story by now that the cigarette was burning away between her fingers and her West Jutland accent was more noticeable.

"Well anyway, I wasn't expecting anything like that and it was nearly dark—when he just grabbed me sudden like—I tummelt ower."

Einarsen stared at her blankly. "You what?"

"That's the local expression for fell over," explained Morck.

"Oh, I see," said Einarsen stonily. "Did he fall on top of you?"

"I didn't say that. There was no such suggestion—not frae me anyway—but, yes, he did. It was the heels on my shoes."

"Heels?"

"Aye, they were high ones, and you couldn't stand on them right."

"Oh, yes. So he pulled you so that you fell down with him on top of you. Then what?"

"I told him to let go. 'You don't think I'm going to lie here and mess about with you, do you?' I said. But he hugged me tae him, and that's not the worst of it—he was greetin' all the time."

"Greetin?" said Einarsen. "What do you mean greetin?"

"What do I mean?"

"She means sobbing," said Morck.

"Yes, that's it. And he wouldn't let go of me," said the girl. "I don't know what got into him. But I managed to pull myself away. Maybe it hurt him—but what about me? Anyway, I put the knee in."

"You put the knee in?"

"Aye, right in the groin. You can't very well let them just get on with it, can you?"

"No," said Einarsen. "Certainly not."

"So he cleared out. And when he'd gone, I said to myself, well that's the last time you go out with him; and ever since then he's kept well out of the way. He very near puts his head in a poke if he as much as sees me."

The girl had come to the end of her story and Einarsen said, "You're going to burn your fingers."

"What?"

"With the cigarette."

It had burned down as far as her nails, and she threw it hastily into the ashtray.

"Aye, it's an easy thing to get yourself into trouble," she said.

"Do you think you would remember where all this happened if you saw the place again?"

"I canna say for sure."

"We could try tomorrow."

"Try what?" she asked suspiciously.

"Are you off tomorrow afternoon?"

"Yes, between two and four."

"Then we can all drive out together and see if you can find the spot where it happened."

"But I don't want to get mixed up in anything."

"Of course you don't," said Einarsen.

She glanced doubtfully from one to the other as she left. They sat in silence, listening to the sound of her footsteps receding downstairs.

"How can you bring yourself to do that kind of thing?" said Morck.

"Oh, I could see a mile off she was one of those rather droopy but worldly-wise fillies, with a weak spirit and a willing flesh—so I reckoned it was worth a try. And she rose to the bait beautifully."

"You're a complete and utter cynic."

"There's every opportunity to be that in my job; and I'm not one to miss an opportunity."

"No, you're not," said Morck.

"If I can get her to confirm that the incident took place on the same spot as the murder . . . then I'll go for the boy."

"If *you* can get her to confirm . . ?"

"Maybe I should have taken her out there right away to avoid the risk of her cooling off by tomorrow," said Einarsen. "No, she seems accommodating, don't you think?"

"She certainly wasn't lying," said Morck; "but how far the whole episode has been dramatized in the course of recollection . . ."

"She'll stick by her version. That could be a good bit of testimony. What about our tea now that that's over? Have you a shot of something to go with it?"

Morck had but did not want to prolong Einarsen's stay. Sometimes he felt a sudden revulsion at his presence, just as at other times Einarsen found it difficult to tolerate his. Nevertheless he fetched the bottle from his coat pocket, laid out the cups and poured the tea, adding a dash of spirits to each.

"A truly maritime drink," said Einarsen, having succeeded in trapping him.

The town's relics of past glory as a seaport, the view over the bay where the sailing ships had ridden at anchor, the ships on the walls, including the five-masted barque *Copenhagen* over the bed—all these things had provided him with a pretext for buying none other than— a bottle of rum.

9

THEY DRANK THEIR tea, laced with the rum. Einarsen had one of his infrequent attacks of caloric abstinence, withdrawing the hand that had reached out for the home-made biscuits, a speciality of Mrs Petersen and of the Vesterso Inn. Morck took one, not because he was hungry, but out of a vague idea that if the girl had gone to the trouble of bringing them biscuits on her own initiative (or the landlord's) it would be improper to leave them untouched.

He poured out more tea, passed the bottle across to Einarsen, and took out the pictures from the technical department which Jessen had handed over to him.

Her legs were not bare, even if they had looked so in the photograph of the body he had already seen fleetingly at Petersen's. Maybe the photographer had used extra light to bring out the face, which was hidden in the shadow of a sapling? It was really no longer a face. Some teeth glinted in the middle where the upper lip was pulled away from them, and one eye was open. The other was hidden in the shadow.

"No, you don't ever get used to it."

"What did you say?" asked Einarsen.

"Nothing."

He must have been muttering to himself, but fortunately not loudly enough for the words to be made out. Why couldn't Einarsen slip out and find himself a bar where he could sit moping over his drink, wondering what his wife was doing in some other bar in the far south? It was of prime importance that Morck should study these pictures. But he would have preferred to do so without Einarsen, thus being spared the comments Einarsen was liable to make.

The lump of brick lay close beside the body, as if the murderer had let it drop as soon as he had used it. There were some separate photographs of the brick, taken from various angles. It was on a table; the technical people having taken it away for closer scrutiny, the results of which were obvious from the start—congealed blood and traces of skin were found.

"Did you see——" began Einarsen, but Morck interrupted him.

"Sorry, I'm looking at these photographs just now."

"Oh, if that's how you feel, I'd better watch my step," Einarsen made a knowing face at him. He understood Morck's ways.

Next came a picture of her cotton coat. The bottom button was missing, and where it had been, there was a slight tear in the fabric. Herting said that two men with dogs had combed the surrounding area but hadn't found the button. Of course, it could have been missing beforehand. But was that self-evident? How many women would like to be seen in a coat with one button missing? Yet if she'd been in a hurry, especially when she'd just got out of bed, maybe she had not even given it a second thought.

There was a general view of the clearing where she had been found, apparently taken from the path leading out to the Beach Road. At that distance, her body looked like a rag doll, sprawling awkwardly in the grass. The photograph told him nothing: pictures of bodies don't reveal very much about the living person. Nor did it tell him anything about the crime that he didn't know already.

There were other photographs like the first he had seen, close-ups, but with different exposures. She was wearing tights; her skirt was caught up, and the cotton coat, with the white nurse's coat underneath, was flung open to one side. There was something helpless and prayerful about this twisted posture, with the knees drawn upwards.

"Gosh, she wasn't a bad bit of stuff," said Einarsen. "Fine pair of thighs there."

"Oh, shut up," said Morck gruffly.

"I only happened to be looking at this one here."

Einarsen chucked a photo across the table with the gesture of a card-player. It landed on the one Morck was looking at.

She was in a bathing suit, standing on a white beach, and smiling radiantly at a man nearly a head taller than her, who in turn was smiling at her. He was in swimming trunks. They weren't touching one another, but they were clearly just about to. The picture had frozen the turning motion of her body as she stretched

68

up towards him; and his hand was moving towards her right breast.

"The joker in her pack," remarked Einarsen. "Nice fellow. Handsome guy. I wonder who he can be?"

"So do I," said Morck.

The picture could have been taken on any beach under the sun. They were almost at the water's edge, and the sea was the only background. He looked at the reverse side of the photo and noted the date.

"Five years old," he said.

"Same as the passport photo," added Einarsen. "What about this one then?"

It was a portrait of the man, on the same scale as hers. Morck laid them side by side. The same greyish tints, the same cardboard mounting.

"Togetherness, eh?" said Einarsen.

The face was angular, his unruly hair brushed back from the forehead. Morck compared it with the small photograph of them both: the little hollow above the cheek bones was the same, and so was the setting of the eyes.

"I'd say that one was five years old too."

"Quite remarkable," said Einarsen. "I find it hard to believe people still do that sort of thing nowadays. Having their photographs taken at the same studio indeed."

"That's precisely what they did," said Morck rising. He held the man's picture under the lamp so that the light fell obliquely on the mounting. The name of the photographer was very faint.

"José Mala . . . something or other. Spanish. Palma. Yes, there's no doubt about it—di Mallorca."

"You don't say," said Einarsen. "Can't we find some other place to talk about?"

"Some other place?"

Einarsen didn't reply. He was staring into space, preoccupied with his own reflections.

"I wish I knew what those two bitches are up to at this moment. They do have each other for company, but the circle's bound to be widening."

Morck refrained from comment. He looked at the pictures till Einarsen awoke from his reverie.

"Well, all that was presumably five years ago . . . the late Miss Kirsten Bunding's brief but hectic hour of bliss on a Spanish beach. Unless anything else crops up in this connection, I see no point in

69

ferreting around for her playboy. Let's stick to what we have here already."

"But we must try to establish his identity."

"O.K.," said Einarsen, "but I reckon he will have melted into the background when the summer was over, while she came home and found herself humming the melody of 'For you it was only a game, dear, But I have lost my heart to you-oo-oo.' And all she saw of him ever after was the picture in her dressing-table drawer."

"She was called Jonsson," said Morck.

"Who?"

"The girl who used to sing that song—Karen Jonsson. It must have been in the forties."

"Bloody odd scraps of information you come out with," said Einarsen. "Do you have some special storage space for them all?"

"Yes. It's called the Jonas Morck Museum of Irrelevant Information—oh, are you going?"

Einarsen had got up, and he nodded at him with a yawn. Halfway to the door, he turned round and said, "Jonas, how did you guess what the boy was doing when he went for her?"

"I'm not sure we can say he went for her."

"All right, but about him sobbing all the time? *Sobbing.* As if that was the obvious thing for him to do."

"I tried to put myself into his frame of mind at the time."

"Put yourself into——?" said Einarsen incredulously. "Lord above! I'm off to have a beer somewhere. Goodnight, Jonas."

10

It was nearly 8.30 p.m. when Morck turned into Barkway. Although it wasn't really dark yet and people hadn't yet drawn their curtains, lights were showing in most of the houses, mellowing the harsh blue glare of the TV screens.

There is something about a lighted window that never fails to attract the gaze of the passer-by. You cannot but glance towards it and a special effort is needed to avoid turning your head. Morck was reminded of the boy, twenty-two-year-old Otto Bahnsen, who could not curb his instinct to stare in at people.

A lighted window, a fleeting glimpse of other people's lives in which one has no part. Is that where the fascination lies? In the excitement of seeing people as they are when one isn't there, when they are really themselves?

Detective-Inspector Jonas Morck had his average share of human curiosity, though perhaps this was conditioned by his profession. There were five lighted windows along the short stretch of road. He found himself looking in at the first three. Through the first he saw only an empty room, through the second, an elderly lady in an armchair, not reclining, but sitting up straight, with her hands folded in her lap, concentrating intensely on the blue screen. Beside her, a man's shirt sleeves and hands could be seen holding open a newspaper. Through the third window, he saw a naked baby lying on a quilt on a table, with its legs uppermost, as in its mother's womb. The mother was leaning over it, apparently dividing her attention equally between the TV programme and changing the child's diaper.

People's lives, mused Morck, finding no more profound expression for his own thoughts, nor a suitable quotation from anyone else's. For no obvious reason he suddenly felt depressed and alone, walking along this blind side-alley. At the end of it was the beach, shrouded in evening shadow, and the bay gleaming dully under the grey sky. The wind had died down.

Morck went up the garden path with the key in his hand. He let himself into the murdered woman's flat, as his lawful business required; yet he closed the door hastily behind him, as if he didn't really want anyone to see him there. This sense of forcing an entry into private property, without having asked the owner's permission—he shook his head at the thought.

In the semi-darkness of the hallway his hand brushed against something soft. A woman's coat. He caught sight of himself in the mirror; the shadow of an uninvited guest. Was it so that the neighbours shouldn't hear him that he trod lightly and made a mental note not to step on the threshold between the hall and kitchen? The boards creaked there.

She had left a coffee cup and a wine glass on the draining board. Had she brewed coffee earlier in the evening and had a glass of wine later? Or the other way round? As if it mattered.

He didn't open any of the cupboards. He hadn't come to search the flat after all, but only to take a look round to form some impression of—yes, of what?

This was anything but clear. He didn't mean an impression of the room, with its furniture and other contents. But rather of the individuality with which each person permeates the atmosphere of his own house; so that anyone who can interpret the language can construe the individual.

There were two doors to the bathroom; one opening on to the hallway, and a locked one leading to the bedroom. He lingered on the step. The bathroom looked quite new, with its pale-green tiles, and the bidet Einarsen had remarked upon in typical Einarsenian fashion.

He closed the door and released the handle cautiously, making the lock function noiselessly. There was no real point in creeping about so quietly, as if there was a danger in being overheard; but he did it all the same.

The twilight had deepened by now, and the contours of the furniture were becoming vague. But he didn't turn on the lights, or take off his coat or sit down. He hadn't been invited—was that the reason? Or was it more on account of the suspicion—which he would be hard pressed to explain rationally—that certain things can be seen more distinctly in twilight, just as sometimes when one looks at a sharply-focused portrait with half-closed eyes, the most essential and dominant characteristics of the face emerge with greater clarity?

The black embossed volumes on the dining-room shelf were the twenty-six volumes of the *Nordic Encyclopaedia*, published at least fifty years ago. Blicher and J. P. Jacobsen, Zola and Ibsen, all in old-fashioned leather bindings. Heirlooms, no doubt. And Thor Naeve Lange. Though the middle name wasn't on the spine, he suddenly remembered it. An almost forgotten poet from around the turn of the century. He took down the small, thin volume. It stuck to the other books. By chance he came upon the lines:

> I dare tell no one of my tender love.
> I fear the song made of the dream I dreamed
> Will break this heart, which ne'er before knew love
> With too great bounteousness of joy.

Naeve. Yes, a gentle celebrant of the soft emotions. There was once a time when such verse could be written, but nowadays it was no longer possible.

He replaced the book on the shelf. The next volume was Shelley's, *The Sensitive Plant*, which also stuck to its neighbour. He pulled it out halfway, then pushed it back again, not having read much literature of that period.

Then he went through to the comfortable low-ceilinged living-room. The light had begun to fail, so that the colours of the embroidered cushions on the divan could hardly be distinguished, though the colours of the flowers by the window were still visible in the evening light. In each of the three windows was an English Pelargonium. A delicate touch. Geraniums seemed to be at home in these old houses. Sitting in the twilight. People used to do that once. Nowadays they switched on the TV. Her television stood in one corner, facing the divan. Had she watched it that evening? She had been alone, to judge from the small amount of washing-up left in the kitchen. Had she lain on the divan with the glass of wine at her elbow, watching—what? He wanted to know what had been on—not because the knowledge would be relevant, but for his own satisfaction.

They had switched on that night themselves back home, but only for a few minutes, in the middle of a film review. The scrawny critic with the subtle line in mild sarcasm had been saying:

"You now see a shot of a pale mystical moon after rain."

"He might as well be speaking in Chinese," he had commented to Marie. Apart from the word "mystical".

"Do we want to sit through all this?" she'd said.

"Shall we switch off?" He had pressed the button as the critic was saying,

"The famous Japanese film——"

Maybe the woman—he always thought of her as the woman, not as the murdered nurse, thirty-three-year-old Kirsten Bunding—maybe she too had seen that shot of a pale moon after rain? Very likely she had, but what did that add to his picture of her?

He could see her face before him now, the warm, vigorous laughing face of a woman in love. But that had been five years ago, the product of a holiday romance that had gone no further. She had come home to be caught up in the daily grind, yet she kept the photograph carefully in a drawer by her bed—"I dare tell no one of my tender love"—. A sentimental reminder for a thirty-three-year-old who was well on the way to becoming an old maid.

Another verse from Thor Naeve Lange's sensitive poem came back to him.

> I fear the song made of the dream I dreamed
> Will rouse the gentle sighs of the wind
> In the slumbering woods of night
> To mighty storms whose rage will shake the earth.

Ah, how can we ever be sure? A matter of some considerable debate. He wouldn't be any the wiser for standing here in her living-room indulging in all manner of vague speculations.

He happened to have the photograph in his jacket pocket, having put it there as he rose from the table in his hotel room. Why did you do that? he asked himself, but there was no reply. He had simply done it, just as perhaps he also . . . he felt around in his other jacket pocket; yes, it was there, and he didn't even remember having put it there. He had brought Marie's little meerschaum pipe with him. You certainly are a rum character at times, Einarsen would have said. The pipe was his own affair, but he hadn't brought the photograph along

74

to contemplate it in her domestic surroundings. He only wanted to have an idea of her everyday appearance.

There was a bookcase beside the divan, containing what must have been her own books—the ones she read herself. By now it was so dark that he could scarcely read their titles. *The Nursing Handbook.* Yes, that was obvious. *Mallorca—Holiday Island.* This would prove where the photographs had been taken, if it was five years old. He took the book from the shelf. Yes, the date of publication was six years ago. There was a large number of novels. His gaze rested by chance on some particular ones. *A Seat in the Garden, Night Visitors, Evil Fortune.* He had read this last one, by Tove Ditlevsen. The title came from the old rhyme about the raven that flies off towards evening, but must not stir by day. How did it go?

> The raven shall have evil fortune,
> For good it may not gain.

He thought better of looking at any more book-titles as he had a penchant for becoming engrossed in stray ideas. You can read what you like into anything—as Marie said. But from a psychological point of view, nothing is undetermined—as Morck said, usually in making a flimsy excuse for his tendency to interpret pure coincidences as significant sequences of events.

Facts. That's what the solving of a murder depended on. But surely the person who has been murdered is also a fact? Was he any nearer the solution—or rather nearer to *her?*

She must have gone to bed after the late news on television and about 1 a.m. she had been roused by the telephone ringing. The phone was in the dining-room, so she must have had to go through the whole flat to reach it, though there could have been another connection in the bedroom. As she was a nurse, she would be bound to receive calls from time to time at night.

He went into the bedroom. There was an extension but not on the dressing-table. Hadn't Einarsen been prattling about pictures on the dressing-table? The telephone was on a little chest by the bed. The quilt was flung aside and on it, her nightdress lay in a heap. It was either blue or turquoise, maybe green, but there was too little light to tell.

She had been roused by the telephone and had talked to somebody who asked her to come right away. She must have known who it was, surely?

She had got up immediately and put on her clothes—what, in the dark? No, she was in a hurry to leave so she had put the light on. But the curtains were not drawn. Not drawn? Why?

Morck stood motionless for an entire minute, maybe two, staring past the murdered woman's bed at a double window with six panes, and curtains—not drawn. Could she have forgotten in her haste to get dressed? Surely not. Does a woman living alone forget such a thing? Wouldn't she draw the curtains automatically, obeying an unfailing reflex? Someone could peer in at her getting dressed; and there was just such a person in Vesterso.

The Peeping Tom, as Einarsen had called him. She must have known about him, as everyone did, according to Petersen, and known that he wandered restlessly about the town late at night, sometimes irresistibly attracted by the sight of a lighted window.

The window faced south, like the living-room windows. At the foot of the garden there was a public footpath. The boy must have been walking along it some evening when there was a light in her bedroom window, and he could easily have broken through the hedge into her garden unnoticed; maybe there was even a gate, and there were no street lights nearby. All this she must have realized.

And yet she had forgotten to draw the curtains, unless . . . yes, unless she had forgotten precisely because she wasn't in the habit of doing so and she didn't even draw them when she was undressing for bed. Though she must have known. Did she leave them because she knew? That someone could be standing out there in the darkness watching her?

Was this a possibility? Exhibitionism was the word—an unhealthy desire to expose oneself to the opposite sex, reflected Morck. Labels are attached to actions in order to fulfil the need for a common name covering all shades of meaning. One could equally talk of an unful-filled desire for love, which in some cases leads to extravagances.

This thirty-three-year-old woman who—we are forced to admit it —still hankers after a man she fell for five years ago, and still looks at the picture of him she has hidden in a drawer by her bed; this woman cannot accept that he no longer so much as glances in her direction, that he no longer finds her desirable.

Could she have derived a kind of comfort—if one could use such an expression—a dreamlike, nocturnal solution of emotional tensions, from the knowledge that sometimes there was another man out there as she was going to bed? Only a reticent twenty-two-year-old, admittedly, but still a man of sorts in the darkness outside her window, looking in at her with passive and hopeless longing? Then, after she had turned out the light, she may have lain listening to his footsteps receding through the garden—a miserable way of being loved. But possibly better than not being loved at all.

How can we tell? About such things, we cannot. It was only his imagination, deluded by the dusk and the sound of the night wind's breath in the shrubbery bushes, heard through the open window, that was filling him with all manner of extravagant notions. All because of the merest triviality—that, by chance, she had forgotten to draw the curtains. Have a care, he cautioned himself, you're losing your grip. Random association, as they say in the psychiatric reports.

Anyway, there was another possibility, which until now had not occurred to him, namely that Jessen, Herting, or the two men from the technical department had opened the curtains during their inspection of the flat.

Herting had given him a number to ring if he wanted to get in touch with him. Should he ring up and ask? If only to settle the question right away and put it out of his mind. He made these and other excuses for himself as he crossed to the chest with the telephone on it. He found the slip of paper in his pocket and there was just enough light from the window to read the number.

"Herting?"

"Yes, speaking."

Herting's voice was thick and he sounded surprised, as if the phone had woken him up. Was he in bed with his bird? There was a faint rustling and something reminiscent of a whisper in his vicinity. He was definitely in bed.

"Morck here. Sorry for disturbing you."

"It doesn't matter," said Herting, half-heartedly.

"There's just something I wanted to ask you: Did you open the curtains in her bedroom?"

"Did we what?"

"Did either you or Jessen or any of the others open the curtains in her bedroom?"

"No, we didn't."

"You're quite sure you didn't? Were you the first to go into the room?"

"I went in immediately after Jessen," said Herting, "and the curtains weren't drawn. I daresay we didn't pay special attention. After all, it was daylight at the time. But I did notice there's a tree bang up against the window and it keeps the light out; that was why I thought——"

"Yes, I quite understand. Thanks very much, Herting."

"You're in the flat now?"

"Yes," said Morck absent-mindedly. He had turned to face the window. There, confronting him less than two yards away, was the tree that kept the light out, a tall and sturdy fir, full of vitality. In the half-light it looked black. He only became aware of a paler patch against the blackness when it moved ever so slightly.

"You must obviously think the curtains are of some importance," said Herting.

"Goodbye, Herting." Morck didn't realize he'd said it. He replaced the receiver as Herting was making some puzzled reply. The moving patch was a human hand; and now he made out another grey patch, which must have been the man's face, all but hidden in the dense fir tree.

11

MORCK MADE HIS way rapidly and noiselessly through the house. Fortunately there was no furniture blocking the passage from one door to the next, so he didn't have to worry about colliding with anything in the dark. He closed the outside door gently and crept through the front garden on the row of paving stones that lay close to the house. He straddled the fence then hurried round by the garage, along the side of the building, where another fence surrounded the back garden. There was a gate, but it might have made a clicking sound, so rather than use that, he straddled the fence again. Then along the south side of the house on another row of paving stones, and on towards the fir tree by her bedroom window up against the neighbour's fence.

"Are you still there?" he said sharply. The man started, then emerged from his hiding place, like a shadow detaching itself from the gloom of the fir tree.

"Yes, I'm sorry. I suppose you must be from the police?"

"Yes."

"I thought so. But since the light wasn't turned on . . . I thought I ought to make sure. You never know, do you? You see, she is my neighbour . . . I mean, she was. I'm Henrik Steffensen, customs officer, retired."

"And I'm Detective-Inspector Morck."

"Oh, then I see why . . ." He mopped his brow with a large pallid hand, the gesture of an old man. There was still a faint tremor in his precise but pleasing voice.

Morck said, "I must have startled you."

"Oh, a little. I didn't see you or hear you coming. As I said, I thought I ought to take a look . . . just in case. We usually do—we usually did—keep an eye on one another's houses if either of us was away. Just the occasional look."

"I expect you must have known quite a lot about Kirsten Bunding?"

"As a neighbour, yes——" the old man began, then broke off as he realized he was about to repeat himself. "Yes," he added, "of course we knew each other."

"Could I have a word with you?" said Morck. "That is, if you can spare a few minutes?"

"Surely. But I don't think I can add anything to what I've already told one of your colleagues—or rather, two of them. I had to make a statement to PC Petersen first."

"I'm not so much concerned about the plain facts as——"

"As what? If you'll pardon my asking?"

The question was shot at him abruptly, as if the retired customs officer wished to indicate he'd had enough of all this probing, which was not to his liking.

"As to forming an impression of Kirsten Bunding's personality, and her nature in general," said Morck.

"I'm sure I won't have anything important to tell you, but perhaps you'd care to come in?"

"Thank you."

Conversation is impossible with a man whose face you only see as a grey mask in the darkness, with black sockets for eyes and a pale glimmer for a nose.

"Do come this way."

He led the way through a gate in the fence that divided his property from Kirsten Bunding's. Morck shut it behind him, noticing that the posts were pitted and rotting. They were decaying away in the shade of the tall fir, the result of rain dripping off the thatch; there was no form of lock. It closed with a dull thud, and he followed the upright figure of Steffensen, who had a springy gait not to be expected in an old man.

"I'll go and put the lights on," said Steffensen, entering the darkened house by an open garden door, and turning on the lights.

"Is your place the twin of the one next door, Mr Steffensen?" asked Morck entering the house.

"Yes, as a matter of fact, it is," he replied, raising his eye-

80

brows in remote surprise. "Perhaps you'd like to see the other rooms?"

Almost a polite invitation—almost, but with that familiar undertone, thought Morck, that signified, "Here comes one of those nosey snoopers who thinks he has a right to pry into the private lives of respectable, law-abiding citizens just because he's out to catch a criminal." Sometimes people said as much to his face. Their reaction was as common as that almost imperceptible turning up of the nose at his occupation which he had experienced among these same respectable, law-abiding citizens: "What an unpleasant job it must often be for you." How right they were. It was often highly unpleasant.

"That wasn't what I had in mind," he said. "It just occurred to me that the two flats were the same, except that yours must be the mirror image of hers."

"Er . . . mirror image? Yes, one could put it that way."

"And so your bedroom is through the wall to hers?"

Steffensen looked at him for a moment in silence. A silence of disapproval or incomprehension. Then he nodded agreement.

"So that's why you were able to hear the telephone ringing?" went on Morck following Steffensen into one of the rooms.

"Yes. But I absolutely forget . . . oh, do please sit down."

"Thank you."

Steffensen motioned him to a heavy old-fashioned wing chair, upholstered in leather, beside a large desk which also served as Steffensen's daily dining-table. He removed a tea cup and a plate, putting them somewhere out of sight, and sat down on the other side of the desk in a high-backed chair with elaborately carved arms, and upholstered in rather worn chequered embroidery.

Against one wall was a cupboard with shelves above and drawers below, and against the other was a dark plush sofa with grey covers on the arms and seat. There was a smell of stale tobacco in the room. On one window sill was a stand with seven or eight pipes, on the other, a drooping green plant in a pot. Only one picture hung on the walls: one of a blue lake with golden-brown reeds at the edge, from which a flight of ducks had risen in formation. Steffensen opened a drawer in the desk.

"Cigar? Mr Morck, isn't it?"

"I'll have one of my own cigarettes, if you don't mind."

Steffensen put the box back in the drawer, without taking one.

"Yes, I was woken up by her telephone. My window was half-open, and at my age, you sleep lightly."

How old was he? About sixty, or more like seventy? His narrow but powerful face with its long weathered furrows, and clear unwavering eyes did not give the impression of old age.

"The time was either eight or twelve minutes to one, I'm not sure which."

"Did you switch on the light?"

"No. My alarm clock has a luminous dial."

"And you thought it unusual for her to be rung up so late?"

"It didn't happen very often. But she was a nurse, after all, and people are sometimes taken ill in the middle of the night."

"How much of her telephone conversation could you make out?"

"Only the odd word or two. I remember her asking something about the doctor, and eventually she said she'd come immediately. But I've told your colleagues all this twice already, as I said."

"And you haven't had any further thoughts since then?"

"No, why should I?"

"Something could always have come back to you on further reflection; her tone of voice, for example. Was it reluctant? Did she sound as if she already knew the caller?"

"I couldn't commit myself there," said Steffensen with some signs of irritation, taking a tobacco-pouch from the drawer and filling his pipe decisively and with precision, as if to indicate that the interview was virtually at an end.

"You didn't notice either whether she used the polite or the informal 'You'?"

"No."

He laid the filled pipe down in the ashtray without lighting it.

"You see, Mr Morck, I am not in the habit of listening to other people's telephone conversations."

"I'm not suggesting that you are. But in this case . . . it was more or less unavoidable, surely? Your window was half-open, and so was hers; the two windows are close together, so that you . . ."

Morck fell silent, suddenly feeling the need to be on the defensive. His sometimes unpleasant job—how often it seemed to consist of asking people questions which they saw as a form of aggression.

"From what you heard, did it appear she was being asked to visit a patient?"

"That was my impression."

"And she drove off shortly after, I believe?"

"Yes, at about two minutes past one, I'd say."

"You didn't look at your alarm?"

"No. I'd gone through to the kitchen for a glass of water, when I heard the car back out, drive up to the main road and turn left."

"How could you tell that it was turning left?"

Steffensen did not answer, but looked down at the tobacco-pouch. He moved it so that it lay parallel to the edge of the desk, pondering his reply.

"Perhaps I didn't express myself accurately," he said. "I could hear from the sound of the engine that it was going north, and consequently, she must have turned left. You realize that in a small town like this, you know a little about nearly everybody, at least, you know who they are. So you automatically wonder who could be needing the nurse at that time of night."

"But you didn't come up with any ideas?"

He shook his head, evidently not relishing the question. Morck lit his cigarette, having held it in his hand for some time. He began to show the familiar signs of nervousness and tension that resulted from his having gone about something in the wrong way. This time he was on the point of failure. He had annoyed the old man by asking him the same question again, as if he wanted to put his honesty to the test by seeing whether the answer would be the same. But elderly gentlemen of a certain worth, of a fossilized turn of mind, can be utterly unhelpful if they think their honesty is being doubted. Nevertheless, Morck went on in the same vein, without really knowing why.

"Mr Steffensen, did you put on the kitchen light when you went for the glass of water?"

"Did I . . . ?" He fell silent again, adjusted the tobacco-pouch, and frowned. "Yes, I may well have done . . . yes, I remember doing it now. But I honestly can't see why it should be of any interest to you."

"Perhaps it was to the murderer."

"What do you mean?"

"Supposing he was nearby at the time, he might have been worried if a light had gone on in your place, and afraid you might have caught sight of him and recognized him—in the street, for example."

"I didn't see anyone," said Steffensen.

"You didn't see anyone?"

"No, that is, not before I put the kitchen light on."

"Did you look out of the window?"

"Not really . . . that is, I didn't go to the window and look out," said Steffensen after a short pause for reflection. Morck sensed that a change had come over him, in the space of a few seconds, as if he had suddenly come to accept his rôle in the proceedings and was beginning to find it quite intriguing.

"But you realize, Inspector . . . er . . ."

"Morck."

"Yes. I beg your pardon, Mr Morck. My memory plays me tricks now and again. You realize if you come into a dark kitchen you automatically look towards the window before putting the light on. I didn't see anyone on the street at the time: anyone I saw would have had to be more or less right outside the window. May I ask if you have reason to believe there was somebody?"

"No, I wouldn't say I had. I was merely considering the possibility. But you said 'at the time', Mr Steffensen."

"What?"

"You said you didn't see anyone at the time."

"So?"

"That prompts me to ask you if you noticed anyone on the street earlier in the evening, whose presence there you thought significant?"

"No, I can't say I did, really," Steffensen said deliberately. "No, I wouldn't call it significant . . . after all, it has happened so often, that it can scarcely be of much importance."

"What has?"

Steffensen hesitated. He picked up the pipe from the ashtray, struck a match, and lit it thoughtfully. Not until the tobacco was burning smoothly, and he had waved the smoke out of the way did he go on.

"I've no wish to make things difficult for other people; as I say, this town is a small place, where people know one another, and I can't imagine that young chap having anything to do with it . . . he's said to be a bit peculiar, but otherwise quite harmless. Still, now that you ask, I have to admit that he did go by here late at night, as he does from time to time—frequently in fact."

"I assume you're talking about Otto Bahnsen, the boy who works at the inn?"

"Ah, so you've heard about his unfortunate habit of peeping in at people? Yes, of course you're bound to have."

"What time did you see him?"

"About eleven-thirty, or maybe eleven-forty-five. I'd opened the garden door to let some air in before going to bed. I was standing outside smoking my pipe and looking at the weather for perhaps five minutes. During that time, the light went out next door at Kirsten's, and soon after——"

He broke off and bowed his head a moment, as if to conceal a look of pain. Then he pulled himself together, puffed audibly at his pipe and blew the smoke away.

"Where was I?"

"The light went out next door . . . meaning the bedroom light, I assume?"

"Yes, and soon after that I saw him come round the corner, along the path that runs past the foot of both gardens, then follow my hedge down to the opening on to Barkway. From there he went up to Main Street."

"Did you see him do that?"

"Yes, I'd gone through to the kitchen with my cup and plate," said Steffensen. "As you no doubt noticed, I'm a bit lackadaisical about clearing up after supper, so without paying any special attention, I watched him from my kitchen."

"You don't know whether he had been in her garden?"

"No, I didn't see him. But he has been in there several times; I've caught him hanging about."

"And what did you do?"

"I just gave him the rough edge of my tongue and told him to clear out."

"Did you ever tell Kirsten Bunding about it?"

"No, I didn't see any point in making her feel uneasy—especially as he has always been considered quite harmless in other respects. Anyway, he's not the sort you could easily imagine would . . ." Steffensen tailed off, shaking his head, then after a pause, he said, "You mustn't suppose I'm eager to tell you all this."

"No, I don't," said Morck.

"But now that I've started, I might as well tell you that one evening a week or two ago, as I was going out for a walk before bedtime, I caught him sitting in her car."

"In the garage?"

"Yes. It was raining, and whether he'd got inside to shelter or not, I couldn't say. I asked him the reason, but he just muttered his usual answer, 'I don't know', and hurried off. He hasn't much of a brain, so he finds it difficult to understand his own actions, let alone explain them to others."

"Was he sitting in the driver's seat?"

"Yes, he was. But I don't think he had any intention of starting the engine. He was just sitting there."

"I see," said Morck. "And you didn't tell Kirsten Bunding about that incident either?"

"No. I didn't see the point of telling her. I didn't think it mattered much, nor would she have thought so. She knew as much about his quirks as anyone else did. I have told you all there is to know now, I believe."

"Indeed," said Morck, putting his cigarette out in the ashtray. "May I ask, Mr Steffensen, what was your own relationship to Kirsten Bunding?"

Before the words were out of his mouth, he knew that they were an unfortunate choice.

Steffensen raised his eyebrows and sat bolt upright in the chair.

"What do you mean by relationship?"

"As neighbours you doubtless saw something of one another?"

"Only as neighbours do."

"Did you ever meet in more convivial circumstances?"

"If the occasional cup of coffee can be called convivial, then yes. We used to meet much as everybody else in the street does. Only a few weeks ago we both had an invitation from the engineer across the way, and several other people from Barkway were there. Then occasionally the family further along would ask people in. That's the way we go about it here."

"Sounds very friendly."

"Yes, very. And as I've already said, if either of us was away, the other would keep an eye on things."

"Did you leave keys with one another, to make sure the flowers would be watered? I noticed Kirsten Bunding had quite a few geraniums."

Steffensen smiled a faint and curious smile which deepened the lines on his face.

"No, I wasn't entrusted with watering the flowers; she didn't have any confidence in my talents for that sort of thing . . . with good reason. The cleaning lady saw to that when she came twice a week."

86

Morck nodded.

"Who was the cleaning lady?"

Steffensen shrugged his shoulders, then he said, almost regretfully, "Mrs Bahnsen, I'm afraid—the boy's mother."

"Really," said Morck. There was a long silence. "So he sometimes came here when his mother was doing the cleaning?"

"Yes, sometimes."

"And Kirsten Bunding was often around too?"

"Yes, I suppose she was," said Steffensen, fidgeting and shifting his position in the chair. He looked older than before, and had an air of uneasiness or impatience.

"I have answered your questions, Mr Morck," he said; "but hasn't the subject been explored sufficiently by now? I certainly have nothing else to tell you."

"Not even about your impression of her personality?"

"That would only serve to confirm what your colleagues have already learned from talking to the neighbours."

The old man seemed tired, impatient and less accommodating. He had had enough.

"Just one further question, before I go," said Morck; "she has lived here for . . . isn't it four years?"

"More. Four and a half years."

"Do you know if, during that time, she has had any close relationship with a man?"

"I don't know what you mean by 'close relationship'," said Steffensen curtly. "As far as I'm aware, there weren't any men who visited her regularly, and I would hardly have failed to notice such a thing."

"That wasn't exactly what I meant. I was wondering whether there might have been a man who visited her occasionally, or even only once."

"I'm not aware that there was."

"Or possibly a man she sometimes went to visit, even once in a while?"

"No, I really couldn't say . . ."

"Even if she didn't mention him directly, something she said might have suggested——"

"We never talked about such matters, Mr Morck, not even in a suggestive way," said Steffensen curtly. Yet his disapproval was momentarily overcome by curiosity. "Who could this man be?" he asked.

"I don't know. But I have a picture of him here. Perhaps you might recognize him."

Almost reluctantly Morck took the photograph from his jacket pocket and handed it across the table. Steffensen laid it aside while he looked for his spectacles.

"My eyes are not as good as they used to be," he said, "but I can always take a look." He put the spectacles on and squinted at it by the light of the lamp. Then he started, and for a split second registered shock or immense surprise.

"Do you know who he is?" said Morck.

"No, I don't," said Steffensen. "I can only just recognize her in that photo. She doesn't look at all like she really was . . . if you see what I mean."

"Quite," said Morck, as the old man pushed the photograph away with a frown that suggested he found it offensive. A half-naked woman, leaning invitingly against an unidentified man, and laughing up at him in the elation of love—this didn't fit the picture Steffensen had formed of his neighbour.

12

WHEN HE GOT back to the inn, Morck locked himself in the marine room and hurriedly typed out a report of his conversation (or interview, as he called it) with Henrik Steffensen, retired customs officer. He was able to condense it into a few lines, which largely concerned Otto Bahnsen's behaviour in the vicinity of Kirsten Bunding's house prior to the murder. He also added two notes to the text. One was a rough estimate of the time—11.30 p.m.–11.45 p.m. "namely one hour before the phone call"—a superfluous addition—and the fact that "Steffensen was standing at his garden door taking the air, when he saw Otto Bahnsen come along the path at the back of the house, go round by the meadow then turn into Barkway and up to Main Street. Steffensen says that he has seen Bahnsen in Kirsten Bunding's garden on a number of previous occasions, peeping in at the windows. Two weeks ago . . ." Then came the bit about the car. "He was only sitting in it, according to Steffensen."

Morck wondered whether Steffensen had switched off the light in the dining-room before going to the garden door. If not, Otto Bahnsen would have realized that he was being watched. He'd forgotten to ask Steffensen. Something always gets left out. But surely the light hadn't been on; it wouldn't be. He was willing to bet that Steffensen was in the habit of switching out lights as soon as he had left a room—good old-fashioned thriftiness. He had turned the lights off this evening before going into his neighbour's garden to see if whoever was in the murdered woman's house had any business to be there. It hadn't occurred to him that it might have been the police. Maybe that wasn't the most obvious of answers. Morck heaved a sigh. For some reason or other, his thoughts instinctively turned to his wife, "and you a policeman", she would say.

But the business of the car . . . the boy hadn't been sitting in the driver's seat intending to drive the car, nor just to shelter from the rain. Why then? "I don't know." He found it difficult to understand his own actions, let alone to explain them to others. Yet who doesn't, in certain frames of mind, no matter what their level of intelligence?

Would he, Morck, for instance, be able to give a rational explanation of why he had remained in Kirsten Bunding's house in semi-darkness? In the attempt to form an impression of—of what? Her nature? The phrase carried even less weight in reporting jargon than the boy's timid muttering of "I don't know". Or was he trying to sense her presence, to conjure her up, in some way? Such questions were meaningless and if he were asked them, he would simply look blank.

"And you a policeman." Ought he to have rung home tonight? He hadn't thought of doing so till now, and it was a quarter to eleven, rather late to ring. Anyway, Marie wouldn't be at home. She usually went over to visit their daughter, Dorit, and her husband in Hillerod the first night he was away. He hoped for his wife's sake that their eight-month-old grandchild wouldn't sleep too soundly, but wake up yelling, so that she could make a fuss of it. Grandma! How incredible—and to think of himself as Grandpa was utterly impossible.

He puzzled over the other note he had made on his pad. "To the left." Then its significance came back to him. Steffensen had heard the nurse drive off along the Beach Road in a northerly direction, and next morning, while he was taking his usual walk down to the beach, he'd begun to worry about her, on seeing the car parked in that deserted spot by the pine scrub . . .

Morck finished writing his report. On paper, it all seemed to add up. The relevant facts. And there was every temptation to draw the one conclusion that stared him in the face.

Yet how could that poor timorous creature, with his bottled-up emotions, have driven himself to do such a thing? Always poised for flight, for escape.

What had Einarsen said? In a panic situation, he might well swing over to the other extreme. And the opposite of flight is attack. No doubt Einarsen was right. They did come across cases of a sudden volte-face, and many things pointed to . . . at least they hadn't yet discovered any evidence to the contrary. True, there were still two unexplained factors they would have to look into. One was the telephone call, which might be accounted for in one of the summer houses. And the other was the unidentified man by her side on a Spanish beach. Maybe they would never find him. A holiday affair of five years ago, who had evidently not been in touch since then.

Morck got up, took the report over to Einarsen's table and fixed it firmly in the roller of his typewriter. Bloody good stuff this, Einarsen would say tomorrow, declaring the case closed. So now he'd wade into the boy.

Suddenly Morck felt dead tired. He locked up the marine room, went to his room and got into bed. He was a long time in falling asleep. The case sounded fairly straightforward but he was tormented by guilt, as if he had overlooked some essential point. Something of decisive importance for the solution of the murder.

During the night, he had to go to the bathroom along the corridor. When he came back, he stood at the window for a while to clear his head, and gazed out at the harbour. Five past two. Two fishing boats, each about twelve or fifteen tons he reckoned, were moored to the long pier which served as a harbour. There was no enclosed basin. In the town's heyday, two- and three-masted sailing ships had lain at anchor out in the bay. Through the open window he could hear the subdued cackle of a flock of seagulls in nocturnal conference.

The street lights went out as he watched; then the harbour and the whole town was in darkness, apart from a lighted window here and there. But there was still a flood of light from the phone booth by the harbour—where the call had come from. Tomorrow he would have to——

"Oh, give over," muttered Morck. This was no time of night to be anticipating the tasks of the next day.

He went back to bed, and while he was settling himself, he wondered whether his wife had taken the last train home or was spending the night in Hillerod with Dorit. She must have come home. "I'd love to stay," she'd have said, "but it's best to get back to your own bed."

For almost a minute, Morck listened to the sound of the seagulls mingling with the wind outside, then he fell fast asleep.

13

THE NEXT MORNING was overcast. Under the grey sky the wind whipped the grey waters of the bay into crisp white crests. Morck sat drinking his coffee by the farthest window in the dining-room. Already this had become his usual table. There were two others apart from him, obviously regular customers. Both were youngish office-workers, in their early thirties. Their customary table, laid ready for them, was over by the wall. They were locals, and from the remarks they made over breakfast, Morck deduced that one worked in the bank in Main Street, the other in the post office. A bank clerk and a post office cashier, thought Morck, wondering how, in a town with a very limited number of salaried and pensionable jobs, they had contrived to preserve their bachelor status for so long; so much so that one of them was beginning to put on weight and the other was bald on top.

The girl, Eline, wasn't serving this morning, her place being taken by the landlord's wife, a powerful, angular woman in her late fifties. Her grey hair straggled untidily due to the steam of the pots in the kitchen. It was a face that seemed to be at a constantly high temperature. In contrast to the landlord's fussy servility, her conversation was sparse, and her voice was remarkably throaty.

"Do you think it will rain today?" Morck asked, for the sake of something to say as she was laying the table.

"Not wi' this wind."

She sounded as if she was directing a threat at the rain. Just let it try . . .

She went off to the kitchen for the coffee pot, and having poured it out, completed her forecast.

"It's grey enough, though . . . just call if you want more coffee."

"Thank you."

On the way back to the kitchen, she opened the corridor door and shouted, "Bahnsen, tak these empties oot."

The sound of the vacuum cleaner stopped. Before Morck realized who she'd been shouting at, the boy came in from the corridor and shot a shifty glance in his direction. Then he slunk behind the bar and didn't take his eyes off the ground as he carried the two crates of empty bottles into the kitchen. He didn't come back through the dining-room. Soon the vacuum cleaner started up again in the corridor. He must have gone round by another way, maybe out into the yard by the back door and round to the front entrance, to avoid Morck's presence.

The two office-workers had eyed him curiously as he was taking the crates out. The one sitting with his back to the bar had even turned round. They knew the police suspected him, and were surprised he hadn't been arrested yet, which was why they were putting their heads together and talking in such low voices that Morck couldn't hear what they were saying. No matter, for it was the talk of the whole town.

What had Einarsen said? It would do the boy no harm to soften him up a little.

"Damn rotten job you have sometimes, Jonas," he said to himself. He seldom used his own Christian name and whenever he did, it was a bad sign.

The bank clerk and the post office cashier—if these were, in fact, their occupations—left just before eight-thirty. As soon as they were gone, the landlord's wife emerged from the kitchen, and opened the door of the corridor. It was empty, but the vacuum cleaner could be heard faintly somewhere else in the building. She made for Morck's table, fixing him with a "rigid" rather than a merely "steady" stare. (There is a difference, he thought later, like the difference between Danish proper and Jutlandish.)

"Not that it's any of my business," she said, "but Eline says you're going to set to work on that boy."

Morck had no idea how to reply, so he said nothing. She kept staring rigidly at him.

"Whatever else he may get up to," she said, "—we know what that is, and I don't like the sound of it—but I can't see how it could have been him; I know him too well, nae matter what you think."

"We don't think anything at present, Mrs Mehlsen."

"Then what are you doing?"

"We're investigating a murder, Mrs Mehlsen, and surely you can see that we have to interview anyone who is connected in any way with the victim."

As if he had to state his case to her, the case for the defence. It looked as if he might have to, the way things were going.

"Aye, I understand," she said in her throaty Jutlandish. "I can't say anything against that. What else can you do? It's just that . . ." She paused, searching for the right words.

"Well?" said Morck.

"He's a poor fish and he lets people get the better of him. That's one thing."

"And the other, Mrs Mehlsen?"

"That Eline girl . . . now, how can I put it? because there's nothing wrong with her work. Now, I know it's none of my business, but she's a bit of a flibbertigibbet and likes putting on airs."

"What do you mean by putting on airs?"

"Well, making an exhibition of herself somehow or other. And you never know what that might lead to."

"No," Morck added in agreement, meaning that he saw what she was driving at.

"So maybe," she said, choosing the words with caution, "you can't take her at her face value all the time. That's all I felt I ought to say . . . you'll excuse me interfering."

"That's quite all right, Mrs Mehlsen," said Morck; "I'll bear in mind what you've said."

He nodded at her, and she withdrew her gaze, feeling the side of the coffee pot with one hand.

"This could do with being a bit warmer," she said, and took it back to the kitchen. Quite a character, thought Morck, and worthy of some degree of respect.

She brought him more hot coffee, but this time they merely exchanged courtesies. Then Einarsen came in.

"Can I have a weak coffee and a bitters, please? Do you want one, Morck?"

"No thanks."

Mrs Mehlsen brought him a cup and a glass for the bitters.

"Aren't you having anything to eat?" asked Morck.

"No, just this stuff for my sins," said Einarsen, draining the glass. In the morning he always looked gloomy and flushed.

"How were the pubs in Esbjerg?"

"Not up to much if my spot-checks are anything to go by. All exactly the same, I'd say."

"How do you mean the same?"

"Well, you see, I went into the first pub and it was deadly dull. I went into the next, and it was deadly dull. And the third——"

"Deadly dull too?"

"In all probability. But I was prevented from going in."

"Why, were you drunk?"

"Not in the least. Crazy, that's all. A passing attack of insanity," said Einarsen. "I somehow had the mad idea that the fault didn't necessarily lie with the pubs. It was just possible there was something the matter with me. Me! Can you imagine that?"

"No, that's quite beyond my powers of imagination," said Morck.

"I'm glad you're on my side," said Einarsen, looking at his empty glass. "What did I do with that glass of bitters?"

"You drank it."

"So I did, damn me. But it should be working. Do you know what I think, Jonas? I've come across this time and time again. It's a pure con trick. Somebody's messing about with the bitters these days. They're managing to extract the fuses from them. What do you think of that theory?"

"Not in my line," said Morck, "you'd have to consult the bomb squad."

"But there's no question," said Einarsen; "or would you claim that it was my own fuses that are faulty?"

"What are you talking about?" said Morck. "Why don't you just eat that spare half roll and you'll feel a lot better."

"There isn't anything wrong with me."

"Yes, sure. But get that inside you all the same."

"Very well, as you've been so understanding, I'll have a go just to oblige you."

Einarsen drank his coffee and ate the half roll. Neither seemed to agree with him, but he did begin to look a little better.

"Where's Herting?" asked Morck.

"Sitting in the marine room. We arrived at the same time. He said he'd had breakfast before he left."

"I can well imagine he did."

"Can you?" said Einarsen. "And how come you can? Have you been drilling proper eating habits into him too?"

"No, but I did talk to him on the phone last night, and I had the impression he wasn't coping with the housework unaided. I called him about a curtain that hadn't been drawn."

"In the lady's bedroom?"

"Yes."

"Hm. Where else? Did you get any more joy out of your visit to the house of the departed?"

"I got rather more from a visit to her neighbour. I've written it all down. There's a page of notes on your table. Shall we go through now and discuss the plan for today?"

When they came into the marine room, Herting was stooping over Einarsen's table looking at the sheet of paper protruding from his typewriter. He straightened up somewhat uneasily.

"I thought it'd be all right for me to read it," he said.

"Sure. Go ahead," said Morck.

"Steffensen didn't say anything about all that when Jessen interviewed him."

"Then Jessen couldn't have asked him in detail about the events of the whole evening," said Morck, shrugging his shoulders. "He must have just questioned him about what happened later that night and, anyway, Steffensen himself didn't attach any importance to the business about the boy."

"Let me have a look," said Einarsen, taking the paper out of the machine. He read it through rapidly.

"Well, blow me," he said, sitting down in the chair and starting to go through it again, this time slowly and thoroughly. "You've got a hot line on him there," he said to Morck. "I don't fancy his chances now, let me tell you."

"Let's not be in too much of a hurry," said Morck. "There's no conclusive evidence in that document. It could have been pure chance that he went past her house that night."

"And purely by chance, he tagged along behind her when she drove along the Beach Road," said Einarsen. "Purely by chance he waylaid her in the bushes and when she failed to go along, he went berserk, and purely by chance succeeded in killing her."

"Yes, that's one possibility, but it's nothing more."

Einarsen set the paper on one side, leaned back in his chair and looked at Morck in a challenging manner.

"What have you got against it?" he said. "Too straightforward for your taste, is it? Too uncomplicated?"

Morck didn't answer. Herting would have said he wasn't even listening to Einarsen.

"An emotional crime. Unpremeditated," said Einarsen.

"Yes," said Morck.

"And what gives rise to such a crime? Coincidence? A chain of coincidences?"

"Very often."

"Well, what about it?" said Einarsen. Then, apparently answering his own question, "You don't like it."

"We can't commit ourselves to that theory yet," said Morck. "Several things have still to be explained. Will you go over the summer houses this morning and the flat later?"

"Yes, I'll do that," said Einarsen; "then the waitress in the afternoon. If I can only get her to admit that the scene of the murder was the place where he had the overwhelming urge to mount her——"

"Don't go too far," warned Morck; "it mustn't be a case of you getting her to admit anything. That's not what you have in mind, I trust."

"Oh no, of course not," said Einarsen, and Herting couldn't fail to detect a note of sarcasm. "She'll do it of her own accord. What do you take me for?"

"I'll come along too," said Morck.

"Jawohl, Herr Inspector. I take your meaning."

"Good," said Morck distractedly. "Then we're agreed so far."

"What, us?" Einarsen laughed, but he didn't show any further signs of the enmity which had momentarily arisen between them. This, thought Herting, was part of their long-standing polarity, established as a more or less routine element in their team-work.

"Herting, what was it you were to do this morning?"

"Find out where the bunch of tulips in her living-room came from."

"Oh yes, that's right. It's not of much importance, but I suppose you might as well. Then after that you can try and dig up something about a man she was on holiday with in Mallorca five years ago, and whom she found very attractive."

"He means she fancied him," put in Einarsen.

Morck looked at the picture he had taken from his jacket pocket.

Ignoring the interruption, he laid it down beside the larger portrait of the man.

"Herting, do you know what height she was?"

"Five foot six."

"What! As small as that?" said Morck, though it wasn't really small, but medium height. Still, he had unwittingly imagined her as being taller, altogether bigger than that.

"Then he must be five foot nine to ten. Are you taking this down? A broad, angular face with shallow depressions under the cheek bones, darkish, low-set eyebrows, average nose, slightly indented at the top, large mouth, the lips neither narrow nor full, hair probably sandy, although it may have gone grey since the photo was taken, and I'd say he would be about forty by now. Of average build, square-shouldered, slim——"

"Five years ago, that is," said Einarsen.

"What?"

"He was slim."

"Quite. But he doesn't look the sort that puts on weight."

"Clothing?" asked Herting.

"Bathing trunks. Here, you can see for yourself." He passed Herting the photo.

"Anything else from that source, Einarsen?"

Einarsen's large blue eyes were gazing into space and there was a sceptical twist to his lips. He had made his own observations of the photo.

"He's no manual worker. Look at his hands."

The man had raised one hand to rest under her left breast—a slender hand with narrow fingers.

"He's a white-collar worker, isn't he?" said Einarsen. "Some sort of executive or professional man? Or something quite different? It's anybody's guess, I suppose."

"I can always try ringing up her aunt in Grenaa," said Herting. "She might have confided in her. Then I can ask the doctor, though I don't hold out much hope there."

"There's not much hope of finding anything other than a five-year-old layer of dust on that one," said Einarsen. "But, if you insist, have a word with the doctor's wife first. Women prefer to confide in one another about the tender secrets of the heart."

"You put it so delicately," said Morck. "Still, you could well be right."

98

"Did you get that, Herting?"

"Get what?"

"A nasty slip of the tongue," said Einarsen. "He said I could well be right. Are you losing your grip then, Jonas?"

"Yes, I must be," said Morck, rising. "Shall we be going? I'll go and have a word with Otto Bahnsen's mother, for a start."

"After Steffensen's revelations, she's going to find it difficult to maintain he was at home all evening," said Herting.

"Not a bit of it," said Einarsen. "She's his mother—and he's a heel. And a heel's mother doesn't make any bones about it. Anyway, the son's been a heel for long enough."

14

THEIRS WAS NOT one of the thatched houses. The roof was of
dark slate between whitewashed gables. The remaining walls were
of red brick, but their colour had faded. There were two windows
on each side of the green front door. The street doors of the older
houses in the town were nearly all green. The nameplate read
B. BAHNSEN; but above this, two white cards had been pinned up
on the right-hand side of the door frame. Mrs Bahnsen let out rooms,
and clearly only occupied half of the house herself—the left half, as
was evident from the curtains and the plants. The living-room was
on the street side, one bedroom and the kitchen at the rear, and
through one of the door-panes he could see a steep staircase leading
to the upper floor, where the boy's room must have been. The house
had no attic.

Morck rang the bell, but there was no answer. One of the cards
on the door-frame was a printed visiting card. J. PETERSEN, CASHIER.
Maybe the one who took his meals at the inn? On the other, the
name F. OLSEN, with no further designation, had been printed in
block capitals by someone who didn't seem to be in the habit of
making daily use of a pen. Petersen's card was firmly fixed with four
thumbtacks, whereas Olsen's curled itself rebelliously round a single
one. Olsen certainly wasn't—what was the expression Einarsen had
used?—a white-collar worker. Much could have been deduced about
the two lodgers by looking at their cards, but that wasn't what he'd
come for, and anyway, even the most well-founded predictions were
often contradicted by reality.

He pressed the bell again and listened; but he couldn't hear it
ringing inside the house. It must have been out of order. So he went

round the side of the house into a little cobbled yard. There was a faint smell of poultry. Some white hens were scratching about in a hen-run attached to the outhouse. Through the window by the back door, he could see her standing at the kitchen sink.

She must have seen him too, but she didn't answer his knock. He opened the door and said good-morning before he went inside. He had an occasional habit of coming through a door sideways, a throwback to some childhood embarrassment which had never really been conquered. Sometimes he went out in the same way.

"Excuse me," he said, "I am Detective-Inspector Morck. May I have a few words with you?"

She looked at him as if the request was unpardonable. She didn't even say good morning but went on scraping the salsify she was holding. There was going to be soup for lunch as some leeks and carrots were being prepared as well. He was still hovering in the doorway. Suddenly she dropped both the salsify and the knife into the sink, and leant on it with both hands.

"Why can't you leave him alone?" she said. "I tell you, he was at home all evening."

"That wasn't a wise thing to do, Mrs Bahnsen," said Morck, who had come in by now and shut the door. He wished he wasn't there.

"I don't know what you mean," she said, "but he was here anyway."

She was small and thin, a head shorter than her son, and had almost no figure. She was wearing a dress of indeterminate colour, and a big old-fashioned apron, tied at the waist. Her features were grey and worn, scarcely noticeable in detail. Morck was conscious only of their pale, forbidding glare and implacable severity. He didn't doubt but that this concealed the kind of despair that turns hard as stone through constant concealment.

"We watched television until ten—I suppose you want to hear the lot all over again?" she said. "Then I went to bed and Otto stayed on until the programmes finished. I heard him switch the set off and go upstairs to bed. And that's where he remained. I didn't sleep very well and he couldn't have come down these stairs without my hearing him."

"The newsagent has a different story," said Morck. "He says he saw your son outside his shop around midnight."

"Him and his dirty magazines and goodness knows what else . . . he's a one to talk about other people."

"And Mr Steffensen, the customs man——"

"What, him! I expect they must have been putting their heads together. Steffensen could never stand the boy; he's always gunning for him, so I wouldn't give a fig for what he says. Anyway, Otto was here all the time. That's what I'm telling you."

She took the knife and the salsify from the sink and set them beside the other soup vegetables, as if to put things in their proper order. Through the open door of the living-room, Morck could see a television set in the corner by the window, a table with chairs round it in the middle of the floor and a small round table—the kind that used to be called a sewing table. There was also an old club armchair with splayed, curving arms. He would certainly not be invited into this domain.

"I won't try to make you say otherwise," he said and somewhere in the recesses of his consciousness, his wife was saying, "What, and you a policeman". "But I think I ought to tell you Steffensen has testified that he saw your son hanging about Kirsten Bunding's house around midnight."

"Does that mean you're going to pin it on him?" The question rang out shrilly, almost as a shriek.

"We won't be pinning anything on anybody, Mrs Bahnsen."

"Won't you? I must say it sounds as if you will."

"Don't you see that since we have this evidence, we are obliged to investigate your son's movements on that evening? But this doesn't mean that a charge is being preferred."

Or did it? He felt an utter hypocrite, and to her he must have sounded as if he was lying.

"I don't honestly think it will help his case to deny——"

"But he couldn't do a thing like that."

"Nevertheless, we must establish what he was up to that night."

"He was at home. I don't care what they say—they won't make me say anything else."

By "they" she meant the newsagent, Steffensen and the whole town, including Herting and himself.

"They've always been against him. They've always wanted to set him in a bad light. It's been the same ever since his schooldays, and lately they've tried harder than ever, so that it's a wonder he hasn't come off worse than he is."

She remained at the sink, while Morck stood at the end of the

102

kitchen table, making no attempt to intervene. She looked him straight in the eye and said:

"There are some people who are always being got at by others . .. I don't care if that makes sense or not. But that's how it is; and this is not the first time he's been got at. Maybe he's not . . . not quite like other people in certain ways . . ." She had to struggle to make herself say this; for a split second, her lower lip trembled, but she managed to control herself. Was this as near as she could get to acknowledging her son's habit of running round at night in search of lighted windows? It might even be the nearest she had come to facing the truth herself. "But he's never done anyone any harm," she went on. "He's not like that at all. He's more of a softy—too soft, in fact—and always being defeated by things. He just couldn't bring himself to do such a thing. Anyway, he was very fond of her. Yes, I do know that much. Whatever you may think."

"I won't insist on your answering any further questions about your son, Mrs Bahnsen," said Morck.

"As I've already told you, he was at home."

"But there is one question I'd like to ask you about Miss Bunding. I believe you used to go and clean for her twice a week. How long had you been doing that?"

"About two or three years, I'd say. Sometimes when I was at her place, he would run errands for her. So that's why I'm telling you he was very fond of her."

"What I want to ask you doesn't concern him, but someone else."

"Someone else?"

She turned from the sink to face him.

"I'd like you to look at this photograph."

"I'll have to fetch my glasses."

She scurried into the living-room, drying her hands absent-mindedly on her apron. He overheard her exclaiming impatiently, "Now, where are they?" then she returned with them on. He removed the picture from its envelope. He had brought the large portrait of the man.

"Have you ever seen this man at Kirsten Bunding's flat?"

She looked closely at the picture and took it over to the window to view it in daylight. Then she shook her head.

"No, I can't say I have."

"And you didn't ever hear Miss Bunding talking about a man in connection with a holiday in the south some years ago?"

103

"No, I don't recall any such thing," she said, seemingly absorbed in the picture. At length, she looked up at him eagerly, seeing a glimmer of hope.

"Could it have been him?" she said.

"We haven't the faintest idea," said Morck. "That photograph is five years old. We don't even know who he is."

She didn't pass the photograph back to him but laid it down on the kitchen table and returned to the sink.

"Then maybe you should be concentrating on finding out," she said.

He retreated through the doorway, half-sideways. The back passage was very narrow, only perhaps a yard across. There were two pails in the one available corner, one with a floor cloth draped over it. He pulled the back door to behind him and stood a moment on the stone step looking through the wire netting at a hen clucking and scratching at the ground. It took a step back to examine the little scrap of earth it had scraped up, then pecked at it. What would it find? Morck found the tactics familiar. Exactly the same as ours, he thought, scraping the surface a little and picking up a seed here and there.

He couldn't resist a quick glance out of the corner of his eye at the kitchen window as he went by. Mrs Bahnsen had picked up the knife and the salsify again, but her hands were below the edge of the sink, her wrists resting on it. He couldn't see her face, but felt sure there would be no change in her expression now that she was alone.

Was he talking aloud, muttering to himself? He was indeed, as he hurried out of the little yard. "Let's get on. Let's put her out of my mind. Oh, damn it all."

15

WHEN HE REACHED the inn and was on his way along the corridor, he noticed the door to the phone booth by the stairs was wide open. Einarsen had twisted himself round to make room for his broad shoulders in the narrow space available, and he was facing the door in order to be able to breathe. His bright eyes looked piercingly at Morck, as he continued with his phone call.

"He's busy just now, Mrs Petersen, but not for long, you said. Yes, I can hear him pulling the chain. Well, if you'd tell him to come down to the inn. What has he got to do? Go into Esbjerg to organize passports at the police station. Yes, of course it's important if people are waiting to leave. And a juvenile court case—Yes, I know that's important too. Isn't there something he has to fetch for you while he's about it? How do I know? Oh, the general run of things. This week's offer, did you say? At the cut-price butchers in Norre Street? Yes, I see. He mustn't forget that, at all costs. And if you'd kindly tell him to drop by at the inn before he leaves for Esbjerg. Yes, thank you, Mrs Petersen. Goodbye."

Replacing the receiver, he continued to look at Morck, who had halted halfway up the stairs and was leaning over the bannister.

"What a complete idiot," said Einarsen. "He should be stuffed down his own gullet."

"What are you getting so worked up about?"

"You'll soon find out. Wasn't he a sergeant in Esbjerg once?"

"Yes, I believe he was."

"Then I see why they sent him out to the sticks."

They went into the marine room. Morck sat down at his desk. There was a note on his blotting pad which read, "The flowers were from a patient. H." It took him a second to realize that "H" stood for Herting and the flowers were the seventeen tulips. They didn't figure in the case. He slid the note under his blotter.

"Well, has anything come up?" he asked.

Einarsen fished in his breast pocket, and produced a wrapped white lady's handkerchief which, unfolded, contained a small glass cylinder. Holding it up gingerly with the tips of his fingers, he turned it to the light—an empty phial—and read the label syllable by syllable: "Dex-tro-mora-mid. What does that mean to you, Jonas?"

"A synthetic preparation with effects similar to morphine. Also known as Palfium."

"Thank you, Professor Morck."

Einarsen wrapped the phial up in the handkerchief again.

"That suggests she wasn't called out on false pretences," he said, "but really was visiting a patient."

"In one of these summer houses?"

"Yes."

"So she could have been murdered on the way back."

"Yes," said Einarsen.

"And the handkerchief—did you find that too?"

"No, it's Cilia's," said Einarsen. He had remained by the table, rocking himself to and fro, with his hands in his trouser pockets, the bulge of his stomach hanging over his belt. He added, as an afterthought, "When I was packing, there were none of my own in the drawer, but hers were heaped up by the dozen, the bitch."

"Come now," said Morck soothingly, "there's no point in making a fuss."

"That's exactly what she'd say too."

"We'd better have that thing checked for fingerprints. Petersen can take it into Esbjerg with him."

"That bird-brained nincompoop," said Einarsen.

There was a knock at the door.

"Just keep calm now."

"I wouldn't dream of doing anything else." He turned towards PC Petersen as he came in, and said ingratiatingly, "Ah, Petersen, I wonder if you could spare us a minute or two of your valuable time, although we know how fearfully busy you are."

"But of course."

Petersen's grey, furrowed face looked from one to the other in confusion.

106

"What is it about?"

"Do take a seat."

Einarsen motioned him to his own chair, and Petersen sat down. Einarsen remained standing at the end of the table behind Herting's chair. He was still rocking back and forth, taking his time. Morck had seen him in similar situations before and wondered, as he had also done before, why he enjoyed this sort of thing. Why did he enjoy it? In the back of his mind, the ghost of an answer appeared, but he preferred to refrain from formulating it. Einarsen and he would have to go on working hand in glove for some time yet.

"The thing is this, Petersen," said his gentle colleague, "the day after the murder, you went through all the summer houses near the scene of the crime—correct?"

"Yes, but I wasn't inside any of them. They were all locked up."

"And there were no signs of recent occupation?"

"Not that I could see," said Petersen. His face tensed up as if he were suddenly less certain or as if at some sporadic pain. "Were there any?" he asked.

"That's exactly what we're trying to find out," said Einarsen. "You didn't find any a few days ago. But did you look in the rubbish bins?"

"Yes. They were all turned upside down. Bottom upwards, that is. They're always in that position out of season when they're not in use. It keeps them from rusting."

"So they were all upside down?"

"Yes. I've just said so."

"Remarkable."

"What's remarkable?"

"That they're all upside down. Yet half an hour ago I had my nose in one that wasn't."

"You can't have. I looked everywhere . . ." Petersen fell silent.

"Did you?" said Einarsen.

"Yes. I mean, except that there was one place without a bin."

"Without a bin? What do you mean?"

"Well . . . unless I overlooked it."

"Really?" said Einarsen, solicitously. Then he too fell silent. After an awkward pause, Petersen said:

"If so, I'm sorry, of course."

"Of course," said Einarsen. "I should damn well think so."

"Einarsen, come to the point," Morck said.

107

"I will," went on Einarsen. "The point is that at all of these summer houses the rubbish bins are so placed that you can't fail to fall over them if you go round the side of the house. Apart from one of them, where it was stuck out of the way and hidden in a fir-hedge at the end of the garden."

"Perhaps in your hurry, Petersen, you forgot to look for it?" said Morck.

"Yes, I must have. I am sorry . . . how exasperating."

"Well, yes, but what the hell, it's only a trivial little case of murder," said Einarsen, turning round sharply as the door opened. It was Herting. He stopped in the doorway, sensing the tension in the air. Then, without saying a word, he went into the adjoining den—the boxroom, full of shelves and linen cupboards.

"What kind of summer house was it?" said Morck.

"If you go eastwards along the narrow path from where she was murdered and carry on through the scrub, you come first to two smaller houses with turf roofs. Immediately to the left and behind them, there's a wooden thatched house of a more expensive sort. The tourist office doesn't have the key and both the back and front doors had security locks, so I wasn't able to get in."

"Do you know who the owner is, Petersen?"

"No, I don't, to be honest. There are hundreds of summer houses in this area and they're constantly changing hands, so it's impossible to keep track of them all."

"Herting."

"Yes?"

Herting came in. "You heard what was said about the position of the house," said Morck. "Well, go down to the tourist office and check up on it; and if they don't know who the owner is, you can find out at the council offices."

Herting hurried out, and Einarsen said, "Did you notice anything particular about the house, Petersen?"

"No, I can't say I did."

"But you presumably looked in at the windows?"

"Yes."

"Was there anything special about them?"

"The bedroom curtains were drawn, but not the living-room ones, if that's what you mean."

"No, that's not what I mean," said Einarsen. "What about the glass, the window panes. Were they misted up?"

Petersen nodded. "Yes, now you come to mention it."

"How far?"

"About halfway up."

Einarsen nodded back. "There were even drops of water in the bottom corners and the frames were wet," he said. "That would seem to indicate that the heating had recently been on. Even the most——"

He shrugged his shoulders and said no more, but there was no doubt about what he meant. He folded his wife's handkerchief around the phial.

"Apart from this," he said, "there were the remains of at least one meal in the bin. They'd had a cold supper. Do you have an envelope?"

Morck gave him an envelope for the exhibit.

"Take this to Esbjerg, Petersen, and ask them to test it for fingerprints," he said. "If there are any, they should be compared with Kirsten Bunding's."

Petersen rose, his face even greyer than before.

"I will," he said. "I'm sorry, but this isn't the sort of case I have to handle every day."

"No, of course you don't," said Morck, "but if you'll be good enough to have this tested for us——"

"Preferably before you go round to Norre Street," put in Einarsen, crossing to the window and turning his back on them. Petersen turned greyer still, and opened his mouth to say something. Then he thought better of it and left without another word. The door closed behind him and there was silence for a while. Then Morck said:

"What was that about Norre Street?"

"This week's special offer from the cut-price butcher. I reminded him about it so that he wouldn't come home to his wife empty-handed and get a telling-off from her as well."

"You're a bit hard on people sometimes, Einarsen."

"Who, me?"

"There was no need to go for him the way you did."

"Why the hell not? If there's one thing I can't stand, it's in-efficiency."

"But he's probably a first-rate policeman for a small town like this. Moreover, he's not getting any younger and he doesn't look at all well to me."

"Well, now that's over, I'll go round and view the premises," said Einarsen, striding out of the door.

"All right," said Morck.

The premises—in other words Kirsten Bunding's flat.

16

Morck spent a quarter of an hour leaning back with his hands behind his head, looking at the opposite wall of the marine room, with its double row of ships' pictures: brigs, schooners, galleys, one barquentine, and the one in the bottom corner next to the window, which must have been a yacht, or maybe a sloop? His attention was, however, fixed more on a third row of pictures in his mind's eye.

First the spectacle of Petersen's face while Einarsen had been tormenting him—devil take Einarsen and his belief that being in the right entitled one to ride rough-shod over another person's feelings, regardless of human dignity. This may often have proved an effective method of extracting a confession—of gouging one out by terrorizing the suspect, so that bitter resistance would be mysteriously transformed into an almost submissive devotion to Einarsen, the criminal showing the utmost willingness to come clean in order to please him, taking him into his confidence as one criminal to another. Morck was unable to take part in this curious game.

Second, a woman at a sink. Mrs Bahnsen. A dark epitome of dejection, her hands drooping over the sink so that the knife and the vegetables fell into it. "Why can't you leave him alone?" He would gladly have avoided the scene—maybe this was why he had felt such a strong obligation not to? The boy . . . she had used this word too, but with good reason. He was twenty-two so she could hardly have been more than about fifty herself. But whether she was fifty or sixty could not be told from her face.

To hell with it all.

What can one make of appearances and how can one understand human beings?

Thirdly, the boy himself—visible only rarely, as if he were hovering on the limits of perception, though so far he had been the centre of attention, slinking about at night in the dark streets and gliding rapidly out of sight if anyone looked at him. Playing a mute and minor rôle, until suddenly he was dragged into the limelight as the protagonist everyone was waiting for.

Morck felt vaguely guilty whenever he thought about him, suspecting he was betraying a minor. Irrespective of whether he had committed the crime or not they were softening him up, as Einarsen had said, letting him wither away inside with fear.

A scapegoat, he mused. The boy's made for the part, with his gauche and reticent manner. Isn't it always the same? When a crime of this magnitude is committed, not only do we want to track down and punish a criminal, but equally there is an urge to find a scapegoat, someone to be punished—a whipping boy.

Still, he shouldn't be devoting time and energy to such thoughts. He would just have to shake them off and concentrate on his professional business here in Vesterso—namely, looking for the murderer of Kirsten Bunding, thirty-three, unmarried, a skilful and popular district nurse.

When he tried to picture this nurse's face, it seemed as anonymous as her uniform. But, at the same time, he could picture the radiant, laughing face of a woman in love with a man on a Mediterranean beach. The two faces would not merge. But that other face, a dark blotch in the shadow of a fir tree, the glint of one open eye, the other out of sight, that would not merge either with any living face.

He had looked at the pictures of the spot last night. They hadn't revealed anything to help the inquiry. Now he took them out, laid them on the green blotting pad and went through them minutely. Not because he expected them to give any new insights, for if they had contained any, Einarsen would, presumably, have grasped the point with almost instinctive accuracy—in a great many ways he was dependent upon Einarsen. Then why? Perhaps purely because he shrank from looking at the pictures, he felt he ought to look at them again more closely.

In the panoramic photograph, she looked like a rag-doll tossed away into the pine scrub by some child. Her handbag, somewhere in the region of five feet to the left of the body, was unopened, he knew. The forensic laboratory had examined it and found traces of her finger prints on the lock, but nothing to suggest that the man who killed her had snatched it from her. They had sent a list of the contents, which Einarsen had read over that morning. "There's nothing here," he had said, meaning nothing important. So there wasn't anything. Einarsen could be relied upon.

There were some close-ups of the body. He couldn't by-pass them, though what they could tell him wasn't clear. She was lying there helplessly, in a pleading posture. Einarsen be damned! "Fine pair of thighs there," he'd said; now Morck found it impossible to look at the close-ups without hearing his remark in the background. But no, he was being unjust. Einarsen had been talking about the picture of her while she had been alive, the one taken with the man five years ago. Not the one he should have been looking at; yet here he was with it in front of him again. Einarsen was right, only his way of putting it was idiosyncratic. They were nice and shapely, like her breasts, prettily moulded by the bathing costume. A grown woman, past the age for wearing bikinis—five years ago.

He pushed the picture aside. He should be concentrating, not on a holiday snap, but on a body with a smashed-in face. These pictures, taken from a variety of angles, and with different lighting. What did they tell him?

Nothing, except that they made him feel acutely depressed. He seemed relieved when Herting returned with the phone book, one finger marking the place.

"It was simple enough."

"Is there anything that is?" said Morck.

"Yes, finding out who owns a summer house."

"Oh, yes, quite so."

Herting looked at him sceptically. Morck more or less seemed to have forgotten what he had told him to do, though the matter was of some importance.

"The name is Erik Sogaard and he's a doctor in Aarhus," said Herting. "He has a practice in town, but his private address is in Riiskov. Here's the number."

He looked it up in the book.

"I also discovered that he bought the summer house about six months ago," he said. "Shall I ring him up?"

"Yes, do that."

"In his consulting hours?"

Morck hesitated. He was musing on the fact that a man who had called for a nurse from the phone booth in the harbour square would not be the one who needed her assistance. But his wife might have.

"No, try his home number first," he said. "If his wife answers, get her to describe their stay in the summer house, and ask if she had been in need of the nurse. Then ring him up immediately afterwards at his practice, if he's there."

"You mean, so that she doesn't have time to give him any warning?"

"Yes, I'd prefer she didn't," said Morck.

"It does sound a bit strange—a doctor sending for a nurse to give an injection," said Herting.

"Ask him why he did."

"Yes, I will," said Herting departing in eager excitement.

Morck bundled the photographs together and put them away, wondering whether he should really have made the phone call himself. No, he had to think of Herting too. It wouldn't be right for the young man to feel he wasn't an equal member of the team, but only an errand boy who was not to be trusted with matters of importance.

Herting came in again.

"There was no answer from the private number," he said. "So I rang his practice in town and spoke to the receptionist. There are three surgeries—the practice is a shared one, if that's the word. The girl said Dr Sogaard was out visiting a patient but he would be back around noon. I told her to get him to ring here—was that the right thing to do?"

"Yes, quite right," said Morck, though he would have preferred not to identify himself or give a contact number. He would have said the call was a personal one and he'd ring back later—for the sake of what he sometimes called "immediacy of response". He wouldn't want the other party to have premeditated answers. A man who has no answers prepared gives himself away more readily. But fair's fair. If you trust a man with a job, you have to have confidence in his ability to do it in his own way.

"What shall we do now?" asked Herting.

"Have some coffee . . . or maybe it's nearly lunchtime?"

"It's just gone eleven o'clock."

"Well, let's call it a pre-lunch break," Morck led the way into the dining-room. The girl, Eline, was serving. "Eline sang her artless song." She cast an expectant glance over her shoulder at him, but the expectancy waned when she saw not Einarsen but Herting following in his wake.

Four men were sitting drinking their midday beer. The brewer's delivery man was recognizable by his cap and blue apron, the postman by his uniform. More difficult to identify was the man in the white coat with the moneybag slung over his shoulder. He could either have been a milkman, a cheese-vendor or a grocer—someone going his rounds at any rate. The fourth man was in a boiler-suit with oil stains on the front. He was saying that the only place you would ever come across such a rotten old crankshaft as that was in a graveyard. So he was presumably a mechanic. Like the rest of them, he lowered his voice when Morck and Herting came in. They left soon after and the girl cleared their table and set it for the office-workers' lunch.

Morck picked up the telephone on the bar. He found Kirsten Bunding's number and dialled.

"Is that you, Einarsen?"

"Who else do you think it could be?" said Einarsen irritably.

"Have you had any luck?"

"No, it's a sheer waste of effort. A Christmas card from Auntie in Mols, an Easter card, a postcard from Florence, where she writes that she had the time of her life in the Uffizi Gallery—what the hell does she mean by that? Then there are receipted tax bills and such-like, a savings-book with a balance of 6,700 kroner——"

"But nothing significant?"

"No, and there's not going to be either. I've gone through most of it and there's not a single scrap of any interest, as far as I can see. How are you managing to kill the time?"

"We've just ordered coffee and sandwiches."

"The hell you have. How many?"

"Two each."

"Order me four. I'll be along in about a quarter of an hour."

"All right," said Morck. "Bye for now."

"No, hang on."

"Yes?"

Morck waited a few moments while Einarsen, he guessed, was conferring with his better self.

"Oh well, make it only three, for goodness sake," he said, obviously not pleased at having lost the argument. "That won't keep me going for long, will it?"

When Morck replaced the receiver, he was confronted by the girl behind the bar. She stopped smiling, and looked shiftily at him, as if she wanted to ask something but didn't have the courage. He nodded at her, but before he could ask her what was up, she burst out:

"I'm not going to do that—what you said—this afternoon."

Mrs Mehlsen must have been at her.

"It was Einarsen who made the arrangement, Eline. Hadn't you better tell him?"

Did he give this answer to avoid making a decision?

"But he's not here," said the girl.

"He'll be along in a few minutes and he wants a coffee and three sandwiches. When do you begin serving lunch?"

"The first lot comes in just after eleven-thirty."

"In that case we'd better have our coffee in the marine room, if you don't mind. Shall we go in now, Herting?"

Herting had already risen from the table by the window. At this point, the telephone rang and the girl answered it.

"Vesterso Inn," she said, and waited. "Detective Insp——. Yes, Herting; he is, yes. One moment, please. Do you want to take it here?"

"No, out in the phone box."

Herting hurried out, and the girl transferred the call.

"Was it three he wanted?" she asked. "He" meaning Einarsen.

"Yes, please," said Morck, going through to the marine room.

17

EINARSEN CAME IN. They sat down at their respective tables facing one another. Herting was still on the phone.

"There wasn't enough to cover the tip of my little finger," said Einarsen, referring to the results of his search of Kirsten Bunding's flat. He lit a cigarette, and his previous remark drew Morck's attention to something he hadn't taken any notice of for a long time—that the heavy growth of hair on the back of Einarsen's hand was nearly red although the hair on his head was fair.

"There weren't any old love-letters, either?" said Morck.

Einarsen sniggered. "What did you say? You're rather a quaint old codger from time to time, Jonas. Was that the in thing several centuries ago? Love letters indeed."

"What's the modern expression, then?"

"There isn't one. Nobody writes them nowadays."

"There's some truth in that."

"Did you tell the girl they should be thickly buttered?"

"What should?"

"The sandwiches."

"I didn't make a point of it."

"Well, usually I don't care about your lack of concern for the important things of life," said Einarsen, "but when I'm the victim, that's another matter. Oh, I suppose as long as we get something to bridge the gap——"

"You'll be bridging it in five seconds," said Morck.

There was a knock at the door and the girl appeared with a tray. Herting held the door for her, and followed her in.

"Just put it down here on my table," said Einarsen. "I'll dish them out and assign the four I like least to the rest of the party. What's up, Eline?"

She had to come out with it, even before she set the tray down. The words were the same as those she had used to Morck, but their order was changed.

"What you said—I'm not going to do that this afternoon."

"What won't you do?" asked Einarsen.

"You know what I mean," she said, setting the tray down in front of him, then lingering a moment, unsure of her next move. Einarsen said nothing until she turned to go, then he stopped her.

"Eline," he said.

"Eh?"

"Ma Mehlsen's been at you, hasn't she?"

Goodness knows how he'd guessed, for Morck hadn't told him what Mrs Mehlsen had said that morning.

"You didn't fall for that one, did you? Now don't tell me you're so dumb as to imagine there's anything in it. You promised her you'd try though, eh?"

"Yes, I did."

"But what good would that do her?" Einarsen broke in with a shake of the head. "You can never tell with some people, can you?"

"There's nothing wrong with her," said the girl.

"Did I say there was?"

Einarsen leaned back in his chair and raised his eyebrows in feigned surprise—and the girl knew it was feigned. In their encounter, the unspoken was understood to be as important as what was actually said. He went on without any clear follow-on from his previous remark: "So you just couldn't resist talking to her."

"Well, I'm allowed to, am I not?" the girl retorted sulkily, her Jutland accent coming out in the throatiness of her vowels.

"As far as we're concerned you are, but that's up to you, my lass."

Morck had never heard Einarsen use the expression before, and he wondered where he'd picked it up. It was, however, ideally well-chosen for an argument with this particular girl. "That's up to you, my lass." Einarsen lacked only the long throaty vowels.

"Yesterday, we agreed to keep all this to ourselves," he said. "Don't you think we should stick to our guns, especially from now on? You wouldn't want people to get wind of the story, would you? And all this talk about not doing it. Why on earth shouldn't you?"

"Because," the girl said, "maybe it wasn't him."

118

"Who? Otto? But surely you know who you were out with that evening?"

"Yes, but I mean him that—did it."

"That's not what we're talking about. You don't know anything about that, do you?"

"No, I don't."

"And nobody's asking you either, are they?"

"No . . ."

"We're only talking about the time you were out there with him when such and such happened—as you told us yesterday evening. That's all true, isn't it?"

"Yes . . . quite true."

"Then shouldn't we let things stand as they are? Surely you can see. Yes, dammit, Eline, why get yourself into trouble by hampering the police in their investigations? Why? Of course you see the point. You said you were free at two o'clock, I think?"

The girl nodded, but her face expressed confusion and defeat.

"Then let's meet here and drive out in my car."

"Well, I suppose, if I must," she said, still hesitant.

"Good girl, Eline," said Einarsen, with an amicable grin. "See you later."

He leaned back in his chair and followed her to the door with his eyes. The door closed behind her.

"Silly cow," said Einarsen, leaning forward in the chair to survey the plate of sandwiches. "Is beef and horseradish anybody's particular favourite? I hope not. Good, then I'll have it. Pass the cups round, Herting, will you?"

"Demagogue," said Morck.

"What, me?" said Einarsen. "How do you mean?"

"In certain circumstances you're not my special favourite."

"I know. But sometimes one has to—demagogize if there's such a word, in order to attain some end. What's all this fine language, anyway? Herting, you should know; you look as if you went to a decent school. What is a demagogue?"

Herting was handing round the cups and pouring the coffee. He didn't seem anxious to take part in the discussion.

"There certainly isn't any direct equivalent," he said.

"But you must know what sort of a creature it refers to," said Einarsen, "surely you must. Come now, Herting, tell us. What is a demagogue?"

Herting poured out his own coffee and sat down.

"I read recently that it meant someone who was experienced in the art of ensnaring fools," he said.

"Exactly what I thought," said Einarsen with evident relish. "Unless anybody begrudges me that roast pork sandwich I think I'll have it as well. Did you find out who owns the summer house?"

"Herting has cleared that one up," said Morck. "The owner is an Aarhus doctor; was that who you were talking to on the phone?"

"Yes, and they were here—he and his wife, that is—on the night of the murder. He was the man who rang for the nurse."

Herting took out his notebook and flicked through the pages.

"His name is Erik Sogaard and he has a practice in Aarhus. Private address, a villa in Riiskov, or at least a semi-detached. Age forty-two. His wife's name is Nancy, née Petersen, aged thirty-seven. No children."

'Did you ask him all that about his age, his wife and children?"

"No, I didn't think I could, in the circumstances. His explanation seemed quite plausible, so after I'd finished talking to him, I rang the public records people in Aarhus. I thought it might be as well to check up."

Morck nodded, and Einarsen said, "How did his plausible explanation run?"

"He said that he and his wife had arrived at the summer house about 6.30 p.m. direct from Aarhus. They had intended to spend a few days at the house, as they'd only been there for two weekends since they first bought it last autumn. They didn't speak to anyone after their arrival, nor had they stopped in Vesterso to buy anything, as they'd brought provisions from home.

"About midnight, his wife had a violent attack of kidney trouble and Sogaard drove into town to find a doctor able to administer a pain-killing injection. I asked him why he didn't have his medical bag with him so that he could give her the injection himself. He said he did have it with him, but, like many doctors, he wasn't too keen on treating his immediate family."

"That's quite a common attitude," said Morck.

"Especially towards injections," said Einarsen. "Among doctors, there's an adage that says if a doctor lifts a finger to inject his wife, he's risking his whole arm."

"Why his whole arm?" said Herting.

"Well, she might easily acquire a taste for it, mightn't she? Then he'd never have any peace from her nagging at him for the daily dose."

"Oh, I see. Well anyway, he drove into Vesterso to find a doctor. I asked him why he didn't ring from the phone booth next to the Marine Hotel. He said he tried but the phone was out of order. That is, in fact, true, because I checked up with the exchange. About twelve-thirty then, he rang the doctor's door bell, but there was no answer—he was out helping at a birth. So he had the idea of driving down to the harbour and ringing up the district nurse from there."

"Did he say he had the idea?" asked Morck. "Were these the words he used?"

"No, I must have added them," said Herting. "I think he just said he drove down to the harbour and rang up Kirsten Bunding."

"Did he use her name?"

"Use her name?" Herting looked a little puzzled. "Why, is that important?"

"I don't know, but if you can think back——"

"No, he didn't use her name—except once, when he said Miss Bunding. But that was later——"

"Really? Go on."

"He rang her up then and, as he said, 'put her in the picture'. She agreed to come at once and give his wife the pain-killing injection."

"Did he have the necessary drug for the injection?"

"I didn't get round to asking that—I mean, I just didn't ask—but I suppose he must have had. Nurses don't usually keep a stock of that kind of substance, do they?"

"They administer it to patients, so there could well have been some left over," said Morck.

"I hadn't thought of that."

"It wasn't necessarily the case either," said Einarsen. "Jonas, you're getting tied up in knots with all these vague possibilities. Don't forget the guy had his medical bag with him."

"You could be right. Very well, let's confine ourselves to that possibility. She agreed to come at once—what then, Herting?"

"She arrived at exactly ten minutes past one and knocked at the door."

"Having left the car on the Beach Road and cut through by the path?"

"He didn't know if she had or not."

"Didn't he hear the car approaching?"

"No, but he said you couldn't drive nearer to the house than eighty to a hundred yards, and there was a wind blowing. I asked him if he'd seen the car headlights, as it's very dark out that way at night —no streetlamps or anything. But the living-room and the bedroom both face the other way."

"Let's not make things more complicated than they are already," said Einarsen. "We can surely assume she stopped the car on the Beach Road."

"Why?" said Morck.

"Because I've looked at the geography of the place. We can also assume that she knew her way about. You can drive further along the Beach Road and turn left on a road that runs along by the dunes, then, shortly after, turn left again and drive a little further. But you still can't get nearer the house that way than you can by the path from the Beach Road."

"But would she want to walk through a pitch dark plantation at night?"

"There was moonlight," said Einarsen; "the moon didn't wane until about two am. And the other road, or rather path, runs by a pitch dark fir hedge, so it's six of one and half a dozen of the other."

"Right then, we'll stick to the first theory," said Morck. "How long was she in the summer house, Herting?"

"Five or ten minutes," said Herting. "She was only giving an injection. I asked him if he saw her on her way. Only to the door, he said. His wife was in pain, so he stayed beside her and early next morning, just after six, they left for Aarhus, so that she could get hospital treatment. And that's the whole story."

Morck asked, "He neither saw nor heard anything after she left? Nothing struck him later, on reflection?"

"No," said Herting, closing his notebook, "he hadn't anything more to say."

"How did he seem to you?"

"Seem to me?"

"Yes. How did his voice sound over the phone?"

"He . . . well, his explanation was lucid and objective enough, but maybe . . . yes, he did sound a little on edge. He'd only read the news in the paper that morning and he said he would have rung us up if our call hadn't forestalled him."

"Did he say that towards the end of your conversation?"

"No, that was the first thing he said."

"Eat up, Herting," said Einarsen.

"What?"

"You've forgotten your sandwiches."

Herting set to work on them, and Einarsen looked up at Morck. "A lucid and objective explanation," he said. "Any further questions?"

"No," said Morck, shaking his head, "none whatsoever. But we'll have to have a signed statement from him."

"We can get our people in Aarhus to send someone to see him one of these days," said Einarsen. "How did you get on with Auntie in Mols, Herting?"

"She couldn't tell us anything," said Herting. "Her niece had visited her from time to time at weekends and on her days off, and she'd also been to see her in Vesterso a few times. But she knew nothing about any man, nor about our suggested tie-up with the holiday in Spain five years ago. She wept over the telephone and said she couldn't believe Kirsten had been murdered; how could it have happened? She just couldn't understand it, she said."

"Well, we can forget about her," said Einarsen. "But I'd say it's becoming increasingly clear what happened."

"Do we have any other leads?" asked Morck, ignoring him.

"I haven't spoken to the doctor's wife yet—the one in Vesterso, I mean," said Herting. "We could also make some inquiries at the engineer's across the road from her in Barkway. I thought of doing that this afternoon, unless there's anything else you want me to do?"

"No, that'll do fine."

"I'd thought of having a stab at the boy this afternoon," said Einarsen, "but I'll deal with the girl first."

18

HE WOULD DEAL with the girl first. She knocked at the door of the marine room at a quarter past two, having changed into jeans and an Icelandic sweater, and put on a pale-mauve headscarf, not particularly well-chosen to set off her pale features and creamy lipstick.

"I'm ready then, if you insist," she said, trying for the sake of modesty to sound cross and unwilling, though she was quite clearly looking forward to the expedition.

"Good girl, Eline," said Einarsen. "We'll drive over right away."

He made sure he had the girl in the front seat beside him. Morck sat behind, but he didn't feel part of the act. Einarsen amused himself by chatting to the girl, or rather, he amused her with his chat as they drove along Main Street and out by the Beach Road. Wasn't it a morgue of a place, this, in the off-season?

"You bet it is," the girl said, "completely dead. There's hardly anything apart from the cinema, and that's only open three nights a week."

"What about dances? They must hold these from time to time?"

These were dead too. Always the same faces. And anyway, there weren't enough of them. Sometimes a whole month could go by from one dance to the next, except around Christmas time.

Were there any other events?

No. And she wasn't going to stay another winter, that's for sure.

Einarsen said he could well see why. But in summer, in the holiday season, things would be different, of course, with dances every night at the Marine Hotel, and young people in tents at the camping-site. They were driving past the place that very moment.

"I don't go there," said the girl sulkily.

"Don't you?" said Einarsen. He had made a minor slip. She said she hoped he didn't think she was the sort of girl that went a-roving among the tents.

Einarsen hastily replied that he didn't think so for one minute.

"If you do that kind of thing, there's no end of gossip," she said; "and I don't mean to give people's tongues any excuse to wag."

"Of course not," said Einarsen.

Just then she pointed out of the window at the gap in the scrub where the path began.

"Wasn't this the place?"

"Yes, but you came from the other direction, didn't you? You went out along the beach, came through the dunes somewhere then back by the summer houses. Let's try to find the way you went."

The girl said nothing as Einarsen drove on to the hotel and turned left on to a gravel road behind the dunes. There were summer houses on both sides of the road.

"Where did you normally come up from the beach?" he asked.

"You remember, don't you?"

"Yes . . . but I don't like this, honest I don't, even if I had been with somebody else."

"You mean someone other than Otto? You don't like his company much then?"

"No I do not."

"But it so happened it was him you were with. There's no getting away from that. So let's go through with it, and the sooner the better. Just tell me when we get near the place."

"That must be it, there at that signpost."

The sign said TO THE BEACH. They had driven about 200 yards along the road by the dunes. Einarsen stopped the car and they got out. As Morck slammed the back door, the girl turned her head to look at him in a speculative sort of way, as if she didn't quite see why he was there. Maybe she'd forgotten he was, for he hadn't said a word throughout the journey. He thought it was time he said something.

"Did you always take this track up from the beach when you went out with Otto Bahnsen?"

"Why the always?" she snapped back. "There were only those few times I've told you about, and I don't know what you——"

"Well, what about those few times?"

"Yes, we came up through the dunes here."

"And you didn't take this road along by the dunes back to the Marine Hotel?"

"If we were going there we did."

"But on the evening in question, you went through this terrain in the direction of the town?"

The girl looked at him vacantly.

"You went through by the summer houses," Einarsen translated for her.

"Yes, isn't that what we've been talking about all the time?" she said with mild exasperation, as if she thought Morck was rather slow on the uptake. "If not, what was it?"

"Quite," said Einarsen, and Morck refrained from intervening further. The girl didn't seem to approve. Nor did Einarsen.

"Let's try to take the same path, if you can remember it," said Einarsen. "Did you look in at any of the summer houses on the way?"

"No. It was still summertime and you never know, there might have been people there still."

"Yes, but it was very late summer. About the beginning of September, would you say?"

"Yes, probably," the girl replied. "It got dark quite early. We must have taken this path, and then kept roughly to the boundaries."

A handful of summer houses were dotted among the low, grey dunes between the gravel road and the scrub. Here and there they would make a detour to avoid marshy hollows. Einarsen let the girl walk a little in front of him but made it appear they were walking side by side. "You lead," he said; "we'll take our cue from you."

She stopped at the western end of the fir hedge.

"Now, I'm not sure what . . . did we go along by these firs, or did we go straight across past that house?"

Behind the fir hedge a thatched house could just be made out. By Morck's calculations this must have been Dr Sogaard's.

"Maybe there were people in it," said Einarsen, "and they might not have taken kindly to you tramping over their land. So maybe you——"

"Yes, this is the way we went," she said confidently and walked on along the fir hedge by a narrow path that seemed to be well used. It continued between two plots of land. The houses on them were identical, with turf roofs. Then the path divided. One branch skirted the pine scrub; the other disappeared into it. The girl stopped again, uncertain which of them to take.

126

"Now, did we go up to the Beach Road through here?" she said. "There's another way farther on; yes, there are two ways——"

Einarsen said, "You'd be more likely to go through here, wouldn't you?"

He sounded unusually subdued. One couldn't blame him for trying to influence the girl, thought Morck. But wasn't he guiding her where he wanted by asking that question?

"Yes, we would," she said, "otherwise you'd go right up past their windows."

She meant the windows of the thatched house. But would that have stopped them going along by the edge of the scrub? Yes, it might have. For the same reason Morck himself would have chosen to cut through by the path she was now turning into.

"That's what we did all right," she said. "Yes, I'm sure we did."

"Do you know where it leads to?"

"Out to the Beach Road like the others."

Then she turned abruptly to face him.

"Is this the path where——?" she said, awe-struck.

"Go on ahead, Eline," said Einarsen, and she went on in front of them along the narrow path through the scrub which, on the western side, was only a few feet high, brown and wilted after the winter, but growing higher and thicker and developing into full-size trees around the clearing into which she now disappeared with Einarsen at her heels.

Morck followed them with a strangely ill-defined resistance. Was he resisting on account of the passive rôle now assigned to him, or was it the expedition as a whole he was against, together with the notion that they were hatching a sly plot against the person to be charged with the crime? The feeling was by no means unfamiliar to him.

When he reached the edge of the clearing Einarsen and the girl were standing on the path in the middle.

"Was this the place?" she was asking him, her voice sinking to a reverent whisper.

"Well, wasn't it?" said Einarsen. "Was this where you sat with him that evening?"

But that was not what she meant. "I don't really know; one spot looks much like any other here."

"What about that pile of bricks; don't you remember them?"

"Yes. I've certainly been here before. But whether I was here that evening——"

"Take a look around, something might suddenly click."

The girl surveyed the clearing, taking in the place where Morck was standing, but seeming not to notice him. Her gaze was wide-eyed and vacant.

"Yes," she said, "this may well have been the place."

"You recognize the area at least," said Einarsen.

"Yes, but I still think this isn't quite like what I remember."

"Ah, but that was in summer; the grass was green and so forth."

The grass was yellowed and brown now as well as being trampled down at the foot of the hollow.

"And it was beginning to get dark when you sat down," said Einarsen.

"Yes," said the girl.

"And then, when you got up to leave, and he atta—— fell upon you——"

"No!" said the girl, "I didn't say that. I've already told you."

"Yes," said Einarsen, "but that's what it seemed like at the time, didn't it? You hadn't been expecting anything of the sort, had you?"

"No. Honest to God, I hadn't. And I don't think he had either. It just kind of welled up in him."

"Yes, it welled up in him, and he suddenly threw you to the ground, but you were lucky enough to evade his—what can we call it but an attack?"

"I suppose it was in a way."

"Then you left together?"

"Yes, more or less," she said. "I was hopping mad, of course, and there was nothing more to be said."

"But you still went together?"

"Well, we both had to get back to town and it was dark."

"Come up here," said Einarsen. Now it was his turn to lead the way. He went on through the clearing and emerged on the wide path, nearly a road, that led up to the Beach Road. He turned to her with confidential irony: "Are you telling me you stepped politely out of the scrub side by side, as if nothing had happened?"

"What, with him?" she answered scornfully. "You don't know him. He just slunk along behind with his tail between his legs, the stupid clot."

"But was this where you came out?"

"I suppose it must have been. Yes, I'm almost sure it was."

"You can't remember more exactly?"

She shook her head and Morck, registering an angry look from Einarsen at his uncalled-for interjection, said, "But you don't actually recall that the episode took place just here?"

"What . . . ?" she faltered. "I've told you I do. What more can I say?"

"All right," said Einarsen to calm her, "we'll stick to your story. But there's just one thing more, Eline. Where would you say you sat down, if you can say."

She turned round to survey the clearing and pointed at a grassy hollow to the right of the path.

"Over there."

It was the only convenient place you could sit: the choice was almost inevitable. But it was also the place where the body of the murdered nurse had lain.

"Good," said Einarsen. "That seems to be the lot then. Let's get back to the inn."

19

WHILE THEY WERE away Herting had had a phone call about the results of the autopsy. He had left a slip of paper on Morck's table which Morck read and then set aside. Shortly, he would read it again as was his wont, even though there was no surprising news in it.

The door to the little room off the marine room was open. Einarsen was tapping at the typewriter.

"Full name?" he asked.

The girl said it was Eline Kristine Abelone Jensen, but she didn't go for the Abelone much. She'd only been given it because her grandmother——

"OK, we'll give ourselves a treat and leave it out," said Einarsen. "Date and place of birth?"

"17 June, 1954, in Vrad."

"Where?"

"Vrad. That's the name of the parish."

"Would you spell that for me?"

The girl spelled the name, and Einarsen picked it out on the typewriter.

"You state then, that one evening last summer, presumably about the beginning of September, you were violently molested by Otto Bahnsen."

The girl said, "Molested? I don't know that word."

"It means being approached too intimately, being embarrassed by another's behaviour."

"Well, that's no exaggeration."

"He came a damn sight closer than you thought he would, didn't

130

he?" said Einarsen. "You further state—just let me write it down first."

He wrote it down first. Then he would read out to her what she had stated. Morck picked up Herting's note again.

The investigator reports that the woman was *first* the victim of a strangulation, effected by the pressure of the thumb upon the larynx, which has suffered the damage normal in such cases. Nevertheless, it can probably be assumed that the direct cause of death was the severe injury caused by several blows to the face. There were fractures of the cranium.

It was signed "H". Herting set great store by correctness of presentation. Morck put the note on his desk on top of a pile of papers, then he changed his mind, took it across to Einarsen's desk and laid it on his blotter. In the inner room, the rattle of the typewriter stopped. Einarsen was saying:

"You further state that on the evening in question, you and Otto Bahnsen had gone for a walk along the beach in a southerly direction from the Marine Hotel. Your route home cut through the summer houses, then you followed a path through the pine scrub, emerging on the Beach Road. On the way, you stopped in a clearing and sat talking for a while. So far, no approaches of any sort were made either by Bahnsen or by you——"

"By me!" the girl exclaimed angrily. "As if I would even dream of it."

"That's exactly what I've written," said Einarsen, "so that there won't be any misunderstanding. Then I say that when it began to get dark, and you rose to leave, you were set upon by Otto Bahnsen who flung his arms round you without warning, so that you both fell to the ground, with him on top. He held you fast, despite your protests and your efforts to escape. You couldn't very well see this as anything other than an attempt to force you to have intercourse with him——"

"I'm not so sure," said the girl. "That's not quite how—do you have to put that bit in?"

"What else could he have been playing at? Anyway, we then say you managed to struggle free by kicking him in the groin."

"I don't like the sound of that either."

"What don't you like?"

"People knowing I might be tempted to kick them . . ." ('Them' meaning the male sex in general.)

"But wasn't that the explanation you gave?"

"Yes, but still . . ."

"Well, what else can we say?"

The girl said nothing. Einarsen tapped the typewriter and concluded.

"Today, you took part in a reconnaissance in the presence of the undersigned and Detective-Inspector Morck, during which you thought you recognized the spot where all this took place, although you cannot be absolutely certain. Is that correct?"

Einarsen had to repeat his question.

"Is that correct, Eline?"

"Yes, I suppose so," she said reluctantly.

Einarsen took the report from the typewriter.

"Read this through," he said, "but take your time."

There was a lengthy silence, then the girl said, "I don't like the bit about kicking him . . . anyway I only used my knee."

"Right," said Einarsen, "we'll put that in too. With your knee. Any other objections?"

"I suppose not."

"Then sign here."

The statement had been read over, and signed by Einarsen. Underneath, she signed her name—Eline Jensen.

"That's all settled then," said Einarsen. "Thank you, Eline. Do you know what Otto Bahnsen's doing at the moment?"

"I expect he's helping in the kitchen," the girl said.

"Will you do me a favour? Go and tell him we'd like to speak to him."

That was a bit much, thought Morck, Einarsen sending her to summon the boy. But she didn't object. On her way through the marine room she halted halfway, looked at Morck with misgiving and said:

"I had to say what actually happened, didn't I?"

Morck nodded. "Yes, you did," he answered. He had no objections to make, or if he had he was in no position to articulate them. Einarsen's reported version of her statement was just as she had made it, in a manner of speaking. And it was convincing enough.

Even the part about her being a little uncertain about the exact spot where the episode had taken place could only serve as a further proof of her trustworthiness.

Einarsen came into the marine room and caught sight of the note Morck had left for him.

"The autopsy?"

"Yes, the results so far."

He read it through.

"Ugh, hell and damnation, the filthy swine!" he said.

And there was a knock at the door.

20

EINARSEN TOOK HERTING'S chair and put it at the end of his table.

"Sit down," he said.

The boy fumbled his way tentatively on to the chair, as if it were rickety and might collapse under him. He crouched rather than sat on it, gripping the edges of the seat tightly, and his large body, clad in a scanty, faded jerkin, slouched pear-shaped and round-shouldered between the arms. His hair was fair and bristly, falling over his forehead, yet not long enough to hide his eyes. His mother must have made sure that he kept it short.

He didn't dare to look either up or down. Timorous as a hare and frightened as a mouse, that was how Einarsen had described him yesterday. Today, he said nothing. He just made the boy sit there for what seemed an age, while he thumbed through some papers, looking across at him now and again, to show that his presence was not forgotten, and that he would be attended to in good time. Morck had already realized which method of interrogation Einarsen would choose. Einarsen used two methods which he sometimes thought fit to expound: method one was—Ask him everything. Keep asking questions, both key questions and trivial ones, going into all the details. Repeat them again and again. Then take the reverse side of the coin and ask him the same questions in different contexts, without giving him time to recover. Be on top of him the whole time until he begins to falter and tie himself up in contradictions. Then you've got him.

Assuming the man is guilty, of course. But an innocent man might also begin to contradict himself if he were sufficiently bamboozled.

Method number two was—Tell him you know everything. You don't have to ask him anything. You know all about him and what he has done. If there's anything he's not sure about, then he just has to ask you. You're not in the least interested in explanations. You've already understood. Give him the impression that he's trapped and, if he's the right type, he'll almost immediately break down and confess.

This was the method Einarsen would use. He would declare, if anyone asked him, that Otto Bahnsen was more or less an ideal subject.

Eventually Einarsen set the papers to one side, retaining only a single sheet, which he arranged on the blotter, although there wasn't a word about Otto Bahnsen on it. Then he began to speak in short sentences, with a short gap between each.

"Your name is Otto Bahnsen. You are twenty-two. You live at home with your mother, and always have done. You are employed at this inn. Before that you worked at a packing-case factory. But they didn't keep you on. They fired you. Why?"

The boy gazed at him in complete silence. Einarsen returned his gaze with lofty contempt.

"You couldn't hammer the nails in quickly enough, could you? Answer."

"N . . . no," the boy stammered in confusion.

"So you came to the inn and you have been here ever since," said Einarsen. "At night you prowl round the town when people are going to bed and peer in at their bedroom windows."

The boy had stopped holding on to the seat and jammed his hands between his knees. He was shaking his head in panic, but this was more a defensive gesture than a denial.

"There's no point in denying it," said Einarsen, "because we know you do. Everyone does. The whole town knows—isn't that so?"

The boy had stopped shaking his head and was merely staring fixedly at Einarsen.

"You have looked in at Nurse Kirsten Bunding's window too."

"No . . . no," said the boy, tripping over his words. "No, I haven't ever——"

"That's a lie. Steffensen has caught you in the act several times. He also found you once sitting in her car. Or are you saying Steffensen is lying? Are you?"

"N . . . no."

"So you have looked in at her window? Have you? Answer."

"Mm . . . yes."

"You did so on the very night she was murdered."

"No, I . . ." said the boy, making an apparently desperate effort to pull himself together now that Einarsen had come to the question he knew he would ask. "No, I didn't. Not that night anyway."

"Why?" asked Einarsen quietly, leaning back in his chair. As soon as the boy began his answer, he butted in.

"Because I was——"

"Because you were at home watching television. Thank you very much. We've heard all about that. You watched television all evening then went to bed. What was on?"

"I . . . I . . . I don't know; I can't remember."

"Wasn't the last programme a football match?"

"Eh . . . yes."

"A football match?" Einarsen repeated. "You remember all of a sudden, then?"

"Yes."

"And you're sure you saw it? Quite sure?"

"Yes."

"Late that evening?"

Einarsen shook his head. "That's a lie," he said, "nothing but a pack of lies. There wasn't a football match on television, and Steffensen saw you lurking around Kirsten Bunding's house about midnight. The newsagent saw you too through his shop window. You were in her garden. What were you doing there?"

"Nothing."

"What kind of answer is that?"

"I don't know."

"Do you think we'll believe you?"

"I don't——"

"You don't know," cut in Einarsen. "Very well, then, I'll tell you. You went there for the usual reason—to peep in at her bedroom window. Did you see anything?"

The boy shook his head.

"You're lying again. Wasn't the light on?"

"Mm . . . yes."

"And the curtains weren't drawn? Were they? Will you kindly answer me?"

"N . . . no."

"Yet you saw nothing. Does that seem likely? Does it?"

The boy didn't dare make any further reply. His large features, still not fully developed, were contorted in dismay. Einarsen glared at him viciously, his fair complexion flushed with anger.

"You spied on her while she was undressing for bed," he said. "And you stayed there till the light was switched off. What did you do next?"

"Nothing."

"So you stayed where you were?"

"No. I went home."

"You went up to Main Street and looked at the porn in the newsagent's window. Did that get you roused at all?"

The boy shook his head again.

"Don't you understand what I said? It made you want to get between her legs all the more. Is that putting it plainly enough?"

It wasn't merely putting it plainly but going too far, and Morck thought it was time he intervened with a word of warning.

"Einarsen," he said firmly.

"All right, all right," Einarsen said irritably. He made a gesture indicating that if Morck wanted to take over the interrogation, then he could go ahead.

"Bahnsen, you'll have to explain what you were up to that night," said Morck, "and you'd be best to stick to the truth, otherwise you could get yourself into serious trouble."

He nodded to Einarsen to continue. Einarsen shot a contemptuous glance at him, still exuding the aversion he clearly felt for the boy. Then he set to work again.

"Let's hear what you did, then, after you'd been to the news-agent's. Or would you rather I told you?"

"But I went home."

"You went home again? So you're still not any the wiser—after what you've just heard? You're not doing yourself any good main-taining this attitude, I assure you. You just went home, did you? No you didn't. You went back to Barkway."

"N . . . no . . ."

"Quite right. That must be the first time you've told the truth. Carry on. You might pick up the habit. No, you didn't return to Barkway the second time round, you took the footpath through the gardens at the back of the houses. Why did you go back?"

"I . . . I don't know."

"There's a great deal you evidently don't know," said Einarsen. "So shall I tell you the answer again? You returned because you had a mad idea that some possibility might arise whereby you could have a stab at her. The house was in darkness, but maybe the lights would go on again. And they did, didn't they? Answer me."

"Yes."

"You were in the garden again, and you saw her putting her clothes on," said Einarsen. "Then she drove off in her car. What did you do then?"

"I went home."

"What, again. You kept going home. The hell you did. Didn't you follow the car along the Beach Road?"

"No . . . I . . ."

"You followed her."

"No, I turned round."

"And went home," said Einarsen. "For God's sake, Bahnsen; you followed her."

"No, I didn't."

"But you've just said you did. Don't you know at all what you were up to? Maybe you don't even know what you're up to now? Sitting here telling us a pack of lies."

"But I turned back at the camping-site. I didn't go out as far as that. . . . It wasn't me that did it."

"Did what? Did what, I'm asking you."

"K . . . k . . . killed her. It wasn't. Honest. It wasn't. It wasn't."

The boy jammed his hands between his knees, unable to look Einarsen in the eye. He began to sob quietly.

"You admit you followed the car," said Einarsen. "Why did you do that?"

"I don't know."

"Did you want to see where she was going?"

"Yes."

"And you say you turned back at the camping-site. Why?"

"I don't know. But I didn't go as far as . . . that."

"As far as what?"

"There, where she——"

"Where? What?" said Einarsen. "Out there in the scrub where you tried your hand at the same game once before, eh? With Eline from the inn? The same place? Yes, we know all about that. You knocked her over and threw yourself on top so you could have her then and there, didn't you?"

"N . . . no," said the boy with a long wail. "That wasn't it."

"What was it then?"

"It . . ."

The words wouldn't come.

"So you don't know again."

"But I didn't do it."

"How do you know, when you don't seem to know about anything else you do, or why?" asked Einarsen angrily. He had gone over the score again. The boy was sobbing.

"Leave him alone for a bit," said Morck, more sharply than he meant. Einarsen gave him his what-the-hell-do-you-think-you're-up-to look, then, with a nod, lit a cigarette and leaned back in his chair, puffing the smoke across the room. No let-up, that was his way. Push right through to the end, as he said. "Be on top of him all the time." On the other hand, he knew that further questioning would be useless for the present.

The silence lasted for several minutes. The only sound in the marine room was the boy's sniffing. After a while that subsided too and he sat slumped in the chair, hanging his head and scarcely daring to breathe. Morck took his cigarettes from his pocket and tapped them half out of the packet. Going over to the boy, he laid a hand on his shoulder which immediately shrank from his touch.

"Do you smoke?"

"I . . ."

Was he going to say he didn't know?

"Have a cigarette."

"No thanks."

"We'll have to have a written statement from you now, you know."

"A statement!" exclaimed Einarsen. The boy began to sob again.

"But I didn't do it."

"In that case, nothing will happen to you," said Morck. "But you will have to account for everything you were up to that night; and I mean everything, without lying or leaving anything out or skipping over anything for your own good. Do you understand?"

The boy nodded. Not because he understood an exact account would be to his advantage, Morck thought. He was revolted by the entire situation and with himself. He felt he was playing a confidence trick on the boy. And he was revolted by Einarsen who longed to be after his quarry again.

"Which of us is going to carry on?" he said. At that moment, there was a knock at the door.

"Take him into the back room," said Morck. "We can't stay here with people running in and out all the time."

"Come on you," said Einarsen, rising and beckoning the boy to follow him. He led the way into the store-room, and Morck answered the door. It was the portly landlord.

"Telephone for Mr Morck," he announced, endeavouring to look past him into the room. "I've transferred it to the phone box in the hall."

"Thank you," said Morck, closing the door in his face. He watched the boy follow Einarsen submissively into the small back room.

"Sit down," said Einarsen. Morck heard the sound of paper being wound into the typewriter. "Now, let's start from scratch, and let's have the truth this time: nothing but the truth. I don't want to hear anything else, and you can leave out all that stuff about not knowing. We'll just keep on until you do know. Is Otto Bahnsen your full name? Date of birth?"

"3 February," sniffed the boy.

"Year?"

"1946."

"Where? Here in Vesterso? Right. Then we'll put the rest down." Einarsen pounded at the typewriter, reading aloud as he went along.

"He was interrogated concerning the circumstances of the case. He—that's you, of course. After first stating that he had not left home at all during the evening in question, and then having involved himself in conflicting accounts of his movements, he admitted . . . and that brings us to the point. You'd better get it right this time."

On they went, about the "circumstances of the case". There was no other way. Morck went out and found the landlord still standing in the corridor, staring at him open-mouthed.

"Has he said anything yet?" he asked in a hoarse whisper, "Otto, I mean?"

Morck had to struggle to repress the anger which suddenly flared up inside him. He managed not to reply "Get the hell out of here."

"What do you mean by 'said anything yet'?"

"I mean . . . whether . . . whether it was him?"

"Him who murdered her?"

The landlord made no reply. The tense look on his face faded, and he blinked. Morck regarded him in stony silence.

"No," he said, "he hasn't said anything about that. Have you any good reason to think he is the killer?"

"No. None at all."

Mehlsen retreated sideways then managed to turn round and vanish through the door that led to the kitchen. Morck glared after him. The effrontery of some people knows no limits. They add spite to curiosity without a second thought. The technique is not entirely unknown in police methods, Morck thought. He went into the box and picked up the phone.

"Yes, hello?" he snapped angrily. (But who was he angry with?)

"Hullo, Jespersen here."

(Who the hell was Jespersen?)

"We've had a look at that thing Petersen brought."

Petersen? Thing? If only people would express themselves clearly.

"What thing?" he said.

"The phial Petersen brought in, of course. The one he said you were particularly interested in," said Jespersen, somewhat offended. "Perhaps you no longer are? He also said you wanted the results in a hurry."

"We are interested," said Morck, "Certainly we are. Sorry, but I just went blank for a second. Things are a bit hectic down here."

"Oh, really. I can well understand that," said Jespersen. "Are you on to something then?"

"We just might be. But it's none too clear yet. Have you discovered anything that might help us?"

"Yes, I think so. The fingerprints on the phial are hers. The left-hand index-finger is clearest, but there's part of a thumb-print too."

"Good work, Jespersen; that confirms our suspicions. Many thanks."

"Things are hotting up, you say?"

"Yes. Nothing to complain of really ... I'm in the middle of interrogating someone right now."

"Oh, I see. Well, best of luck."

"Thanks. And thanks for your help."

Certain provincial police personnel had to be handled with the utmost tact, sometimes even with exaggerated solicitude. Otherwise they were inclined to grumble "here come the top brass from the flying squad, thinking they can do better than we can". Jespersen had sounded as if he might belong in that category.

Morck replaced the receiver. The thumb and index-finger of the left hand. The information wasn't of any particular interest now. It only served to confirm what they already knew from Herting's phone call to the doctor in Aarhus.

21

THE SMALL STORE-ROOM, with its blue-painted linen cupboards and shelves for china, was far too cramped for three people. It was far too warm as well, even though the door into the marine room had been left open. Einarsen had tried to force open the window above the table to let some air in; but it was jammed shut and he had merely succeeded in cracking one of its six small panes. His face was glowing and rubicund with the heat. There was hardly a yard between him and the boy across the table. The boy's eyes were swollen, which made his features appear even more podgy and immature.

Morck wasn't sweating, but he felt uncomfortably hot and faintly nauseous, and wasn't sure whether this was due merely to tension or to imminent sickness, or both. His feet were tingling from having stood up for so long. He had brought a chair in from the marine room but couldn't bring himself to sit down. He seemed to find it more tolerable to remain at a distance from the other two, deeply immersed in this claustrophobic cross-examination. He leaned alternately on the doorpost and on the shelves opposite.

So far the interrogation had lasted two hours, and they were not out of the woods yet. The boy had slumped even lower in the chair. He was sitting slightly askew, with his left shoulder raised in a defensive position. He was answering sluggishly and staring fixedly in front of him. Indeed, they were all getting sluggish, and would soon have to call a halt, or at least pause for a while.

Einarsen embarked on the same question, for the fourth or fifth time.

"You say you turned back when you reached the camping-site. Why?"

"I just did."

"That's not an answer."

"But if I did . . ."

"Did you? Where exactly did you turn back? At the entrance?"

"Entrance?"

"All right, the way-in," said Einarsen impatiently. "Did you turn back by the way-in to the camping-site?"

"Y . . . yes, I think so."

"You think so? But you're not sure?"

The boy shrunk back from the chasm that yawned before him. "Yes," he said, nodding vigorously. "Yes, it was just there."

"You think so," said Einarsen, "and you want us to think so too." He sat back and gazed at the boy.

"Just a minute," said Morck. "Listen, Otto . . . Otto."

He was using the boy's Christian name for the first time, and Otto looked up, not with confidence, but with a faint glimmer of hope that someone might be about to show him some sympathy.

"You see, we do have to know exactly what happened," said Morck gently.

Of course the boy would not be able to see that, but he might at least react favourably to his tone of voice. "You didn't actually turn back at the way-in; you went on a little further, didn't you?"

"Yes," said the boy, "but not much further."

"How far then? Try to remember. There's a bend in the Beach Road and a willow hedge running along the edge of the camping-site. Did you walk along by that hedge?"

"Yes, but then I turned back."

"Where the willow hedge stops and the Beach Road continues straight on to the Marine Hotel?"

"Yes, right there."

"You're quite sure?" It was on the tip of Morck's tongue to call him Otto again, but he stopped himself. There was no longer any need to. He had him where he wanted him, and the consciousness of his treachery was unpleasant enough. He didn't have Einarsen's instinctive talent for communicating with a suspect at his own linguistic level. But he had another talent, which he sometimes cursed himself for using: the talent for getting the suspect to put his head in the noose by giving an impression of sympathy, warmth and understanding.

"Yes, it was just there I turned back," the boy said, eager to please him.

"Ah, yes," said Einarsen, nodding vigorously. He had cottoned on immediately. Morck checked him with a glance; Einarsen's inquisitional methods were not needed here. He followed up stealthily, drawing his conclusions with a trace of mock surprise: "But then you must have seen her car parked at the side of the road, by the pine scrub, mustn't you?"

The boy didn't answer. He merely hung his head.

"Since the road is straight from where you turned back, you couldn't have avoided seeing it, could you? The distance wasn't very great, and it was moonlight. Her car was there, wasn't it?"

"Yes," muttered the boy.

"Why didn't you say you had seen it?"

"Because . . . I thought . . ."

"Well, what did you think?"

"I thought I would get the blame for having done it."

Morck said no more, though not because he had run out of questions. There was something reprehensible about what he was doing to the boy, and this bereft him of words.

"No more questions?" said Einarsen with mild disdain, a sign that he knew very well why Morck was speechless. He turned to the boy and took up where Morck had left off.

"So the next thing you'd have us believe is that you turned back when you caught sight of her car?"

"Well, I did."

"You keep saying that," said Einarsen. "What'll you be saying next?"

"But I did turn back."

"Why?"

"Because I . . . I couldn't understand why the car was there."

"By the pine scrub? And because you couldn't understand why it was there you turned round and came back. Do you think that sounds likely? Look up at me and answer."

"I . . . I don't know."

"I'm sure you don't. But I'll tell you what really happened. Because you couldn't understand why the car was there you went to take a closer look, then realized she'd gone through the scrub by the path you already knew so well; and when you got as far as the clearing where you monkeyed about with the girl from the inn, you saw that nurse walking back from one of the summer houses. You were itching to have another go at her——"

"That's not true. It's not true. I didn't do it. It wasn't me." He began sobbing.

Morck said, "Don't you think we should stop now?" He went over to the boy and touched him lightly on the shoulder. "Just sit here and calm down a little." Not that there was any reason why he should. "We could probably all do with some coffee. How about you?" There was no reaction. Morck left him sitting there and, with an eloquent glance at Einarsen, went through to the marine room. Einarsen shrugged and followed him out, leaving the door ajar.

Herting had just come back and was sitting waiting for them.

"How are things?" he said. "Are you in full swing?"

"Yes, and the pay-off won't be long," said Einarsen. Then, turning to Morck, "Do you think it's really wise to let him recover just when . . . well, I thought he was just about to spill the beans."

"Let's wait and see," said Morck. "You mustn't . . ." He searched for the right expression but couldn't hit upon what it was they mustn't do . . . or rather, in all honesty, ought not to do. Squeeze a lemon to the last drop? Milk the cow dry? Yet wasn't it precisely something of the sort they were bent on doing?

"Wait and see what?" said Einarsen. "It's in the bag, I tell you."

Morck wondered if the boy could have overheard him.

"We'll take a coffee break now," he said. "Herting, would you mind bringing some through from the dining-room? There'll be four of us; and how about a cheese sandwich all round?"

No objections were raised.

"Bring some cigarettes too. Have you had a profitable afternoon, by the way?"

Herting said he'd talked to several people, but hadn't come upon anything he thought might interest them. At least, not now that—he gestured towards the half-open door of the . . . meditation chamber; wasn't that how Einarsen had described it? Then he went off to get the coffee. Morck and Einarsen sat down at their respective tables in the marine room and stared vacantly into space. In the middle of an interrogation a break can often seem monotonous.

In a few minutes Herting gave a muffled knock at the door with his elbow, having both hands occupied. Morck opened the door for him and he came in with the coffee and the cups rattling on a tray. Just then, Einarsen heard another soft thud, like the noise a broom

146

makes falling on the floor. He got up and looked in to see what the boy was doing, then flung the door wide open, took a couple of steps into the room, and glared at the opposite wall for a second.

"Complete, bloody idiot, that's what I am!" he exclaimed, dashing through the marine room and disappearing down the corridor. "He's cleared out."

Herting turned in his tracks, still holding the tray, and watched him disappearing.

"You'd better put that down before you drop it," Morck said to him, entering the store-room.

Einarsen had assumed that all the cupboards were linen cupboards and hadn't bothered to open any of the doors. But the last one was a broom cupboard. Two brooms had been knocked over, and one could now see it was accessible from both sides. Instead of a blank wall, there were two inner doors, both wide open, leading out to the corridor.

"I'll nip out and pick up his trail," said Herting.

"No, stay where you are," said Morck. "If Einarsen hasn't already caught him, he'll be a long way off by now."

Three minutes later Einarsen came stomping back through the marine room puffing and sweating. He glowered furiously at the escape route through the cupboard.

"Bloody fool," he said, "it just didn't occur to me."

"Nobody's perfect," said Morck, "not even you. They say it's good for people to admit that."

"Oh, shut up! I didn't even have the foggiest idea which way he'd gone, with all those narrow streets and winding alleys. He might even be clean out of town by now, safely in some hideout in the bush. What do we do about that?"

"He'll turn up somehow, sure as fate," said Morck. "Certainly during the night or early in the morning, if not before. There wouldn't be any point in mounting a full-scale search, not just yet."

"I'll get Petersen to keep a look out for him. That gent hasn't made himself too useful so far; and at least he's known in the neighbour-hood."

Einarsen went out to phone Petersen, doubtless not in his most cordial manner. He would have to find somebody to take it out on. He came back and went over to the window, buried his hands in his pockets and rocked edgily back and forth on his heels. He had taken up his stance of sullen scepticism, but for once it happened to be directed inwards at himself.

"What can we do?" he said.

"We'll have our coffee now for a start," said Morck, reaching for the pot. "Don't just stand there chewing over the problem, old man."

"Let me be," snarled Einarsen, turning on him. Herting rapidly wiped the smile from his face. "It's all very well for you to take it calmly, isn't it?"

"Well, there's no point in——"

"Don't you think it'll be cold by the time our little friend turns up?" He was looking at the tray, and Morck realized he had poured out four cups without thinking.

"Very probably."

"We'll have to arrest him now," said Einarsen.

Morck emptied the boy's cup into the coffee pot.

"Yes, I suppose we'll have to," he replied.

22

AT NINE-THIRTY THE flaming red torch in an attic window across the bay was extinguished, as the sun set somewhere far out to sea. Morck was standing at his own window at the inn, and when the shadows of night had blotted out the bay, he took his clothes off, put on his dressing-gown and went along to the bathroom for a hot shower—not so much because he needed a wash, but in the hope that it would make him feel better, in particular by relieving some of the painful tensions in his neck and the headache stabbing into his forehead.

The symptoms were familiar. He knew them from previous disturbing cases—but was "disturbing" the right word? It was one hell of a case. The interrogation of the boy had left him with an indelibly bitter taste in his mouth. Once, in an expansive moment, while he was mildly flushed with red wine, he had employed a particular phrase to describe this to his wife—"the hangman-feeling".

But if the boy was guilty . . .

He would still have that feeling, and if so, the crime would have claimed two victims: the woman who was murdered and the boy whose misfortune it was to have killed her.

"I couldn't help it," he'd say, just like a child, when he eventually cracked up. "I didn't mean it . . ." No, he had had no intention, no end in view. At the time he hadn't been aware of it happening. If he'd done it, that is.

Nothing pointed to any other suspects. The overall picture of his behaviour and his movements that night had singled him out. So Einarsen was quite right. They would have to arrest him when he turned up again; and turn up he would—what else could he do? He certainly wouldn't be able to hold out for long, curled up in his bolt-hole, wherever that might be—in a dark corner of some barn or shed, or in a thicket in the middle of the plantation, with the wind whistling in the pines overhead, and night coming on, as he stared out with blank terror in his eyes.

Then, later, when he emerged, they—Einarsen and he—would make him crack up. That was what they were here for. That was the task they had been set, and they would doubtless carry it out. If he was guilty he would, in all probability, break down and confess before long. And if he wasn't? They would torment him until he broke down—even though he didn't confess. This was the price they might have to pay for their interrogation: they ran the risk of exceeding even the feeble limits of psychic endurance which this reticent lad possessed, and doing him serious damage.

The price! The implications of the terminology were clear. Sadly, it was a price which had to be paid. A price the boy and his mother would have to pay—and if he turned out in the end to be mentally defective? No. Whether he was or not, it didn't seem to accord with any worthy principle that the administration of justice, so called, should be carried out by inflicting mental injury upon someone, guilty or otherwise.

Yet it did accord with judicial practice. There, inflicting mental injury was indispensable: breakdown. The interrogation of a suspect was directly solely to this end. "If people didn't in general break down and confess, the Danish legal system could not function."

He had seen the quotation only yesterday in a newspaper interview with a well-known criminologist and police-chief. "Is police interrogation itself a form of mental torture?" the journalist had asked.

"We all shrink from the idea of torture, and mental torture is one of the cruellest forms it can take. The phrase is, of course, emotionally charged; it gives rise to certain feelings of outrage. Thus if we discover by the very act of interrogation we are inflicting mental torture, a problem arises as to whether we ought to give up the practice."

He was right on the first point; but the sequel sounded rather too righteous. He ought to have known better. Regardless of whether mental torture is part and parcel of interrogation, interrogation as such cannot be abandoned. If he had argued that way . . .

He would have aroused a storm of protest.

Nevertheless, it was true. A basic principle in any law-bound society is that the enforcement of law relies upon power, and the weapons of power are subjugation, violence, mental torture; all of which he and Einarsen would continue to employ when the boy turned up again. Interrogation could not be abandoned.

What else had the criminologist said about interrogation?

"Being interrogated by a journalist is not much fun either."

Morck was tempted to borrow Einarsen's exclamation "Lord above!"

He turned off the shower and shook off the drops of water, but not the hangman-feeling. A policeman should really be inoculated against such scruples. They only hampered his work and reduced his efficiency. He knew one or two who evidently had been so inoculated on entering the force—if indeed there had been any need for inoculation in their case.

He went back to his room and put his clothes on. The nagging stiffness in his neck had worn off a little. The room was in semi-darkness but he didn't need to look in the mirror to comb his hair and tie his tie. Instead he looked out of the window. Twilight obscured the harbour and not a soul was to be seen. No, that wasn't true. There were two souls, in fact, walking along the quay with their arms round one another's waists. Once or twice they stopped, turned to face one another and went into a clinch. All very passionate. But the girl couldn't have been a day over fourteen, surely? They start early these days, thought Morck. And when you begin to have such thoughts, he reflected, you're getting old yourself.

One of the two fishing boats had already set sail. The engine of the remaining one was chugging irregularly. Was it about to set sail too or had it just arrived? The sky, framed by the right-hand half of the window, was still sunset-red. Two black night birds flew across; then from the underside of their wings in flight, he saw that they were white. A pair of gulls. One shouldn't be taken in by appearances.

Yet appearances were so much against Otto Bahnsen that they would have to charge him with murder.

The courting couple were walking hand in hand now, a little apart. That meant either that the girl had had qualms of conscience or there was another soul on the quay besides them.

In fact, it was not a soul, only a policeman—Herting, out to take a look round the town, as he'd said he would. He trudged purposefully past the couple, and Morck couldn't resist watching to see whether he'd guessed his destination correctly. In order to do this, he had to open the window and put his head out.

Sure enough, Herting was making for the ramshackle shed at the far end of the breakwater. A blue flag fluttered on the roof, and in front three or four small pleasure boats had been beached in the channel, while a couple of larger ones rocked with the tide, moored to buoys.

Herting disappeared round the end of the shed. He was acting even less intelligently than the boy himself, who would hardly dare to seek shelter in the sailing-club's pavilion at the end of May when all the boating enthusiasts would be gathering every evening to work on their craft and drink beer to usher in the season.

Morck tied his shoelaces, and, on looking out of the window a second time, saw Herting returning empty-handed from the harbour and making for the town.

What of Einarsen?

He'd said he would go and see if the boy had run home to his mother.

"That's the one thing he wouldn't do," Morck had said.

"How do you know?"

"I'm quite sure." But how could he be so sure?

"Despite your singular perceptive gifts, I'm going to have a try," Einarsen said.

"Better let me do it."

"Why?" Einarsen and his perpetual "Why?".

"Because . . . well, I've spoken to her already."

Einarsen glowered at him. His manner had been exceptionally stony since the boy's escape.

"So has Herting: that makes it my turn," he said, and swept out.

What would he say to Mrs Bahnsen? "He sneaked off before we'd finished interrogating him, and we can't tolerate that sort of thing, you know. . . . Not that I'm doubting for one moment the truth of what you say, but I'd like to look and make sure that he's not here. He might have slipped in without your hearing him."

He'd ask to see the boy's room, and he'd go through the house from top to bottom, outhouses as well, and no doubt knock up the lodgers for good measure. Without success. Morck could well imagine how Mrs Bahnsen would react.

"But I told you he was here at home all the time, on the night of the murder. What more do you want with him?"

152

"We want to interrogate him."

This would be Einarsen's only reply. He'd tell her to make sure the boy reported to the inn for further questioning, should he come home. He'd certainly not mention that he would immediately be arrested and charged with murder. The first she'd hear of that would be after the event. And Einarsen wouldn't be the bearer of the news.

Why couldn't Petersen go? She knew him, after all, so it would be better for him to. . . . No, you won't wriggle out of it that way, thought Morck, by finding an excuse for someone else to do it, then calling it a good reason.

Morck did his best to put these worries about the future to the back of his mind. He put on his jacket, took his coat over his arm and went down to the marine room. Herting had come back.

"I've had a look round," he said. "There's no knowing where the most likely places are."

"Sure, Herting." Morck sat down and leafed through the reports and other papers on his desk. He couldn't concentrate on any of them. Einarsen came in a few minutes later.

"Any success?"

"No," said Einarsen morosely.

"He hasn't shown his face at home?"

"Not according to his mother."

Morck got up and put his coat on.

"You're off to bring him in now, I suppose?"

"It's still too early in the evening for him to turn up."

"Ah yes, you'd know about that," said Einarsen sarcastically. "Of course you would. I'd forgotten you'd used your imagination to put yourself in his frame of mind."

"But even so we should keep a sharp lookout," said Morck.

He went northwards out of the town, and three youths on motorbikes flashed past him three abreast, considerably faster than the speed that type of vehicle was restricted to. They buzzed noisily between the houses along the narrow Main Street. Before he reached the end of the street they came careering back towards him, having made an about-turn out by the Marine Hotel. How often did they do this of an evening? Apart from them he met nobody. The rest of the population was sitting at home round the tube, looking in at a world outside Vesterso, or rather the fictional representation of that world which television was obliging enough to give them.

He continued along the Beach Road, passing the "way-in" to the camping-site, and following the curve of the willow hedge that surrounded it. At the end of the hedge, he stopped. He stood pondering a while, not thinking of anything in particular, except that this was where the boy had turned back, according to his most recent admission, when hard-pressed. He and Einarsen hadn't succeeded in forcing Otto Bahnsen further along the Beach Road—not this time round anyway.

The street lamps were lit, or rather the only two on that stretch of road were; one right out at the Marine Hotel, the other just past the point where the path led into the scrub. The boy had said that when he caught sight of her car there, he had turned back.

No, it was Einarsen who had asked the question. "So the next thing you'd have us believe . . ."

"Well, I did . . ."

"Why?"

"Because I . . . I couldn't understand why the car was there."

". . . And because you couldn't understand why it was there, you turned round and came back. Do you think that sounds likely?"

Not at all. It sounded highly unlikely.

". . . But I'll tell you what really happened. Because you couldn't understand why the car was there, you went to take a closer look . . ."

This was more probable, and the police, like the courts, deal in probabilities. The most likely hypothesis was what they had to stick to in an investigation, as much as in a court case. People have to be judged according to such hypotheses—the circumstantial evidence. The unlikely hypotheses have no special name. They are merely rejected. Yet from time to time, the improbable does happen.

Morck sighed, not knowing what to believe, though in the end, he didn't need to bother his head about believing anything, but merely stick to the probabilities. And the probability was that the boy had gone on further. He was on the point of doing the same himself, continuing out to the scrub where the murder had been committed. But instead, he turned on his heel and made his way back along Main Street. On the way, he made a detour down one of the side streets. There was a faint glimmer of light behind the yellow blinds of Mrs Bahnsen's two front windows; one of the blinds was torn at the top. There was a light also from one of the lodgers' windows. He stopped outside the house but there was nothing he could do. So he returned to the inn.

154

Herting was sitting all by himself in the marine room. He said Einarsen had gone out with some comment about not usually setting much store by old adages . . . the criminal returning to the scene of the crime and so on, but this one was idiot enough to do just that.

Morck nodded. He had had a similar idea himself. Einarsen and he often did come up with the same ideas, though their methods of arriving at them were usually very different.

Einarsen came back, looking peeved. He didn't say where he had been. By this time it was ten o'clock. They had more coffee, having already had some after dinner. Morck had heartburn and an acid feeling in his stomach from all the coffee, and, added to this, an acute lethargy which slowed his reactions. He topped up his cup.

"Let's go through the case again, from the beginning," Morck said wearily.

"What, again?" said Einarsen. "I'm sick to the back teeth of it."

"There may be some aspect we haven't noticed, some detail we've overlooked so far."

"There bloody well is."

"What's that?"

"That damn broom cupboard. Just let me get my hands on that son of a——"

Einarsen couldn't forgive himself for the blunder.

"Let's consider Kirsten Bunding," said Morck. "Aged thirty-three. Unmarried. District nurse in Vesterso for the last four years. And prior to that——"

"She had a job at the general hospital in Esbjerg," said Herting.

"Well-liked by her neighbours; popular with her patients. Lives a quiet life alone. As far as one can see, there isn't a man in her life. There was one, five years ago, but he was only a holiday acquaintance. What else is there to say about her?"

Herting shook his head. "I haven't anything startling to add."

"No dark corners?" said Morck.

"How do you mean?"

"There's a proverb my grandmother used from time to time: No room's so light that it doesn't have a dark corner somewhere."

"You and your grandmother," said Einarsen.

"Kirsten Bunding was rung up about one in the morning by Dr Sogaard from Aarhus . . ."

They went through the whole story, and ended up knowing no more than they knew already, by which time it was getting on for eleven o'clock. Herting took the coffee pot into the bar to have it filled up again. Morck rose and picked up his coat.

"I'm going for a stroll."

Einarsen showed no sign of interest. He didn't even bother to retort that as far as he was concerned, Morck could go to hell.

23

THE THREE MOTORBIKES, if they were the same ones as before, had become two by this time of night. They droned past him yet again—for the fourth time at least. He had almost grown accustomed to them. Did the people whose bedrooms faced the road also grow accustomed to them so that they didn't wake up every time they went by? He had trudged the length of Main Street and found himself nearly at the camping-site again, without really knowing why. Not because he expected to find the boy; he was just having a stroll. A rather aimless stroll. He had paused only to go down one or two of the many dimly lit side streets. Barkway was one of them, and he had passed Kirsten Bunding's house, noting that the lights were out in the house next door. Customs officer Steffensen, retired, had done as his title suggested.

In another side street, a faint glimmer of light was still visible through yellow blinds.

On his way back to the inn, he was browsing in the bookshop window, scanning the titles of the meagre stock on display without really taking them in. Two people came towards him. As they drew nearer they stopped talking and only began again when they were well past him. From the sound of their voices, he knew he was the topic of conversation: "That must be Detective . . ."; then they disappeared round the bend of Main Street two street lamps away. As soon as they had gone someone hurried across the street, and the lights in the bookshop window were turned out, as they must have been by now in almost every house in Vesterso.

The boy would be sure to turn up early next morning. If he didn't, they would have to mount a search.

There wouldn't be any point in keeping a watch throughout the night, so he would go back to the inn and tell Einarsen and Herting the meeting was adjourned, and they could go off to Esbjerg if they wanted.

The car Petersen drove was easily recognizable—an old Volvo with the two-piece hood and the big bulbous body. He was turning out of the side street where Mrs Bahnsen's light was still on, and the blinds were drawn in the side window. Petersen put his pale, scrawny face out.

"Are you still on the lookout for him, Petersen?"

"He's just this minute given me the slip. Didn't you see him sneaking across Main Street?"

"Well, I did see someone a few minutes ago, but I wasn't near enough to see who it was; and anyway he was going in the opposite direction."

"I'll turn the car around."

"Don't bother. Leave it here."

Petersen got out and they started walking back along Main Street.

"He was standing by the fence outside his house, not daring to go in to his mother. So when I drove by and caught him in my head-lights, he ran off through the back garden. These paths lead any-where and everywhere."

He presumably meant the little footpaths running between the garden fences.

"So before I could get out of the car—and my legs aren't as good as they used to be . . ."

"Let's take it easy then," said Morck, slowing down and taking Petersen by the arm to curb his enthusiasm.

"But they're not that bad," he replied, "as long as I don't have to sprint. Hey, look, there he is!"

"Yes, that looks like him sure enough," said Morck. Just where he was on that fateful night, he thought.

He had only seen his back, but Otto Bahnsen's large ungainly shape, with the sloping shoulders, was immediately recognizable. He was standing outside the stationer's on the corner, with his hands in his pockets, looking in the window. They approached carefully, so that he wouldn't hear them coming.

When they were only fifty yards away, he moved on down Main Street, still slouching with his hands in his pockets, without having seen them. Then he went past the end of a house that protruded at an angle on to the street and disappeared from view.

"He's turned into Barkway."

They increased their pace, but when they reached Barkway he was gone.

"I'll follow him," said Morck. "You take the path along by her back garden down to the field. It'll be dark, but even if you have your torch with you, don't use it, and don't hurry, even if you see him. Speak gently to him, we don't want to startle him."

"All right, I get the idea," Petersen nodded, and went along Main Street, turning down the next side street where the footpath branched off. Morck continued down Barkway with his own words ringing in his ears. Speak gently to him, we don't want to startle him. Then we'll be able to corner him and arrest him.

During the evening, the wind had died down, and by now all was still. Only the faint sound of his footsteps on the pavement could be heard. Then, as he passed the only lighted window in the street, he heard someone talking. The voice came from the house where, on the previous evening, he had seen the young woman with the baby lying naked on the table on its quilt waiting to be dressed. This time, the curtains were drawn but the friendly glow of a red lamp shone through them. The window must have been ajar, for the words floated out to him through the darkness, in a forced whisper.

"Oh . . . oh, darling. Yes . . . yes. Keep going, you're so . . ."

Morck didn't hear the rest, but there was no difficulty in guessing what was going on. What could be better than a woman who enjoys sex? As he passed by, he was struck by the memory of . . . no, not of his wife, but of the woman who had become his wife and who enjoyed it too. He hastily brushed the thought aside, sensing that it might be sullied by contact with his present undertaking.

There was no other sound in Barkway. He stood motionless by Kirsten Bunding's gate and listened, then went on past Steffensen's house to where the sidewalk gave out. A pair of wheel ruts disappeared into the darkness of the field. He came back and stood looking into her front garden, listening again. The two neat spruce trees were coupling in the darkness, swelling themselves up into female shapes that reminded him of—but what the devil was wrong with him? She was murdered, and he had come out to arrest the person to be charged with the murder. Speak gently to him, we don't want to startle him. He was oppressed by the hypocrisy of it all but at the same time he was thinking about a woman's breasts.

The strangest and most incompatible thoughts can be in our minds at once.

What thoughts had been in the mind of the boy, Otto Bahnsen, and what thoughts were in it now? Where was he hiding? Surely not in Kirsten Bunding's back garden, or behind the tall pine where, at night, he had stood gazing in at her? No, what could have induced him to return there? Some obscure yearning which can make people seek out a place where once they had enjoyed . . . the expression was hard to find . . . a "moment of tenderness"? As with love letters, the idea wasn't in any more.

But that would be sheer madness. Or would it? For this boy to have stood outside her window at night, giving vent to the feelings we call love. "I dare tell no one of my tender love . . ." and he could not declare his passion to her openly.

Not only madness, but improbable as well. "The heart's fond yearning," as they used to say in the old days, is reserved for people of a certain mental capacity and favourable appearance who have the means of expressing it in an appropriate manner. This could not be said of Otto Bahnsen—an overgrown lump of a boy, a hopeless good-for-nothing who gaped forlornly in at bedroom windows.

Yet how can one be sure? Morck set off round the back of the house to look for him there, behind the tree, but he didn't get that far. Her Volkswagen was still standing in the garage at the side of the house. The light from one of the street lamps was reflected in the side windows, and the glass had a milky sheen in the darkness. So the game was over. This was the second misted window pane in the case. The case of the misted windows?

Morck went round the car and opened the front door. The dark mass straddling both front seats immediately shrank away from him.

"So this is where you've been hiding," he said. "Sit up, Otto." The boy did as he was told, pressing himself against the other door as far as possible from Morck, who couldn't see his face in the dark. What should the next move be? Morck sat down next to him.

"You shouldn't have run away, you know," he said.

"But he kept on asking me questions," the boy replied. "And since I didn't do it . . ."

His voice had the helpless whimper of a tired child, although he towered over Morck. His short legs, long, sloping shoulders, and fat body were those of a child writ large. And child he was, thought Morck: he had reverted to the infant state, from which he had never really escaped. What was Morck taking upon himself in prolonging his harassment, even if his duty forced him to?

"If you didn't do it, then you've nothing to fear," he said.

"But he kept on and on at me . . ."

The childish whimper was superseded by the adult voice of Otto Bahnsen insofar as he was an adult. A note of dumb defiance was creeping in:

"And since I didn't do it . . . and I didn't. I wouldn't do any such thing . . . so I wasn't going to let him just . . ."

"Now listen, Otto."

The use of the name was enough to soothe him.

"Why can't you let me alone?"

"Because we have to interrogate you and you have to answer our questions," said Morck. "Surely you can see why?"

The boy said nothing. Silence was his simplest way out.

"Where were you hiding?"

"At the very back of the garden."

"Where, at home?"

"Yes."

"Is there a toolshed there?"

"No. Nothing. Just some bushes."

Morck remembered them now: some old overgrown elder bushes that had spread all over Mrs Bahnsen's garden behind the chicken coop. The elder is in leaf early in the season, and since by then they were in full leaf, it would be easy to hide in semi-darkness among their dense foliage.

"Did you stay there on the ground the whole time?"

"Yes," the boy said defensively, as if to ask if there was anything wrong in that. After a short silence, he added, by way of explanation: "I used to have a den there."

"When you were a boy?" asked Morck.

"Yes, when I was a boy."

"And sometimes you used to go and hide there, eh? When?"

The boy considered the question. "I remember now," he said: "I used to hide there mostly when some rotten bullies were after me and I couldn't get away . . ."

"You couldn't get away," Morck said sadly. But he had to go through with it now, whether he wanted to or not. There was no other way. He heard Petersen coming up from the field.

"You still shouldn't have run away, Otto. Because we'll have to arrest you now." This was not quite true, for they would have arrested him in any case.

"Arrest me?"

"Yes, so that we'll know where to find you tomorrow. Then you'll get a fair hearing . . ."

Had the boy taken in what he'd just said? There wasn't any sign that he had. But just then, Petersen loomed up at the open door of the car. He had heard their voices.

"Is that him you've got there?" he said.

"Yes, I've found him."

"Well, that's a stroke of luck. . . . What are you doing in her car, Bahnsen?"

"I don't know," the boy said. "I just got in . . ."

Petersen shook his head. "The same old story," he said. "He just does things, and never knows why."

"Petersen," said Morck, "would you bring your car around?"

"Yes, sure." He hurried off along Barkway. As the sound of his footsteps died away, Morck returned to his previous point.

"Now, you do understand . . ."

As if there was the faintest chance he might. Morck began again.

"Listen now, Otto. You'll be spending tonight in custody."

"In a bed?"

"Yes, of course, in a bed. You'll get something to eat; I'll see to it that you do. You probably haven't eaten anything for some time, so you must be hungry."

Morck found himself assuming that false jollity people use with children when they want to cover up the truth or explain away facts. But the facts could not be explained away.

"I don't know if I am hungry," the boy said. "I think I am . . . but I don't care, if they'll only stop saying I did it . . . because I didn't. But they think I did, even so. Do you think so too? Do you?"

"It doesn't matter what I think."

"Then you do think so," the boy whimpered. "If that's what you say."

"Not at all. I don't think either that you did or that you didn't. That's not my business, you see . . ."

Morck felt ill at ease. He stopped trying to explain to Otto Bahnsen what his business was. The boy could not be expected to understand.

"Otto," he said, "the next time you're interrogated, you must answer truthfully whatever questions you're asked. If you didn't do it, then nothing will happen to you."

"It's easy for you to say that. But if everyone thinks I did . . ."

"Oh, nonsense, Otto."

"It's not nonsense. I know they do . . ."

"Try to be sensible, Otto."

"I am. They'll blame it on me because they want to."

"Now, listen, Otto . . ."

"No, I won't."

He wrenched himself away angrily, hiding his face to sniff back the tears. The atmosphere in the car was oppressive although the door was open. Otto Bahnsen seemed to fill it entirely; a whimpering 168-pound child, nearly six feet tall. His body smelled of sweat. What was to be done with him?

"Just stick to the truth now, Otto," said Morck.

"Thanks for the tip."

"Tell me, why did you get into the car—her car?"

"I don't know."

"But you've done the same thing before," said Morck.

The boy didn't answer and he went on cautiously: "Was it because you were fond of her?"

"Yes. I was."

"So you had the sensation of . . ."

Would the boy grasp the sense of the phrase? No. Morck used another:

"So you imagined you would be near to her, if you sat here. Was that what you thought, tonight as well?"

"I don't know," the boy said uncertainly. There was silence. He wasn't snivelling any more. Then all of a sudden, he turned to Morck in a moment of self-discovery:

"I could have imagined that, couldn't I, since I was fond of her?" he said.

"Yes, you could," said Morck, and Otto Bahnsen asked him a further question, frightening in the confidence it betrayed:

"Should I say that . . . that was the reason? Then they won't think I did it, will they?"

"You should simply tell the truth," said Morck. He was spared the agony of saying more, for Petersen's ancient Volvo was coming down Barkway towards them.

24

THEY STOPPED OUTSIDE the inn.

"I'm going to drop in here for a second," said Morck. "Petersen, will you look after . . ?"

Petersen moved into the back seat of the car next to Otto Bahnsen. Would he be unhappy about being left alone with the boy? Neither of them had said a word during the short drive from Barkway to the inn, but now Petersen started talking.

"We'll just sit here quietly until Inspector Morck comes back. You understand, Bahnsen?"

"What have I to understand?" the boy said suspiciously.

"That you'd better not get up to any of your tricks again—that wouldn't be any use."

Did Petersen imagine he was putting the boy at his ease with a remark like that? Morck hurried into the inn, leaving the hall door open, and walked purposefully into the marine room. Herting and Einarsen looked up.

"So you've smoked him out," said Einarsen, stating a fact rather than asking a question.

"Yes, he's outside in Petersen's car," said Morck. "Herting, would you mind going into Esbjerg with Petersen?"

"What, and put him into custody there?"

"Yes. Make sure he gets something to eat."

"Why not feed him here?" Einarsen butted in. "Then——"

"Herting, you'd better be going."

"Then keep at him while his resistance is low," said Einarsen, as Herting went out.

"No. There'll be no further interrogation tonight."

164

"Jonas, you're too bloody soft with him."

"Maybe I am," Morck snapped back, "but there'll be no more interrogation tonight. It wouldn't be . . ."

He was still searching for the right word—was it "fair" or "reasonable"?—when shouts were heard from outside, evidently cries of anger or pain. Einarsen leapt past him into the corridor. But he stopped at the outside door, with Morck close behind.

"No need for us to interfere," he said.

Otto Bahnsen was outside the car, gasping for breath and groaning helplessly. Herting had his left arm in a half-nelson, while Petersen was lying on the back seat, halfway out of the car, still holding on to his right wrist.

"You can let go now, Petersen," said Einarsen. "What the hell do you think you're doing anyway?"

Petersen let go of the boy. He squeezed himself back into the car first, then got out on the other side.

"He was trying to escape," he said.

"I was not!" yelled the boy. "But they keep saying it was me."

"Calm down now, Otto, if you please," said Morck just as one says to a child to make it behave. The effect was immediate; maybe this was how his mother spoke to him when she wanted him to toe the line?

"Herting, you can let go too. Otto, get into the car again."

"All right, but he's not to say it was me."

"Now, look here," Petersen protested, "all I said was that if it was you, the best thing to do was confess on the spot."

"Who the hell asked you to say anything of the sort, Petersen?"

The force of the question surprised even Morck himself: it wasn't at all like him to explode in this way. It didn't fit his image.

"Yes, what's the game, Petersen?" said Einarsen taking advantage of his hesitation. "Have you been put in charge of confessions, or what?"

Dismay spread over Petersen's drooping features. Before he could reply, the boy lent his voice to the apparent storm of protest.

"Yes, and he wanted to put these on me; but since it wasn't me, I wouldn't let him. I wouldn't."

"Be quiet, Otto," said Morck. "Get into the car beside Herting."

"But you said you didn't think I did it."

"Into the car with you," said Herting, taking a step towards him, and looking at Morck for permission to seize his arm again. Morck shook his head.

"Otto," he said, "what I told you was that if you didn't do it, nothing would happen to you."

"Won't it?"

"Of course not. Now, will you do as you're told?"

Otto Bahnsen looked at him in sullen silence, then climbed into the car. Herting got into the back seat beside him, and Morck held the door open to speak to him.

"I'll tell your mother where you are, and I'll be seeing you tomorrow."

"But it wasn't me," came the reply from the shadowy interior of the car. "Honest, it wasn't."

What more was there to say? He always gave the same answer, made the same ineffectual plea.

"Then you've nothing to be afraid of," said Morck, shutting the door and standing back. Petersen was still waiting by the car.

"Take over, Petersen, if you feel up to it."

"I'm quite all right," said Petersen. "That business of the handcuffs . . . I thought I saw him fiddling with the door handle, so I thought I'd better make sure——"

"Great!" interrupted Einarsen. "Then why didn't you?"

Without waiting for an answer, he turned on his heel and went back into the inn. Morck watched the car move off towards Main Street, then followed Einarsen into the marine room.

Einarsen brought his typewriter from the store-room, placed it on the table and sat down. He lit a cigarette and filled his lungs, but seemed to find the taste unpleasant. He had smoked too many in the course of the evening: they both had.

"Hell of a scene, eh? Hysterics and all that," he said. Maybe the memory of it, not the cigarette smoke, had left a nasty taste in his mouth. "But isn't that just what's true? Idiots are never in short supply."

Morck said nothing, and Einarsen, with a glance at the store-room door, added in a distinct, if casual undertone: "There's so many of them about, you bloody well get mixed up with them yourself."

"It's high time you stopped fretting about that episode," said Morck, suddenly feeling dead tired. But dead tired or not, he had to go on. Stubbing out the cigarette he had just lit, he rose and put his coat on. Einarsen had set up his typewriter.

"I'll finish this report so that we'll have it for tomorrow. What can we say? That during the interrogation, he disappeared? No, that won't do. That during a pause in the interrogation he took off? What do you think, Jonas? Can we leave it out altogether?"

"You'd better make up your own mind," said Morck wearily.

"Thanks for your help. Are you going out again?"

"I'm going round to let his mother know."

"The pleasures of this life are many and various," said Einarsen, with a wry grin.

There was still a light shining behind the yellow blinds, but so faintly now that he could scarcely make it out. Only a single lamp could have been lit, just sufficient for a vigil. He tried the front door, though he knew it would be locked, and the bell was out of order. Why did he bother trying it then? To put off the evil hour?

He went round the side of the house. The little yard was dark and smelled of poultry: he could feel the rough cobbles under his feet. The kitchen window glimmered in the darkness, and he stumbled over the doorstep, found the back door and knocked. There was no chance that his knock would be heard, and the door was certain not to be locked. So he let himself in, felt his way along the narrow passage to the kitchen door, knocked, and listened. Then he knocked again, and this time, he thought he heard a voice answering.

The door into the dark kitchen opened and somewhere behind it the angry voice of Mrs Bahnsen was saying:

"So, you have the nerve to show your face here again."

"Excuse me, Mrs Bahnsen," Morck took a step into the kitchen. She was framed in the doorway to the lounge, with the light behind her. "I've come to let you know that we have had to arrest your son. I'm sorry, but it was necessary."

"Arrest him!" she gasped, just as Otto had done.

"As you know, he ran off and went into hiding in the middle of an interrogation."

"Yes," she said, "does that surprise you? He may be stupid, but he'd soon see what you were driving at."

"What were we driving at?"

"You know very well." Her voice was sharp and a little shrill. "It's the easiest way out, of course—to pick on someone like him."

"You're quite mistaken, Mrs Bahnsen. We'll be doing our very best to . . . to clarify the situation." Morck thought how lame this must have sounded. "Your son will undergo a preliminary examination tomorrow; but this doesn't mean——"

"What does it mean, then?" she broke in.

"We are continuing with our investigations," he said. "Fresh evidence can always come to light, so that even if he is charged, I trust he would turn out to be innocent."

"Do you indeed?" she said acidly. "You trust he would be innocent——"

The only possible course was to leave. "Goodnight, Mrs Bahnsen."

She did not return the greeting.

He closed the kitchen door and the outside door behind him, crossed the rough cobbled yard, went along the side of the house and out through the front garden. On his way back to the inn, he could see her still in his mind's eye standing motionless in the doorway, a lean, grey silhouette with the light behind her and the high-pitched voice on the point of cracking.

25

BY THE TIME he got back to the marine room, Einarsen had gone, leaving a hastily scribbled note for him: "Pick you up tomorrow between nine and ten? If not, ring Hotel Esbjerg."

Morck stood by the desk gazing at the note. If he had sat down then he would merely have remained there scowling into nothingness, rather than pulling himself together and going straight to bed. Between nine and ten would be fine. Time for a decent sleep before they started interrogating him again. Or rather, before Einarsen did. Quick-witted Einarsen, the tough-guy of the team.

Morck was neither quick-witted nor tough, especially at that moment. He was plagued by an anxiety which often, and never without good reason, pervaded his work: the feeling that he had overlooked something; that he had walked straight past an important piece of evidence which he ought to have noticed; the terror of the unguarded moment.

Besides, he had a splitting headache, and the painful tension in his neck had come back. With the dregs of that talent for synthesis peculiar to detectives, he contemplated a half-empty Coke bottle which Herting had left on his desk, and hit upon the idea that its contents might be usefully combined with the remains of a bottle of rum up in room number seven.

Taking the Coke with him, he locked the marine room door, then, with one foot already on the bottom stair, he turned round and went through into the darkened dining-room. There he pressed the uppermost of a row of buttons by the door. A light went on behind the bar. He looked at the switchboard, thinking he should be able to operate it—in his remote past as a young policeman he had operated switchboards at a number of different police stations. Room seven. What was he thinking of, ringing his wife at this time of night? Yesterday he'd decided eleven was too late and now it was nearly one; not an appropriate hour to ring, but he had made up his mind to do so.

He was startled out of his reverie by the stern voice of Mrs Mehlsen.

"Yes, what can I do for you?" She was standing in the doorway that led from the bar to the kitchen; her grey hair straggled over the collar of her white overall.

"I'd like to make a phone call from my room, if I may."

"I'll put you through; but it'll be charged at the higher rate at this hour." She went over and pressed two buttons on the board.

"That's all right," said Morck.

She stared at him, her fiery face overcast in the dim light. "So you couldn't leave him alone," she said.

"No," replied Morck, "there were certain circumstances that made his arrest inevitable."

The prolixity of this answer made it sound like an excuse.

"I'd be interested to know what you mean by 'circumstances'," she retorted. "Goodnight, sir."

He went up to room seven, took the glass from the shelf above the washbasin and emptied the rum and Coke into it. The glass was nearly full, and he swallowed half of it at one gulp then undressed and put his dressing-gown on. He sat down at the little desk by the window, took another sip and felt a delicious warmth permeating his body. He picked up the telephone and dialled.

"Vesterso exchange."

Was it the mother or the daughter who was on duty? No matter; Herting had said they sounded exactly alike. He gave the number.

"Is that you?" said Marie.

"Yes, it's me. Did I wake you up?"

"If you did, I'm glad you did. But I wasn't asleep. I went to bed too early."

"What are you doing?"

"You always ask me that," she said. "What do you think I'm doing? Lying here beside the tall dark man the fortune-teller once told me I'd get hitched up with? Not a bit of it. He's away just now, as he is most of the time. He's taken from my bed two nights in every three——"

"Yes, so he is," said Morck.

170

"Why don't you say something?"

"You're the talker."

"But you called up. So you must have something to say."

"No, I called just to hear your voice."

"Are you miserable, Jonas? Isn't the case going well?"

"Not really. We've just arrested a young man——"

"But you didn't want to? And you don't think he's the murderer?"

"I don't know. But I didn't want to arrest him."

"No. I can tell from your voice you didn't."

Had she heard him heaving a sigh of distress? What was he doing phoning his wife up in the middle of the night and howling in her ear? He took a sip from the glass.

"I can hear you slobbering something down. Surely you're not sitting there getting sloshed in the middle of the night, little Jonas?"

"You're good at making elementary deductions; we could use you in the flying squad," said Morck. "Yes, that's what I'm endeavouring to do."

"All alone? Good lord! On what?"

"Rum and Coke."

"You don't stint yourself when you're away from home."

"Well, I have to have my little bit of fun."

"Sounds as if you're having that all right. What else are you doing, as you usually ask me?"

"I've just been talking to a lady . . ."

"Oh, so you talk to ladies as well. Not just to me?"

"No, to ladies and to you as well. I was talking to the landlord's wife—rather a caustic, impressive, or rather imposing, lady."

"Just your type."

"Yes," Morck said absently. "She was asking me——"

"Jonas, you weren't listening."

"Wasn't I? What did you say?"

"That she was just your type."

"Nothing like it. You're my type."

"That's a bit better," said Marie, who was neither caustic nor impressive. "What was she asking you about then?"

"About what we meant by circumstances."

"We? That is, you and Einarsen, I take it; what did you say?"

"Nothing. But it's a good question. I'm still turning it over in my mind."

"And getting sloshed all alone in a hotel room in the middle of the night. Some policeman you are. It's nearly one-thirty, so just you settle the question and polish off the booze and fall into bed, darling."

They said goodnight but he remained by the phone long enough to empty his glass and finish his cigarette. Beneath the window, the street lamps by the harbour were surrounded by shimmering haloes. He couldn't say for certain whether they were due to fog, or a combination of fatigue, rum and Coke; nor did he answer the questions he was turning over in his mind. But one part of her instructions he did obey by going to bed. He would be able to sleep until eight o'clock.

At a quarter past six he was up again, brushing his teeth at the washbasin. He took a mouthful of cold water from the tap and shivered. After a shower he dressed and went out before seven for a walk round the harbour, thinking about Einarsen. If this was how he felt every morning of life, his lot was not to be envied.

26

MORCK PASSED THE sailing club's pavilion and went along the shore by a deeply rutted track covered in puddles after the previous night's rain. It had been made passable for motor traffic by the addition of a layer of bricks and broken slates, but was so unpleasant to walk on that he soon turned back. As the early mist was lifting from the grey waters of the bay, his hangover began to clear up. He noticed for the first time that the fishing boats were not in the harbour. The last vestiges of Vesterso's fleet had put to sea. Outside the inn, a small hunched figure was sweeping the sidewalk of Harbour Street. It was Mehlsen, the landlord, out with the broom himself now that the boy. . . .

Yes, this morning Einarsen and he would have to go on interrogating him in Esbjerg police station. In the afternoon he would appear before a magistrate, charged with murder, and be remanded in custody.

The sequence of events was inevitable, unless something unexpected were to turn up in the course of the day. But what?

"Damn it all," Morck said aloud to the tranquil morning air, without directing the imprecation at anything in particular. One target was clearly the hangover, which seemed to have disappeared merely to make room for a more general queasiness. Maybe this would wear off after breakfast.

He came to a standstill and fell into a daydream with one foot on the edge of the sea wall, gazing out to sea. The water, the mist, and the sky merged at the horizon, grey with grey, epitomizing his early morning mood. He continued along the wall, and a man in a green overcoat came striding stiffly towards him, and, raising his rather old-fashioned brown hat, said:

"Good morning, Mr . . . eh, Morck."

Customs officer Steffensen, retired, seemed somewhat embarrassed at the encounter, as if the obvious wish to satisfy his curiosity was a breach of his usual etiquette.

"I hear you've arrested Otto Bahnsen," he said.

"The news appears to have travelled fast," said Morck coldly, knowing he was being unfair. If only he could have had breakfast before the inevitable leading questions were asked.

"I had a word with Mr Mehlsen on my way down."

"Yes, I'm sure you did," said Morck. Then he tried to sound more friendly: "You've stopped taking your usual walk down to the beach then, Mr Steffensen?"

"Yes . . . I'm afraid I have, of late."

Morck nodded. It was understandable that he wouldn't be inclined to start the day by walking past the scrub where the body of his murdered neighbour had been found.

"You know, I simply can't imagine that boy doing such a thing," Steffensen went on, taking the plunge at length. "As I believe I told you the other evening."

"You did indeed," said Morck.

"I'm quite sure he couldn't possibly—he's not like that. Will he be charged? Yes, I suppose he will; otherwise why would you have arrested him?"

Steffensen's face was grey and heavily lined in the early morning. No doubt he wasn't at his best at this time of day. He seemed troubled, probably by some scruples that his reporting of the boy's presence in Kirsten Bunding's garden may have hastened his arrest and helped to bring the murder charge upon him.

"He can hardly avoid being charged on the evidence so far available," Morck said. "But we are still continuing with our inquiries."

"Yes, I expect you are." The old man seemed to be racked by doubt. He shook his head feebly.

"Goodbye, Mr Steffensen," said Morck, and walked away. Halfway across Harbour Street he looked back and saw Steffensen going slowly along the sea wall. Morck went up to the bookshop in Main Street. A teenage girl was behind the counter.

"Have the papers come yet?"

"Only the local paper," she said, knowing full well who he was. Obviously the whole town must have known.

"OK. That'll do."

174

He went back to the inn, sat down in the dining-room, and ordered breakfast from Mrs Mehlsen. The post office cashier and the bank clerk—as he now thought of them—were sitting at their usual table, stealing furtive glances at him. He buried his head in the newspaper and did his best to look preoccupied, hoping to prevent them yielding to the overwhelming urge to start a conversation.

The main item of local news was splashed across the front page: STILL NO ARREST IN VESTERSO MURDER CASE. The arrest had been made too late last night for the paper to publish the news. The central flying squad, the report said (that would be he and Einarsen), were at present in charge of the investigations being made by the regional crime squad (that would be Herting) "and, according to our correspondent's latest communication, several lines of inquiry are being pursued".

They must have had Einarsen on the telephone. He didn't care much for journalists, and Morck, being familiar with his methods of dealing with them, could guess how the conversation had run:

"Would you say that several lines of inquiry are being pursued by the police?"

"We're always pursuing lines of inquiry. What the hell else would we be doing?"

"So you do have a line of inquiry to pursue?"

"As a rule we do. There's a corpse to start with."

"Can you say anything about the direction of these inquiries?"

"If I could, I wouldn't be able to take time off to talk to you."

The report went on to say that it was still too early to say whether these inquiries were of such decisive importance that an early arrest of the murderer might be expected but the impression gained was that the police were taking an optimistic view of the case, a rapid conclusion of which would soon solve this gruesome murder.

Typical journalese—a gallon of soup made from a single stock cube. Yet, as a follow-up tomorrow, the paper would be able to say "As we predicted yesterday, a rapid solution of the murder seems to be imminent. A young man has been remanded in custody and charged."

Morck put the paper down without finishing the article. The effort of reading both today's and tomorrow's news at the same time was too much for him.

The two office workers left the dining-room for their respective jobs, and he was left alone with Mrs Mehlsen, who came in with his breakfast. She asked no questions: they had been asked already. Apart from the usual courtesies, she merely said:

"You may as well have this, it came this morning."

The postcard was of blue Mediterranean waters breaking as white foam upon a beach crowded with people in bathing attire, some with deckchairs and sunshades. In the background, there was a white hotel like a cream cake, complete with palm trees and balconies, silhouetted against a pale blue sky. There was no need to look at the reverse side of the card to find out the name of the addressee.

It was nearly nine when Einarsen arrived. He sat down heavily in the opposite chair, and glowered at the card Morck passed him with even more bloodshot eyes than usual.

"What does she say?"

"I don't know. I haven't read it."

"Why not? You're always sticking your nose into other people's affairs. Go on."

"No. Go on yourself."

"Oh, go on, read it to me," said Einarsen.

"I have no intention of reading your postcard. What gets into you in the mornings? Don't you feel well?"

"No. Why the hell should I?"

"A cup of coffee will do you good, and you can have——"

"That half roll you've left, if I can stomach it—thanks very much," said Einarsen, leaving the card face downwards on the table until he had drunk his coffee. Then, turning it over he read it through, munching the roll the while.

"Bitch!"

"Now, now," said Morck gently.

"Everything's so marvellous there, they've decided to stay another week, since I won't be at home anyway, she says."

"Well, you won't."

"She must think I'm a bloody idiot," said Einarsen.

"Why?"

"Why not. The card was sent the very day they arrived, probably from the arrivals lounge at the airport. They'll have sat hand in hand during the flight, getting it all settled between them. A pair of lovey-dovey little lesbians!"

"Oh, forget it, Knud. That's a far-fetched conclusion to come to."

"You can talk like a criminal report if you want but I happen to know that little slut. Shall I tell you what I'd like to do to her—no, to both of them?"

"You don't have to," said Morck. "I can well imagine."

Einarsen glared at him. "What, you? Imagine the likes of that? Lord in Heaven, I wouldn't have believed it of you, Jonas. Oh, let her pack her bags and go; except that she's gone already."

He put the card in his pocket and lit a cigarette.

"I think we may possibly be on our way too," he said.

"How so?"

"Well, that's what I reckon anyway. Before I left I dropped in at Esbjerg."

"Where, at the yard?"

"At the police station," said Einarsen, who only recognized one yard—in Copenhagen. Anything in the provinces was a plain station.

"I had a word with Detective-Superintendent Olsen. The big white chief was on the job so early this morning it's proof positive there's a big flare-up on the way to do with this drugs case they're plugging away at. They've made nine arrests so far, and it turns out there are contacts in Hamburg too. So last night, Olsen rang Graumann to ask him to send LSD over."

LSD was the usual abbreviation in the flying squad for the two narcotics experts, Sergeants Lau Simonsen and Detlef.

"Graumann refused. He said he couldn't spare anybody for the moment. But that was last night. The superintendent's going to phone him again this morning, so it's my guess that——"

He stopped talking as Mrs Mehlsen came in from the kitchen and advanced upon their table.

"Telephone for Mr Morck," she said, "from Baltrup, Funen."

"Just as I thought," said Einarsen.

Morck went out to the phone booth in the hallway.

Deputy Chief Superintendent Graumann had a repertoire of two voices in his capacity as head of the flying squad. With one he discussed calmly and deliberately what policies should be adopted; with the other, a sharp bark, he put an end to further discussion once a decision had been reached. That's settled, so let's get on with it.

This time he used his second voice.

"According to what I hear from both the senior inspector and from Olsen, all you need now is a confession. Am I right?"

"It may appear so," Morck said doubtfully, "but——"

"But what? Have you any evidence to show that Otto Bahnsen is not the murderer?"

"Nothing too precise. But I'd like to continue with our inquiries."

"You don't think Detective Jessen would be competent to take over then?"

"Of course Jessen would be competent."

"Well?" said Graumann.

Morck was silent. He couldn't very well point out to Graumann that Jessen was competent enough as a police officer but as a person he was hidebound and unimaginative, and would do no more than run the later stages of the case according to the rules, neglecting to keep a weather eye open for other explanations. "What other explanations?" Graumann would retort. And Morck wouldn't be able to give them.

"I've managed to get through to Otto Bahnsen, which wasn't easy——"

"For Jessen you mean?"

"No, for anyone. But it so happens he regards me with a degree of confidence, and I've promised to go in and talk to him again this morning."

"Promised? What do you mean you've promised? You sound as if you were going to visit an invalid."

"That's not so far from the truth as it may seem. But, in any case, there would seem to be some point in not losing a suspect's confidence——"

"So you're giving me a bloody lecture in police methods now, are you? Thank you, Morck. So what?"

"In short, I think he would talk to me more readily."

"You mean confess?"

"Yes, if he is the killer."

"And isn't he?"

"I don't know; even if the evidence points to him, I still have the feeling that——"

"Damn it all," said Graumann, at the end of his tether. "Now look here, I've got seventeen men working on this robbery with violence case on Funen, and all the time the big-wigs are pestering me for reinforcements; then you start confiding in me about your feelings—you can keep these for your wife, as far as I'm concerned. How is she, by the way?"

"Very well, thanks," said Morck.

"Give her my regards when you see her. And get that case wound up this morning then go over to Skaelskor. A taxi driver was shot dead early yesterday. He was found in his cab near Lystskov. You'll get all the details at Skaelskor. All right?"

The last two words could elicit only one response.

"Yes," said Morck. "Whatever you say."

"If the unexpected should happen, we can always recon—— Yes, coming. Goodbye, Morck."

Morck had no chance to say goodbye, as Graumann had already replaced the receiver. He went back to the dining-room.

"We're being taken off this case."

"Great," said Einarsen with a yawn. "Anything to get out of this provincial dump. Where do we go next?"

"To Skaelskor," said Morck. "A taxi driver's been murdered. Found early yesterday morning, shot dead in his cab, in a back road near a place called Lystskov."

"I know it well," said Einarsen. "There's a dinner-dance place where I once went in my innocent youth and, being a gentleman, offered to see a young lady home. On the way we took a little rest. Unfortunately it had been raining so it was wet underfoot in the woods, but we managed to find a beech tree—at least I think it was a beech—whose trunk was sufficiently solid and unyielding for us to be able to demonstrate our mutual intentions in comfort. What, are you going, Jonas? Aren't you interested in my youthful memoirs?"

"You've already told me that story," said Morck, "several times. I'll go and settle the bill."

27

THEY TOOK THE ferry across to Sjaelland in the early afternoon and drove to Skaelskor along a country lane that twisted through the rolling hills. Leaving the car outside the police station, they were received inside by an elderly constable, who peered at them over his spectacles, and said:

"It's good of you to come, but he'll be with the police in Korsor by now."

"Who, the killer?"

"Yes, he gave himself up about noon, saying he hadn't meant to shoot. But Jensen, the taxi driver that is, refused to hand over the money. He was trying to grapple with the man when the gun went off, a 9mm. Parabellum. The bullet entered his head under the chin. Damned idiot!"

The last expression referred to the gunman.

"Do you know what his motive was?" asked Morck.

"Couldn't he pay his fare?" said Einarsen.

"No, it wasn't that: he couldn't pay the next instalment on his new car. His wife had given him the money but he'd spent it all on drink—she has a better job than him, you see. But he couldn't very well go home and tell her, so—do you want some coffee?"

"Let's be on our way," said Einarsen, "we're not needed here."

"Yes, thanks," said Morck. "I'll have a cup."

"Come on through into the back then."

They followed the constable into the guardroom, and he served up coffee from a thermos flask. He had the station to himself so was glad of an audience.

"I've known Jensen for years. He once had a plot of land next to

180

mine, and his eldest boy is at the same school as my youngest. We see a lot of the boy at home. Jensen was a decent, respectable sort, without so much as a driving offence to his name. Then he comes up against a complete nincompoop like that. What can you say? The fellow comes in here mid-morning, puts his gun on the counter and cracks up. He's sorry about what happened, he says, but he didn't mean it." He shook his head and drank some coffee. It was lukewarm and had a muddy flavour.

"Did the taxi driver have a lot of money on him?" said Morck.

"Money? He'd just nipped in to see his wife half an hour before and he'd told her it had been a slack night so far—just a few short trips. So he didn't have much more on him than he'd left home with."

"How much was that?"

"Enough to change a hundred kroner note," said the constable. "Yes, human lives are worth less and less these days. Even here in Denmark."

It was sixty-seven miles from Skaelskor to Copenhagen. Later that afternoon, Einarsen stopped the car in Crocodile Street but wouldn't go in. He drove off to some unspecified destination, and Morck went in through the front door which wasn't locked. Marie must have been in, but he couldn't find her in the living-room or the kitchen. He took a sly peep through the window into the backyard, and there she was, with her back to him, busily engaged in hanging some clothes up on the line. He went out by the back door.

"Jonas, you're back." She dropped the checkered bag with the clothes pins and embraced him. "And I've just taken down the living-room curtains and washed them."

"I don't see why you should do that for my sake, and anyway, I didn't even notice."

"You didn't notice that they were down? Oh, really, Jonas. I just can't understand how you can be like that."

"Sometimes I can't either. How have you been?"

"What about you?" she said. "Did the case work out properly in the end?"

"I don't know. But there wasn't really any other way it could."

"Well anyway, it's nice to have you back. And they're nylon, so they'll be dry in a matter of minutes."

"What are?"

"The curtains, silly. And he's had another tooth while you've been away; that's the third. And if you ask me who has——"

"I won't, Granny."

They put the living-room curtains back up and after they'd had a meal, washed up and made coffee, Morck dialled the number Herting had written down for him the other evening.

"Hello, Jens, is that you already?" said a girl's voice, which he thought he had heard before, though only in a distant and unintelligible whisper.

"It's not Jens, it's Jonas."

"Who?"

"My second name's Morck."

"Oh, Mr Morck," she said. "What a pity, he——"

"I'm sure it is," he replied with a readiness of wit that could only be put down to the bottle of red wine they'd had with supper.

"No, I meant he only went out half an hour ago. And I don't know when he'll be back."

"Oh, I see. Well, you'll never know when he'll be back. I hope he's given you plenty of warning?"

"I've had ample opportunity to find out," she said, "but that doesn't make any difference."

"No indeed it doesn't. I hear you're going to marry him in two weeks."

"In ten days," she replied.

"He told me two weeks. But of course that was two days back."

"Then he should have said twelve days."

"You're better at counting the days than he is."

"Yes, but he has so much else to think of. You just have to get used to it."

"You're right there. Ask my wife, for instance—— Just a minute. What did you say Marie?"

Marie repeated what she'd said in a deafening whisper: "Ask her what her first name is."

"I heard her," said the girl. "My name's Jonna. But that's not what you're calling about, I take it."

"No, I wanted to ask Herting how the hearing went today—in the Otto Bahnsen case."

"Jens said he'd been remanded in custody for a week. With some justification, they said."

"Yes," said Morck with a sigh. "That's just what you'd expect they'd say."

"Jessen had interrogated him for two hours beforehand. But he couldn't get a single word out of him. He just kept saying he hadn't done it. Jens doesn't think you're so sure he did, either."

"Give your Jens my regards."

"Shall I tell him to phone you, if anything comes up?"

"I haven't really anything to do with the case now," said Morck, "but if anything does come up I'd be glad to hear from him."

He wished her all the best for the wedding, and hung up. Going back to Marie, he took the cup of coffee she'd just poured him.

"We'll have to send a bouquet," she said. "What's her name?"

"Jonna. But why do you want to know?"

"Really, Jonas, surely even you can see that. We can't just address it to The Hertings, can we?"

"Eh . . . no, I suppose not."

"Jonas."

"Hm?"

"You're home now, eh? At least I can see you sitting there."

"Yes . . . oh, then I'd better move over beside you."

He went and sat beside her on the sofa.

"So that I can touch you as well as see you—" she said. "Yes, you're here sure enough. Do you know when you might have to go off again?"

"No, I didn't tell the department when we were coming back, in case they immediately chased us off somewhere else."

"Sometimes you show great presence of mind."

"Yes, when the occasion strongly demands it, such as now, in our case."

"But at our time of life, surely it's not that strong?"

"No, but it is a demand, isn't it?"

"Well, is it?"

"Yes," he said, readily recalling a late hour of the night in Barkway, Vesterso, when he had heard a woman's whisper through a half-open window and had been reminded of his wife.

"What did you say, Marie?" he asked.

"I just said it was only eight o'clock in the evening."

"Yes, dear," said Morck.

28

THAT SAME NIGHT, a patrol car was on the lookout for drunken drivers on one of the northern approach roads to Copenhagen. Among the vehicles stopped was a van with two stone-cold sober men in the front seat. Unfortunately for both of them, one of the policemen recognized the driver and greeted him with surprise and delight, as if by sheer good luck he'd bumped into an old acquaintance.

"Goodness, Mathiesen, fancy meeting you," he said. "What have you been doing in North Sjaelland at this time of night?"

Mathiesen hadn't been doing anything. And, in any case, that was his own business.

"Sure, if it really was your business," said the policeman. "But we'd better make sure, just to be on the safe side."

The other policeman opened the back door of the van and helped a third man out. He had been curled up on the floor of the van in the tiny space left over after it had been loaded up with cigarettes and spirits following a break-in at two North Sjaelland supermarkets. He was young and a newcomer to the job so he was the one who blabbed. The other two said as little as possible, obdurately denying they were part of a larger organization known to the Sjaelland police for some time.

Einarsen and Morck were assigned the mopping-up operation which went on for several weeks and resulted in seven arrests, all of them small-fry; a few small twigs in the ramifications of a much larger empire. The big cheese—or cheeses—the men at the top, the managing directors, all slipped through the net. It proved impossible to pin them down. The inquiries were trivial and wearisome, involving a lot of to-ing and fro-ing in Sjaelland but nothing much elsewhere. Still, they at least had the advantage of being able to get back to Copenhagen most nights.

On June 10, Marie Morck went into the florist and ordered a bunch of roses for the newly-weds, Jens and Jonna Herting. She gave clear instructions to the florist:

"When you ring Esbjerg, tell them not to send any that have been lying around in the shops for days. And at all costs, they mustn't be salmon-pink."

A few days later, an acknowledgment came, and in the envelope, Herting—or maybe the new Mrs Herting—had enclosed a newspaper cutting.

"Just take a look at this," said Marie when Morck came back from North Sjaelland that night. "What do you think of a judge who acts like that?"

"Acts like what?"

"Read it and see."

The cutting was from the local paper:

CONFESSION IN VESTERSO MURDER CASE

But in a subsequent court-hearing, Otto Bahnsen,
the accused, retracts his confession.

Under police interrogation, hotel porter Otto Bahnsen (22) confessed yesterday to the murder of the nurse, Kirsten Bunding, in Vesterso. But in a hastily convened hearing he retracted this confession shortly afterwards. On being cross-examined in court, Bahnsen entangled himself in a number of falsehoods and inconsistencies, but still maintained he was not the murderer. On being asked by Chief-Superintendent Ehner why he had confessed, he replied:

"Because they kept on and on at me."

Ehner: "What do you mean by that?"

Bahnsen: "They wouldn't stop asking me questions, and I only wanted to be left in peace."

Ehner: "That cannot be true, Bahnsen. Since you've confessed and made a statement to the police, you must be guilty."

Bahnsen: "No, I'm not."

Superintendent Ehner then outlined the movements of the accused on the night of the crime, according to the statements he had made to the police Defence Counsel Mr Schmidt, QC, asked if the police report contained a transcript of the actual confession and was told that Otto Bahnsen, in reply to the question "Did you kill Kirsten Bunding?" eventually said "Yes, I did. And now leave me alone."

Ehner: "Bahnsen, don't you see that the evidence is against you, and moreover, you have confessed, haven't you?"

Bahnsen (almost inaudible): "Yes."

Ehner: "Why should you confess, if you're not guilty?"

Bahnsen: "I don't know. But anyway, it wasn't me."

At this point, Judge Jacobsen intervened and took charge of the proceedings with his customary authority, asking the accused:

"Why have you told us all these lies, Bahnsen? Are you in your right mind?"

No reply.

Judge: "Don't you know the difference between truth and falsehood?"

The accused bowed his head and muttered incomprehensibly.

(What was he muttering? Morck wondered. No doubt his usual response: "I don't know.")

Judge: "Speak up."

The accused raised his head but gave no answer, upon which Judge Jacobsen addressed him with great earnestness, exhorting him to tell the truth.

Judge: "You have no choice, Otto Bahnsen. You're only making things worse for yourself, both physically and spiritually. You are bound not only by the laws of man but are also answerable to a Higher Power. You will be in torment till your dying day if you are guilty of this crime; so you had best tell the truth and set your conscience at rest. Don't you think that is what you should do?"

Otto Bahnsen, struggling to get the words out, eventually managed to say:

"No, I won't."

Judge: "Now tell me the truth, Bahnsen. Did you murder Kirsten Bunding?"

Bahnsen: "No, I didn't. I didn't."

186

Judge: "Then we shall have to wait for another occasion."

At this point the hearing was adjourned, it having been decided that a psychiatric report on Otto Bahnsen should be prepared by the official doctor.

"Is a judge really entitled to say that sort of thing?" Marie asked indignantly. "He's worse than any fire-and-brimstone preacher at a mission. Surely it's not part of his job to preach repentance? Is it?"

"No," said Morck.

"Yet he talks as if he already knows the boy is guilty and so he condemns him out of hand." Marie had also begun to call Otto Bahnsen "the boy".

"Yes, the report makes it sound as if he had."

"And tell me, why didn't the defence counsel do more for the boy?"

"He doesn't get much of a mention in the paper."

"I simply don't believe it," said Marie in a conclusive tone of voice. She had taken sides by now.

"What don't you believe?" said Morck.

"He's almost bound to be innocent, if they go on brainwashing him like that," she said. Marie was not always strictly logical, but she compensated for that with the passion of her pronouncements.

Some weeks passed, and cool, breezy June came to an end. Summer was at its height now and the days grew shorter. Neither Einarsen nor Morck had been given the week's holiday due to them in the spring. It was high time they had their summer holiday, but that too had to be shelved. The flying squad staff with school-age children were first on the list, and even then, they couldn't all time their holidays to coincide with the school holidays.

Einarsen's wife had long since returned from her Mediterranean holiday with the girl friend, and their marriage had been stabilized again as it often had been whenever threatened with breakdown. Or maybe it would have been nearer the truth to say that Einarsen had put both Cilia and the girl friend in their places. That, at least, was his story.

Morck couldn't be sure of the details, but he had formed some idea of them from a few cryptic remarks Einarsen had let slip.

"When they came home, still bosom pals, I had the bright idea of taking up temporary residence with the fashion-shop manageress, though she isn't exactly my number one favourite female. So when I confessed to dear Cilia that I'd been feeling up her friend behind her back, she was predictably eager to scratch her eyes out and skin her alive. So now they're the deadliest of enemies and I can twist Cilia round my feet."

"Surely you mean your little finger?"

"No, I mean my feet, godammit. She's developed quite a taste for them."

No doubt all this was partly bravado, but even so Einarsen had quieted down considerably, and was less volatile and bloodshot these days. As a result, he had lost six or seven pounds. But the temperature was still soaring, and the normal seasonal drop in the crime-rate showed no signs of occurring.

The papers said that in the past year there had been more murders and crimes of violence in Denmark than during the German occupation. In this second category, armed bank robberies were in the majority. In general the robbers had succeeded but the same couldn't be said of the police attempts at catching them.

Morck and Einarsen were put on a bank robbery in a South Sjaelland village, where a man in his mid-twenties, or possibly his mid-thirties, had come into the local bank two minutes before closing-time and politely asked the lady cashier, although at gunpoint, to fill a white shopping bag he was carrying with notes. She was able to hand over 20,200 kroner. He had then asked the bank manager for the keys to his car, and had driven off in it with his shopping bag. A few hours later the car was found in a copse on the other side of the village not far from the main road to Copenhagen. The tyre marks of the car he had switched to were clearly visible on the woodland track. They were of a pattern currently to be found on every second or third car in the land; apart from that, the only clue to his identity was the description given by the cashier and the bank manager, who had been the only staff in the bank at the time. A young or youngish man, of average height and appearance, with a pleasant manner, the middle-aged lady cashier said, trembling with excitement. He had obviously given her the greatest thrill of her life. Well-spoken too, though he'd been wearing grey or khaki overalls and a cap.

"They were green," said the manager. She disagreed.

"Like my tie?" said Einarsen.

"Yes, just like that," she said; "they were more or less the same colour."

Einarsen's tie was pale green and the cashier was obviously colour-blind; but she refused to be swayed.

While searching for the bank robber (they never found him), they stopped one afternoon at a wayside inn on Highway 2 just north of Vordingborg and, as they were having coffee, Morck produced a letter. It had lain unopened in his pocket since the morning, when he had met the postman on his way out of the house. A newspaper cutting had been enclosed. Another one. While he was reading it, Einarsen remarked:

"What's wrong? You've gone all red in the face."

"You know that Otto Bahnsen business?"

"What? Oh, you mean that miserable little creep in . . . Vesterso, was that the name of the place?"

Morck wondered if he too might have forgotten the boy if this particular clipping hadn't reminded him—the third or fourth he'd received—together with the conversations he'd had about the case with his wife, who kept harking back to the topic.

"Yes, the miserable little creep in Vesterso," he replied angrily. "I've bloody well never heard anything like this before—no, I'm damn sure I haven't."

"Jonas, really. What kind of language is that for you to be using?" said Einarsen. "It's not like you at all. I hope you haven't been getting into bad company of late?"

"Oh, shut up," said Morck. "Just read this."

Einarsen read the cutting and returned it to him with the comment: "Well, they've sewn him up good and proper now. But he was the killer after all, and now he's confessed."

"Or else they've forced a confession out of him?" said Morck.

"A confession's a confession and it's time you stopped all this——"

"All this what?"

"All this tinkering about with old cases that don't concern you any more," said Einarsen. "It can be positively dangerous. You know the famous unsolved double murder that was committed in Frederiks-berg years and years ago? Well, I've heard there's an old detective out there who spends all his leisure time ploughing through the fifty thousand or a hundred thousand or so pages of information gathered in the course of the investigations. He's got it on the brain."

189

"Damned newspapers," Morck muttered, paying no attention to Einarsen. He was reading the cutting again.

"What did you say?"

Morck didn't repeat the general imprecation. "The style is repulsive, snivelling and melodramatic," he said.

"They've certainly gone the whole hog this time," said Einarsen. "And you can rest assured their readers lapped it up . . . just the sort of sickly guff the public like. What was the name of the girl behind the bar at the inn?"

"Eline."

"Ideal for the part, isn't she?" said Einarsen, taking the coffee pot back to be filled up.

The headline read:

OTTO BAHNSEN GIVES IN AND CONFESSES

During a dramatic confrontation at the scene of the crime in Vesterso yesterday evening, hotel porter Otto Bahnsen, broke down and confessed for the second time that he had committed the gory murder. The confrontation was arranged thanks to the testimony of a female witness during a vital court hearing. The witness, a young girl from the neighbourhood, related how, last summer, she had been attacked by Otto Bahnsen in the scrub brush outside Vesterso, where the murder had actually taken place. He had knocked her over without warning and thrown himself on top of her. However, she had managed to struggle free, and he had not pursued her, or renewed the attempt, which, at the time, she had interpreted as a totally unsolicited incitement to intimacy. The girl thought that the attack had been made in the same place as the murder had been committed; thereupon the court decided to arrange a confrontation at this spot that same evening.

The hearing had begun late in the afternoon, and it was nearly dark when the court re-convened and drove to the scene of the murder in a long convoy of police vehicles, which aroused considerable interest on its way through Vesterso in the calm of the evening. A large crowd of people followed the convoy out to the scene of the crime.

In the first car were the chief witness, the judge, and some police personnel, and in one of the others, Otto Bahnsen, the accused. The girl indicated the place where they should stop on the Beach

Road, and in the glare of several powerful floodlights rigged up by the police, she led the party along the path through the scrub to the place where Otto Bahnsen had attacked her.

She stopped immediately next to where the murder had been committed.

"This is the place," she said, confidently.

A fascinating and highly dramatic scenario was then enacted, as orders were given that Otto Bahnsen should be conducted to the spot under police escort. In the blustery wind of this dark evening, the suspense of all those present was well nigh unbearable as Otto Bahnsen appeared in the clearing in the scrub between two police officers. The powerful floodlamps pierced the darkness with rigid shafts of light. The wind and the scudding clouds completed a picture which will not be readily forgotten by any of those who witnessed the drama.

Otto Bahnsen was then confronted with the girl, on the very spot where the murder had been committed. She looked steadfastly at him, as she described how, on that very spot, she had sat talking to him without any ulterior motive after a walk they had taken, and how, when they were about to leave, he had tried to overpower her.

"That's not true," Otto Bahnsen protested at first. She looked him straight in the eye, and he withdrew his gaze. "It wasn't here. I've never been here," he said. "No, never."

"This was the place," she replied, again looking him in the eye, "and you know very well it was."

"I don't think it was. It was further on."

"It was here," she said. At this point Judge Jacobsen intervened.

"You've heard what the girl says, Bahnsen; and she appears to be a great deal more sure of herself than you are. Wouldn't you be better to admit that this was where the episode took place?"

Otto Bahnsen mumbled an inaudible reply.

Judge Jacobsen: "Speak up!"

Otto Bahnsen: "All right, I will."

Judge: "What, admit it, you mean? I should think so. So you recognize the spot?"

Otto Bahnsen: "Yes, maybe I do."

Judge: "Do you or do you not? Kindly give us a straight answer, one way or the other."

Otto Bahnsen: "Yes."

Judge: "So, you do recognize it. Are you aware of where we are,

Bahnsen? You are standing on the very spot where Kirsten Bunding was murdered."

Otto Bahnsen: "I . . . I . . . I don't know anything about it, I didn't have anything to do with it."

Otto Bahnsen seemed confused and fearful. He hung his head, not daring to look up, and the inevitability of the impending confession was clear to everyone.

Judge Jacobsen said: "Don't you think you should tell us the truth now? Will you or won't you?"

Otto Bahnsen: "Yes, I will."

Judge: "Then tell me: Did you murder Kirsten Bunding here, where we are standing?"

Bahnsen: "No, I didn't, I didn't, I didn't."

Judge: "Think it over, Bahnsen. We have plenty of time."

Bahnsen: "But it wasn't me."

Spotlighted by blinding shafts of light, Otto Bahnsen was conducted round the little hollow where the terrible deed was done. There were tears in his eyes, but he still maintained that he knew nothing about the murder.

Judge Jacobsen then recommended him to speak to his defence counsel, Mr Schmidt. The discussion lasted several minutes. Otto Bahnsen was heard to say "Will they leave me alone if I do?" and, soon after that, he yielded to persuasion, confessing to the judge without any sign of emotion:

"Yes, it was me."

Judge: "So you confess to the murder, Bahnsen. Will you abide by this confession?"

Bahnsen: "Yes . . . yes, I will."

He no longer seemed to be affected by the situation but, on the way back to the police car he began to cry.

"He did, did he?" said Morck aloud. His fury had increased after his second reading of the newspaper cutting. "Did he really? My, what a surprise. These bloody——"

"There, there," said Einarsen, reaching over to pour him out more coffee. "Another cup? And stop shouting like that in public, Jonas."

"Shouting in public is exactly what someone should be doing," said Morck.

29

"WHAT DO THEY think they're doing to that boy," said Marie, when he came home two days later. She handed him a paper: "Just read that."

"Where did you get it?"

"At the news stand in Osterport Station."

"But how did you know——?"

"Because Herting rang up wanting to talk to you . . . he told me the whole story and I wanted to read it for myself. I just had to," she repeated hotly. "Go on, read it."

Morck complied:

Yet another sudden and sensational turn of events took place this morning in the Vesterso murder case, as sentence was about to be passed on Otto Bahnsen, who recently confessed to the murder at the very spot where it had been committed.

Bahnsen caused a stir as soon as he entered the court room. He came up from the cells sobbing, almost unable to utter a coherent word.

"What's wrong with you?" asked the police superintendent.

"I didn't do it. It wasn't me," Bahnsen stammered in tears. The hearing was further complicated by his incessant crying, and it proved nearly impossible to make sense of what he said. On being asked by the judge why he was retracting his confession yet again, he eventually managed to reply:

"Because it wasn't me . . . I just said it was because I couldn't stand it any longer. I was scared . . ."

Superintendent: "Scared of what, Bahnsen? Surely not of the police?"

From then on no intelligible answers could be got out of him, and the hearing had, consequently, to be abandoned.

The official psychiatric report is now at hand indicating that Otto Bahnsen is backward to an exceptional degree, emotionally undeveloped and mentally retarded. The report recommends that he be regarded as a psychopath. In view of this recommendation, Otto Bahnsen is being confined to a mental hospital for further observation.

"How can they do it?" said Marie. "How can they, Jonas? Do they really have any right to run rings around him and torment him?"

"Yes, they have a right to, the law says they have, and that's how the law operates. And, incidentally, I'm another factor in the operation of that law."

"But if he's not guilty, and they still go on at him—what's the word I want?"

"Nowadays they probably say he's being manipulated."

"Till he doesn't know whether he's coming or going. And so he confesses for the sake of peace—isn't that possible?"

"I don't know, I suppose it might be. But to get at the truth——"

"Well, they should make sure. Otherwise how can anyone condemn a poor creature like him?"

"They can and they will."

"Then he'd be put in a mental hospital as a psychopath, regardless of whether he did it or not."

"No, he wouldn't," said Morck. "He's only backward, and despite the official doctor's recommendation, which the medical consultant's lawyer will certainly uphold, a judge doesn't usually treat backward people as special cases. If he were found to be in the least mentally deficient he might be considered unsuited for punishment and be put into care. But he's just backward, so that can't happen. In fact, there's only one possibility if he's found guilty."

"What's that?"

"Life imprisonment."

"Good God. What kind of a country is this?"

"You may well ask," Morck said. "Or backward people may."

They were both silent for a while.

"And that official doctor," she went on. "The poor soul behaves like an unhappy child and is informed that he's 'emotionally under-developed'. What does that mean?"

"That's only the technical jargon they use for people who have difficulty in expressing themselves."

"You mean the doctor can't express himself any better? I'd certainly go along with that."

"No, I mean the boy."

"Maybe the doctor couldn't get across to him though."

"You can't be sure."

"Yet he has to pass judgment on his mental state. How can an ordinary doctor be qualified to do that?"

"He'll probably have taken some superficial course in psychiatry," said Morck. "But anyway, the court assumes that those whom the State has chosen as its official doctors have arrogated from God the power of evaluating other people's psychic condition."

"But think of all the little, powerless people, who don't find life easy—they're at the mercy of the system. How can the right-thinking people in our society stand by and watch that happening?"

"I don't know what you mean by 'right-thinking' or 'our society'. Whose society? The doctor's?"

"You know very well what I mean. I mean everyone who is responsible for the system being as it is."

"Well, they can simply refuse to face the facts, can't they?" said Morck, reaching for the telephone to ring up Herting.

30

"I DON'T KNOW if this is of any importance or not," Herting said over the phone; "I've told Jessen but he's not interested. He thinks the case is as good as finished, at least as far as the police are concerned. Otto Bahnsen's bound to be found guilty and so on."

"Yes, I can see that," said Morck, "but tell me more."

"You know the girl in the telephone exchange at Vesterso—the daughter?"

"The one that looked like a younger, watered-down version of the mother?"

"Yes, that's the one. Did you talk to them both yourself?"

"No, but that was the impression you gave me from your encounter."

"She came up to me yesterday afternoon on King Street in Esbjerg," said Herting. "She was in town on a shopping expedition and she caught sight of me on the opposite side of the street. I think she must have crossed over to my side on impulse. 'There's something I should tell you after all,' she said, 'even though I can't be absolutely sure, and it won't matter anyway now that he's confessed.'"

She had been pale and trembling with nerves, obviously because Mama had dared her not to breathe a word. But, for some reason she had taken Herting into her confidence.

"You remember the doctor, don't you?" she said, "the one who rang Kirsten Bunding that night and asked her to come out and see to his wife in the summer house? Well, I said I'd only heard him ask for the number, but that's not quite true. I heard a few words more, only half a sentence or so. But mother didn't think I should say anything about it, since I wasn't quite sure exactly what was said and, besides, people might think we listened in to their conversations."

"What did the doctor say?" Herting asked her. "And what are you not sure about, Miss Bergquist?"

"Only about whether he used the familiar you or the formal one."

"In what context? Now, if you can recall his exact words . . . he rings up and asks for the number, then?"

"She lifted the receiver and said 'Nurse Bunding'. Then I think he said, 'You'll have to come right away'—using the familiar form."

"And was that all? He didn't even give his name?"

"No. But he might not have used the familiar form. I just thought——"

"And you didn't hear any more?"

"No, because just then someone rang for a taxi. Anyway I wouldn't have gone on listening to what they were saying. I only heard what I did hear because I wanted to make sure the call had gone through. After all, it could have been an emergency. You see what I mean, don't you?"

Herting had said yes.

"What do you think, Morck?" he said.

"The same as you," said Morck. "As you've already suggested: he doesn't give his name, but says, without further ado, 'You'll have to come right away'. Or else he uses the formal you. In either case, given that Miss Bergquist's memory is correct——"

"The doctor assumes that Kirsten Bunding would know who was speaking merely by hearing his voice."

"Yes, that's the way I see it."

"Then they must have known one another extremely well," said Herting.

"Yet he said nothing about that when the police in Aarhus interrogated him. I've just read the report again. There's nothing in it to suggest he was asked the question, but even if he wasn't, he made no mention of this knowledge of his own accord."

"Your reasoning's solid enough," said Morck.

"Yes, but what does it point to?" said Herting. "There isn't necessarily any great significance in that fact alone, is there?"

"Perhaps not, but we still ought to go more deeply into the question. What do you have on your plate just now?"

"We're rounding up a gang of youths, about half-a-dozen of them, mostly minors, but some older ones too. They specialize in highly organized shoplifting. It's no joke, I can tell you—breaking the news to their parents, I mean."

"No, it can't be."

"Three of our men are on holiday too, so there's a lot of extra work, and we're having great difficulty in keeping up to date with the job in hand, let alone anything fresh."

"Your wife included?"

"Yes, her especially," said Herting. "She's very understanding—but there's another thing I thought of. Maybe no more than a wild idea; but when I began to turn the case over in my mind again, the picture of the man on the beach five years ago came into my head. Do you remember him?"

"Yes, beside her in a bathing suit."

"No, bathing trunks."

"I was thinking about her," said Morck. He conjured up a picture of them side by side on a Mediterranean beach, she smiling radiantly at the man she loved. He did not have as clear a memory of him.

"I know you were," said Herting, "but you see what I'm driving at?"

"Yes, an unknown man from five years back, and now a man who won't admit to having known her—that's the tie-up, isn't it?"

Neither of them spoke for a few seconds.

"But the worst of it is," Herting went on, "it's disappeared."

"What has, the picture?"

"Yes, I've tried my best to trace it, but I can't. It must be tucked away somewhere, but nobody's reported it missing yet. It's sure to be lying around somewhere; maybe Jessen has it somewhere in his files, but he's away at present."

"Wait a minute," said Morck, "I've just had an idea." He called out to Marie, who was still in the kitchen. She came to the door and looked at him with eyebrows raised. "You remember that jacket I had with me in Vesterso?" he said.

"Yes, the shabby tweed one—I told you it would be too cold to pretend the summer had come——"

"Yes, I know, dear. Would you go upstairs and look in the left-hand pocket?"

"For what?"

"For whatever you happen to find," he said curtly, preoccupied with his own train of thought: ". . . like going round with a key you've borrowed from somewhere and forgotten to return. If it should turn out to be—if only it were——"

"If only it were what?" Herting's voice said in his ear.

"Sorry. I must have been talking aloud to myself. I must be getting old—though my wife says I've been like that for years and years. What was I saying, by the way?"

"Something about a key," said Herting. "And that's exactly what we may have found. Anyway, this is the first time we've come up with a new hypothesis."

"Let's not read too much into it yet. Early days——" Morck said as Marie came in carrying the photograph.

"Yes, it was in my pocket all the time. I don't know what could have come over me. Hold on a minute—— What did you say, Marie?"

She pointed at the picture and repeated in a whisper, "Is that her?"

Morck nodded.

"And who's the man?"

"We don't know yet. What's the time?"

The question was addressed to Marie, but the reply came from Herting.

"Five to eleven."

"Then I've just got time to catch the night train to Aarhus. I happen to be free tomorrow because Einarsen and I have given up trying to catch a bank robber. What's that, Marie?"

Things were beginning to get confusing with Marie on one side and Herting saying something else in his other ear.

"So you think he might be the doctor from Aarhus, the one in the picture?"

"Don't jump to conclusions, Marie. What did you say, Herting?"

"I'll go up and pack your overnight bag."

It was still Marie talking. She hurried out of the living-room and went upstairs.

"Herting, are you still there?"

"Yes, what do you want me to do?"

"Five years ago, Kirsten Bunding was working in Esbjerg, do you remember how long she was there?"

"Only a few months. She was transferred from Randers Cottage Hospital."

"And the doctor—what's his name?"

199

"Erik Sogaard."

"Where was he five or six years ago?"

"That didn't emerge during the interview, after all no one had connected them in this way before; but I'll find out and ring you back in ten minutes."

"Thanks, Herting. I'll just manage to have a shower in that time."

As if that mattered to Herting. Morck replaced the receiver and took the phone with him up to the bedroom. He was halfway through the shower when it rang again.

"Shall I take it?" said Marie. But he came out of the shower and took it himself.

"Was he in Randers?" he said.

"Yes, Sogaard was on call at Randers at the time."

"Well, that settles one point."

"Yes, they must have known one another."

"Thanks a lot, Herting. You'll be hearing from me. Bye for now."

Although the conversation was over he remained by the phone. "They knew one another," he said blankly to the bedroom wall.

"And you've only discovered that now?" said Marie.

"Yes. And that only because a telephone operator from Vesterso happens to catch sight of Herting in the street."

"And a mere coincidence like that could be the deciding factor?"

"Yes, there's a faint possibility."

"And sentence might have been passed on the boy by now, mightn't it?"

"Yes."

"But Jonas, that's utterly horrific, don't you agree? That such things should depend on sheer——"

"Yes, but first let's see if there's any truth in it."

"Truth? How do you mean?"

Morck didn't reply: was he even listening? She passed him a towel.

"You're obviously on your way already," she said, "but you might as well dry yourself; you're dripping wet. And look at that huge puddle on the floor."

"Yes, that huge puddle," he echoed. "What did you say, Marie?"

"You've just repeated what I said, but you weren't even listening."

"No."

"Jonas!"

She had to shout at him. He stared at her in astonishment. "What's up?"

200

"If you want to catch the night train, you'll have to get your skates on."

Morck dried himself rapidly with the towel.

There was still time enough for them to walk slowly along Great King Street and through the shopping centre to the station. Marie kissed him goodbye on the platform and he boarded the train. He waved at her from the window watching her go down the steps to take the subway home. The night air was cold for summer and she had had the sense to put on a tweed coat, not very different from the one that had been hanging in Kirsten Bunding's hallway. The thought struck him that the murdered woman, Kirsten Bunding, reminded him strongly of his wife in many ways—but this was mere fantasy. Though a fantasy he firmly believed in. Marie disappeared beyond the lamplights.

And what of the man, Sogaard?

The train pulled out of the station and Morck went along to the buffet car, ordered a beer and sat down to study the photograph. His eye was repeatedly drawn to the woman, and in the end he covered her up with his hand in order to concentrate solely on the man. A pleasant, average-looking individual. What more was there to be said? He was only a man after all.

31

HE OPERATED FROM comparatively modern business premises in central Aarhus. At street level there was a car showroom on one side and a travel agent on the other. Between these, double glass doors gave access to some stairs and an elevator leading to the upper floors. Behind a glass plate in the passage way, the words DOCTORS' SURGERY stood out in white letters against a black background. Three names were printed underneath, and Erik Sogaard's was the top one.

Telephone messages 8.30 a.m.–9.30 a.m. Consulting hours 12.30 p.m.–2.00 p.m. The same for all three—sure sign of a well-organized business. Reception was on the first floor. It was just about nine-thirty, so Morck went up by the stairs. A brass plate with the words OPEN and CLOSED showed CLOSED, but he knocked and went in.

"I'm sorry, but if you want to make an appointment . . ." The doctors' secretary was sitting at her desk behind the counter. She was young and chic, in a becoming white coat, but she frowned in a less becoming manner when he came barging in, in spite of the time restrictions indicated.

Morck said he didn't want to make an appointment, then, introducing himself as Detective-Inspector Morck, asked to speak to Dr Sogaard.

"Is it about the same case as before?" she said.

"Yes."

"Dr Sogaard's very busy this morning, but if you could come back later I think I could fit you in . . . later this afternoon."

"I'm sorry, that will be too late. I must see him immediately."

Now it was Morck's turn to sound annoyed. These doctors, he thought, who—apart from their measly hour-and-a-half in the middle of the day—turn a deaf ear to the patients they grow rich on.

"Well, if it's that important, I'll see what can be done."

"Yes, please do," he said. She picked up the phone.

"Dr Sogaard, there's someone from the police who says he must speak to you, at once, if possible. A Detective-Inspector Morck."

He hadn't said if possible. What he had said was—— She waited for the reply with some signs of surprise and confusion. Was the doctor unduly long in answering? Was that why she was surprised?

"Dr Sogaard?" she repeated. This time the doctor did reply. She nodded. "Yes, I will," she said and replaced the receiver.

"Dr Sogaard will see you now. First door on the left."

The desk wasn't made of wood but of some greenish material. The legs were enamelled steel, and the total effect was artificial and aseptic. The few objects on it had suffered a distressing regimentation. Dr Sogaard was closing a cupboard behind the desk and had his back to the door. He was wearing his white coat. Would he usually wear it to receive phone calls in the morning, Morck wondered. Or had he just put it on on impulse, when Morck's arrival was announced? So that he'd just hung up his jacket in the cupboard? Sogaard turned round.

"Good morning. I believe you want to speak to me."

"Yes, about the murder of the nurse, Kirsten Bunding, in Vesterso."

His tone was official, as if in the next sentence he was going to charge Sogaard with the murder. Sogaard was the man all right. There could be no doubt about that. The white-coated doctor and the man in bathing trunks were the same person. The broad, slightly lop-sided face, with little hollows below the cheekbones was unmistakable, though somewhat thinner now, and the hollows a shade deeper. But still the same face. The brow seemed higher, for the hair had receded and thinned out on top. He was also beginning to go grey. Standing on the other side of the desk, he stooped slightly forward (who had said he had a stoop?).

"I've already told everything I know to those colleagues of yours who came to interview me."

"I don't believe you have," said Morck.

"What do you mean, you don't believe I have?"

"I can't put it more simply than that."

In the photograph he was young and suntanned—one should say he was still young. But in the bright morning light streaming through the window from the south-east, his face was sallow, almost haggard. Five years had passed and his youth was gone.

"I really don't understand what you mean," he said, and Morck did not trouble to enlighten him. He had put him off his stride, which was exactly what Sogaard had done to other people by keeping silent. And this silence had meant that other people—one in particular, the unfortunate Otto Bahnsen—had been blamed for a murder which he, the respectable Dr Sogaard, could throw more light on. That was the long and the short of it. Somebody or other would have to make sure he did penance for his silence, and it so happened that that somebody was Jonas Morck. Yet it wasn't like Morck to relish the mild cruelty he was indulging in.

"May I sit down?" he said.

"Of course. Excuse my forgetting."

They both sat down, Morck in the patient's chair and Sogaard at his desk. Sogaard's nerves were on edge and he began talking compulsively, in explanation of his remark.

"Your colleagues brought the statement and asked me to read it through. There was nothing I could add, so——"

"You signed it?"

"Yes, I did."

"But presumably you intended to lend further support to your declarations when summoned as a witness in court? Otherwise, the consequences could be fairly serious, as you are no doubt aware," said Morck, though he knew the warning was unnecessary. Still, Sogaard was pushing his luck.

"I really don't know what you're talking about," he said, endeavouring to sound righteously indignant. "I've already explained——"

"Yes, you've explained sure enough; and as a consequence of your explanation and a combination of other factors, a young man has been accused of murder and is in danger of being sentenced to life imprisonment."

"Yes, but tell me how I——?"

"Very well," said Morck, taking the photograph from his pocket and passing it over to him. "I assume you recognize yourself in that photograph?"

Sogaard picked up the photograph and looked at it, then he went deathly pale.

"My God," he breathed, with something remotely resembling a smile, if only a twisted and morose one. He sank back in his chair, no longer the doctor in the white coat but the man in the picture, then young and bronzed, now grey and middle-aged.

"Yes, she . . . she was . . ." he muttered incoherently, and Morck did not trouble to ask what he meant, for the syllables were not addressed to him. He looked away, waiting for Sogaard to make the next move. He was no longer angry.

At length Sogaard looked up from the picture. "Well, there's no way of avoiding the issue now."

"None whatsoever," said Morck.

"You see, I have certain . . . strictly private reasons for keeping our . . . relationship a secret. There were compelling reasons for keeping it a secret."

"From whom?"

"From my wife. Her nerves are not very strong, and I was afraid she might go to pieces if it ever came out."

"What? That you were having an affair with Kirsten Bunding?"

"Yes, I suppose that's the only phrase we can use. There'd be no use in trying to describe it any other way."

He kept looking at the picture he still held in his hand, at the half-naked woman smiling at him across a distance of five years, and now murdered.

"Perhaps you'd prefer to say it was a close relationship?" Morck suggested.

"Yes. I suppose I would," he replied, with a sigh of relief tinged with gratitude. Then, for the first time, he confessed what he had never confessed before.

"You see . . . I . . . we . . . I was in love with her, but it was impossible——"

"Because of your wife?"

"Yes. After all, I was responsible for her, and she wasn't in the best of health even then."

Sogaard stopped, almost at a loss for words, then he pulled himself together again.

"Look, I'm prepared to answer any questions you ask," he continued, "but couldn't we go somewhere else? I'd find it so much easier on neutral ground, and there'd be less chance of being interrupted."

No one was interrupting them where they were and it would have been hard to imagine surroundings more neutral than the clinical chill of this impersonal consulting room. Nor could a less suitable place be imagined for confessing love for a woman who had been murdered: "I . . . we . . . I was in love . . ."; spoken by a man in a doctor's coat. The room may have induced patients to trust their doctor, if only with minor confidences. But Morck acknowledged that in this case, when it was the doctor's turn to confide in someone else, the room was far from suitable.

"Very well, let's go," he said.

"I'll just have to tell the secretary."

Sogaard went through to the outer office and spoke to the secretary, then came back and took his coat off.

"Do you normally have that on in the morning?" said Morck.

"Eh . . . what? No, actually I don't."

"So you must have decided to put it on when you heard I'd arrived?"

"Yes. But I really don't know why I did," Sogaard sounded faintly surprised.

"Wasn't it because the white coat is your uniform? For one thing, a uniform gives civilians the protection of anonymity. And for another, it allows them to assume the authority which the uniform asserts."

"Yes, that must have been roughly what I had in mind, although I wasn't fully conscious of it," said Sogaard with a weak smile. "There wouldn't be much point in claiming that the strategy worked though, would there?"

"No. For it to work you have to assume first that the party you're trying to impress is not clued in."

"To what the civilian is hiding you mean? You're very thoroughly clued in, more's the pity."

"So you regret that I am?"

"Very much so. But I'll have to cope with that now, whatever the outcome may be."

He hung up his coat in the cupboard and put on his jacket.

"Shall we go? There's a quiet little restaurant along the street."

Sogaard was not the kind of man who would frequent pubs. A white-collar worker, some kind of executive or professional man— exactly what he looked like, as Einarsen had guessed from the merest glance at a photograph of him in bathing trunks.

The little restaurant along the road, haunt of the local businessmen, was precisely *comme il faut*. The tables, covered in plain white cloths, were set in alcoves separated by wickerwork partitions. At the tables nearest the street, three or four of the white-collar brigade were ensconced with their morning coffee and newspapers. Morck and Sogaard went into the inner part of the restaurant, where the light was dimmer, and sat down in an alcove with a smoked glass window in a blue frame looking out on to an invisible yard.

"Beer or coffee?" said Sogaard.

"Coffee, thanks," said Morck, a little startled. Beer during an interrogation seemed as unthinkable to him as beer after a funeral.

"Yes, of course," said Sogaard, giving the waitress the order. They sat in silence for her to bring the coffee. Morck laid a notebook and a pen on the table.

"Well, Dr Sogaard, I have to ask you to give me some further details of your relationship with Kirsten Bunding. Did you first get to know her in Randers?"

"So you know that as well?" said Sogaard. "I suppose I was naïve enough to think you wouldn't find out."

"Yes, you were," Morck laughed, thinking how near he had been to not finding out. "And I must advise you at the outset not to withhold any more information. Otherwise you could very probably land up in an extremely difficult situation."

"You mean I could be prosecuted for having withheld it?"

"No."

"What then?"

"You were with Kirsten Bunding immediately before she was murdered. That is a fact. It is also a fact that in your first statement to the police—the one you signed as being a complete account of your movements and which was recorded as such during the pre-liminary hearings—you said everything you could to implicate yourself——"

"But not in the m——"

"Yes, in the murder."

"You surely don't think I——"

"I don't think anything," said Morck. "I'm only trying to set out your position as the court might view it. You ring her up in the middle of the night. She comes out to your summer house, and a few yards away she is found murdered; subsequently you try to cover up the fact that you knew her—which you succeed in doing particularly well, it happens. You had been having an affair with her for several years, hadn't you?"

Sogaard looked at Morck in mute incredulity.

"Hadn't you?" Morck repeated.

"Yes."

"So you had to do your utmost to prevent your wife finding out?"

"Yes," said Sogaard again.

"Presumably you can see the interpretation that could be put on all this?"

"But that's preposterous."

"No more preposterous than the supposition that someone who hardly knew her should have murdered her."

"But he's confessed to it."

"He has withdrawn his confession," said Morck. "You probably know that from time to time false confessions are made in murder cases, and Otto Bahnsen is mentally retarded——"

"So now you're going to try to pin it on me!" Sogaard made this announcement as if he'd never heard anything so incredible in his life. Morck was even surprised at the vehemence of his own attitude to the man. But didn't this stem from a particular liking he had for him, an inclination to understand him, to put himself in his place?

"What I want is a frank statement of the truth—with nothing left out," said Morck.

"And that's exactly what you'll get," said Sogaard with some degree of animosity. There was something encouraging about the fighting spirit he showed and Morck suddenly felt they were on equal footing. Wouldn't Morck himself have reacted in the same way had he been in Sogaard's position? He hoped he would have.

"Let's begin with Randers then," he said. "That was where you met Kirsten Bunding, wasn't it?"

"Yes."

"You were on call at the hospital and she was a nurse."

"Yes, I . . . we fell in love."

"And that led to your having an affair with her?"

The obligatory questions came, not from Morck himself so much as from a policeman by the name of Morck. Sogaard looked across the table at him.

"That's what people would say," he said. "Yet it sounds so . . . banal, almost profane. The same old story, eh? Always the same as ever, I guess."

"Yes, it is," said Morck, "except for the people involved. How long did the affair last in Randers?"

"Only a few months, by which time everybody at the hospital knew about it. By everybody, I mean the nurses, the doctors—and principally, the doctors' wives. As far as I know, one of the last-named category was kind enough to let my wife know. She was already suffering from . . . a nervous disposition, and the result was that she had a breakdown and had to be given hospital treatment."

"In the neurological ward?"

"Yes. For her sake we decided to discontinue our——" Sogaard could not bring himself to use the one word he disliked so much.

"But you didn't in the end?" said Morck.

"No. We fully intended to. But when it came to the crunch, we couldn't stay apart. Not for more than a month anyway."

"After you'd moved to Aarhus and she had taken up her job in Esbjerg?"

"Yes. And although I'd sworn blind to my wife that it was all over and done with—that doesn't sound too good, does it?"

"I've heard roughly the same before now," said Morck wryly.

"Yes, I imagine you have. Quite a run-of-the-mill case really, isn't it? However, I had to swear the whole thing was over, or else she'd have . . . well, at least I was afraid she might . . . eh, do something desperate."

"What, again?"

Sogaard looked at him without saying a word then nodded slowly.

"Yes," he said gently. "So you got to know about that as well?"

"Not exactly," said Morck. "Did she first begin to take sleeping pills when she found out that you . . . that you were meeting Kirsten Bunding?"

"Yes," said Sogaard. "How did you guess?"

"Oh, that's the usual sequence of events, and with you being a doctor, she wouldn't have any difficulty in obtaining them, I take it?"

"No. She had ample supplies. I suppose that's the way it usually goes but the unusual factor was that she already had weak kidneys and the dose she was taking only served to weaken them more. Since then, she's had one removed. So you can see why, in the circumstances, I couldn't very well—but perhaps that has no bearing on your report?"

Again he managed to summon up the semblance of a grin, although his face was glistening with sweat.

"I seem to have given myself the wellnigh impossible task of justifying my actions to you. I don't think I can."

"I don't see why," said Morck.

"Really?"

"As far as I can make out, you felt you were responsible for your wife's condition and, consequently, could not desert her."

"Elementary," said Sogaard, not really meaning to be derogatory to Morck. "If only it had been as simple as that. The motive you ascribe to me sounds almost respectable. After all, I had responsibilities in another direction."

"To Kirsten Bunding, you mean?"

"Yes. You know, I don't really know why I'm telling you all this. I've never breathed a word to anyone before."

"Presumably because you've never had occasion to."

"Yes, but now I have. Yes, you're quite right. The time is ripe."

Sogaard went no further, but sat for a while in silent meditation. Morck did not disturb him. He hadn't touched either the pen or the notebook, and both still lay on the table in front of him. The coffee was rapidly getting cold.

"I admit my weaknesses, Mr Morck," Sogaard said.

Morck shrugged his shoulders, wishing merely to convey the thought Who doesn't? But he did not put it into words.

"Strangely enough, I don't mind admitting this to you, I don't know why. Maybe you can enlighten me?"

"From time to time, we all have to talk about ourselves to someone else, if only to clarify our thoughts. It so happens that I'm around on this occasion, and, as you don't know me personally——"

"This is the obvious time to choose. You see—it's all decided for me. Now, what was I saying?"

"You were weighing one responsibility against the other," said Morck.

"You put it so very concisely. That was just how things stood. I had to make a choice, and you can always look back afterwards and try to preserve the illusion of having done so. But really I had no choice. I stayed where I was."

"With your wife?"

"Yes. You might say that by a happy coincidence I lacked the resolution which could have driven me to reject my responsibility . . . to my wife."

"Yet you and Kirsten Bunding didn't split up?"

"We did," said Sogaard, "but only for a month. Then one morning, I rang her. We had agreed not to meet again. I only wanted to hear her voice. But that was just as disturbing."

"As meeting her?"

"Yes. Then we did meet, whenever possible, which wasn't often. We had the week in Spain that same summer. My wife was convalescing by then, and my excuse was a medical conference which might have had some bearing on an article I was writing at the time. I never finished the article. But we had that week together. Unfortunately, it led to my wife having another breakdown."

Suddenly Sogaard stopped talking and looked intently over at Morck.

"Why the blazes am I telling you all this? I don't have to. Why should the details of my past concern you? Do you have any cigarettes?"

"Yes, here, help yourself." Morck took one too, and passed Sogaard the matches.

"And I'd just given up smoking," said Sogaard with a sigh. "Then I began again. One keeps stopping and taking it up again."

"Yes," said Morck. "When you were talking before about your wife having a breakdown, what you actually meant was that she attempted to commit suicide. Isn't that so?"

"Yes. I was trying to avoid the issue. But after the holiday . . . you see, I'd arranged with a colleague from another hospital who had to attend the conference, that a series of postcards should be sent to my wife."

"As an alibi?"

"Yes," said Sogaard, "but of course I was nowhere near the conference. Anyway, he managed to get the sequence of cards mixed up (I'd written them in advance) and my wife became suspicious and quizzed another of my colleagues who'd also been at the conference. So she found out I hadn't been there."

"But with Kirsten Bunding in Spain instead?"

"No, I swore I hadn't. I said I'd only wanted a few days peace and quiet."

"From your wife?"

"Yes, or that's how she saw it," said Sogaard. "I chose what I thought was the lesser of two evils, both for her and, especially, for myself: I had to be brutally frank to her about my feelings. I said I'd been longing to escape from the effects of her nervous condition, if only for a few days—though God knows, she needed to even more than I. Not that that was the full extent of my longing, as you know. A piece of downright deception, wasn't it?"

"That's not for me to say," said Morck. "I'd have thought it was debatable."

"Why? Because you're more used to dealing with criminals?"

"Criminals are just the same as anyone else on the whole. Most of us are capable of deception as you call it. But few of us are aware when we are being deceitful. We rationalize our behaviour and ascribe worthy motives to what we've done."

"How very sympathetic of you, Mr Morck," said Sogaard ironically. "No doubt this attitude helps you to make people spill the beans?"

"Yes, occasionally it does," Morck replied impassively. "You were saying, about your wife."

"She had a nervous breakdown and was taken to hospital. After that, she was in and out of hospital several times."

"While you went on meeting Kirsten Bunding?"

"Yes, particularly when my wife was away; which provided our most favourable opportunities. We used to meet in various places in Jutland."

"And your wife never found out?"

"No, she never did, and she still doesn't know," said Sogaard, "but even so . . ."

Morck didn't ask what he meant by even so, but presently Sogaard asked him, or rather himself, another question.

"I'm no psychiatrist, but at the time I often used to wonder exactly how genuine such a breakdown might be. The patient tends to dramatize a situation in order to put pressure on the factors menacing him."

"Also for another reason," added Morck, "namely the fear that these same factors will refuse to take his condition seriously."

"Quite so. Now, if I'd had the chance, I would have . . ." Sogaard did not finish his sentence, but reached over to stub out his cigarette in the ashtray, holding it down until the end had stopped burning.

"You said she was frequently in hospital after that?" Morck said.

"I didn't say frequently."

"That's what I took you to mean."

"All right," said Sogaard, "let's say several times."

"For long periods?"

"Yes."

"And did she have to go into hospital after she was taken ill in Vesterso that night?"

"Yes, and she's still there."

"On account of her kidneys?"

Sogaard hesitated for a second.

"Yes," he said with unprecedented bitterness, "because of the one she still has. There was some talk of a transplant under certain circumstances. But her . . . general condition at the moment isn't such that they . . ."

He shrugged his shoulders. "She'd have to be in better shape to risk the operation."

"So she's suffering withdrawal symptoms?" Morck couldn't quite decide whether this was a question or a conclusion. Sogaard's reaction was immediate. He sat bolt upright in his chair.

"How the hell——! They've no right to divulge that kind of information," he exclaimed.

"Who? The hospital authorities? But that's not where I got it."

"Then how can you have found out? How?"

"From what you've told me about your wife, together with what I already know about your movements that night in Vesterso, I concluded——"

"Isn't there anything you can't work out for yourself?"

"Yes, several things, otherwise I wouldn't be here," said Morck. "But why conceal the fact that your wife is a drug addict?"

"Because she wouldn't approve of it being made known," said Sogaard, flushed with anger. "Haven't you discovered enough about my wife by now?"

"You're the one who kept on talking about her."

"Am I? Yes, I suppose I am." Sogaard relaxed again, and stroked his chin wearily. He looked grey and middle-aged. "From time to time I ask myself. . ." he murmured, then fell silent shaking his head.

"But one's never any the wiser, eh?"

"About oneself? No. Getting reconciled to one's own inner contradictions can be hard—fidelity and infidelity, for example."

"Especially when the second is the stronger," said Sogaard, with his little twisted smile, scarcely worthy of the name. "But let's not try to be profound for goodness sake. Things are bad enough without all these solemn utterances. Where were we, if anywhere?"

"At your summer house in Vesterso, on the night of the crime."

"So we've come to the full-stage interrogation now, have we? That'll take time; and my consulting hour begins at twelve-thirty."

"Well, we can stop now, if you want, and carry on later, either here or at your house."

Sogaard didn't seem to like the idea. For a moment he remained undecided.

"No, I'd rather get it over with now," he said at length. "I'll ring up and cancel my consulting hour on some pretext or other."

He got up and added, in his mildly mocking way, "What do you suggest—a stomach-ache, or some pressing family business?" Then he went out without waiting for Morck's answer.

Morck picked up his cup, but didn't drink any of the contents. The coffee was cold and grey, so he called the waitress and ordered a fresh pot, and two cheese sandwiches—as he often did in breaks during an interrogation. So far, this had turned out to be one of the strangest he'd ever experienced.

When Sogaard returned, they ate the sandwiches, then he asked if he might order them a Cognac. He looked as if he needed one. They downed the first and ordered another.

This was highly irregular—quite unheard of, in fact.

Morck was vaguely nervous on his own account; he suspected himself of being influenced by the regard he had for the man. As if to restore order to the situation, he took his pen and wrote one or two things on the pad before they set to again.

32

"YOU BOUGHT THE summer house six months ago," Morck said, "to enable you to meet Kirsten Bunding there?"

"Yes, I hoped we'd be able to meet more often. During that time we managed to meet twice, at weekends."

"Vesterso isn't a big place. Had you considered that sooner or later people would begin to take note and their tongues would begin to wag?"

"Yes, we had; but in these circumstances one tends to ignore the problems of the future, and Kirsten had no ties, after all." He made an apologetic gesture. Possibly his lack of caution was the only drawback to be reckoned with—one which Kirsten Bunding had to reckon with; a weak man, thought Morck, yes, a weak man. And he toyed momentarily with the question of which of his own weaknesses would come to the surface in a similar situation.

"But your wife could have got wind of it too," said Morck.

"She doesn't know anybody in Vesterso, and anyway, I assumed she wouldn't want to come there. She doesn't like the west coast."

"And she had no idea that the nurse in Randers was called Kirsten Bunding?"

"She still doesn't have any idea; and I hate to think how she'd react if she got to know Kirsten was the nurse I called in that night. I realize how utterly silly this must all sound to you, if not worse."

Morck did not contradict him.

"Let's go back a bit," he said, "I want to hear exactly what happened in the correct order. You say you assumed your wife wouldn't want to come to the summer house. Yet she did come."

"Yes, but only that one time. It was my own fault; I pressed her to come with me, expecting her to say she couldn't bear to. That way, it would have seemed . . . what's the word . . . legitimate in her eyes for me to spend the odd day there now and again, when she was away visiting relatives and such-like——"

"Or in hospital," put in Morck.

"Yes."

"And did things turn out as you expected?"

"I dare say they did."

"Your wife didn't like the summer house?"

"She didn't like the house itself or anything else to do with it—the house wasn't comfortable enough, the setting was too barren, nothing but sand and sea and a cold wind. All in all she thought she'd be bored to death there, even for a weekend."

Yes. A weak man. He'd hoped his wife would react the way she had, and even so there was an unmistakable bitterness in the way he described the fulfilment of his expectations.

"After supper, she went straight to bed. There would have been no point in staying up. No television, not even a radio."

The words were her own; he was merely repeating them, as a betrayal, yielding to the grudge he bore her, though he was also tied to her by his own guilt.

"Later, an attack came on."

"Kidney stones?" Morck asked.

"Yes, possibly."

"You said so in your statement."

"Then you might as well put that in this report too. I don't want to withdraw what I said. In fact, it's impossible to tell whether they really are in pain or whether they're pretending; or even inducing real pain in order to get what they want."

Now it was Sogaard the doctor talking. By 'they' he meant drug-addicts such as his wife.

"Over and above that, there were deprivation symptoms. I don't know if she'd forgotten to bring some of the tablets with her or if she'd simply lost them."

"Which tablets? Were they hard drugs?"

"Yes. She didn't get them from me, of course, but from other doctors. As you know, that's no problem, especially for a doctor's wife. Failing that, she would write a prescription herself, then sign my name and take it to a pharmacy where she was known as Dr Sogaard's wife."

216

"But when you realized what was going on, didn't you try and stop that pharmacy serving her?"

"Yes, several times over. But Aarhus is a large town. There would always be other doctors and other pharmacies—they always find some way of getting the stuff."

"They" again referring to drug-addicts.

"So your wife was taken ill later that evening?" said Morck.

"Yes. The usual symptoms occurred, only they were exceptionally severe. Violent abdominal pain, possibly pain in the kidneys too, as I've already mentioned. She was shivering with cold and vomiting and so forth. She could scarcely stand up, so I more or less had to carry her to the bathroom. About midnight she was so ill that I was afraid she might have a heart attack. So I decided to contact the doctor in Vesterso to get him to give her an injection."

"Why couldn't you have given her one yourself if her condition was so serious?"

"I didn't have my syringe," said Sogaard.

"But what about the stuff to fill it—the Palfium?"

"Yes, I had brought two capsules with me, bearing precisely this situation in mind. It had happened before."

"Yet you hadn't brought your syringe. Why?"

"I have never given my wife an injection, nor would I ever dream of doing so. That would be——"

The thin end of the wedge did he mean?

"If I were to give her even one, she would go on plaguing me until I gave her another—and so on."

A weak man.

"No, that is to be avoided at all costs, especially when one's wife is the addict in question."

"So you tried to contact the doctor in Vesterso?"

"Yes. I tried to ring him from the phone box at the Marine Hotel, but it was out of order. So I had to drive to his residence; but he wasn't in, so there was nothing for it but to——"

"But to ask Kirsten Bunding to come?"

"Yes," said Sogaard. "I hadn't the faintest idea what else I could do—and it was a real emergency."

He fell silent, at a loss for words.

"So you drove down to the harbour and called her from the phone booth there; and when she picked up the phone you said, 'You'll have to come right away'. "

"Yes, I did, but——" Sogaard stared at him in amazement and alarm. "How do you know I said that?"

"The girl at the telephone exchange admitted yesterday that she'd overheard you. So of course that gave you away as well."

"How do you mean?"

"You were obviously a close friend of Kirsten Bunding," said Morck with studied carelessness. "But go on."

Sogaard didn't reply immediately. When at length he did, he had wandered from the point.

"Such a small detail."

"Yes, such a small detail," said Morck. "So you drove back to your wife and the nurse arrived soon after."

"Yes."

"Can you describe the encounter?"

"What do you mean, the encounter?"

"The encounter between your wife and Miss Bunding," said Morck mercilessly, fully aware of why he was suddenly calling Kirsten Bunding Miss for the first time: that was what Mrs Sogaard would have called her. Sogaard seemed to know why too. Anger flared up in him.

"There wasn't an encounter in any sense of the word. She simply did as she would do in any other case."

"Where a nurse has to give a patient an injection?"

"Exactly."

"What did they say to one another?"

Sogaard was perspiring. He made a feeble attempt to ward off the question.

"Surely you don't have to ask? What's the point?"

"An answer is required—maybe you'd rather give it in court? No matter what happens, you'll have to answer it then. What did your wife say?"

"Nothing, she was just groaning. She was in a very bad state."

"And Kirsten Bunding?"

"What do you mean?"

"What did she say when she went in to your wife?"

"Only the kind of thing a nurse says to a patient. The whole business only took half a minute. It can't be of any importance what——"

"Oh, yes, it can," said Morck, though he would not have been able to say why at the time. Still, he wanted to know, and he wanted

Sogaard to repeat the words to him. Morck leaned back and looked straight at him.

"Kirsten Bunding arrived at the house," he went on. "You took her into the living-room and told her what was required of her. She filled the syringe before she went in to your wife——"

"How do you know?"

"You told her to."

"But how can you——"

"I can't. But I can say she did. And now you've confirmed what I say. So she went in to your wife. You do, of course, recall exactly what she said?"

"She . . . uh, endeavoured to be completely professional. She said, 'I'm going to give you a little shot, and then you'll feel much better'."

Sogaard had stopped perspiring, but his face was ashen. He looked crushed and humiliated and Morck knew how important it had been—to make him so. He heard the voice of the policeman in him saying, Now you have him where you want him.

"I see," he said with a nod, and asked no further questions. He left Sogaard to his own thoughts and lit a cigarette, noticing for the first time that a number of lunch-time customers had come into the restaurant; but they were all sitting in the brighter section near the street. They were still alone in the inner room.

Sogaard was the first to speak.

"What are you getting at?" he said. "Don't you think I'm telling the truth?"

"You are, in part," said Morck, "but you're adding to it."

"I don't know what you mean."

"You . . . if I can put it this way: you overplayed your wife's rôle. If she really was as ill as you say, and could scarcely stand up, and you were afraid she might have a heart attack, you wouldn't have left her alone in the house. You would have taken her to the doctor in Vesterso in your car, and then, when you found he wasn't in, you would have driven on to Esbjerg to see that she got the proper treatment. Esbjerg's only another fifteen to twenty minutes' drive away. But you didn't take this course so I reckon the crisis wasn't as serious as you made out."

"Maybe I was exaggerating," murmured Sogaard.

"Were you afraid you wouldn't sound convincing enough?"

He did not reply.

"You thought you should give a particularly urgent reason why Kirsten Bunding should have had to come to the house. Was that it?"

"I didn't have to. What are you suggesting?"

Sogaard was speaking aggressively at the top of his voice.

"I first tried to contact the doctor in Vesterso, do you hear, and, since he wasn't in . . . moreover it was absolutely essential for her to get that injection."

"But not because she was as ill as you first said she was," said Morck. "Wasn't it rather because she was pestering the life out of you for it?"

"All right, what if it was? She still had to have it. If you'd lived with an addict you'd understand. They don't give up until they get their fix. There's no option."

"But there were so many other alternatives open to you when you found you couldn't contact the doctor. You could still have driven your wife to Esbjerg. You could have gone to Barkway and borrowed a syringe from Kirsten Bunding——"

"No, I couldn't have, I'd promised never to go there, for her sake."

"You talk a great deal about her sake," said Morck. "When you rang, you could have asked her to meet you somewhere in Vesterso and bring the syringe with her. You didn't do either of these things. You say you loved her, yet——"

"I did," said Sogaard shrinking at the thought, and something made Morck shrink inwardly too—the hangman-feeling. But he was forced to go on. There was no option, as Sogaard had just said of his own predicament.

"You put Kirsten Bunding in a position which must have been the most awkward, hurtful and infuriating in her whole life, the most . . ." Morck could not find one word to cover the various shades of meaning. "Sogaard," he said, "why did you do it? What drove you to it?"

The look on Sogaard's face made Morck aware of his own only as a mask, frozen in a dark fury of condemnation. So he looked down at his hands on the tablecloth.

"I . . . I don't know. . . . Anyway, I didn't mean to . . . I couldn't be sure . . ."

Stammering miserably like some Otto Bahnsen. Yet this was Dr Erik Sogaard of Aarhus, a man whose intellect, knowledge and

220

experience were vastly different. Though, as far as the third is concerned—insight into our own life—how experienced are we? Morck thought, looking silently at Sogaard, that here was a man of his own calibre, yet possessed of scarcely more self-awareness at this moment than Otto Bahnsen.

"But the one and only reason I drove to Vesterso was to contact the doctor," said Sogaard.

He seemed to be reassuring himself that this was so, clinging to the alibi as much for his own benefit as for Morck's.

"I don't doubt that it was," said Morck. "But I think that after you found the doctor was not at home—only then did the idea come to you."

"What idea?"

"The idea of getting Kirsten Bunding to come to the summer house. Here was your opportunity to do what you had always wished to do, deep down inside—to bring the two women face to face."

"That's not true . . . I . . . I wasn't thinking along those lines at all."

Sogaard's words of protest died on his lips. He was defeated. Staring glassily into space, he murmured, "At least I wasn't aware that I was."

"Nevertheless, that's what you did," said Morck, pausing for a moment to ask himself what he was doing to this man, and on whose authority. That his duty as a policeman demanded it was no excuse . . . yet he couldn't stop now.

"You may well be right," said Sogaard hoarsely.

Morck didn't care about being right.

"Wasn't that your idea?" he said.

"Now you're telling me what my own ideas were."

"I find it easy to imagine that you found your position distasteful—sometimes quite intolerable—always being marooned between these two women. So, that night in Vesterso, you thought to yourself, now's my chance."

"But I really wasn't conscious of the thought."

"Maybe not, but that was the upshot; you suddenly thought that if you seized this opportunity of bringing the two women together, face to face, then perhaps—even though neither knew the other—some kind of solution or liberation would result—for you, that is. In this way you'd have been able to do something, to deal with the predicament you were in. But did you really have any clear idea of what the result of this confrontation might be?"

Sogaard shook his head. He looked at Morck with growing horror, though possibly the horror stemmed more from what he saw in himself than from external fear.

"No . . . no. How can you possibly make out . . . I didn't . . . but I can't deny that . . . that I hoped for something or other."

"Which would set you free . . ." Morck was about to add, to the detriment of Kirsten Bunding, but he refrained. Gratuitous cruelty would get him nowhere and Sogaard knew very well what he meant. If he hadn't been fully aware of what he was doing before, he certainly was now.

"But nothing happened?"

"No, it was foolish of me to think anything might."

"Kirsten Bunding went in and gave your wife the injection. Where were you at the time?"

"I must have been standing by the bedroom door."

Just as one might expect, thought Morck. Sogaard had brought the two women together, then found himself excluded from their meeting. His rôle was confined to that of a mere spectator.

"What happened next?"

"No more than I've told you. It was all over in a matter of seconds."

"And Kirsten Bunding came back into the living-room with you?"

"Yes."

"Did you speak to one another?"

"We couldn't really . . . the bedroom door was open."

"What did you say to her? It's very important that I should know exactly what was said."

"Why?"

"The living-room curtains weren't drawn, were they? So somebody could have been watching you from outside."

"Do you think——"

"That's one possibility. What did you say to Kirsten Bunding?"

"We had to act like complete strangers. I said what one normally says at times like these. 'I'm very grateful for your help', or something of the sort."

"And what did she say?"

"She only said goodnight."

"Had she realized by then?"

"Realized what?"

Morck did not answer. Sogaard lowered his eyes. His hands were clasped on the table, index fingers linked together. He swayed a little from the waist, then suddenly he unclasped his hands and exclaimed in anguish:

"Yes. She had. She looked at me."

"How?"

"As if . . . I suddenly knew . . . that I had finally betrayed her. And as a way of concealing from myself——"

"Concealing what?"

"That I was on the point of losing her for ever—I kept thinking, Now you're going to lose her—I put my arms round her, at the door, and kissed her. I shouldn't have done it, of course, with my wife lying in bed only yards away; but, still, I don't think that was the only reason why she turned away and walked off . . ."

"You mean you had lost her at that very moment?"

Sogaard nodded. He had clasped his hands together again on the table in front of him. At length, with his eyes fixed on them, he broke the silence.

"But what does that matter now? She's dead and gone and there's an end of it. Does it matter?"

"Nothing else was said?"

"No."

"She left the house immediately and you remained behind with your wife?"

"Yes."

And not long after, only a matter of minutes, Kirsten Bunding was murdered in the pine scrub. This would have been Morck's concluding remark; but there was no need for him to make it explicit, they both knew what the other was thinking. Some time passed before Sogaard resumed the converstion.

"Do you really believe I followed her and . . . did it?"

"I don't believe anything," said Morck. "Beliefs are not my stock-in-trade. I only deal in facts."

What he had just discovered, however, was scarcely fact in the sense accepted in criminal detection.

"But between you and me, I don't believe you did," said Morck, thinking to himself: A weak man, hm? Weaker than who? And doesn't a man's very weakness often surface as an urge to murder? Not with Sogaard though. Otherwise he wouldn't have described

223

the parting with Kirsten Bunding in the way he did—as her having left him.

"What about another Cognac?"

He didn't wait for Sogaard to agree but rang for the waitress.

"Doubles," he said.

This was quite unheard of and Morck could not believe he had said it. Sogaard drank half of his Cognac at one gulp. But he wasn't the only one who needed reviving. Morck followed suit.

33

THE OUTER SECTION of the restaurant was empty. The lunch-time clientele had left and it was two o'clock now. The interrogation had been going on for more than four hours. Morck looked at his pad. It was made to fit exactly in a jacket pocket, and had a plastic cover. When one pad was filled, another could be slotted in. But the current one only had one solitary page of notes.

"You haven't made many notes," said Sogaard wearily.

"No, I haven't."

There were only a few words to jog his memory, including a couple of lines that were really superfluous, since he would be sure to remember the words Kirsten Bunding had used: "I'm going to give you a little shot and then you'll feel much better".

Mrs Sogaard would have been given the injection immediately. Morck suddenly remembered her Christian name: Nancy. And what else? She was born Petersen, aged thirty-seven, and has no children. Herting had told him. But during the interrogation, she had been mentioned only as Sogaard's wife. Nancy . . . Nancy. The name failed to suggest a face to him. She remained an anonymous, emaciated, grey figure, whining, tortured and unreasonable in his picture of that night in the summer house.

She had gained instant relief from the injection Kirsten Bunding had been obliged to give her. But the relief would not have lasted for long. In reality, no one was comforted. Kirsten Bunding had been murdered, and Sogaard would be going through hell, if not for the rest of his days, at least for a great number of them.

Yet people do recover from the most harrowing, repulsive and tragic experiences. Or they learn to live with them. At least one can endeavour to believe they do, if only for the sake of one's own peace of mind. Morck sighed. He hated the next question which had to be asked.

"Which hospital is your wife in?"

"The State Hospital," said Sogaard, roused suddenly from his lethargy. "But you don't intend to interrogate her too, surely? Why? A moment ago you said you didn't think I——"

"Irrespective of what I may think, we still have to check the accuracy of your statements."

"But if she heard what I've been telling you . . . it could be the death of her."

"Is that your professional opinion, Dr Sogaard?"

"I'm not my wife's doctor, but I——" He stopped in mid-sentence and shrugged his shoulders. "You're quite right," he said. "It was only hot air. When they've gone beyond a certain stage . . ." (By "they" Sogaard once more meant his wife and similar addicts.) "There's only one vital problem that interests them—how to get hold of the stuff. At present, she's on a cure, which we can only hope will work; but if she hears all this about me, she's bound to revert to her old ways. I know her too well. Either that or she'll find something even stronger. She has tried to kill herself a number of times, after all. I don't think she will again, admittedly, but does anyone ever think so before the event? So, if you can find some way of preventing her getting involved . . ."

"I would if I could," said Morck, "but that depends on the solution of the case, if any."

"You don't think I'm the murderer," said Sogaard, "What about Otto Bahnsen? Even though he's confessed, you don't think he is either, do you?"

"Let's just say, I doubt if he is."

"Then who else is there? Do you suspect anyone?"

"No. I've no idea who might have done it."

Sogaard looked at him curiously. Maybe he had said something slightly peculiar: as if he were talking of someone he had fleetingly glimpsed without being able to identify him, and moreover would be unable to recognize him if he ever saw him again. Still, this was only his impression.

"Are you sure that during the time you knew her she had no close relationship with any other man—not necessarily an affair, I mean?"

226

"I'm as sure of that as I am of anything," said Sogaard. "She would have told me: you see, she was always utterly frank with me."

Could Sogaard be said to have been the same with her? Morck thought not. But what difference did that make?

"And in any case, a second affair would have been inconceivable," said Sogaard.

"Why?"

"That's just how she was: she was made that way."

"Meaning that if she took up with a man, she became completely involved?"

"Yes," said Sogaard—the man she had been completely involved with. "What else do you want to know?" he added sharply.

"Had she told anyone in Vesterso about her affair with you?"

Sogaard shook his head, "I don't think she had."

"So she really had no one to confide in? No close friend?"

"Well, I suppose, in a way, Steffensen was one."

"Her next-door neighbour, the customs officer?"

"Yes, but she wouldn't have told him about that kind of thing, in any case."

"What do you mean by that?"

"By what?"

"By the phrases 'in a way' and 'in any case'?"

"I meant Steffensen wouldn't have taken at all kindly to the news," said Sogaard. "He was virtually an uncle to her, and his feelings towards her were roughly those of a father. As you know, he'd known her since she was a child."

"As I know?" said Morck. He felt tempted to use Einarsen's felicitous retort—I bloody well know nothing of the sort.

"But surely Steffensen mentioned——" said Sogaard.

"He didn't breathe a word."

"But why?"

"That's exactly what I'd like to know." Morck emptied his glass and felt a sudden gentle glow inside. The light from the blue-framed window, falling on the table, had a certain quivering clarity, and for a moment the outline of Sogaard's face was faintly blurred. This could not have been entirely the effect of the Cognac—they had only had a few over a long period.

"Sogaard, how much do you know about Steffensen?" he said. "You said he was virtually an uncle to her."

"Yes, but he isn't a blood-relation. Kirsten told me——"

Sogaard stopped short. His face darkened. He had used her name.

"What about another Cognac?" he said tentatively.

"All right. But let's make that the last."

When their glasses were filled, Morck went on: "Tell me then. What did she say?"

There could be no more beating about the bush now. Sogaard drank half his Cognac.

"It all took place so long ago," he said. "It can't matter very much now. She told me Steffensen had been a boyhood friend of her father's. The two families had lived cheek by jowl in Fredericia and the two boys had always been close companions. The story goes that they fell in love with the same girl——"

"Kirsten's mother?"

Morck had begun calling her Kirsten too, and Sogaard showed no surprise. His eyes had become a little clouded; perhaps the extra Cognac was one too many for this time of the afternoon.

"Yes. They were both nuts about her," said Sogaard using a phrase he would not normally have cared to use. The story evoked a fragrance of rose petals and lavender.

"She couldn't decide between them; but in the end she had to. And she didn't choose Steffensen. He must have taken it very hard, and he never married later. But he sometimes visited them——"

"Her parents?"

"Yes. Until Kirsten was about seven or eight years old. Then her mother died. Steffensen went to Esbjerg, and some years passed before she saw him again, this time by sheer chance on the street in Esbjerg. She said the encounter had been extraordinary. She was walking along the street when a man, whom she didn't immediately recognize, stopped in his tracks and stared at her, utterly dumbfounded.

" 'Are you Karin's daughter?' he'd said instantly, 'Surely this can't be . . .' He was evidently much moved by the meeting."

"Because of the similarity between them?"

"Yes. He said it had been like seeing her alive again—Karin, that is. And later he found himself (or maybe Kirsten had heard him) calling her Karin—though she was dead and gone years ago."

Sogaard gazed mutely down at his glass. Then he emptied it. Karin was not the only one who was dead and gone.

"Highly romantic, don't you think?" he said. "They had such

228

tremendous regard for sentiment in the old days. What about another Cognac, though this one was to be the last?"

"Thanks, I will," said Morck, "but finish your story first."

Sogaard finished the story, then ordered two Cognacs. Morck asked the waitress for a train timetable.

"Are you going to see Steffensen?" said Sogaard, while Morck was looking up the trains. The next one was at 4.05 pm.

"What's the time?"

"Ten to four."

"Then I must have a taxi right away," said Morck. "Yes, I'm going to see Steffensen."

34

HE MANAGED TO catch the train, and on the journey down through
East Jutland he sat half asleep in a window seat. His head lolled
forward several times on to his chest. The elderly lady opposite
frowned at him from time to time in secret disapproval, being
clearly of the opinion that he was an undesirable character whose
proximity was an intrusion. Maybe he smelled of Cognac, which
strengthened her conviction. How can one tell?

Sogaard and he had certainly polished off a few, he couldn't recall
how many. He could scarcely even remember the restaurant. But
what he did remember was the fluctuating expressions on Sogaard's
face. He thought he could even visualize his expression when he had
been standing by the bedroom door, introducing Kirsten Bunding
to his wife—that look of vacuous despair which came over him when
he began to realize what he had done in yielding to some obscure
inner temptation to bring the two women together: "I hoped something or other might happen"; "But nothing did?"; "No, it was
foolish of me to think anything might".

Something or other? A thing quite different from the something
he had stupidly hoped for had happened. She had come back into the
living-room and realized what his intention had been with the two
women: "She looked at me".

Had she known merely by seeing his face that he had—what was
the word Sogaard had used?—had betrayed her?

Morck was unable to picture his face at that particular moment,
though he was able to at the next, when the awful thought had
occurred to him—Now you've lost her.

"What did you say to her?"

"I only thanked her for her help."

As he had to do within his wife's earshot, with the bedroom door open.

"And what did she say?"

"She just said goodnight."

And that was the whole story. All was over between them. Then she went out and was murdered.

Good God! said Morck to himself, though not out loud, he hoped. The train jolted to a halt and he nearly slipped off the seat. It must have been Skanderborg.

"I'm so sorry," he said. His knees had contrived to come into contact with the highly respectable knees of the lady opposite. She paid absolutely no attention, but went on staring icily past him out of the window. He couldn't have been her type.

In fact they were in Horsens. They must have stopped in Skanderborg while Morck had been dozing. He hadn't noticed. For the rest of the journey he was wide awake. He had a headache, which was normal after an interrogation, but this one was worse than average, throbbing rhythmically with the regular rattle of the wheels on the rails. The interrogation too had been out of the ordinary.

He took the pad from his pocket and looked at his solitary page of notes. The last entry read "Promise never to show up at K.B.'s residence". Reporting jargon.

For her sake, Sogaard had said, "For her sake, you say".

When he had taken up the same point later, Sogaard had modified this: "Maybe I should really say for Steffensen's sake. He would not have been able to stomach the truth about our affair."

"Do you mean he would have been jealous?"

"Yes, you might say he would have been, in his own way."

"You might?"

"He was inclined to look upon himself as her self-appointed guardian."

"And did she play along?"

"I couldn't say for sure, but at least she didn't object. I understood that she felt strongly dependent on him somehow."

"You said earlier that his feelings towards her were roughly those of a father."

"Yes. She lost her mother when she was seven or eight, and her father died shortly after she'd begun training to be a nurse. So quite probably, although she was in her late twenties when she

231

met Steffensen again, there was some unfulfilled emotional need."

"Yes, that does seem probable," Morck said to Sogaard. He knew from his own experience that age had nothing whatsoever to do with it. His own mother, who had not been married, had died when he was twenty-two.

"A kind of parent-substitute, you might say," Sogaard had said.

In Steffensen, Kirsten Bunding had possibly seen a long-awaited replacement for her dead parents. But the need to feel this sprang from another source which Morck also knew from experience—the need for protective love, which he had found when he met his wife.

In the dismal terminology of needs and their fulfilment, Kirsten Bunding had not had this need satisfied by the man she had fallen in love with. On the contrary. Love fosters the wish to be together always. But their love kept them constantly apart: it had excluded them from the very town where they had met. Yet she still had Steffensen, whom she had met shortly afterwards in the street in Esbjerg, just when she must have been feeling at her most lonely and forsaken. Some months later, when the flat next to Steffensen's became available, she gave up her job at the hospital and moved to Vesterso to become district nurse.

Steffensen must have loomed up before her like a childhood memory. "Are you Karin's daughter?" He had been in love with this Karin who was Kirsten Bunding's mother, and the daughter must have borne a striking resemblance to her. It would have been almost like seeing her alive again.

"Extraordinary," Kirsten Bunding had said to Sogaard.

But there was something even more extraordinary, not to say inexplicable: a remark Steffensen had made later. In describing the effect upon him of having seen her walking towards him along the sidewalk, he had said it was "Like having you back with me in flesh and blood". Why you, Morck wondered, nursing his headache over the points. According to Sogaard, Kirsten had asked the same question.

"Me? What on earth are you talking about, Steffensen?" She had good reason for asking. Was that the kind of remark that slips out unawares when the heart is brim-full? Morck thought this over, studying his notes. They made no mention of the episode, and he went on thinking it over until the train arrived in Fredericia, where he had to change. He had twenty minutes to wait, so he went through to the main concourse and rang Esbjerg police station. Herting wasn't there but the officer he spoke to undertook to give him a message.

When he came out of the phone box, he felt faint and there was a hole in his stomach; he recalled that he hadn't eaten anything since having that cheese sandwich in the restaurant. There would be no buffet car on the train, but he had time for a couple of frankfurters before it left. He pursued his train of thought as he was eating.

A strange romance. The curiously outmoded word 'romance' was what immediately sprang to mind. A romance which ended many years later—a generation later—with her being murdered.

Her? he thought. Karin or Kirsten? Scarcely more than a random notion: a nebulous phantasm in which the two women seemed to merge into one. He was interrupted by the announcer:

"We repeat, the train now standing at platform . . ." The announcement had already been made and he hadn't been paying any attention.

The train crept along at a snail's pace, stopping at every station. He took out his pad from force of habit and looked at his notes, though they could add nothing to what he already knew. There was only one scrap that seemed to be of any significance: "Promise never to show up at K.B.'s residence". For Steffensen's sake. He would not have been able to stomach the truth about our affair, Sogaard had said. And he had more to say.

"Once Kirsten was afraid he had his suspicions despite our precautions."

"Why?"

"Well, it all started when I rang her up once, about six months ago, I think, just after I'd bought the summer house—it was a man who answered the phone. He gave her number and I was put out of my stride. I had no idea it was Steffensen. I asked to speak to Kirsten then he asked who was speaking. Automatically, I gave my name."

"You said your name was Erik Sogaard?"

"No, I said what I normally would to strangers: 'This is Dr Sogaard'. It was purely a reflex, and I didn't think at the time. Of course, it was rather foolish of me, but my conspiratorial talents aren't very well-developed, I'm afraid."

Morck had not had the heart to gainsay this. The telephone conversation had come to an end when Steffensen asked if he could take a message and Sogaard had said no, he would ring later.

And that was all; except that Steffensen hadn't mentioned the call to Kirsten Bunding when she came home. The simplest explanation, of course, was that the old man had just forgotten about it. But what had he been doing in her flat?

"Kirsten wondered why he'd been there too," Sogaard had said. "She had only gone out shopping. But he had a key so that he would be able to keep an eye on things when she was out of town."

Keep an eye on what? And, anyway, she wasn't out of town.

Morck closed the notebook and put it back in his pocket. The train had stopped again; this time it was Vejen. There was several minutes' delay. Still, this was West Jutland. The train eventually got under way.

"But a few days later he made a remark that might have had some connection."

"With your phone call?"

"Yes. Something about young girls running the risk of being thrown away on married men."

"Being thrown away."

"It did sound vaguely ridiculous, and Kirsten thought so too. I wonder if he was trying to warn her about me. I suppose it could have been a mere coincidence."

A ridiculously old-fashioned remark to make. But when one reflected that she had indeed been thrown away—murdered in the scrub outside Vesterso . . .

Morck sighed. The train made another lengthy halt at some minute station. Weren't they nearing the end of the journey? And wasn't he making progress in his deliberations too? How was the truth of the matter to be arrived at?

If there was any, he wasn't able to detect it. The way was shrouded in mist, the destination formless and elusive.

The window was splattered with rain and, outside, night was already falling under a clouded sky. He had been travelling for three and a half hours.

At seven-thirty the train stopped in Esbjerg. Herting was on the platform waiting for him.

35

HERTING GREETED HIM heartily like some old friend he had greatly missed, although, in fact, they didn't know one another very well. The Vesterso murder case was their only piece of common ground. Yet Morck was surprised at how glad he was to see the young man again.

The young man. Herting was probably at least thirty. Nevertheless, Morck tended to regard him as such. Suddenly, it seemed less strange to him that Steffensen, who was even older, had regarded Kirsten Bunding as a young girl in need of cautionary advice about going off the rails through lack of experience.

"Do you want to eat first?" said Herting. "Or shall we drive over right away?"

"Let's get going now."

Herting's car—an old Volkswagen with worn seat-covers, almost the twin of the one Morck had in Copenhagen—was in the garage opposite the station. They drove down by the harbour. It had been raining in Esbjerg, and the reflections of the street lights glittered on the wet roads.

"So you want to see Steffensen," said Herting.

"Eh, what's that?" Morck felt tired and dull-witted after the long journey. His reactions were slow. "Yes, I have one or two questions to ask him—if that's what you meant," he added after a pause. "I don't know if it'll lead anywhere."

"I see," said Herting.

To tell the truth, Morck had only a vague idea of what questions he wanted to ask Steffensen. He had certainly not prepared any, hoping they would formulate themselves when he found himself face to face with the old man.

"But I'd like you to come along," he said.

Herting nodded and let matters rest there. They spoke about other things, leaving the street lamps behind and following a dark country road that was almost devoid of traffic. Morck asked how Herting's wife was.

"Very well, thanks, but I must say, I haven't been at home all that often."

"You have as much on your plate as ever then?"

"Yes, sometimes when I get home, she says 'Fancy seeing you— are you really the man I married a couple of months ago?' "

"And you try to make excuses?"

"Yes. I try to bring her round as best I can; things are bound to brighten up eventually."

"Just like in those thirties' street songs."

"Just like what?"

Why had this occurred to him at this particular moment? Another piece of random association. He ransacked his memory for their topic of conversation.

"Street songs," he said at length. "There was one that went:

> Some day the skies will brighten,
> And I'll come home to stay,
> And I'll go no more a-singing
> When a bit of work comes my way"

"Oh, now I see what you mean," said Herting, though he didn't sound as if he did. "Yes, times have changed since then."

Since the thirties—which for young Herting was a purely imaginary period. For Morck they were not the remote past, but only round the last corner. An individual's past, his personal sense of history one might say, has amazingly fluid dimensions. At certain times, the memory of what happened thirty years ago can appear more vivid and immediate than the events of the previous day. But what had this to do with the case? He ought to be working out what he was going to ask Steffensen.

Steffensen had fallen in love with Karin in the thirties, and ended up by being jilted. Thirty years went by, more than thirty in fact. Then she was murdered. Kirsten.

"Then they passed the hat round," said Herting.

"They——? Oh, yes, of course they did, and people used to

throw down a few coppers from their kitchen windows. There was a second verse to the song, something about:

> I go from door to door and hope,
> Knocking at every one . . .

Not very different from what we do in our job, eh?"

"No, you have a point there. But how the heck did we get on to the subject?"

"I've no idea."

"Neither have I. I've completely forgotten."

Soon the headlamps played on pine trees on both sides of the road, and once through the plantation, they saw the lights of Vesterso.

"Let's stop at the post office," said Morck. He wanted to walk the rest of the way, to reaccustom himself to the atmosphere of Vesterso —and perhaps rehearse his meeting with Steffensen? No; there would be no rehearsal. But when he set eyes on him . . .

Outside in the fresh air, he stood for a moment listening. But the wind was in the wrong quarter. He couldn't hear the sea tonight.

They didn't meet a soul on the way. In the thatched houses set sideways to Main Street, the curtains were all drawn. It was television time. As they turned into Barkway, the wind blew directly in their faces, sweeping over the moorland between them and the bay, and laden with the smell of salt. Her house was in darkness. The car had gone from the garage, there was no light in the windows and the curtains had been taken down. All her furniture and belongings had been removed. There was nothing left of her. Of course not. What had he expected?

"I can't see any lights on in Steffensen's place," said Herting.

"He must be in the living-room at the back of the house. Let's go in."

They went through the front garden past the stunted junipers. Morck knocked on the outside door and tried the handle. It wasn't locked. He couldn't find the light switch in the hallway, but he remembered the layout of the house as being the mirror-image of Kirsten Bunding's. So he walked straight along the dark corridor and came to a door at the end. He knocked again. There was no answer, but a thin shaft of light spilled out over the threshold. He opened the door.

"Good evening, Mr Steffensen," he said.

Steffensen looked up at him without returning the greeting. Had he failed to recognize him? He was sitting, as before, in the high-backed chair behind the desk; but his appearance had altered. Morck was not even sure that he would have recognized him in any other setting. He stood in the doorway, waiting.

"Oh, so you've come at last," Steffensen said eventually.

"Were you expecting me, Mr Steffensen?"

"In a way, I was," the old man said.

36

AN OLD MAN—that was what he had become in the two months since the murder of Kirsten Bunding. He was wearing a dressing-gown over his nightwear and seemed to have become older and smaller, sinking into the high-backed armchair as if only kept upright by the pressure of his arms on the curving armrests. His formerly powerful features had collapsed and were now in ruins. He looked over his shoulder at Morck and said:

"So there are two of you, are there?"

"Yes," said Morck, stepping aside to make way for Herting; "no doubt you remember my colleague, Sergeant Herting."

"Do I? Ah yes, you generally come in pairs when it's a question of . . . please do sit down."

Morck sat down, as he had at their last encounter, in the leather wing-chair beside the spacious desk. As before, there was a teacup and a plate on the desk; the teacup was half-empty, but two thin slices of bread lay untouched on the plate. On one window sill was the pipe-rack with its seven or eight pipes, on the other a stunted green plant. Steffensen leaned over and opened a drawer in the desk. His movements were frail and unstable, making Morck fear for a moment that he might simply topple over as he let go of the armrest.

"Cigar, Mr Morck?"

"I'll have one of my own cigarettes, if you don't mind."

It was exactly as before, apart from the transformation in Steffensen which even affected his voice, now faint and quavering. Herting, who had sat down discreetly on a chair by the wall, was not included in the offer. This could well have been because Steffensen no longer remembered he was there, for he had old-fashioned ideas of politeness. Perhaps his sight had deteriorated too; a sort of pale film had spread over his eyes. Yet, behind that, deep down, an unquenched fire still smouldered.

"I have some questions to put to you," said Morck.

"You've been a long time getting round to them, Mr Morck."

"Maybe so, but I've made it in the end."

Now there were only the two of them present, not Herting, though he was sitting only a couple of paces away, with note pad and pencil at the ready and one leg crossed over the other.

"You haven't quite made it, Mr Morck. I'm going to cheat you again."

"Again? Does it make any difference that you've done it once already?"

"None whatever," Steffensen nodded. "It was only my little joke."

A polite little joke. But now it was no joking matter.

"You have cheated yourself, Mr Steffensen," said Morck.

"You don't understand—or do you? If you do, explain how."

"Mr Steffensen, why——" Morck broke off and took a deep breath, holding it a moment in an attempt to control himself. As he did so, it struck him that he was continually addressing the old man as Mr Steffensen—the man who had murdered Kirsten Bunding by strangling her and smashing her face in. Angrily he said; "Why should I do any explaining? Now, it is your turn to explain."

He stopped short, and Herting, seeing him in profile, was surprised at the expression on his face. He seemed almost ashamed of having gone further than he had intended. Steffensen raised himself a little in the chair by pushing on the arms. He laid his head back and his pale ruin of a face seemed to regard Morck with authority.

"Go on, light it," he said. "I don't object to your smoking, although I don't smoke myself any longer. I've gone off it, as I have most things."

Morck reacted as if this were a mild reproof, and was prompted to resume the conversation in a way the old man would find convenient and tolerable. He glanced at the unlit cigarette in his hand and made as if to put it into his breast pocket, then stopped, as if that would hardly be good manners in the presence of Steffensen. Instead, he laid it down on the desk and said, "If I could accept your original offer".

"Of course you may," replied Steffensen, leaning over again in

240

his frail unstable way. He opened the drawer, reached forward and took out the cigar box.

"Cigar, Mr Morck?"

"Thank you."

"And you, young man?" He had momentarily remembered Herting was present. Herting did not smoke cigars, but even if he had, he would have refused politely, conscious that what was going on between the two men was a game of equals which he did not understand and would be best to stay out of. Deliberately Morck lit his cigar, and, having waved the smoke away and ascertained that the top was burning evenly, he began:

"You have obviously been ill, Mr Steffensen."

"Yes. I left hospital a week ago after an operation. They opened me up then sewed me together again, having decided nothing more could be done. They didn't tell me that, of course, but I realized all the same. So I insisted upon being discharged. I knew it was cancer of the stomach, and that I would die before very long."

"You are quite sure?"

"I trust you don't pity me," said Steffensen, his faint voice almost enlivened by a suggestion of profound mockery.

"No, I don't pity you."

Steffensen appeared to be waiting for a sequel to this, a question. But Morck sat there himself in quiet expectation, smoking his cigar and watching the smoke curl away. It occurred to Herting that the old man looked disappointed, even a little downcast. Things aren't going as he expected, he thought, just as Steffensen broke the silence.

"It is rather odd, having to die in the way I imagine I shall, and yet being compelled to perform a final act of consequence and significance."

"Not a final act—your very first," interpolated Morck.

"What do you mean, Mr Morck?"

"Don't you know what I mean yet?"

Morck looked around for the ashtray on the desk and laid his cigar to one side. It was a kind of delaying tactic, to forestall the old man's reply, to give himself a few seconds' respite before going on:

"Before you die, it will become clear to you that what you call the significance of your life is a mere distortion, and what you call its consequence is the outcome of insanity."

"You don't know what you're talking about."

"Indeed I do," said Morck, "only you fail to face up to it."

"You haven't understood anything. I could . . . yes, I could possibly make it all clear to you. But I don't have to. Why should I? The choice is mine."

"Is the choice always yours?" asked Morck quietly, and in a remarkably respectful tone of voice.

"I wasn't obliged to summon you here, Mr Morck, but I chose to do so since I assumed that what you wanted was a formal confession."

"Yes," said Morck, still in the same tone of voice, and without showing any surprise at the extent of his delusion. "So you confess?"

Steffensen nodded.

"I can't really say I think much of the expression, but I assume that 'confess' is the word that you, as a policeman, have to use. Yes, I have come to see the necessity, or rather the sense, in publicly assuming responsibility for the murder."

He opened a drawer in the table in front of him. At this point, the thought occurred to Herting, The man must be off his head. He stared at his note pad, where, in his private shorthand, he had written "publ. assm. rsp. fr. mrdr?" Unwittingly he put a question mark after it, but in parentheses, to indicate a private reaction. When he looked up, Steffensen had laid on the desk a closed portfolio of the sort designed for keeping personal papers and documents. He opened it, took out a sheet of paper and handed it to Morck. The words on it, in an old man's shaky handwriting, were blurred, as if vibrating on the page:

I, Henrik Steffensen, retired customs official, of Barkway, Vesterso, hereby declare myself responsible for the murder of the nurse, Kirsten Bunding.

The date and signature underneath were barely legible, while the name sprawled across the paper was half-rubbed out, like a name written in sand by the shore then swept out of recognition by the wind.

"Unfortunately, I could not recall the exact date," said Steffensen.

"Of the murder?"

"Yes. But in this case it can presumably be added later."

"That will not be necessary."

"Moreover, my handwriting has become a little unsteady. Perhaps

242

I ought to ask you and the young man to witness the signature and the general authenticity of the document?"

"That will not be necessary either."

"Then you think everything is in order? It is what you require, isn't it?"

Morck agreed politely, without showing much interest.

"It does certainly have some significance, but of course . . ."

He handed the paper across to Herting. The old man frowned uneasily, puzzled at his indifference. He raised himself a little in his chair, and when he next spoke it sounded as if he had prepared what he was going to say beforehand, but suddenly felt unsure whether this was the right occasion to say it.

"You must understand that I give you this document out of concern for that poor idiot, Otto Bahnsen, who was bound to attract suspicion by his stupid behaviour, and then proceeded virtually to condemn himself by making his even stupider confession."

"Isn't your concern for the boy a bit late in emerging?" replied Morck.

"That I can explain, but you needn't expect any further explanations from me. I assumed to begin with that, since he was mentally retarded the worst that could become of him would be to be put into a remand home. Judging from my acquaintance with him I thought that his interests would be as well served there as in his present situation, if not better; and as soon as his mother died he would, in all likelihood, be put in a mental home anyway."

"So you didn't think it mattered very much?"

"Not taking all the circumstances of the case into account; after all, one has to weigh one consideration against another. But when I found out during my stay in hospital that he might be risking life imprisonment, I changed my mind. That was, of course, something I could not justify."

"Couldn't you?" Morck broke in. "Yet you thought you could justify your first little ploy? Who on earth do you think you are, Steffensen?"

"Who——"

"Yes, since you think you have the power of life and death over an innocent human being—no, two——"

"Two?"

"The second being Kirsten Bunding, whom you murdered."

"She wasn't by any means——" began the old man. Then he

243

broke off, or rather was interrupted by a spasm of pain, which doubled him up and contorted his face horribly. He recovered and sat up again, saying: "No, you won't be able to understand, and what is more I don't have it in mind to explain any further. I only wanted you to come here in order to accept the confession, while there was time."

"You wanted me to come? On the contrary, I came of my own accord."

"You came——?"

"You're deluding yourself, Steffensen. You didn't summon me. Maybe you thought about doing so, but you couldn't bring yourself to do it."

"But I wrote the confession," the old man whimpered uncertainly. He raised one hand to his brow, but lowered it again to regain his hold of the chair. "I'm sorry, I . . . one doesn't always manage to . . . do I remember correctly?"

"You certainly wrote the confession. But was that in order to give it to me? Wasn't it more for your own personal use? You had to have some sort of alibi for refusing to let someone else be condemned on your account, and so you confessed, or rather, as you wrote, declared yourself responsible for the murder. Nevertheless, you couldn't bring yourself to declare that responsibility during your lifetime, could you? You wanted to be safe in Abraham's bosom first. The confession would, of course, be found after your death——"

"You've no right to talk to me like that. It isn't true about——"

"It isn't true about what, Mr Steffensen? Doesn't it tally with the fantasy of yourself you cling to so desperately?"

"You can't, I say . . . I am a sick man. I came home to . . . to set my house in order and write my confession."

"What? Eight days after the date you put on it? It lay in that drawer until I came in this evening and you realized I knew the truth about you. Then you dragged it out. It was the only way of maintaining your . . . what the blazes is it called . . . your respectability. You confessed purely and simply to avoid being stigmatized as one of the lowest sort of criminal—one who lets another take the blame and suffer the punishment for his crime."

Morck was speaking gently, at one level, and with immense self-control. He was leaning forward in his chair so that the light from the table lamp fell on his face. The lines in it were heavy and of a sudden he looked elderly, an old man with a marked resemblance to

244

—Yes! He looks like Steffensen, thought Herting, with discomforting accuracy. Steffensen in better days, that is, not this trembling wreck of Steffensen sitting before them, opening and closing his mouth without managing to utter so much as a whisper.

"Wasn't that how it was, Steffensen?" went on Morck mercilessly.

"I don't want to talk to you any more," whispered the old man.

"It's not that. You shrink from examining yourself."

"I absolutely refuse——"

"You refuse to look at yourself for fear of what you might see. But you know what is there: you can't avoid seeing it any longer."

It was no longer an ordinary interrogation—if it ever had been, thought Herting. It was the day of reckoning.

"You have the power to arrest me," muttered the old man.

"In that case I arrest you."

"But you can't force me to——"

"No, and there would be no point. I know the truth about you already. I know why you murdered her."

"You can't possibly know. No one can know."

"Yes, they can," said Morck, rising impetuously from his chair. Standing on the cupboard by the wall was a framed photograph which had been moved forward since the last time he had been in the room. It was an old picture. The hair style was of the period when girls wore their hair parted and used shiny lacquer. Each generation seems to have its individual expression distinct from all others. A young girl smiled shyly out at him from the picture—or was it confidentially, mysteriously? He didn't know how to interpret that smile, or rather, how Steffensen had interpreted it; but the likeness to Kirsten Bunding was unmistakable, even to one who only remembered her from the other picture taken on the beach, where she was smiling radiantly at the man she loved.

"Is that Karin?" asked Morck. "It could almost be Kirsten Bunding. I'd like to know whom you really see when you look at that picture, Steffensen? Maybe you don't know yourself."

"Leave her alone," the old man said. Morck took no notice of him. He continued to look at the picture.

"Kirsten or Karin?" he resumed. "It can't be Karin because she jilted you. It can't be Kirsten either. You murdered her. So it's neither of them."

"Leave me alone . . ." Steffensen was on the point of pleading for mercy; but he was unable to utter the words.

"It is a woman who has never existed outside your own imagination. A phantom. And you became a murderer purely because of that phantom."

"Morck!" said Herting, interrupting him in a precautionary tone. This could well be the end of old Steffensen, he thought. Morck turned round. Steffensen's face was deathly pale, a mass of interlacing wrinkles that resembled a broken spider's web. For a second time, he doubled up with pain, one hand clutching his stomach.

"Herting, fetch a glass of water," said Morck, going rapidly round to the far side of the desk. "You're bound to have some painkillers. Where are they? In the drawer?"

Steffensen brushed his hand away, opened the drawer himself and rummaged about till he found a box of pills. His hand was trembling too much for him to take the lid off, so Morck took the box from him and got hold of a tablet. He was putting it in the old man's mouth as Herting came back from the kitchen with the glass of water. Steffensen spilled most of it in his efforts to swallow the tablet, and Herting waited, ready to take the glass from him. He put it on the desk and retreated to his chair, awkwardly, without looking at the invalid. Morck did likewise. All his anger had left him. He looked distractedly at his hands. All that remained was a strange feeling of shame, at having made, as it were, a furious and violent attack upon some defenceless—even innocent—party: one who could not help having done what he had done. There was silence for a while. Then Steffensen's rapid gasps for breath began to come more slowly. He raised his shrunken face to look at Morck, making a supreme effort to form his words clearly:

"I . . . am . . . sorry. You have witnessed my degradation."

Apologetically Morck said, "You are a sick man, Mr Steffensen, and I shall not be troubling you again."

But the old man had not been referring to his illness.

"I am beginning . . . to see myself," he said.

37

MORCK DIDN'T KNOW what to say. What could he say? He asked himself if what he had done had been necessary. The answer was not that Steffensen's confession, these few faulty lines written by a doomed man, would be unacceptable to the court without greater elaboration of the details of the murder; the answer was that something inside him had driven him to it—something which sallied forth with fire and sword in the cause of what is euphemistically known as justice. But what were the deeper sources of this impulse? He didn't relish the thought, and suppressed it when he had regained his composure. There was no name for it. All he knew was that it gave him the hangman-feeling.

The old man remained staring blankly in front of him, as if no one was in the room. He was evidently still in pain; but he seemed hardly to notice it, although his hand remained pressed to his stomach.

"Do you wish to see a doctor, Mr Steffensen?"

He shook his head.

"Or take another pill?"

"No thank you. They have no effect after a while."

"Isn't there anything we can do for you?"

Steffensen turned towards him and, for a split second, his features twisted themselves into something resembling a smile. Morck immediately thought of the doctor in Aarhus.

"Nothing, apart from arresting me. Isn't that why you came?"

"I wasn't sure when I first arrived."

"But now you are," said Steffensen with a nod. And to his own surprise, Morck replied with some embarrassment.

"May I say that . . . to be quite honest, I am sorry for you?"

"No, you may say no such thing!" The old man's voice was suddenly firm and clear. "You weren't sorry for me when you first came here; so why not be consistent? Or is my memory playing me tricks again? What you weren't sorry about was that I should soon be dead, is that not so?"

"Yes," said Morck.

"Then we agree."

At this point, it appeared to Herting—who was later to assure his wife he had never heard anything like it before, nor ever would again, nor could he describe adequately what passed between the two men—that their rôles in the interrogation had been reversed, and that the old man was interrogating his junior.

"But before you take me away, I would like to know how you came to know the truth about me, as you put it."

"I could only guess," said Morck. There was a brief silence. "Are you quite sure you want to know?"

"Yes," said Steffensen. "I want to have an explanation."

"You know we can call a halt now, and say no more? You can refuse to say anything; you have a right to refuse. You are not required to say any more."

"But I am asking you to do precisely that."

"Very well," said Morck. "On the day you first met Kirsten Bunding in the street in Esbjerg—or maybe it wasn't that day—at any rate, do you recall what you said about the encounter?"

Steffensen said nothing but looked at him expectantly.

"You were deeply moved. You said it was 'like having you back with me in flesh and blood'."

"Yes, I did," said Steffensen.

"But who were you referring to? Not to the woman who was Kirsten Bunding's mother, the woman who had jilted you—I presume that's what she did?"

"Yes, she jilted me."

"So it was not her, but the young girl called Karin from happier days whom you thought you had found again in Kirsten Bunding; or, to be more precise, the thoughts you had about the Karin of olden days—which had been dispelled by the harsh reality of her faithlessness—were re-awakened and transferred to Kirsten. You identified her with a woman who, in the last analysis, had never existed except as an ideal—a phantasm, a dream.

And yet you expected her to live up to this. Is that a true picture?"

"I've never viewed it in such a light before. And besides, there was more to it than that."

"Indeed, yes. There was a certain ambiguity. You were an old man in her eyes."

"In mine too," said Steffensen. "I was an old man. But what do you mean by ambiguity?"

"I mean you had two distinct sets of feelings towards her: the one set I've just described which, in fact, did not relate to Kirsten Bunding as she was, but to what she represented for you. The other was the set of feelings that bound you to the real Kirsten Bunding. In this sense she seemed to be a younger member of the family, so you could see yourself as her guardian in some degree—not interfering directly in her life, yet somehow keeping an eye on her. I'm sorry to say this openly, I may be wrong."

Why was he sitting there making excuses to a man who'd just confessed to murder?

"No, you're not wrong," said Steffensen, "but these feelings weren't distinct. Or rather I couldn't distinguish them one from the other. Do you understand?"

"Yes," said Morck, and there was a long silence between them. The old man shifted in his chair.

"What happened in the end?" he said.

"You know what happened," said Morck. "So why ask?"

"Because I heard about it from others and read about it in the papers," said Steffensen. "But I don't know from my own experience."

"You mean you don't remember what happened?"

"No. But I must know."

"Indeed you must," said Morck. "I would try to tell you myself, but I don't know if I can."

Morck found himself at a loss. He bowed his head in painful concentration—almost as if he were contemplating a confession, Herting thought. Presently, he looked up.

"The night it happened you followed her," he said. "You were lying in bed when you heard her phone ringing."

"Yes," said Steffensen, "I heard her phone ringing from my bedroom. The window was open. But I wasn't undressed."

"Did you know it was Erik Sogaard on the line?"

"Yes."

"And you already knew the truth about her relationship with him?"

Steffensen nodded. "I had only recently come to realize who he was. One day when she was out I had let myself into her flat and he had rung up and asked for her."

"And he happened to give his name," said Morck. "I know. So you found out who he was, then warned Kirsten Bunding against throwing herself away on a married man, as you put it."

"How do you know all this?"

"Sogaard told me. I interrogated him today in Aarhus."

"Ah, I see," Steffensen whispered.

"And you discovered he had bought a summer house in Vesterso, and that she visited him there."

"Yes."

"Had you ever followed her there before?"

"Yes. Once before. One night. I saw her go into the house and . . . I must have gone in order to . . . to . . . what's the word?"

"We needn't trouble about the word," said Morck.

"To spy on her, when they were together . . . yes, that was it," said the old man. "We don't know what we're capable of until suddenly we find ourselves doing it."

"No, no one knows," said Morck. "But you didn't go as far as the house the first time. You turned back?"

"Yes, the first time. But the temptation remained with me, and I knew I wouldn't be able to resist it if I followed her——"

"On the night it happened?"

"Yes."

"So you saw her stop the car on the Beach Road. You took the path through the scrub and went right up to the house, right up to the living-room window?"

Morck seemed to be goading the old man on with the icy neutrality of his voice, if only to keep the narrative moving and get it over with.

"Not quite," the old man whispered. His face was contorted again, foretelling another spasm of pain. "I stopped a few steps from the window, and through an open door in the living-room I saw a woman lying in bed—that must have been his wife. She was ill and obviously in pain. The bedclothes had been thrown off. She looked scrawny and miserable. I shuddered at the sight. Then Kirsten came out of the room——"

"She'd been giving Mrs Sogaard an injection," said Morck.

"She went up to him in the living-room, with his wife lying there in the next room, and I could see from her expression that she was terribly upset. Then he embraced Kirsten as she was leaving, and I saw them kissing one another. I saw them, and I thought it was . . . how shall I say . . . revolting and shameless. My feelings were destroyed in that instant . . . everything was over."

Yet this was not the whole truth, Morck thought. The sequence of events had indeed been more or less as Sogaard had reported, but he had given them a very different interpretation.

"Well, maybe not everything," said Steffensen. "It would be odd to say that everything was over and yet I was appalled at their shamelessness . . . after all, mine was considerable too. I burned with a jealousy which I never knew I was capable of feeling. I desired her then, because she was with him, and also because they revolted me. So . . . something in me snapped . . . how else can I put it? Like a flame bursting out of me. I wandered about in the darkness, not conscious of what I was doing. I remember the pine scrub but I don't remember being there. Do you understand? No, how can anyone? Then she came towards me and I knew I had to do it . . . but I didn't know I was doing it. At the end, her moaning was so terrible that I couldn't bear it any longer . . ."

He couldn't bear it, so, in his panic he had grabbed the lump of masonry, thought Morck. Did he know this himself? Yes, he'd heard about it, read about it in the papers. But it was still unreal for him like something someone else, some other person lodged inside him, had done—wasn't this the real truth of the matter? How can anyone tell? Reality? Truth? When all is said and done, no amount of investigation, no number of confessions and explanations can ever shed any light on these grand abstractions. They remain unattainable. At best one discovers a single truth. But what had been true for Erik Sogaard was false for the old man, whose face now looked to Morck as if the masonry had shattered it too—the skin was pallid, as if life had already drained away.

"I think we should drop the subject now, Steffensen," Morck heard himself saying coldly.

"Yes, there's no point in going on."

The old man's whisper was equally cold—hideously down-to-earth, where he too would be ere long, thought Herting, who was not usually given to such wry subtleties.

Sitting there listening to them talking, though they were not conscious of his presence, Herting shuddered at their unhesitating mutual trust.

"Nor would there be any use in saying it was not what I wanted to do: I didn't want to murder her."

"Maybe not Kirsten, but the one we first talked about—the one you saw in Kirsten. What you wanted to do was to erase her from your psyche. To achieve this you did what you did."

"Yes," said Steffensen. "I see that now."

"And since then you've sat here looking at Karin's picture."

"I tried to understand, but now it's only a . . . a dead photograph. There was one saying that kept coming back to me: 'If thine eye offend thee, pluck it out'. That's what I should have done, but how? Tell me, how does one go about plucking out an offending eye?"

"I don't know."

"No, and I'm no nearer to the answer either," said Steffensen. "We ought to drop the subject as you said. What else can we do? So if you have nothing else to ask me, I'll go and prepare myself to accompany you."

"Just a minute. Maybe . . ." Morck was so long in finishing the sentence that Herting thought he never would.

"Maybe there's something else we should take into consideration."

"We?" said Steffensen.

"Or rather—you. I was thinking of Erik Sogaard's wife, whom you saw that night. She doesn't know who it was he sent for."

"She doesn't know?"

"As far as she is concerned Kirsten Bunding was just a nurse who happened to be on call. She knows nothing about her husband's relationship with her. She is ill and her nerves are in shreds. If she were to find out, her life would be made more of a misery than ever, perhaps intolerably so. And I see no good reason why we shouldn't take this into consideration. Apart from the law, of course."

Steffensen did not ask for an explanation, for Morck was debating the point with himself.

"I had in mind to write a much abbreviated report of your confession, Mr Steffensen. In it no mention would be made of their relationship—if you are prepared to give your consent?"

"You know I am."

"Are you? I would say merely that you were in love with her, but

252

she had rejected you, and under a sudden impulse of uncontrollable jealousy you murdered her."

"Did I?" whispered the old man.

"You thought she had gone out at night to meet a lover, whereas she was, in fact, called out to visit a patient," said Morck. "That is the truth after all. It is a fact, and as such I will abide by it."

"Yes."

"There will be some further interrogation in hospital, should the doctors think your condition allows it. But you will be justified in merely referring to my report and refusing to say any more. That will be up to you, and will not be my concern."

Steffensen was about to say something, but Morck stopped him.

"Don't misunderstand me," he said, "I am obviously not in a position to make any kind of bargain with you. All I can do is tell you that as the accused you need say no more than you wish."

"So you have told me," said Steffensen, again with his deceptive semblance of a smile. "But when the case is heard in court. . . ?"

"Then the whole story will, of necessity, have to come out. But it will be some time before that happens."

Steffensen nodded. They sat looking at one another: two old men, wordlessly plotting in terms of a timely death.

"You have no cause for regret," said Steffensen.

38

MORCK ARRIVED HOME just before twelve the next night. He let himself into the dark house, but his wife woke up and put the light on as he was going upstairs to the bedroom.

"Jonas! What a lovely surprise," she said, getting out of bed, and coming to meet him. "Did you find out, Jonas? It wasn't the boy, was it?"

"No, it was Steffensen, her next-door neighbour."

"The old man who owned the house? Has he confessed?"

"Yes."

"But why did he murder her?"

"Because he'd transformed her into someone other than she was."

"Other than she was? I don't quite understand."

"No," he replied wearily, "who does?"

"Come on now, Jonas," she said, tugging at him gently. "You're home now. Goodness, you must have had a bad time; you look thoroughly miserable."

"Surely I don't," he said, trying to snap out of his mood, but only managing to make a weak joke. "I sank a few—four to be exact—on the Storbelt ferry, to put the finishing touches to my appearance."

"Well, I never; when my husband does come home at last, he's half canned," she said. "Jonas, why are you so upset? I'll go and——"

"What will you go and do, Marie?"

"I'll go down and make you something to eat."

"I don't want anything. I just want to go to bed."

"All right, darling," she said.

When they were in bed, she put her arm round him.

"Go to sleep now, Jonas; you can tell me the whole story to-morrow. It was a good thing anyway you found out the boy was innocent after all."

"Was it?" he murmured. Marie soon fell asleep, but he lay awake, reflecting that it wasn't a good thing by any means. He had found out too late. And he could not shake off the memory of Mrs Bahnsen standing there in her kitchen, a small, thin, almost shapeless figure in her indeterminately coloured dress, incessantly drying her hands on her apron, just as she had done the first time he had set eyes on her.

She had stared at him in such a way that he thought she hadn't understood what he'd been saying. Then when he began to repeat it she had interrupted him.

"What good can that do?" she'd said.

And he hadn't realized what she meant until he rang up the hospital to ask the doctor in charge of the psychiatric ward to tell Otto Bahnsen he would be released immediately and sent home.

"I'm afraid we couldn't allow that," the doctor had said. "He is suffering from a severe psychogenic psychosis as far as we can determine."

"Does that mean that . . . he's had a complete mental break-down?"

"You could call it that," said the doctor brusquely, implying that he didn't approve of such quack layman's expressions. "He is of a singularly low-intelligence level and has only minimal psychic endurance. So when the psyche underwent a more severe strain than it could withstand, as a result of the murder charge—I believe he's innocent, by the way."

"Yes. He was not the murderer."

"Mm," said the doctor, "a regrettable state of affairs, I'm bound to say; particularly as at present he could not be made to understand that he has been cleared of suspicion."

"What are the symptoms of his psychosis?"

"He simply lies in bed with his face to the wall. He has turned his back on the world, so to speak, and refuses to communicate any more with it. Any attempt one makes to penetrate this barrier and make contact with him provokes violent fits of rage. We have had to transfer him to a special ward."

"You're so restless," said Marie, the wife of Detective-Inspector Morck who was taken from her bed two nights in every three. "Can't you sleep?"

"Yes," Morck murmured. And soon he did.

THE ROYAL HISTORICAL SOCIETY
**ANNUAL BIBLIOGRAPHY OF BRITISH
AND IRISH HISTORY**
Publications of 1985

ROYAL HISTORICAL SOCIETY

ANNUAL BIBLIOGRAPHY OF BRITISH AND IRISH HISTORY

Publications of 1985

General Editor: D.M. Palliser

A. Bennett
R. Boyce
J.C.R. Childs
G.R. Elton
R.A. Griffiths
M.W.C. Hassall

A.C. Howe
J.S. Morrill
G. Mac Niocaill
D.W. Rollason
A.T.Q. Stewart
C.A. Whatley

HARVESTER PRESS LIMITED
ST. MARTIN'S PRESS INC.
For the Royal Historical Society

First published in 1986 for
The Royal Historical Society by
THE HARVESTER PRESS LIMITED
Publisher: John Spiers
16 Ship Street, Brighton, Sussex

and in the USA by
ST. MARTIN'S PRESS, INC.
175 Fifth Avenue, New York, NY 10010

British Library Cataloguing in Publication Data

Annual bibliography of British and Irish history.
    Publications of 1985
    1. Great Britain — History — Bibliography
    — Periodicals
    I. Royal Historical Society
    016.941   Z2016

    ISBN 0-7108-1135-7

The Library of Congress Cataloged This Serial as Follows:

Annual bibliography of British and Irish history. Publications of
    ... / Royal Historical Society. —   — Brighton,
    Sussex : Harvester Press ; Atlantic Highlands, N.J. : Humanities
Press for the Royal Historical Society,

        v.; 22cm.

        Annual
        Began with 1975
        Description based on; 1979

        1. Great Britain—History—Bibliography—Periodicals. 2. Ireland—History
    —Bibliography—Periodicals.   I. Royal Historical Society (London, England)

    Z2016.A55   016.941'005   81-641280

    ISBN 0-312-00228-9

Printed and bound in Great Britain by
Billing and Sons Ltd, Worcester
from typesetting by Alacrity Phototypesetters,
Banwell Castle, Weston-super-Mare

THE HARVESTER PRESS PUBLISHING GROUP
The Harvester Group comprises Harvester Press Ltd (chiefly publishing literature,
fiction, philosophy, psychology, and science and trade books); Harvester Press
Microform Publications (publishing in microform previously unpublished archives,
scarce printed sources, and indexes to these collections); Wheatsheaf Books Ltd
(chiefly publishing in economics, international politics, sociology, women's studies
and related social sciences).

CONTENTS

Contents

Contents

PREFACE

The Bibliography is meant in the first place to serve the urgent needs of scholars, which has meant subordinating absolutely total coverage and refinements of arrangement to speed of production. Nevertheless, it is comprehensive and arranged for easy use. Because the sectional headings are those approved by section editors they are not uniform. Searchers are advised to use the subdivisions in conjunction with the Subject Index which, apart from covering all place and personal names, is designed to facilitate a thematic and conceptual analysis.

Pieces contained in collective works (under Bc and sometimes in a chronological section) are individually listed in the appropriate place and there referred to by the number the volume bears in the Bibliography.

Items covering more than two sections are listed in B; any that extend over two sections appear as a rule in the first and are cross-referenced at the head of the second.

Reliance on the British National Bibliography has necessitated the use of its 'Cataloguing in Publication' (i.e. before publication) cards. These have been entered only if the fact of publication has been independently established, but in some cases the item itself could not be seen so that occasionally the pagination has had to be omitted.

The subject index forms an important part of the work, and it covers, so far as is practicable, all major subjects of the books and articles listed, whether or not they figure in the titles. The counties used in identifying places are, for England, those of the pre-1974 counties.

The editors wish to express their gratitude for the assistance received from the International Medieval Bibliography, Leeds (especially Dr R. J. Walsh), Miss Jill Alexander of the Cambridge University Library, and Mrs Kay Austin of the Department of History, University of Hull. They are especially indebted to Dr Alice Prochaska, Miss Rosemary Taylor and the staff of the library of the Institute of Historical Research, London, for undertaking the searches without which the compilation of this Bibliography would not be possible.

Abbreviations

Arch.	— Archaeological
B., Bull.	— Bulletin
HMSO	— Her Majesty's Stationery Office
HR	— History Review, Historical Review
Hist. Soc.	— Historical Society
Inst. Hist. Res.	— Institute of Historical Research
J.	— Journal

Preface

P.	— Proceedings
Q.	— Quarterly
R.	— Review
Soc.	— Society
T.	— Transactions
Univ.	— University
UP	— University Press

A. AUXILIARY

(a) *Bibliography and Archives*

1. Clarke, A.; Collinson, P.; Morrill, J.S.; Parker, G. 'Recent works (1977-1982) on early modern British history: a review essay,' *Tijdschrift voor Geschiedenis* 97 (1984), 517-54.
2. Tobias, R.C. 'Victorian bibliography for 1983,' *Victorian Studies* 27 (1984), 533-613.
3. Hare, S.M. 'The records of the Goldsmiths' Company', *Archives* 16 (1984), 376-84.
4. Parsons, D. (ed.). *A bibliography of Leicestershire churches, pt. 3, fasc. 1: parochial records, parishes A-H.* Leicester; The University; 1984. Pp 89.
5. Jones, J. *The archives of Balliol College Oxford: a guide.* Chichester; Phillimore; 1984. Pp 88.
6. Wilcox, M.: Storey, R. *The Confederation of British Industry predecessor archive.* Coventry; University of Warwick Library; 1984. Pp 51.
7. Aspinwall, B. *The Scots-American connection: a comprehensive bibliography and biographical list extracted from Portable Utopia, Glasgow and the United States.* Aberdeen UP; 1984. Pp 100.
8. Lavell, C.; Dixon, P.W. 'The published works of M.W. Barley,' Bc1, 4-6.
9. Bennett, L. *Richard III in the 1980s: an inprint bibliography.* Normanton; H. & A. John; 1984. Pp 18.
10. Baldwin, M. 'A bibliography of British canals, 1623-1950,' Bc6, 130-91.
11. Ford, J. 'Ackermann imprints and publications,' Bc7, 109-24.
12. (Manuscripts). *St Andrews with Castle Gate United Reformed Church.* Nottingham; University Manuscripts Department; 1984. Pp 45.
13. (Manuscripts). *North Midland Presbyterian and Unitarian Association.* Nottingham; the same; 1984. Pp 17.
14. Manchester, A.H. *Sources of English legal history: law, history and society in England and Wales, 1750-1950.* London; Butterworth; 1984. Pp xiv, 443.
15. Desmond, R. *Bibliography of British gardens.* Winchester; St Paul's Bibliographies; 1984. Pp 350.
16. Nixon, H.M. *Catalogue of the Pepys Library at Magdalene College, Cambridge, vol. 6: bindings.* Woodbridge; Brewer; 1983. Pp xxxii, 45[79].
17. Walsh, K.; Wood, D. 'Bibliography of the writings of Beryl Smalley,' Bc9, 317-21.
18. Not used.
19. Not used.
20. Not used.
21. Millett, B. 'The archives of St. Isidore's College, Rome,' *Archivium Hibernicum* 40 (1985), 1-13.

22. Yates, N., 'Kent Archives Office: major accessions, 1981-1983,' *Archaeologia Cantiana* 101 (1985 for 1984), 313-47.
23. Ville, S., 'The Henley Collection, 1770 to 1831 [in the National Maritime Museum],' *Business Archives* 51 (1985), 45-51.
24. Ross, A.; Morton, A., 'The Hudson's Bay Company and its archives,' ibid. 17-39.
25. Fox-Pitt, S., 'The Tate Gallery archive of twentieth century British art, its formation and development,' *Archives* 17 (1985), 94-106.
26. Lewis, R.W. *Her Majesty's Inspectors of Factories, 1833-1983: a select historical bibliography.* Sheffield; Health and Safety Executive; 1984. Pp 8.
27. Earnest, J.D.; Tracey, G. *John Henry Newman: an annotated bibliography of his tracts and pamphlet collection.* New York/London; Garland; 1984. Pp xx, 234.
28. Barker, B., 'A new Labour archive: the Middleton Collection,' *History Workshop* 20 (1985), 164-ç4.
29. Emerson, R.L., 'Recent works on eighteenth century life and thought [bibliographical review essay],' *Eighteenth Century Life* 9/2 (1985), 92-106.
30. Tite, C.G.T. (ed.). *Catalogue of the manuscripts in the Cottonian Library: Catalogus librorum manuscriptorum bibliothecae Cottonianae by Thomas Smith.* Woodbridge; Boydell & Brewer; 1984. Pp vii, 406.
31. Elton, G.R. (ed.). *Annual bibliography of British and Irish history: publications of 1984.* Brighton; Harvester; 1985. Pp 176.
32. Cohen, B. *The Thames 1580-1980: a general bibliography.* London; the author; 1985. Pp 335.
33. McCann, T.J. (ed.). *The Goodwood Estate archives: a catalogue*, vol. 3. The Estate; 1984. Pp ix, 160.
34. Simpson, K. 'An annotated bibliography of the British Army, 1914-18,' Ii15, 238-265.

(b) *Works of Reference*

1. Edwards, R.D.; O'Dowd, M. *Sources for early modern Irish history 1534-1641.* Cambridge UP; 1985. Pp x, 222.
2. MacKeith, M. *Shopping arcades: a gazetteer of extant British arcades, 1817-1939.* London; Mansell; 1985. Pp viii, 166.
3. Banks, O. *Biographical dictionary of British feminists, vol. 1: 1800-1930.* Brighton; Wheatsheaf; 1985. Pp xi, 239.
4. Williams, M.I. (ed.). *A directory of rare and special collections in the United Kingdom and the Republic of Ireland.* London; Library Association; 1985. Pp xiii, 664.
5. Thomas, C. (ed.). *Research objectives in British archaeology.* London; Council for British Archaeology; 1983. Pp xi, 56.
6. Graham, F. *Maps of Newcastle.* Newcastle upon Tyne; the compiler; 1984. Pp 24.
7. Bellamy, J.; Saville, J. (ed.). *Dictionary of labour biography, vol. 7.* London; Macmillan; 1984. Pp xviii, 301.

8. Hudson, K. *Industrial history from the air.* Cambridge UP; 1984. N.p.
9. Popplewell, L. *A gazetteer of the railway contractors and engineers of Wales and the Borders 1830-1914.* Bournemouth; Melledgen; 1984. Pp 39.
10. Cooper, C.R.H., 'The archives of the city of London livery companies and related organisations', *Archives* 16 (1984), 323-53.
11. Kain, R.; Prince, H. *The tithe surveys of England and Wales.* Cambridge UP; 1985. Pp xvi, 327.
12. Tinch, D.M.N. (ed.). *The Orkney Library 1683-1983: a short history.* Kirkwall; Orkney Library; 1983. Pp 18.
13. Bennet, F.; Frew, H.; Melrose, M. *Index of fellows of the Royal Society of Edinburgh: elected November 1783-July 1883.* Edinburgh; Scotland's Cultural Heritage; 1984. Pp 73.
14. McCann, A. & T.J. *Records of the English Franciscan nuns 1621-1972: a handlist.* Lymbourne Press; 1983. 20 leaves.
15. Edwards, L.W.L. (ed.). *Catalogue of directories and poll books in the possession of the Society of Genealogists* (4th ed.). London; The Society 1984. Pp 63.
16. Jeremy, D.J.; Shaw, C. (ed.). *Dictionary of business biography: a biographical dictionary of business leaders active in Britain in the period 1860-1980, vol. 2: D-G.* London; Butterworths; 1984. Pp xxxii, 690.
17. *A catalogue of historic maps in Avon.* Bristol; Avon County Council; 1984. Pp 98.
18. Gibson, J. (ed.). *Marriage, census and other indexes for family historians.* Plymouth; Federation of Family History Societies; 1984. Pp 36.
19. *Retail price indices 1914-1983 – Department of Employment.* London; HMSO; 1984. Pp vi, 37.
20. Freeman, M.; Aldcroft D. *The atlas of British railway history.* Beckenham; Croom Helm; 1985. Pp 128.
21. Newman, P.R. *Atlas of the English civil war.* Idem; 1985. Pp 127.
22. Poole, H. *Here for the beer: a gazetteer of the brewers of Hertfordshire.* Watford; Museum Services; 1984. Pp ii, 64.
23. Spadoni, C.; Harley, D., 'Bertrand Russell's library,' *J. of Library History* 20 (1985), 25-44.
24. Thompson, D.N., 'Wirral hospital records,' *J. of the Soc. of Archivists* 7 (1985), 421-42.
25. Jones, J.G., 'The Clement Davies papers: a review', *National Library of Wales J.* 23 (1984), 406-21.
26. *Parish poor law records in Devon.* Exeter; Devon Record Office; 1984. Pp 20.
27. Bellenger, D.A. *English and Welsh priests 1558-1800: a working list.* Bath; Downside Abbey; 1984. Pp 254.
28. Popplewell, L. *A gazetteer of the railway contractors and engineers of East Anglia 1840-1914.* Southbourne; Melledgen Press; Pp 40.
29. Sims, J. *A handlist of British parliamentary poll books.* Leicester; The University; 1983.
30. Rowley, G., 'British fire insurance plans: the Goad productions,

*c.*1885-*c.*1970,' *Archives* 17 (1985), 67-78.

31. Broughton, H.E. *Family and estate records in the Leicestershire Record Office.* Leicester; Leics. Museums; 1984. Pp 43.

32. Hawgood, D. *Computers for family history: an introduction.* London; Hawgood Computing; 1985. Pp 72.

33. Raftery, M. *The writers of Leicestershire: a biographical dictionary and literary gazetteer of Leicestershire authors from the 14th century to the present day.* Leicester; Leics. Library Service; 1984. Pp 107.

34. Willsher, B. *How to record Scottish graveyards: a companion to understanding Scottish graveyards.* Edinburgh; Council for British Archaeology Scotland; 1985. Pp 48.

35. McCracken, E. & D. *A register of trees for county Londonderry, 1768-1911.* Belfast; Public Record Office of Northern Ireland; 1984. Pp x, 80.

36. Coupe, J.A. (ed.). *A guide to the registration districts of Manchester.* Manchester & Lancashire Family History Society; 1984. Pp 26.

37. Parbury, K. *Women of grace: a biographical dictionary of British women saints, martyrs and reformers.* Stocksfield; Oriel; 1985. Pp viii, 199.

38. *Guide to Cornish probate records.* Truro; Cornwall Record Office; 1984. Pp 55.

39. Fulton, R.D.; Colee, C.M. *Union list of Victorian serials: a union list of selected nineteenth century British serials available in United States and Canadian libraries.* New York/London; Garland; 1985. Pp xxvii, 732.

40. Lefanu, W.R. (ed. J. Loudon). *British periodicals of medicine: a chronological list 1640-1899,* rev ed. Oxford; Wellcome Unit for the History of Medicine; 1984. Pp xi, 67.

41. Bailey, B. *A guide to Britain's industrial past.* London; Whittet; 1985. Pp 187.

42. Horn, J.M. *History theses 1971-80: historical research for higher degrees in the universities of the United Kingdom.* London; Institute of Historical Research; 1985. Pp ix, 294.

43. Room, A. *Pocket companion guide to British place names.* Harlow; Longman; 1985. Pp 239.

44. Cowen, P. *A guide to stained glass in Britain.* London; Joseph; 1985. Pp vii, 280.

45. Revell, A. *A Kentish herbal: a collection of medicinal remedies taken from original manuscript sources in the Kent Archives Office.* Maidstone; Kent County Council; 1984. Pp xvii, 85.

46. Veysey, A.G. *Guide to the parish records of Clwyd.* Hawarden; Clwyd County Council; 1984. Pp xi, 123.

47. Oakden, J.P. *The place-names of Staffordshire, pt. 1: Cuttlestone Hundred.* Nottingham; English Place-Name Society; 1984. Pp li, 186.

(c) *Historiography*

1. Kettenacker, L.; Mommsen, W.J. (ed.). *Research on British history in the*

Federal Republic of Germany 1978-1983. London; German Historical Institute; 1983. Pp 63.

2. Bann, S. *The clothing of Clio: a study of the representation of history in nineteenth-century Britain and France.* Cambridge UP; 1984. Pp xii.

3. Russell, A.F. *Logic, philosophy and history: a study in the philosophy of history based on the work of R.G. Collingwood.* London; University Press of America; 1984. Pp xxiii, 527.

4. Crook, J.M. 'Architecture and history,' *Architectural History* 27 (1984), 554-78.

5. Elliott, D.C. 'Some slight confusion: a note on Thomas Andrewes and Thomas Andrewes,' *Huntington Library Q.* 47 (1984), 129-32.

6. Moss, M. 'Forgotten ledgers, law and the business historian: gleanings from the Adam Smith business records collection,' *Archives* 16 (1984), 354-75.

7. Bartle, G.F. 'The records of the British and Foreign School Society,' *Local Historian* 16 (1984), 204-6.

8. Neave, D. 'The local records of affiliated Friendly Societies,' ibid. 161-7.

9. Cox, N. & J. 'Probate inventories: the legal background,' ibid. 133-45, 217-27.

10. Parton, A.G.; Matthews, M.H. 'The returns of poor law out-relief — a source for the local historian,' ibid. 25-31.

11. Melrose, E.A. 'Three 18th-century Lincoln libraries,' *Lincolnshire History and Archaeology* 19 (1984), 41-8.

12. Marsden, B.M. *Pioneers of prehistory: leaders and landmarks in English archaeology (1500-1900).* Ormskirk; Hesketh; 1984. Pp xiii, 82.

13. Elton, G.R. *F.W. Maitland.* London; Weidenfeld; 1985. Pp viii, 118.

14. Henstock, A., 'The Nottinghamshire parish registers microfilming project,' *J. of the Soc. of Archivists* 7 (1985), 443-9.

15. Schurer, K., 'Census enumerators' returns and the computer', *Local Historian* 16 (1985), 335-42.

16. Clarkson, L.A. *'According to the fashion of the beetle': inaugural lecture.* Belfast; Queen's University; 1984. Pp 29.

17. Best, G., 'Owen Chadwick and his work,' Bc3, 1-8.

18. Ramsay, G.D., 'Victorian historiography and the guilds of London: the report of the royal commission on the livery companies of London, 1884', *London J.* 10 (1984), 155-66.

19. McLennan, G., 'History and theory: contemporary debates and directions', *Literature and History* 10 (1984), 139-64.

20. Southern, R.W., 'Beryl Smalley and the place of the bible in medieval studies', Bc9, 1-16.

21. Dowling, L., 'Roman decadence and Victorian historiography,' *Victorian Studies* 28 (1985), 579-607.

22. Mandelbaum, S.J., 'H.J. Dyos and British urban history', *Economic History R.* 2nd ser. 38 (1985), 437-47.

23. Georghallides, G.S., 'The management of public records under the British colonial administration in Cyprus', *International History R.* 7 (1985), 622-9.

24. Kenyon, J.P., 'Sir Charles Firth and the Oxford School of Modern History', *Clio's mirror: Historiography in Britain and the Netherlands*, ed. A.C. Duke & C.A. Tamse (Zutphen; De Warburg Pres; 1985), 163-83.
25. Cannon, J. *Teaching history at university.* London; Historical Association; 1984. Pp 35.
26. Prest, W.R., 'Why the history of the professions is not written', *Law, Economy and Society: essays in the history of English law 1750-1914*, ed. R.R. Rubin & D. Sugarman (Abingdon; Professional Books; 1984), 300-20.

B. GENERAL

(a) *Long Periods – National*

1. Burton, A. 'Canals in the landscape', Bc6, 9-22.
2. Norman, E.R. *Roman Catholicism in England from the Elizabethan settlement to the Second Vatican Council.* Oxford UP; 1985. Pp ix, 160.
3. Punshon, J. *Portrait in grey: a short history of the Quakers.* London; Quaker Home Service; 1984. Pp 293.
4. Jones, A. *Welsh chapels.* Cardiff; Amgueddfa Genedlaethol Cymru; 1984. Pp 87.
5. Taylor, C. *Village and farmstead: a history of rural settlement in England.* London; George Philip; 1983. Pp 254.
6. Taylor, C. *The archaeology of gardens.* Princes Risborough; Shire; 1983. Pp 72.
7. Stanley, C. *The history of Britain: an aerial view.* London; Batsford; 1984. Pp 144.
8. Jones, B. *Past imperfect: the story of rescue archaeology.* London; Heinemann; 1984. Pp xii, 164.
9. Cameron, A.; Farndon, R. *Scenes from sea and city: Lloyd's list 1734-1984.* Colchester; Lloyd's List; 1984. Pp 288.
10. Mommsen, W.J. *Two centuries of Anglo-German relations: a reappraisal.* London; German Historical Institute; 1984. Pp 32.
11. Cossey, R. *Golfing ladies: five centuries of golf in Great Britain and Ireland.* London; Orbis; 1984. Pp 256.
12. Ewing, E. *Everyday dress: 1650-1900.* London; Batsford; 1984. Pp 144.
13. Carman, W.Y. *Richard Simkin's uniforms of the British army: Infantry, Royal Artillery, Royal Engineers and other corps.* Exeter; Webb & Bower; 1985. Pp 224.
14. Perrett, B. *The Hawks: a short history of the 14th/20th King's Hussars.* Chippenham; Picton; 1984. Pp viii, 151.
15. Young, A.J. *The swords of the Britons: a military review.* London; Regency Press; 1984. Pp 183.

16. Gulvin, C. *The Scottish hosiery and knitwear industry: 1680-1980*. Edinburgh; John Donald; 1984. Ppix, 163.
17. Pragnell, H. *The styles of English architecture*. London; Batsford; 1984. Pp176.
18. Jones, G.E. *Modern Wales: a concise history c.1485-1979*. Cambridge UP; Ppxii, 364.
19. Ashton, E.T. *The Welsh in the United States*. Hove; Caldra House; 1984. Pp182.
20. Howard, P. *'We thundered out' - 200 years of The Times, 1785-1985*. London; Times Books; 1985. Pp120.
21. Smith, R.M. 'Some issues concerning families and their property in rural England 1250-1800', Bc2, 1-86.
26. Snell, K.D.M. *Annals of the labouring poor: social change and agrarian England, 1660-1900*. Cambridge UP; 1985. Ppx, 464.
23. Fletcher, J.M.; Tapper, M.C. 'Medieval artefacts and structures dated by dendrochronology', *Medieval Archaeology* 28 (1984), 112-32.
24. Field, J. 'Street names', *Local Historian* 16/4 (1984), 195-203.
25. Hutton, B. 'Why this house? Motives for traditional building styles', ibid. 16/6 (1985), 323-6.
26. Gilley, S. 'The Irish' [as immigrants to Britain], *History Today* 35/6 (1985), 17-23.
27. Souden, D. 'Movers and stayers in family reconstitution populations', *Local Population Studies* 33 (1984), 11-28.
28. Levine, D. 'Industrialization and the proletarian family in England', *Past & Present* 107 (1985), 168-203.
29. Schwarz, L.D. 'The standard of living in the long run: London, 1700-1860', *Economic HR* 2nd ser. 38 (1985), 24-41.
30. Roberts, B.K. 'Village patterns and forms: some models for discussion', Bc10, 7-25.
31. Morris, R.K. 'The church in the countryside: two lines of inquiry', Bc10, 46-60.
32. Lockhart, D.G. 'Some aspects of the evolution of small towns and villages in Scotland', Bc10, 187-99.
33. Beresford, M.W. *Time and place: collected essays*. London; Hambledon; 1985. Ppxv, 406.
34. Everitt, A. *Landscape and Community in England*. London; Hambledon; 1985. Ppvii, 362.
35. Everitt, A. 'Dynasty and community since the seventeenth century', ibid. 309-30.
36. Hinde, T. (ed.). *The Domesday Book: England's heritage, then and now*. London; Hutchinson; 1985. Pp351.
37. Steel, T. *Scotland's story: a new perspective*. London; Collins/Channel Four TV & Scottish TV; 1984. Pp358.
38. Neale, R.S. *Writing Marxist history: British society, economy and culture since 1700*. Oxford; Blackwell; 1985. Ppxxii, 319.
39. Aston, M. *Interpreting the landscape*. London; Batsford; 1985. Pp168.
40. Chapman, J.C.; Mytum, H.C. (eds.). *Settlement in North Britain*

1000 B.C.-A.D. 1000. Oxford; B.A.R. (British ser. 118); 1983. Ppxii, 356.

41. Haigh, C. (ed.) *The Cambridge historical encyclopedia of Great Britain and Ireland.* Cambridge UP; 1985. Pp.392.

42. Johnson, P. *The British Travelling Post Office.* London; Ian Allan; 1985. Pp104.

43. Davey, P. (ed.). *The archaeology of the clay tobacco pipe: IX: More pipes from the Midlands and Southern England.* Oxford; B.A.R. (British ser. 146, 2 pts.); 1985. Ppxi, 553.

44. Amussen, S.D. 'Féminin/masculin: le genre dans l'Angleterre de l'époque moderne', *Annales* 40 (1985), 269-87.

45. Stone, L. 'L'Angleterre de 1540 à 1880: pays de noblesse ouverte', ibid. 71-94.

46. Warwick, P. 'Did Britain decline? An inquiry into the causes of national decline', *J. of Contemporary History* 20 (1985), 99-133.

47. Walker, P.J. 'Immigration into Britain: the Chinese', *History Today* 35/9 (1985), 8-15.

48. Prochaska, F. 'The many faces of Lady Jane Grey', ibid. 35/10 (1985), 34-40.

49. O'Brien, P. 'Agriculture and the home market for English industry, 1660-1820', *English HR* 100 (1985), 773-800.

50. Crawforth, M.A. 'Evidence from trade cards for the scientific instrument industry', *Annals of Science* 42 (1985), 453-554.

51. Jones, E.L.; Porter, S.; Turner, M. *A gazetteer of English urban fire disasters, 1500-1900.* Norwich; Geo; 1984. Pp68.

52. Hartcup, A. *Love and marriage in the great country houses.* London; Sidgwick & Jackson; 1984. Pp240.

53. Charleston, R.J. *English glass: and the glass used in England circa 400-1940.* London; Allen & Unwin; 1984. Ppxxx, 288.

54. Burt, R. *The British lead mining industry.* Redruth; Dyllansow Truran; 1984. Ppvii, 344.

55. Elvin, J.G.D. *British gunfounders, 1700-1855.* Llandrindod Wells; the author; 1984. Pp59.

56. Harfield, A. *British & Indian armies in the East Indies 1685-1935.* Chippenham; Picton; 1984. Ppxv, 411.

57. Fisher, S. (ed.). *British shipping and seamen, 1630-1960: some studies.* Exeter; the University; 1984. Ppxi, 109.

58. Hollett, D. *From Cumberland to Cape Horn: the complete history of the sailing fleet of Thomas & John Brocklebank of Whitehaven and Liverpool ...* London; Fairplay; 1984. Pp204.

59. Murray, D.M. 'High Church Presbyterianism in Scotland and England', *J. of the United Reformed Church Hist. Soc.* 3 (1985), 225-34.

60. Oakley, A. *The captured womb: a history of the medical care of pregnant women.* Oxford; Blackwell; 1984. Pp352.

61. Campbell, R.H. *Scotland since 1707: the rise of an industrial society.* (2nd edn.). Edinburgh; Donald; 1985. Ppix, 272.

62. Not used.

63. Faber, R. *The high road to England.* London; Faber; 1985. Pp216.

64. Brock, W.H. *From protyle to proton: William Prout and the nature of matter, 1785-1985*. Bristol; Hilger; 1985. Pp xii, 252.

65. Tranter, N.L. *Population and society, 1750-1940: contrasts in population growth*. London; Longman; 1985. Pp viii, 230.

66. Mansel, P. *Pillars of monarchy: an outline of the political and social history of the Royal Guards, 1400-1984*. London; Quartet; 1984. Pp 207.

67. Bland, J. *The common hangman: English and Scottish hangmen before the abolition of public executions*. Hornchurch; Henry; 1984. Pp 173.

68. Harker, D. *Fakesong: the manufacture of British 'folksong' 1700 to the present day*. Milton Keynes; Open UP; 1985. Pp xviii, 297.

69. Holloway, R. *The Anglican tradition*. Oxford; Mowbray; 1984. Pp 112.

70. Roach, F.A. *Cultivated fruits of Britain: their origin and history*. Oxford; Blackwell; 1985. Pp 349.

71. Scott, P.H. *In bed with an elephant* [Anglo-Scottish relations, 1200-1984]. Edinburgh; Saltire Society; 1985. Pp 48.

72. Ehrlich, C. *The music profession in Britain since the eighteenth century: a social history*. Oxford; Clarendon; 1985. Pp viii, 269.

73. Opie, R. *Rule Britannia: trading on the British image*. Harmondsworth; Viking; 1985. Pp 160.

74. Gillis, J.R. *For better, for worse: British marriages 1600 to the present*. New York; Oxford UP; 1985. Pp xi, 417.

(b) *Long Periods – Local*

1. Greenslade, M.W. (ed.). *A history of the county of Stafford: vol. XX: Seisdon Hundred (Part)*. Oxford UP for Inst. Hist. Res. (Victoria County History); 1984. Pp xx, 250.

2. Allison, K.J. (ed.). *A history of the county of York: East Riding: vol. 5: Holderness: southern part*. Oxford UP for Inst. Hist. Res. (Victoria County History); 1984. Pp xvi, 222.

3. Addyman, P.V. 'York in its archaeological setting', Bc1, 7-21.

4. Hutton, B. 'Aisles to outshots' [Yorks. vernacular buildings], Bc1, 145-51.

5. O'Connor, T.P.; Hall, A.R.; Jones, A.K.G.; Kenward, H.K. 'Ten years of environmental archaeology at York', Bc1, 166-72.

6. Andrews, G. 'Archaeology in York: an assessment', Bc1, 173-208.

7. Dobson, R.B.; Donaghey, S. *The history of Clementhorpe Nunnery*. London; Council for British Archaeology (Archaeology of York 2/1); 1984. Pp 40.

8. O'Connor, T.P. *Selected groups of bones from Skeldergate and Walmgate*. London; Council for British Archaeology (Archaeology of York 15/1); 1984. Pp 60.

9. Smith, H.D. *Shetland life and trade, 1550-1914*. Edinburgh; Donald; 1984. Pp ix, 369.

10. Hume, M.; Boyd, S. *Queensberry House Hospital: a history*. Edinburgh; Directors of Queensberry House Hospital; 1984. Pp viii, 91.

11. Leach, P. (ed.). *The archaeology of Taunton: excavations and fieldwork to*

1980. Bristol; Western Archaeological Trust; 1984. Pp 201.

12. Allan, J.P. *Medieval and post-medieval finds from Exeter, 1971-1980.* Exeter; Exeter City Council; 1984. Pp xix, 377.

13. Philp, B. *Excavations in the Darenth Valley, Kent.* Dover; Kent Archaeological Rescue Unit; 1984. Pp xi, 225.

14. Garrod, A.P.; Heighway, C.M. *Garrod's Gloucester: archaeological observations 1974-81.* Gloucester; Sutton; 1984. Pp v, 114.

15. Crawford, A. *Bristol and the wine trade.* Bristol; Bristol branch, Historical Association; 1984. Pp 28.

16. Perry, C.B. *The Bristol Medical School.* Bristol; Bristol branch, Historical Association; 1984. Pp 24.

17. Dymond, D. *The Norfolk landscape.* London; Hodder & Stoughton; 1985. Pp 279.

18. Newell, P. *Greenwich Hospital: a royal foundation: 1692-1983.* Holbrook; Trustees of Greenwich Hospital; 1984. Pp x, 278.

19. Cooper, N. *Aynho: a Northamptonshire village.* Banbury; Leopard's Head (Banbury Hist. Soc., vol. 20); 1984. Pp xii, 339.

20. Clew, K.R. *The Exeter canal.* Chichester; Phillimore; 1984. Pp 112.

21. Lloyd, D.; Klein, P. *Ludlow: a historic town in words and pictures.* Chichester; Phillimore; 1984. Pp 132.

22. Evans, N. *The East Anglian linen industry: rural industry and local economy, 1500-1850.* Aldershot; Gower (Pasold Studies in Textile History 5); 1985. Pp xiv, 178.

23. Raistrick, A.; Roberts, A. *Life and work of the Northern lead miner.* Beamish; North of England Open Air Museum & Northern Mine Research Society; 1984. Pp 120.

24. Pearse, R. *The land beside the Celtic sea: some aspects of ancient, medieval and Victorian Cornwall.* Redruth; Truran; 1983. Pp 112.

25. Owen, C.C. *The Leicestershire and South Derbyshire coalfield 1200-1900.* Ashbourne; Moorland; 1984. Pp 321.

26. King, A. *Huyton and Roby: a history of two townships.* Huyton; Borough of Knowsley; 1984. Pp 76.

27. Rogers, K. *The book of Trowbridge: a history.* Buckingham; Barracuda; 1984. Pp 156.

28. Wall, B.L. *Sudbury through the ages: a guide to its buildings and streets.* Ipswich; East Anglian Magazine; 1984. Pp 132.

29. Whittaker, M. *The Book of Scarborough Spaw.* Buckingham; Barracuda; 1984. Pp 196.

30. Bessborough, Lord; Aslet, C. *Enchanted forest: the story of Stansted in Sussex.* London; Weidenfeld & Nicolson; 1984. Pp 160.

31. Whitham, J.A. *Ottery St Mary: a Devonshire town.* Chichester; Phillimore; 1984. Pp xiii, 124.

32. Williams, D. *Mount's Bay.* Bodmin; Bossiney; 1984. Pp 120.

33. Hughes, Q. (ed.). *Sefton Park.* Liverpool; Sefton Park Civic Society; 1984. Pp 142.

34. Smith, P.V. *The Nicholson Institute, Leek.* Stafford; Staffordshire County Council; 1984. Pp 65.

35. Mizon, L.; Donoghur, H.M. *Quakers of Haverhill, 1656-1873.* Haverhill; Haverhill & District Local History Group & the Religious Society of Friends; 1984. Pp viii, 32.
36. Hitchman, H.G.; Driver, P. *Harwich, a nautical history.* Harwich; the author; 1984. Pp 151.
37. Maling, J.J. *Colchester through the ages.* Ipswich; East Anglian Magazine; 1984. Pp 136.
38. Green, I. *The book of the Cinque Ports: their origin and development, heyday and decline.* Buckingham; Barracuda; 1984. Pp 144.
39. Crocker, G. *Chilworth gunpowder.* Guildford; Surrey Industrial History Group; 1984. Pp 28.
40. Slack, R. *Brassington Forebears, 1700-1900.* Chesterfield; R. Slack; 1984. Pp v, 117.
41. Webb, C.C. *Writers in Yorkshire: from documents in the Borthwick Institute of Historical Research.* York; Borthwick Institute; 1984. Pp 27.
42. Ryton, J. *Banks and banknotes of Exeter, 1769-1906: a study of provincial banking, with a standard list of banks, banknotes and partnerships.* Exeter; J. Ryton; 1984. Pp 119.
43. Green, E.R. (ed.). *Gravesend and Milton masters and apprentices 1636-1834.* Gravesend; the author; 1984. Pp 31.
44. Hallam, D.J. *The first 200 years: a short history of Rabone Chesterman Limited.* Birmingham; Rabone Chesterman; 1984. Pp 136.
45. Davis, P. *Number one: a history of the firm of Gregory, Rowcliffe & Co; 1784-1984.* London; the company; 1984. Pp 80.
46. Palliser, D.M. *The Company of Merchant Adventurers of the City of York: a brief history of the gild.* York; the company; 1985. Pp 16.
47. Crickmore, J. 'The Old Pit, Upwich, Droitwich', *T. of the Worcestershire Arch. Soc.* 3rd ser. 9 (1984), 13-35.
48. Hurst, J.G. 'The Wharram research project: results to 1983', *Medieval Archaeology* 28 (1984), 77-111.
49. Bateson, J.H. 'The cap of maintenance', *York Historian* 5 (1984), 18-24.
50. Beeston, G. 'Hedge dating on the Broughton estate' [Oxon], *Cake & Cockhorse* 9/7 (1984), 194-200.
51. Nash, A. 'The size of open field strips: a reinterpretation' [Sussex], *Agricultural HR* 33 (1985), 32-40.
52. Jones, M. 'Woodland origins in a South Yorkshire parish' [Tankersley], *Local Historian* 16/2 (1984), 73-82.
53. Harvey, P.D.A. 'Mapping the village: the historical evidence' [Cuxham, Oxon.; Boarstall, Bucks.], Bc10, 33-45.
54. Aston, M.A. 'Rural settlement in Somerset: some preliminary thoughts', Bc10, 80-100.
55. Bond, C.J. 'Medieval Oxfordshire villages and their topography: a preliminary discussion', Bc10, 101-23.
56. Hooke, D. 'Village development in the West Midlands', Bc10, 125-54.
57. Atkin, M.A. 'Some settlement patterns in Lancashire', Bc10, 170-85.
58. Hurst, J.G. 'The Wharram research project: problem orientation and strategy 1950-1990', Bc10, 200-04.

59. Rahtz, P.A. 'Wharram Percy research strategies', Bc10, 205-13.
60. Rudden, B. *The New River: a legal history*. Oxford; Clarendon; 1985. Ppxiii, 335.
61. Saville, A. (ed.). *Archaeology in Gloucestershire: from the earliest hunters to the industrial age: essays dedicated to Helen O'Neil and the late Elsie Clifford*. Cheltenham; Cheltenham Art Gallery & Museums/Bristol & Gloucs. Arch. Soc.; 1984. Pp352.
62. Reid, L.; Goulder, M. *The Links Pottery, Kirkcaldy: a brief history 1714 to 1928*. Kirkcaldy; Fife Local Studies Workshop; 1984. Pp32.
63. Briscall, W.R. 'The Ashford Cage', *Archaeologia Cantiana* 101 (1985 for 1984), 57-68.
64. Langridge, A.M. 'The population of Chartham from 1086 to 1600', ibid. 217-44.
65. Harris, T.M. 'Government and urban development in Kent: the case of the Royal Naval dockyard town of Sheerness', ibid. 245-76.
66. Colvin, H. 'Beaudesert, Staffordshire', *T. Ancient Monuments Soc.* new ser. 29 (1985), 107-23.
67. Baker, T.F.T. (ed.). *A history of the county of Middlesex: vol. VIII: Islington and Stoke Newington parishes*. Oxford UP for Inst. Hist. Res. (Victoria County History); 1985. Ppxx, 246.
68. Davies, I.W.; Elrington, C.R. *The Middlesex Victoria County History Council 1955-1984: an account of its work and a guide to the contents of the Middlesex history*. London; Inst. Hist. Res.; 1984. Pp29.
69. Dunning, R.W. (ed.). *A history of the county of Somerset: vol. V*. Oxford UP for Inst. Hist. Res. (Victoria County History); 1985. Ppxix, 225.
70. Keeling, S.M.; Lewis, C.P. (eds.). *A history of the county of Sussex: Index to vols. I-IV, VII and IX*. Oxford UP for Inst. Hist. Res. (Victoria County History); 1984. Ppiv, 144.
71. Cleere, H.; Crossley, D. et al. *The iron industry of the Weald*. Leicester UP; 1985. Ppxvi, 395.
72. Crouch, K.R. *Excavations in Staines: 1975-76: the Friends' burial ground*. London; London & Middlesex Arch. Soc.; 1984. Pp135.
73. Rogerson, A.; Dallas, C. et al. *Excavations in Thetford 1948-59 and 1973-80*. Dereham; Norfolk Arch. Unit; 1984. Ppxii, 208.
74. Hilton, J.A. (ed.). *Catholic Englishman: essays presented to the Rt. Rev. Brian Charles Foley, Bishop of Lancaster*. Wigan; North West Catholic Hist. Soc.; 1984. Pp59.
75. Martins, S.W. *A history of Norfolk*. Chichester; Phillimore; 1984. Pp128.
76. Eedle, M. de G. *A history of Beaminster*. Chichester; Phillimore; 1984. Ppxiii, 227.
77. Standfield, F.G. *A history of East Meon*. Chichester; Phillimore; 1984. Pp148.
78. Rook, T. *A history of Hertfordshire*. Chichester; Phillimore; 1984. Pp 128.
79. Hawker, A. *The story of Basingstoke*. Newbury; Local Heritage; 1984. Pp87.
80. Bond, M. *The story of Windsor*. Newbury; Local Heritage; 1984. Pp 174.

81. Hillier, K. *The book of Ashby-de-la-Zouch.* Buckingham; Barracuda; 1984. Pp 148.

82. Clarke, J. *The book of Buckingham.* Buckingham; Barracuda; 1984. Pp 176.

83. Farrar, H. *The Book of Hurst: the story of Hurst and the surrounding villages ...* Buckingham; Barracuda; 1984. Pp 152.

84. Davies, J.C. *The book of Market Harborough.* Buckingham; Barracuda; 1984. Pp 128.

85. Busson, C. *The book of Ramsgate.* Buckingham; Barracuda; 1985. Pp 148.

86. Boswell, J. *The book of Shenley.* Buckingham; Barracuda; 1985. Pp 116.

87. Williamson, P. *Yesterday's town: Stafford.* Buckingham; Barracuda; 1984. Pp 116.

88. Sparrow, V. *Remember Stortford: the people and places of the past.* Buckingham; Barracuda; 1985. Pp 112.

89. Parkinson, M. 'The Axe estuary and its marshes', *Devonshire Association Report & T.* 117 (1985), 19-62.

90. Keith, A. *Eminent Aberdonians.* Aberdeen; Aberdeen Chamber of Commerce; 1984. Pp ix, 186.

91. Blackman, M.E. 'The Drake Family of Esher and Walton-on-Thames', *Surrey Arch. Collections* 76 (1985), 89-99.

92. Wakeford, J. 'The royal portraits formerly at Kingston upon Thames', ibid. 109-13.

93. Stell, C.F. 'Calderdale Chapels', *Halifax Antiquarian Soc. T.* (1985 for 1984), 16-35.

94. Bettley, J. 'Post voluptatem misericordia: the rise and fall of the London Lock Hospitals', *London J.* 10 (1984), 167-75.

95. Sellers, I. 'A new town story: the United Reformed Churches in the Warrington-Runcorn urban complex', *J. of the United Reformed Church Hist. Soc.* 3 (1985), 290-307.

96. Ponsford, C.N. *Devon clocks and clockmakers.* Newton Abbot; David & Charles; 1985. Pp 360.

97. Dowler, G. *Gloucestershire clock and watch makers.* Chichester; Phillimore; 1984. Pp xxii, 230.

98. Brooke, C. *A history of Gonville and Caius College.* Woodbridge; Boydell; 1985. Pp viii, 354.

99. Ollerenshaw, N. *A history of the Prebendal School.* Chichester; Phillimore; 1984. Pp xviii, 88.

100. Hornby, F.W.D.; Griffin, P.K. *Katherine, Lady Berkeley's School, Wotton-under-Edge, Gloucestershire.* Wotton-under-Edge; the School; 1984. Pp viii, 236.

101. *Hampshire treasures survey: vol. 9: Test Valley South.* Winchester; Hampshire County Council; 1984. Pp v, 167.

102. Hughes, M. *Man and the landscape.* Winchester; Hampshire County Council; 1984. Pp 41.

103. Beachcroft, T.O.; Emms, W.B. *Five hide village: a history of Datchworth in Hertfordshire.* Datchworth; the Parish Council; 1984. Pp x, 251.

104. Allen, P. *The old galleries of Cumbria: and the early wool trade.* Kendal; Abbot Hall Art Gallery; 1984. Pp 56.

Bb105

105. McIntosh, K.H.; Gough, H.E. (eds.). *Hoath and Herne: the last of the forest.* Canterbury; K.H. McIntosh; 1984. Pp 184.
106. Pam, D.O. *The story of Enfield Chase.* Enfield; Enfield Preservation Society; 1984. Pp 168.
107. Brown, M.B. *Richmond Park: the history of a royal deer park.* London; Hale; 1985. Pp 208.
108. Coxhead, J.R.W. *Honiton: a history of the manor and the borough.* Exeter; Devon Books; 1984. Pp 96.
109. Wells, R.A. *Freemasonry in London from 1785.* London; Lewis Masonic; 1984. Pp x, 165.
110. Cooper, F. *Chevington: a social chronicle of a Suffolk village.* Chichester; Phillimore; 1984. Pp xvi, 148.
111. Dix, F.L. *Royal river highway: a history of the passenger boats and services on the River Thames.* Newton Abbot; David & Charles; 1985. Pp 320.
112. Butt, J.; Gordon, G. (eds.) *Strathclyde: changing horizons.* Edinburgh; Scottish Academic; 1985. Pp x, 294.
113. Holland, A.J. *Buckler's Hard: a rural shipbuilding centre.* Emsworth; Mason; 1985. Pp 233.
114. Jones, R.M.; Rees, D.B. *The Liverpool Welsh and their religion: two centuries of Welsh Calvinistic Methodism.* Liverpool; Modern Welsh Publications; 1984. Pp 119.
115. Yately History Project. *Yateley: a parish through six centuries.* Yateley: W.E.A. Yateley branch; 1984. Pp 65.
116. Barker, J. *Christchurch barracks.* Bournemouth; Bournemouth Local Studies; 1984, Pp 26.
117. Shepard, B. *Newport Isle of Wight remembered.* Newport; Isle of Wight Natural History & Arch. Soc.; 1984. Pp x, 189.
118. Coppock, H.C. *Over the hills to Cherry Hinton: a local history.* Cambridge; the author; 1984. Pp vii, 123.
119. Woodward, S. *The landscape of a Leicestershire parish: the historical development of Groby.* Leicester; Leics. Museums Service; 1984. Pp 42.
120. Bagley, J.J.; Hodgkiss, A.G. *Lancashire: a history of the County Palatine in early maps.* Manchester; Neil Richardson; 1985. Pp 83.
121. Paine, C. (ed.). *Hartest: a village history.* Hartest; Hartest Local History Group; 1984. Pp x, 158.
122. Spicer, C.M. *Tyme out of mind: the story of Shephall near Stevenage in Hertfordshire.* Stevenage; the author; 1984. Pp 102.
123. Payne, M. *Crowborough: the growth of a Wealden town.* Studley; K.A.J. Brewin; 1985. Pp xvi, 140.
124. Arthur, J. (ed.). *Medicine in Wisbech and the Fens 1700-1920.* Wisbech; Seagull Enterprises; 1985. Pp 83.
125. Farmer, A. *Hampstead Heath.* New Barret; Historical Publications; 1984. Pp 173.
126. Smith, T.P. *Brick-tiles (mathematical tiles) in the Faversham area.* Faversham; Faversham Society; 1984. Pp v, 38.
127. Curry, I. *Sense and sensitivity: Durham cathedral and its architects.* Durham; Dean & Chapter; 1985. Pp 35.

128. Pocock, D.C.D. *A mining world: the story of Bearpark, County Durham.* Durham; City & University (Dept. of Geography); 1985. Pp 52.
129. Urwin, A.C.B. *The houses and gardens of Twickenham Park, 1227-1805.* London; Borough of Twickenham Local History Society; 1984. Pp 44.
130. McCann, A. (ed.). *Emigrants and transportees from West Sussex 1675-1889* (2nd edn.). Chichester; W. Sussex County Council; 1984. Pp 27.
131. Childerhouse, T. *Bygone Aldershot.* Chichester; Phillimore; 1984. Pp 118.
132. *Ripley and Send then and now: the changing scene of Surrey village life.* Ripley; Send & Ripley Hist. Soc.; 1984. Pp 96.
133. Ludgate, E.M. *Clavering and Langley 1783-1983.* Clavering; the author; 1984. Pp 81.
134. Ekberg, C. *Grimsby Fish: the story of the port and the decline and fall of the deep water industry.* Buckingham; Barracuda; 1984. Pp 160.
135. Horton Local History Group. *Horton-in-Ribblesdale: the story of an upland parish.* Settle; North Craven Heritage Trust; 1984. Pp iv, 62.
136. Colyer, R.J. 'Early agricultural societies in south Wales', *Welsh HR* 12 (1985), 567-81.
137. Elis-Williams, M. *Packet to Ireland: Porthdinllaen's challenge to Holyhead.* Caernarfon; Gwynedd Archives Service; 1984. Pp 147.
138. Gomme, A. 'The building of Hawkstone Hall [Shropshire]: a reconsideration of the evidence', *Arch. J.* 141 (1985 for 1984), 309-25.
139. Denny, B. *Kings bishop: the lords spiritual of London.* London; Alderman; 1985. Pp vi, 325.
140. Pickstone, J.V. *Medicine and industrial society: a history of hospital development in Manchester and its region 1725-1946.* Manchester UP; 1985. Pp xi, 369.
141. Bidgood, R. 'Churches and gentry in the Abergwesyr area', *Brycheiniog* 21 (1984-5), 34-51.

(c) *Collective Volumes*

1. Addyman, P.V.; Black, V.E. (eds.). *Archaeological papers from York presented to M.W. Barley.* York; York Archaeological Trust; 1984. Pp xiv, 208.
2. Smith, R.M. (ed.). *Land, kinship and life-cycle.* Cambridge UP; 1985. Pp ix, 665.
3. Beales, D.; Best, G. (eds.). *History, society and the churches: essays in honour of Owen Chadwick.* Cambridge UP; 1985. Pp ix, 335.
4. Biddick, K. (ed.). *Archaeological approaches to medieval Europe.* Kalamazoo, Mich.; Medieval Institute Publications; 1984. Pp ix, 301.
5. Craig, E.M. (ed.). *Marriage and Property.* Aberdeen UP; 1984. Pp ix, 192.
6. Baldwin, M.; Burton, A. *Canals: a new look: studies in honour of Charles Hadfield.* Chichester; Phillimore; 1984. Pp 198.
7. Myers, R.; Harris, M. (eds.). *Maps and Prints: aspects of the English booktrade.* Oxford; Oxford Polytechnic Press; 1984. Pp xiii, 124.
8. Fenton, A.; Stell, G. (eds.). *Loads and roads in Scotland and beyond:*

land transport over 6000 years. Edinburgh; John Donald; 1984. Ppvii, 144.

9. Walsh, K.; Wood, D. (eds.). *The Bible in the medieval world: essays in memory of Beryl Smalley.* Oxford; Blackwell (Studies in Church History: Subsidia 4); 1985. Ppxiii, 338.

10. Hooke, D. (ed.). *Medieval villages: a review of current work.* Oxford; Oxford University Committee for Archaeology; 1985. Ppv, 223.

11. Stephens, W.B. (ed.). *Studies in the history of literacy: England and North America.* Leeds; the University; 1983. Ppv, 106.

12. Prest, W.R. (ed.). *Lawyers in early modern Europe and America.* London; Croom Helm; 1981. Pp216.

13. Mayr-Harting, H.; Moore, R.I. (eds.). *Studies in medieval history presented to R.H.C. Davis.* London; Hambledon Press; 1985. Ppxviii, 313.

14. Sheils, W.J. (ed.). *Monks, hermits and the ascetic tradition.* Oxford; Blackwell (Studies in Church History 22); 1985. Ppxiii, 460.

15. Barron, C.M.; Harper-Bill, C. (eds.). *The Church in pre-Reformation society: essays in honour of F.R.H. du Boulay.* Woodbridge; Boydell; 1985. Pp232.

16. Brown, R.A. (ed.). *Anglo-Norman Studies VII.* Woodbridge; Boydell (P. of the Battle Conference 1984); 1985. Ppviii, 245.

(d) *Genealogy and Heraldry*

1. *Index to Cornish probate records 1600-1649: Pt. 1: Surnames A-D.* Truro; Cornwall County & Diocesan Record Office; 1984. Pp74.

2. Wilshere, J. (ed.). *Braunstone parish registers transcripts 1561-1837.* Leicester; Leicester Research Section of Chamberlain Music & Books; 1984. Ppxi, 39.

3. *The Birmingham and Midland Society for Genealogy and Heraldry, 1963-1984.* Birmingham; The Society; n.d. Pp22.

4. Camp, A.J. *An index to the wills proved in the Prerogative Court of Canterbury 1750-1800: vol. 3: Ch-G.* London; Society of Genealogists; 1984. Pp378.

5. Neat, C.P. (ed.). *National index of parish registers: a guide to Anglican, Roman Catholic and Nonconformist registers before 1837: Vol. 11, pt. 1: Durham and Northumberland,* 2nd edn. London; Society of Genealogists; 1984. Ppxii, 76.

6. Grimwade, M.E. *Index of the probate records of the court of the Archdeacon of Sudbury 1354-1700.* Keele; British Record Society; 1984. 2 vols.

7. Major, K. *The D'Oyrys of South Lincolnshire, Norfolk, and Holderness 1130-1275.* Lincoln; the author; 1984. Ppviii, 80.

8. Battiscombe, G. *The Spencers of Althorp.* London; Constable; 1984. Pp272.

9. Kauffmann, C.M. 'An early sixteenth-century genealogy of Anglo-Saxon kings', *J. of the Warburg & Courtauld Institutes* 47 (1984), 209-16.

10. Murray, H. 'The city's shield of arms', *York Historian* 5 (1984), 8-17.

11. Spiers, S.M. (ed.). *Monumental inscriptions for Keithall and Kinkell churchyards.* Aberdeen; Aberdeen & N.E. Scotland Family History Soc.; 1984. Pp20.

12. Spiers, S.M. (ed.). *Monumental inscriptions for Rhynie churchyard.* Aberdeen; Aberdeen & N.E. Scotland Family History Soc.; 1984. Pp 37.
13. Peters, J. *A family from Flanders.* London; Collins; 1985. Pp xii, 219.
14. Andrus, F.S. 'The Paget Family', *T. Ancient Monuments Soc.* new ser. 29 (1985), 137-49.
15. Collins, L. *Monumental inscriptions in the Library of the Society of Genealogists: Pt. 1: Southern England.* London; the Society; 1984. Pp viii, 51.
16. Green, D. *The Churchills of Blenheim.* London; Constable; 1984. Pp 256.
17. Spearman, C.R. *The Northern Spearmans: 1: An index to one Spearman Family of Durham and Northumberland.* London; the author; 1984 (?). Pp 40.
18. Spearman, C.R. *A survey of the Irish Spearmans.* London; the author; 1984. Pp 75.
19. Playfair, H. *The Playfair Family.* Yeovil; the author; 1984. Pp 131.
20. Bagley, J.J. *The Earls of Derby 1485-1985.* London; Sidgwick & Jackson; 1985. Pp xi, 257.
21. Dudson, A.M. *Dudson: a family of potters since 1800.* Hanley; Dudson Publications; 1985. Pp xiv, 284.
22. Huxford, J.F. *Honour and arms: the story of some augmentations of honour.* London; Buckland; 1984. Pp 181.
23. Rideout, A. *The Treffry family.* Chichester; Phillimore; 1984. Pp xiii, 177.
24. Pedler, F. *A Pedler family history.* Chichester; Phillimore; 1984. Pp ix, 130.
25. *Registers of St Michael and All Angels, Great Witley, Worcestershire: baptisms 1538-1874: marriages 1538-1835: burials 1538-1849.* Birmingham; Birmingham & Midland Soc. for Genealogy & Heraldry; 1984 (?). Pp ii, 171.
26. Strachey, B. *The Strachey line: an English family in America, in India and at home: 1570 to 1902.* London; Gollancz; 1985. Pp 192.
27. Maule, J.P.; Barnes, P.G.M. *The Maules of Kings Sutton - their origin and descendants.* Edinburgh; J.P. Maule; 1985. Pp 66.

C. ROMAN BRITAIN

(a) *Archaeology*

1. Drury, P.J. 'The temple of Claudius at Colchester reconsidered', *Britannia* 15 (1984), 7-50.
2. Wilson, D.R. 'Defensive outworks of Roman forts in Britain', ibid. 51-61.
3. Braithwaite, G. 'Romano-British face pots and head pots', ibid. 99-131.
4. Richardson, B.; Tyers, P.A. 'North Gaulish pottery in Britain', ibid. 133-41.
5. Rook, T.; Walker, S.; Denston, C.B. 'A Roman mausoleum and associated marble sarcophagus and burials from Welwyn, Hertfordshire', ibid. 143-62.

6. Neal, D.S. 'A sanctuary at Wood Lane End, Hemel Hempstead', ibid. 193-215.
7. Williamson, T.M. 'The Roman countryside: settlement and agriculture in N.W. Essex', ibid. 225-30.
8. Allason-Jones, L. 'A lead shrine from Wallsend', ibid. 231-2.
9. Clay, P. 'A cheek-piece from a cavalry helmet found in Leicester', ibid. 235-8.
10. Corbishley, M. 'A Roman graffito from Essex', ibid. 238-9.
11. Henig, M. 'Amber amulets', ibid. 244-6.
12. Henig, M.; Taylor, J.W. 'A gold votive plaque', ibid. 246.
13. Frere, S.S. 'Roman Britain in 1983: 1. sites explored', ibid. 266-332.
14. Rodwell, K.A. 'The excavation of a Romano-British pottery kiln at Palmer's School, Grays, Essex', T. of the Essex Arch. Soc. 15 (1984 for 1983), 11-35.
15. Eddy, M.R. 'Excavations on the Braintree earthworks, 1976 and 1979', ibid. 36-53.
16. Priddy, D. (ed.). 'Work of Essex County Council Archaeology Section 1982', ibid. 119-55.
17. Priddy, D. (ed.). 'Excavations in Essex 1982', ibid. 163-72.
18. Rees, S.E. 'A wooden ard-share from Dundarg, Aberdeenshire, with a note on other wooden plough pieces', P. of the Soc. of Antiquaries of Scotland 113 (1984 for 1983), 457-63.
19. Elliot, J.W. 'Three Roman bells from Newstead', ibid. 638-40.
20. Hinton, M.P. 'Seeds from archaeological excavations: results from Sussex', Sussex Arch. Collections 122 (1984), 23-27.
21. Cartwright, C.R. 'Field survey of Chichester Harbour 1982', ibid. 23-27.
22. Bedwin, O.; Orton, C. 'The excavation of the eastern terminal of the Devil's Ditch (Chichester Dykes), Boxgrove, West Sussex, 1982', ibid. 63-74.
23. Rudling, D. 'A hoard of Roman coins from Combe Hill, East Sussex', ibid. 218-9.
24. Allen, M. 'Plumpton Roman villa, a cursory note', ibid. 219-21.
25. Aldsworth, F.G. 'Romano-British quern fragment from Alfodean, Slinfold', ibid. 221.
26. Rudling, D. 'A late Roman gold coin from High Hurstwood, East Sussex', ibid. 221.
27. Todd, M. 'Excavations at Hembury (Devon), 1980-83: a summary report', Antiquaries J. 64 (1984), 251-68.
28. Ling, R. 'Two Silchester wall-decorations recovered', ibid. 280-97.
29. Hunn, J.R.; Blagg, T.F.C. 'Architectural fragments from the vicinity of Verulamium', ibid. 362-5.
30. Edwards, B.J.N. 'Roman bone pins from the Cuerdale hoard', ibid. 365-6.
31. Henig, M.; Leahy, K.A. 'A bronze bust from Ludford Magna, Lincs.', ibid. 387-9.
32. Johns, C.; Rigby, V. 'A Christian late Roman gold ring from Suffolk and a warrior figurine recently found near Torksey, Lincolnshire', ibid. 393-5.

33. Barford, P.M.; Blockley, K.; Day, M. 'A Romano-British steelyard from Marshfield, Avon', ibid. 397-8.

34. Boon, G.C. 'A trulleus from Caerleon with a stamp of the First Cavalry Regiment of Thracians', ibid. 403-7.

35. Henig, M. 'A bronze key handle from Brampton, Norfolk', ibid. 407-8.

36. Ottaway, P. 'Colonia Eburacensis: a review of recent work', Bc1, 28-33.

37. Sumpter, A. 'Interval towers and the spaces in between', Bc1, 46-50.

38. Buckland, P.C. 'The "Anglian Tower" and the use of Jurassic limestone in York', Bc1, 51-7.

39. Allason-Jones, L.; Miket, R. *The catalogue of small finds from South Shields Roman fort.* Newcastle upon Tyne; Soc. of Antiquaries of Newcastle upon Tyne; 1984. Pp 365.

40. Rawes, B. 'The Romano-British site on the Portway, near Gloucester', *T. of the Bristol & Gloucs. Arch. Soc.* 102 (1985), 23-72.

41. Marshall, A. 'A Romano-Celtic carved stone phallic figure from Guiting Power, Gloucestershire', ibid. 212-5.

42. Trow, S.D. 'A second intaglio from The Ditches site, North Cerney, Gloucestershire', ibid. 221-2.

43. Rawes, B. (ed.) 'Archaeological review no. 8, 1983', ibid. 223-32.

44. Crummy, P. *Excavations at Lion Walk, Balkerne Lane and Middleborough, Colchester, Essex.* (Colchester Archaeological Report 3). London; Council for British Archaeology; 1983. Pp 200.

45. Lebon, C. 'The Roman ford at Iden Green, Benenden', *Archaeologia Cantiana* 101 (1985 for 1984), 69-81.

46. Detsicas, A.P. 'A salt-panning site at Funton Creek', ibid. 165-8.

47. Bennett, P.; Blockley, P.; Bowen, J.; Macpherson-Grant, N.; Rady, J.; Tatton-Brown, T. 'Interim report on work in 1984 by the Canterbury Archaeological Trust', ibid. 277-311.

48. Lloyd-Morgan, G.; Reedie, K. 'A new hand mirror from Kent', ibid. 355-7.

49. Kelly, D.B. 'Archaeological notes from Maidstone Museum', ibid. 363-79.

50. Palmer, S. *Excavation of the Roman and Saxon site at Orpington.* Bromley; the Borough; 1984. Pp 67.

51. Crummy, N. et al. *The Roman small finds from excavations in Colchester, 1971-79.* Colchester; Colchester Archaeological Trust; 1983. Pp viii, 183.

52. Burnett, A.M. *Coin hoards from Roman Britain: Vol. 5.* London; British Museum; 1984. Pp iv, 150.

53. Reece, R. 'The Cotswolds: an essay on some aspects and problems of Roman rural settlement', Bb61, 181-90.

54. Miles, D. 'Romano-British settlement in the Gloucestershire Thames valley', Bb61, 191-211.

55. McWhirr, A. 'The cities and large rural settlements of Roman Gloucestershire', Bb61, 212-22.

56. Jones, G.D.B.; Walker, J. 'Either side of Solway. Towards a minimalist view of Romano-British agricultural settlement in the North West', Ba40, 185-204.

57. Bennett, J.; Scott, E. 'The end of Roman settlement in Northern England', Ba40, 205-32.

58. Maxwell, G. '"Roman" settlement in Scotland', Ba40, 233-61.

(b) *History*

1. Braund, J. 'Observations on Cartimandua', *Britannia* 15 (1984), 1-6.
2. Frere, S.S. 'British urban defences in earthwork', ibid. 63-74.
3. Campbell, D.B. *'Ballistaria* in first to mid-third century Britain: a reappraisal', ibid. 75-84.
4. Burnett, A. 'Clipped siliquae and the end of Roman Britain', ibid. 163-8.
5. Bartholomew, P. 'Fourth-century Saxons', ibid. 169-85.
6. Maxwell, G.S. 'New frontiers: the Roman fort at Doune and its possible significance', ibid. 217-23.
7. Bellhouse, R.L. 'G.D.B. Jones, "The Solway Frontier": interim report 1976-81', *Britannia* xii (1982)', ibid. 232-4.
8. Bennett, J. 'Hadrian and the title *Pater patriae*, ibid. 234-5.
9. Didsbury, P. 'A grey-ware cult sherd from Bielby', ibid. 239-40.
10. Fulford, M.G.; Startin, D.W.A. 'The building of town defences in earthwork in the second century A.D.', ibid. 240-2.
11. Hassall, M. 'The date of the rebuilding of Hadrian's turf wall in stone', ibid. 242-4.
12. Jackson, R. 'A Roman stamped shield-boss from London', ibid. 246-50.
13. Sealey, P.R.; Davies, G.M.R. 'Falernian wine at Colchester', ibid. 250-4.
14. Todd, M. 'The early Roman phase at Maiden Castle', ibid. 254-5.
15. Waddelove, A.C. and E. 'The location of Bovium', ibid. 255-7.
16. Wright, R.P. 'Proposed expansion for the iron die found in, or before, 1889, in the City of London', ibid. 257-8.
17. Wright, R.P. 'The problem of the nature of the pliable material to be impressed by leaden dies citing centurions in Roman Britain, in particular at Caerleon (Isca)', ibid. 259-60.
18. Green, C.S. 'A late Roman buckle from Dorchester', ibid. 260-4.
19. Hassall, M.W.C.; Tomlin, R.S.O. 'Roman Britain in 1983: II. Inscriptions', ibid. 333-49.
20. Hind, J.G.F. 'Caledonia and its occupation under the Flavians', *P. of the Soc. of Antiquaries of Scotland* 113 (1984 for 1983), 373-8.
21. Maxwell, G.S. 'Two inscribed Roman stones and architectural fragments from Scotland', ibid. 379-90.
22. Keppie, L.J.F. 'Roman inscriptions from Scotland: some additions and corrections to *RIB* I', ibid. 391-404.
23. Robertson, A.S. 'Roman coins found in Scotland, 1971-1982', ibid. 405-48.
24. Simco, A. *The Roman period*. Bedford; Bedfordshire County Council; 1984. Pp 128.
25. Grew, F.; Hobley, B. (eds). *Roman urban topography in Britain and the western Empire: proceedings of the third conference on urban archaeology organized jointly by the CBA and the Department of Urban Archaeology of the Museum of London.* London; Council for British Archaeology; 1985. Pp xvi, 120.

26. Wacher, J.S. 'The functions of urban buildings: some problems', ibid. 41-2.
27. Salway, P. 'Geography and the growth of towns, with special reference to Britain', ibid. 67-73.
28. Esmonde Cleary, S. 'The quick and the dead: suburbs, cemeteries and the town', ibid. 74-7.
29. Crummy, P. 'Colchester: the mechanics of laying out a town', ibid. 78-85.
30. Jones, M.J. 'New streets for old: the topography of Roman Lincoln', ibid. 86-93.
31. Perring, D. 'London in the 1st and early 2nd centuries', ibid. 94-8.
32. Marsden, P. 'London in the 3rd and 4th centuries', ibid. 99-108.
33. Barker, P. 'Aspects of the topography of Wroxeter (Virconium Cornoviorum)', ibid. 109-17.
34. Brinklow, D.A. 'Roman settlement around the legionary Fortress at York', Bc1, 22-7.
35. Jones, R.F.J. 'The cemeteries of Roman York', Bc1, 34-42.
36. Ramm, H.G. 'The Duel Cross milestone and Roman roads west of York', Bc1, 43-5.
37. Thompson, E.A. *Saint Germanus of Auxerre and the end of Roman Britain.* Woodbridge; Boydell & Brewer; 1984. Pp 160.
38. Crickmore, J. *Romano-British urban defences.* Oxford; B.A.R.; 1984 (B.A.R. British ser. 126). Pp 205.
39. Crickmore, J. *Romano-British urban settlements in the West Midlands.* Oxford; B.A.R.; 1984. (B.A.R. British ser. 127). Pp 137.
40. Swan, V.G. *The pottery kilns of Roman Britain.* London; H.M.S.O.; 1984. Pp x, 179.
41. Sommer, C.S. *The military vici in Roman Britain: aspects of their origins, their location and layout, administration, function and end.* Oxford; B.A.R.; 1984. (B.A.R. British ser. 129). Pp ix, 127.
42. Henig, M. 'Graeco-Roman art and Roman-British imagination', *J. of the British Arch. Association* 138 (1985), 1-22.
43. Hind, J.G.F. 'Summers and winters in Tacitus' account of Agricola's campaigns in Britain', *Northern History* 21 (1985), 1-18.

D. ENGLAND 450-1066

See also Bd9; Ca38, 47, 49, 50, b37; Ea18-26, e22, 23, 26; k12.

(a) *General*

1. Palliser, D.M. 'York's west bank: medieval suburb or urban nucleus?', Bc1, 101-08.
2. Lund, N. (ed.). *Two voyagers at the court of King Alfred: the ventures of*

Ohthere and Wulfstan together with the description of Northern Europe from the Old English Orosius. York; William Sessions; 1984. Pp 71.

3. Haslam, J. *Early Medieval Towns in Britain.* Princes Risborough; Shire; 1985. Pp 64.
4. Hunter Blair, P. *Anglo-Saxon Northumbria.* London; Variorum Reprints; 1984. Pp 340.
5. Reynolds, S. 'What do we mean by "Anglo-Saxon" and "Anglo-Saxons"?', *J. of British Studies* 24 (1985), 395-414.
6. Wood, I. 'The end of Roman Britain: Continental evidence and parallels', De3, 1-26.
7. Dumville, D.N. 'Gildas and Maelgwn: problems of dating', De3, 51-60.
8. Dumville, D.N. 'The chronology of De Excidio Britanniae, Book I', De3, 61-84.
9. Dumville, D.N. 'Gildas and Uinnian', De3, 207-14.
10. Schaffner, P. 'Britain's iudices', De3, 151-6.
11. Muir, R. *The National Trust guide to dark age and medieval Britain 400-1350.* London; George Philip & National Trust; 1985. Pp 256.

(b) *Politics and Institutions*

1. Keynes, S. 'Reading history: Anglo-Saxon kingship', *History Today* 35 (1985), 38-43.
2. Lehman, W.W. 'The first English law', *J. of Legal History* 6 (1985), 1-32.
3. Keynes, S. 'The Crowland psalter and the sons of King Edmund Ironside', *Bodleian Library Record* 11 (1985), 359-70.
4. Fleming, R. 'Monastic lands and England's defence in the Viking age', *English H R* 100 (1985), 247-65.
5. Rosenthal, J.T. 'A historiographical survey: Anglo-Saxon kings and kingship since World War II', *J. of British Studies* 24 (1985), 72-93.
6. Chaplais, P. 'The royal Anglo-Saxon "chancery" of the tenth century revisited', Bc13, 41-51.
7. Abels, R. 'Bookland and fyrd service in late Saxon England', Bc16, 1-25.
8. Hooper, N. 'The housecarls in England in the eleventh century', Bc16, 161-76.

(c) *Religion*

1. Gransden, A. 'The legends and traditions concerning the origins of the Abbey of Bury St Edmunds', *English H R* 100 (1985), 1-24.
2. Tudor, V. 'The misogyny of Saint Cuthbert', *Archaeologia Aeliana* 5th ser. 12 (1984), 157-67.
3. Meaney, A.L. 'Aelfric and idolatry', *J. of Religious History* 13 (1984), 119-35.
4. McClure, J. 'Bede's *Notes on Genesis* and the training of the Anglo-Saxon clergy', Bc9, 17-30.

5. Meaney, A.L. 'Bede and Anglo-Saxon paganism', *Parergon* new ser. 3 (1985), 1-29.
6. Thacker, A. 'Kings, saints and monasteries in pre-Viking Mercia', *Midland History* 10 (1985), 1-25.
7. Witney, K.P. 'The Kentish royal saints: an enquiry into the facts behind the legends', *Archaeologia Cantiana* 101 (1985 for 1984), 1-22.
8. Parker, M.S. 'An Anglo-Saxon monastery in the lower Don valley' ['Donemutha'], *Northern History* 21 (1985), 19-32.
9. Sharpe, R. 'Gildas as a Father of the Church', De3, 191-206.
10. Gneuss, H. 'Liturgical books in Anglo-Saxon England and their Old English terminology', De10, 91-142.
11. Rankin, S. 'The liturgical background of the Old English Advent lyrics: a reappraisal', De10, 317-40.
12. Gatch, M.McC. 'The Office in late Anglo-Saxon monasticism', De10, 341-62.
13. Not used.

14. Not used.

15. Franklin, M.J. 'The identification of minsters in the Midlands', Bc16, 69-88.

(d) *Economic Affairs and Numismatics*

1. Blunt, C.E. 'The composition of the Cuerdale hoard', *British Numismatic J.* 53 (1984 for 1983), 1-6.
2. Gilmore, G.R.; Metcalf, D.M. 'Consistency in the alloy of the Northumbrian stycas: evidence from die-linked specimens', *Numismatic Chronicle* 144 (1984), 192-8.
3. Nightingale, P. 'The ora, the mark and the mancus: weight standards and the coinage in eleventh-century England (part 2)', ibid. 234-48.
4. Robinson, P. 'The Shrewsbury hoard (1936) of pennies of Edward the Elder', *British Numismatic J.* 53 (1984 for 1983), 7-13.
5. Robinson, P. 'Saxon coins of Edward the Elder from St. Mary's churchyard, Amesbury', *Numismatic Chronicle* 144 (1984), 198-201.
6. Nightingale, P. 'The evolution of weight standards and the creation of new monetary and commercial links in Northern Europe from the tenth century to the twelfth century', *Economic H R* 2nd ser. 38 (1985), 192-209.
7. Freeman, A. *The moneyer and the mint in the reign of Edward the Confessor 1042-1066.* Oxford; B.A.R. (British ser. 145, 2 pts.); 1985. Pp xvii, 582.

(e) *Intellectual and Cultural*

1. Page, R.I. 'On the transliteration of English runes', *Medieval Archaeology* 28 (1984), 22-45.

2. Budny, M. 'Striking gold: Anglo-Saxon art', *History Today* 35/1 (1985), 44-8.

3. Lapidge, M.; Dumville, D. (eds.). *Gildas: new approaches.* (Studies in Celtic history, 5). Woodbridge; Boydell Press; 1984. P 244.

4. Lapidge, M. 'Gildas's education and the Latin culture of sub-Roman Britain', De3, 27-50.

5. Wright, N. 'Gildas's geographical perspective: some problems', De3, 85-106.

6. Wright, N. 'Gildas's prose style and its origins', De3, 107-28.

7. Orlandi, G. '*Clausulae* in Gildas's *De Excidio Britanniae*', De3, 129-50.

8. Sutherland, A.C. 'The imagery of Gildas's *De Excidio Britanniae*', De3, 157-68.

9. Sims-Williams, P. 'Gildas and vernacular poetry', De3, 169-90.

10. Lapidge, M.; Gneuss, H. (eds.). *Learning and literature in Anglo-Saxon England: studies presented to Peter Clemoes on the occasion of his sixty-fifth birthday.* Cambridge UP; 1985. Ppxii, 466.

11. Hunter Blair, P. 'Whitby as a centre of learning in the seventh century', De10, 3-32.

12. Lapidge, M. 'Surviving booklists from Anglo-Saxon England', De10, 33-90.

13. Keynes, S. 'King Athelstan's books', De10, 143-201.

14. Sims-Williams, P. 'Thoughts on Ephrem the Syrian in Anglo-Saxon England', De10, 205-26.

15. Cross, J.E. 'On the library of the Old English martyrologist', De10, 227-50.

16. Korhammer, M. 'The orientation system in the Old English Orosius: shifted or not?', De10, 251-70.

17. Godden, M.R. 'Anglo-Saxons on the mind', De10, 271-98.

18. Scragg, D.G. 'The homilies of the Blickling manuscript', De10, 299-316.

19. Stanley, E.G. '*The Judgement of the Damned* (from Cambridge, Corpus Christi College 201 and other manuscripts), and the definition of Old English verse', De10, 363-92.

20. Greenfield, S.B. 'Beowulf and the judgement of the righteous', De10, 393-408.

21. Bately, J. 'Linguistic evidence as a guide to the authorship of Old English verse: a reappraisal, with special reference to *Beowulf*', De10, 409-31.

22. Clark, C. 'British Library Additional MS. 40,000 ff. 1v-12r', Bc16, 50-68.

23. Kiff, J. 'Images of war: illustrations of warfare in early eleventh-century England', Bc16, 177-94.

(f) *Society and Archaeology*

1. Gardiner, M. 'Saxon settlement and land division in the western Weald', *Sussex Arch. Collections* 122 (1984), 75-83.

2. Pritchard, F.A. 'Late Saxon textiles from the city of London', *Medieval Archaeology* 28 (1984), 46-76.

3. Goodier, A. 'The formation of boundaries in Anglo-Saxon England: a statistical study', ibid. 1-21.
4. Rodwell, W.; Rouse, E.C. 'The Anglo-Saxon rood and other features in the south porch of St Mary's church, Breamore, Hampshire', *Antiquaries J.* 64 (1984), 298-325.
5. Mack, K. 'Changing thegns: Cnut's conquest and the English aristocracy', *Albion* 16 (1984), 375-87.
6. Biddick, K. 'Field edge, forest edge: early medieval social change and resource allocation', Bc4, 105-18.
7. Crabtree, P. 'The archaeozoology of the Anglo-Saxon site at West Stow, Suffolk', Bc4, 223-35.
8. Brooks, C.; Mainman, A. 'Torksey ware viewed from the North', Bc1, 63-70.
9. Hall, R.A. 'A late pre-Conquest urban building tradition [Coppergate, York]', Bc1, 71-77.
10. Spriggs, J.A. 'Treating the Coppergate [York] structures — a quest for anti-shrink efficiency', Bc1, 78-83.
11. Tweddle, D. 'A fragment of Anglian metalwork from Blake Street [York]', Bc1, 58-62.
12. Thomas, A.C.; Fowler, P.J. 'Tintagel: a new survey of the "Island"', *Royal Commission on the Historical Monuments of England Annual Review 1984-85*, 16-22.
13. Fell, C. *Women in Anglo-Saxon England*. London; British Museum; 1984. Pp 208.
14. Wilson, D.M. *Anglo-Saxon art: from the seventh century to the Norman Conquest*. London; Thames & Hudson; 1984. Pp 224.
15. Not used.
16. Hines, J. *The Scandinavian Character of Anglian England in the pre-Viking period*. Oxford; B.A.R. (British ser. 124); 1984. Pp viii, 426.
17. Not used.
18. Hartley, R.F. *The medieval earthworks of North West Leicestershire*. Leicester; Leics. Museums, Art Galleries & Records Service; 1984. Pp 67.
19. Bassett, S. 'Beyond the edge of excavation: the topographical context of Goltho', Bc13, 21-39.
20. Adkins, R.A.; Petchey, M.R. 'Secklow Hundred mound and other meeting place mounds in England', *Arch. J.* 141 (1985 for 1984), 243-51.
21. James, S.; Marshall, A.; Millett, M. 'An early medieval building tradition', ibid. 182-215.
22. Hayfield, C. *Humberside medieval pottery: an illustrated catalogue of Saxon and medieval domestic assemblages from north Lincolnshire and its surrounding region*. Oxford; B.A.R. (British ser. 140, 2 pts.); 1985. Pp xi, 730.
23. Heighway, C. 'Anglo-Saxon Gloucestershire', Bb61, 225-47.
24. Vince, A.G. 'Late Saxon and medieval pottery in Gloucestershire', Bb61, 248-75.
25. Aston, M.; Viner, L. 'The study of deserted villages in Gloucestershire', Bb61, 276-93.

26. Leech, R. 'Medieval urban archaeology in Gloucestershire', Bb61, 294-303.
27. Hedges, J.D.; Buckley, D.G. 'Anglo-Saxon and later features excavated at Orsett, Essex, 1975', *Medieval Archaeology* 29 (1985), 1-24.
28. Vince, A.G. 'The Saxon and medieval pottery of London: a review', ibid. 25-93.
29. Cramp, R. 'Anglo-Saxon settlement', Ba40, 263-97.

E. ENGLAND 1066-1500

See also Ca47, 49; Da1, 3, 11, c2, f18, 19, 22-26; Fc23; Kb4.

(a) *General*

1. Chibnall, M. *The World of Orderic Vitalis.* Oxford; Clarendon; 1984. Pp viii, 255.
2. Morris, J. (ed.). *Domesday Book; vol. 33: Norfolk* (ed. P. Brown). Chichester; Phillimore; 1984. 2 vols.; unpaginated.
3. Cook, D.R. *Lancastrians and Yorkists: the Wars of the Roses.* London; Longman; 1984. Pp v, 114.
4. Platt, C. *Medieval Britain from the Air.* London; George Philip; 1984. Pp 239.
5. Williams, G. *Harri Tudur a Chymru* [Henry Tudor and Wales]. Cardiff; University of Wales Press; 1985. Pp 111.
6. Alexander, J.W. 'A historiographical survey: Norman and Plantagenet kings since World War II', *J. of British Studies* 24 (1985), 94-109.
7. Le Patourel, J. *Feudal empires: Norman and Plantagenet.* London; Hambledon Press; 1984. Pp various.
8. Kelly, H.A. 'The last chroniclers of Croyland', *The Ricardian* 7/91 (1985), 142-77.
9. De Cossart, M. *This sceptred isle: Renaissance Italians' view of English institutions.* Liverpool; Janus; 1984. Pp 124.
10. Greenway, D.; Holdsworth, C.; Sayers, J. (eds.). *Tradition and change: essays in honour of Marjorie Chibnall presented by her friends on the occasion of her seventieth birthday.* Cambridge UP; 1985. Pp xvi, 269.
11. Hanham, A. *The Celys and their world: an English merchant family of the fifteenth century.* Cambridge UP; 1985. Pp xv, 472.
12. Vaughan, R. (ed.). *Chronicles of Matthew Paris: monastic life in the thirteenth century.* Gloucester; Alan Sutton; 1984. Pp 286.
13. Krause, H. *Radulfus Niger - Chronica. Eine englische Weltchronik des 12. Jahrhunderts* [An English universal chronicle of the 12th century]. Frankfurt; Peter Lang; 1985. Pp 652.
14. Stokes, G. 'Edward I's links with Wessex and Peking', *Hatcher R.* 2/20(1985), 451-5.

15. Jones, M.; Underwood, M. 'Lady Margaret Beaufort', *History Today* 35/8 (1985), 23-30.
16. Holt, R. 'Thomas of Woodstock and events at Gloucester in 1381', *Bull. Inst. Hist. Res.* 58 (1985), 237-42.
17. Steane, J. *The archaeology of medieval England and Wales*. London; Croom Helm; 1985. Pp xvi, 302.
18. Sawyer, P. (ed.). *Domesday Book: a reassessment*. London; Edward Arnold; 1985. Pp x, 182.
19. Sawyer, P. 'Domesday studies since 1886', Ea18, 1-4.
20. Rumble, A.R. 'The palaeography of the Domesday manuscripts', Ea18, 28-49.
21. Clarke, H.B. 'The Domesday satellites', Ea18, 50-70.
22. Sawyer, P.H. '1066-1086: a tenurial revolution?', Ea18, 71-85.
23. Harvey, S.P.J. 'Taxation and the ploughland in Domesday Book', Ea18, 86-103.
24. Blair, J. 'Secular minster churches in Domesday Book', Ea18, 104-42.
25. Martin, G.H. 'Domesday Book and the boroughs', Ea18, 143-63.
26. Palmer, J. 'Domesday Book and the computer', Ea18, 164-74.
27. Lewis, C. 'The Norman settlement of Herefordshire under William I', Bc16, 195-213.
28. De Bouard, M. *Guillaume le Conquérant*. Paris; Fayard; 1984. Pp 479.

(b) *Politics*

1. Given-Wilson, C.; Curteis, A. *The royal bastards of medieval England*. London; Routledge; 1984. Pp xii, 195.
2. Carpenter, D.A. 'Kings, magnates, and society: the personal rule of King Henry III, 1234-1258', *Speculum* 60 (1985), 39-70.
3. Jespersen, K.J.V. 'Den engelske opstand 1381; fortolkning og dokumentation [The English rising of 1381; interpretation and documentation]', *Historisk Tidsskrift* 84 (1984), 177-97.
4. Hammond, P.W. 'The Funeral of Richard Neville, earl of Salisbury', *The Ricardian* 6 (1984), 410-16.
5. Gillingham, J. 'The art of kingship: Richard I, 1189-99', *History Today* 35/4 (1985), 17-23.
6. Prestwich, M. 'The art of kingship: Edward I, 1272-1307', ibid. 35/5 (1985), 34-40.
7. Harriss, G.L. (ed.). *Henry V: the practice of kingship*. Oxford UP; 1985. Pp xii, 222.
8. Harriss, G.L. 'Introduction: the exemplar of kingship', Eb7, 1-29.
9. Harriss, G.L. 'The king and his magnates', Eb7, 31-51.
10. Hampton, W.E. 'John Hoton of Hunwick and Tudhoe', *The Ricardian* 7 (1985), 2-17.
11. Carpenter, D.A. 'Simon de Montfort and the Mise of Lewes', *Bull. Inst. Hist. Res.* 58 (1985), 1-11.
12. Prestwich, M. 'The charges against the Despensers, 1321', ibid. 95-100.

13. Barron, C.M. 'The art of kingship: Richard II, 1377-1399', *History Today* 35/6 (1985), 30-7
14. Wylie, J.A.H. 'The Princes in the Tower 1483 — death from natural causes?', *The Ricardian* 7/91 (1985), 178-82.
15. Drewett, R.; Redhead, M. *The trial of Richard III*. Gloucester; Alan Sutton; 1984. Pp xi, 158.
16. Hammond, P.W.; Sutton, A. *Richard III: the road to Bosworth Field*. London; Constable; 1985. Pp 238.
17. King, E. 'Walter, count of Meulan, earl of Worcester (1104-1166)', Ea10, 165-81.
18. Roskell, J.S., *Parliament and politics in late medieval England: vol. 3*. London; Hambledon Press; 1983. Pp 345.
19. Crouch, D. 'Robert, earl of Gloucester, and the daughter of Zelophahad', *J. of Medieval History* 11 (1985), 227-43.
20. Stow, G.B. 'Richard II in Jean Froissart's *Chroniques*', ibid. 333-45.
21. Carpenter, D.A. 'The Lord Edward's oath to aid and counsel Simon de Montfort, 15 October 1259', *Bull. Inst. Hist. Res.* 58 (1985), 226-37.
22. McNiven, P. 'The problem of Henry IV's health, 1405-1413', *English H. R.* 100 (1985), 747-72.

(c) *Constitution, Administration and Law*

1. Powell, E. 'The restoration of law and order', Eb7, 53-74.
2. Catto, J. 'The king's servants', Eb7, 75-95.
3. Harriss, G.L. 'The management of parliament', Eb7, 137-58.
4. Harriss, G.L. 'Financial policy', Eb7, 159-79.
5. Hicks, M. 'Attainder, resumption and coercion 1461-1529', *Parliamentary History*, 3 (1984), 15-31.
6. Prestwich, M. 'An estimate by the Commons of royal revenue under Richard II', ibid. 147-55.
7. Powell, E. 'Settlement of disputes by arbitration in fifteenth-century England', *Law & History Review* 2 (1984), 21-43.
8. Millon, D. '*Circumspecte Agatis* revisited', ibid. 105-27.
9. Rörkasten, J. 'Some problems of the evidence of fourteenth-century approvers', *J. of Legal History* 5/3 (1984), 14-22.
10. Helmholz, R.H. '*Legitim* in English legal history', *University of Illinois Law Review* (1984), 659-74.
11. Herbert, N.M. et al. *The 1483 Gloucester charter in history*. Gloucester; Alan Sutton for Gloucester City Council and Gloucester Civic Trust; 1983. Pp 64.
12. Ainsley, H. 'Keeping the peace in southern England in the thirteenth century'. *Southern History* 6 (1984), 13-35.
13. Thorne, S.E. *Essays in English legal history*. London; Hambledon Press; 1985. Pp vii. 282.
14. Rigby, S.H. 'The customs administration at Boston in the reign of Richard II', *Bull. Inst. Hist. Res.* 58 (1985), 12-24.

15. Crook, D. '"Moothallgate" and the venue of the Nottinghamshire county court in the thirteenth century', *T. of the Thoroton Soc. of Notts.* 88 (1984), 99-102.
16. Bates, D. 'The earliest Norman writs', *English H R* 100 (1985), 266-84.
17. Baker, J.H. 'The English legal profession, 1450-1550', Bc12, 16-41.
18. Hollister, C.W. 'Henry I and the invisible transformation of medieval England', Bc13, 119-31.
19. Clanchy, M.T. 'Magna Carta and the common pleas', Bc13, 219-32
20. Brown, S. *The medieval courts of the York Minster peculiar.* York; University of York: Borthwick Paper 66; 1984. Pp 38.
21. Brown, R.A. 'Some observations on Norman and Anglo-Norman charters', Ea10, 145-63.
22. Cheney, M. 'A decree of King Henry II on defect of justice', Ea10, 183-93.
23. Sayers, J. 'English charters from the third crusade', Ea10, 195-213.
24. Clementi, D. 'Constitutional development through pressure of circumstance, 1179-1258', Ea10, 215-37.
25. Turner, R.V. *The English judiciary in the age of Glanvill and Bracton, c. 1176-1239.* Cambridge UP; 1985. Pp xiv, 321.
26. Burns, J.H. 'Fortescue and the political theory of *dominium*', *Historial J.* 28 (1985), 777-97.
27. Spitzer, A.L. 'The legal careers of Thomas of Weyland and Gilbert of Thornton', *J. of Legal History* 6 (1985), 62-83.
28. Meekings, C.A.F. 'A King's Bench formulary', ibid 86-104.
29. Waugh, S.L. 'Non-alienation clauses in thirteenth-century English charters', *Albion* 17 (1985), 1-14.
30. Stoljar, S. 'Of socage and socmen', *J. of Legal History* 6 (1985), 33-48.
31. Clayton, D.J. 'Peace bonds and the maintenance of law and order in late medieval England: the example of Cheshire', *Bull. Inst. Hist. Res.* 58 (1985), 133-48.
32. Arnold, M.S. *Select cases of trespass from the king's courts 1307-1399, vol I.* London; Selden Soc.; 1985. Pp lxxxv, 179 *(bis)*.
33. McDonald, J.; Snooks, G.D. 'Were the tax assessments of Domesday artificial? The case of Essex'. *Economic H R* 2nd ser. 38 (1985), 352-72.
34. Myers, A.R. *Crown, household and parliament in fifteenth century England,* ed. C.R. Clough; intro. by R.B. Dobson. London; Hambledon; 1985. Pp xix, 394.

(d) *External Affairs*

1. Keen, M. 'Diplomacy', Eb7, 181-99.
2. Goodman, A.; Morgan, D. 'The Yorkist claim to the throne of Castile', *J. of Medieval History* 11 (1985), 61-69.
3. Graboïs, A. 'Anglo-Norman England and the Holy Land', Bc16, 132-41.

Ee1

(e) *Religion*

1. Swanson, R.N. 'Universities, graduates and benefices in later medieval England', *Past & Present* 106 (1895), 28-61.
2. Swanson, R.N. 'Thomas Holme and his chantries', *York Historian* 5 (1984), 3-7.
3. Catto, J. 'Religious change under Henry V', Eb7, 97-115.
4. Bennett, N.H. (ed.). *The register of Richard Fleming, bishop of Lincoln 1420-31, vol. 1.* York; Canterbury & York Society; 1984. Ppviii, 149.
5. Burgess, C. '"For the increase of divine service": chantries in the parish in late medieval Bristol', *J. of Ecclesiastical History* 36 (1985), 46-65.
6. Kaufman, P.I. 'Henry VII and sanctuary', *Church History* 53 (1984), 465-76.
7. Dobson, B. 'Mendicant ideal and practice in late medieval York', Bc1, 109-22.
8. Gee, E. 'The topography of altars, chantries and shrines in York Minster', *Antiquaries J.* 64 (1984), 337-50.
9. Brooke, C.N.L. 'The churches of medieval Cambridge', Bc3, 49 -76.
10. Aston, M. *Lollards and Reformers: Images and Literacy in Late Medieval Religion.* London; Hambledon; 1984. Pp xii, 355.
11. Catto, J.I. 'Wyclif and the cult of the eucharist', Bc9, 269-86.
12. Evans, G.R. 'Wyclif's *Logic* and Wyclif's exegesis: the context', Bc9, 287-300.
13. Hudson, A. 'A Wycliffite scholar of the early fifteenth century', Bc9, 301-15.
14. Storey, R.L. 'A fifteenth century vicar of Laxton', *T. of the Thoroton Soc. of Notts.* 88 (1984), 39-41.
15. Foulds, T. 'Unpublished monastic cartularies of Nottinghamshire: a guide to their contents', ibid. 89-98.
16. Robinson, D. 'Ordination of secular clergy in the diocese of Coventry and Lichfield, 1322-1358', *Archives* 17 (1985), 3-21.
17. Bates, D. 'The building of a great church: the abbey of St Peter's, Gloucester, and its early Norman benefactors', *T. of the Bristol & Gloucs. Arch. Soc.* 102 (1985), 129-32.
18. Tanner, N.P. *The church in late medieval Norwich 1370-1532.* Toronto; Pontifical Institute of Mediaeval Studies; 1984. Pp xviii, 279.
19. Lomax, D.W. 'The first English pilgrims to Santiago de Compostela', Bc13, 165-75.
20. Mayr-Harting, H. 'Functions of a twelfth-century shrine: the miracles of St Frideswide', Bc13, 193-206.
21. Swanson, R.N. 'Titles to orders in medieval English episcopal registers', Bc13, 233-45.
22. Brooke, C. 'The archdeacon and the Norman Conquest', Ea10, 1-19.
23. Foreville, R. 'Canterbury et la canonisation des saints au XIIe siècle', Ea10, 63-75.
24. Greenway, D. 'The false *Institutio* of St Osmund', Ea10, 77-101.
25. Cheney, C. 'Two mortuary rolls from Canterbury: devotional links of

Canterbury with Normandy and the Welsh March', Ea10, 103-14.

26. Luscombe, D. 'The reception of the writings of Denis the pseudo-Areopagite into England', Ea10, 115-43.

27. Hudson, A. *Lollards and their books*. London; Hambledon; 1985. Pp xv, 266.

28. Abulafia, A.S. '*The ars disputandi* of Gilbert Crispin, abbot of Westminster (1085-1117)', in Cappon, C.M. et al. (eds.), *Ad Fontes* (Amsterdam; Verloren; 1984), 139-52.

29. Vaughn, S.N. 'Lanfranc at Bec: a reinterpretation', *Albion* 17 (1985), 135-48.

30. Brooke, C.N.L. 'Monk and canon: some patterns in the religious life of the twelfth century', Bc14, 109-29.

31. Herbert, J. 'The transformation of hermitages into Augustinian priories in twelfth-century England', Bc14, 131-45.

32. Davis, V. 'The rule of St Paul, the first hermit, in late medieval England', Bc14, 203-14.

33. Barron, C.M. 'The parish fraternities of medieval London', Bc15, 13-37.

34. Crawford, A. 'The piety of late medieval English queens', Bc15, 48-57.

35. Dunstan, G.R. 'Jean Gerson: Propositio facta coram Anglicis. A translation', Bc15, 68-81.

36. Hare, J.N. 'The monks as landlords: the leasing of the monastic demesnes in southern England', Bc15, 82-94.

37. Harper-Bill, C. 'The labourer is worthy of his hire? — complaints about diet in late medieval English monasteries', Bc15, 95-107.

38. Harvey, M. 'John Whethamstede, the pope and the general council', Bc15, 108-22.

39. Hicks, M. 'Chantries, obits and almshouses: the Hungerford foundations 1325-1478', Bc15, 123-42.

40. Kettle, A.J. 'City and close: Lichfield in the century before the Reformation', Bc15, 158-69.

41. Logan, F.D. 'Archbishop Thomas Bourgchier revisited', Bc15, 170-88.

42. Rosenthal, J.T. 'Lancastrian bishops and educational benefaction', Bc15, 199-211.

43. Rees, U. (ed.). *The cartulary of Haughmond Abbey*. Cardiff; Univ. of Wales P. for Shropshire Arch. Soc.; Pp x, 294.

44. Southern, R.W. *The monks of Canterbury and the murder of Archbishop Becket*. Canterbury; Friends of Canterbury Cathedral; 1985. Pp 29.

45. Owen, D. 'The importance of the Peterborough manuscripts', *Northants. Past & Present* 7/3 (1985), 139-42.

46. Hare J. 'William the Conqueror and Battle Abbey', *History Today* 35/12 (1985), 33-38.

47. Sinclair, K.V. (ed.). Raymond du Puy, *The Hospitallers' Riwle*. London; Anglo-Norman Text Soc., 1984. Pp xlix, 96.

48. Harper-Bill, C. 'Bishop William Turbe and the diocese of Norwich, 1146-1174', Bc16, 142-60.

49. Swanson, R.N. (ed.). *A calendar of the register of Richard Scrope*,

archbishop of York, 1398-1405: pt. 2. York; Borthwick Inst. Hist. Res.; 1985.
Pp xvii, 160.

(f) *Economic Affairs*

1. Henn, V. '"The Libelle of Englyshe Polycye": Politik und Wirtschaft in England in den 30er Jahren des 15. Jahrhunderts [Policy and economy in England in the 1430s]', *Hansische Geschichtsblätter* 101 (1983), 43-65.
2. Jenks, S. 'Das Schreiberbuch des John Thorpe und der hansische Handel in London 1457/59 [John Thorpe's register and Hanseatic trade in London 1457-9]', ibid. 67-113.
3. Dury, G.H. 'Crop failures on the Winchester manors, 1232-1349', *Institute of British Geographers T.* N.S. 9 (1984), 401-18.
4. White, A.J. 'Medieval fisheries in the Witham and its tributaries', *Lincolnshire History & Archaeology* 19 (1984), 29-35.
5. Michel, P. 'Sir Phillip d'Arcy and the financial plight of the military knight in 13th-century England', ibid. 49-56.
6. Seaby, P.J. 'A new "standard" type for the reign of King Stephen', *British Numismatic J.* 53 (1984 for 1983), 14-18.
7. Gittoes, G.P.,; Mayhew, N.J. 'Short cross sterlings from the Rotenfels hoard', ibid. 19-28.
8. Mitchiner, M.; Skinner, A. 'English tokens, c. 1200 to 1425', ibid. 29-77.
9. Bridbury, A.R. 'Thirteenth-century prices and the money supply'. *Agricultural H R* 33 (1985), 1-21.
10. Mate, M. 'Medieval agrarian practices: the determining factors?', ibid. 22-31.
11. Ivens, R.J. 'Medieval building trades', *Cake & Cockhorse* 9/8 (1985), 222-36.
12. Harvey, J.H. 'Vegetables in the middle ages', *Garden History* 12 (1984), 89-99.
13. Welsford, A.E. *John Greenway: 1460-1529: merchant of Tiverton and London: a Devon worthy.* Tiverton; 14 Twyford Place; 1984. Pp 20.
14. Hall, D. 'Fieldwork and documentary evidence for the layout and organization of early medieval estates in the English Midlands', Bc 4, 43-68.
15. Rackham, O. 'The forest: woodland and wood-pasture in medieval England', Bc4, 69-101.
16. Fox, H.S.A. 'Some ecological dimensions of medieval field systems', Bc4, 119-58.
17. Raban, S. 'The land market and the aristocracy in the thirteenth century', Ea10, 239-61.
18. Rigby, S.H. '"Sore decay" and "fair dwellings": Boston and urban decline in the later middle ages', *Midland History* 10 (1985), 47-61.
19. Nightingale, P. 'The London pepperers' guild and some twelfth-century English trading links with Spain', *Bull. Inst. Hist. Res.* 58 (1985), 123-32.
20. Hilton, R.H. 'Medieval market towns and simple commodity production', *Past & Present* 109 (1985), 3-23.

21. Sherborne, J. *William Canynges 1402-1474*. Bristol; Bristol branch of Historical Association; 1985. Pp 30.
22. Smith, T.P. *The medieval brickmaking industry in England 1400-1450*. Oxford; B.A.R. (British ser. 138); 1985. Pp iv, 143.
23. Blanchard, I. 'The British silver lead industry and its relations with the Continent, 1470-1570', *Der Anschnitt* 2 (1984).

(g) *Social Structure and Population*

1. Twigg, G. *The Black Death; a biological reappraisal*. London; Batsford; 1984. Pp 254.
2. Threlfall, J.B. 'John Fressh, lord mayor of London in 1395' (continued), *Genealogists' Magazine* 21/8 (1984), 577-85; 21/9 (1985), 635-42.
3. Campbell, B.M.S. 'Population pressure, inheritance and the land market in a fourteenth-century peasant community [Coltishall, Norfolk]', Bc2, 87-134.
4. Smith, R.M. 'Families and their land in an area of partible inheritance: Redgrave, Suffolk 1260-1320', Bc2, 135-95.
5. Ravensdale, J. 'Population changes and the transfer of customary land on a Cambridgeshire manor [Cottenham] in the fourteenth century', Bc2, 197-225.
6. Blanchard, I. 'Industrial employment and the rural land market 1380-1520', Bc2, 227-75.
7. Dyer, C. 'Changes in the size of peasant holdings in some west midland villages 1400-1540', Bc2, 277-94.
8. Razi, Z. 'The erosion of the family-land bond in the late fourteenth and fifteenth centuries: a methodological note [Halesowen, Worcs.]', Bc2, 295-304.
9. Dyer, C. 'Changes in the link between families and land in the west midlands in the fourteenth and fifteenth centuries', Bc2, 305-11.
10. Kettle, A.J. '"My wife shall have it": marriage and property in the wills and testaments of later medieval England', Bc5, 89-103.
11. Crook, D. 'The community of Mansfield from Domesday Book to the reign of Edward III', *T. of the Thoroton Soc. of Notts.* 88 (1984), 14-38.
12. Richmond, C. 'The Pastons revisited: marriage and the family in fifteenth-century England', *Bull. Inst. Hist. Res.* 58 (1985), 25-36.
13. Slater, T.R. 'The urban hierarchy in medieval Staffordshire', *J. of Historical Geography* 11 (1985), 115-37.
14. Palliser, D.M. 'A regional capital as magnet: immigrants to York, 1477-1566', *Yorkshire Arch. J.* 57 (1985), 111-23.
15. Sawyer, P.H. 'The Anglo-Norman village', Bc10, 3-6.
16. Dyer, C.C. 'Power and conflict in the medieval English village', Bc10, 27-32.
17. Foulds, T. 'The origins of the Hotot Family', *Northants. Past & Present* 7 (1984-5), 79-81.
18. Williams, D. 'From Towton to Bosworth: the Leicestershire community

and the Wars of the Roses 1461-1485', *Leics. Arch. & Hist. Soc. T.* 59 (1984-5), 27-43.

19. Yates, E.M. *Land and life at the Fen edge: as depicted in the medieval muniments of Methwold, Norfolk*. London; U. London, King's College, Dept. of Geography; 1984. Pp 33.

20. Poos, L.R. 'The rural population of Essex in the later middle ages', *Economic H R* 2nd ser. 38 (1985), 515-30.

21. Whatmore, G. 'Whatmore hamlet and the family of Whatmore', *Shropshire Arch. Soc. T.* 63 (1985 for 1981-2), 17-20.

22. Hilton, R. *Class conflict and the crisis of feudalism: essays in medieval social history*. London; Hambledon; 1985. Pp x, 349.

(h) *Naval and Military*

1. Allmand, C.T. 'Henry V the soldier, and the war in France', Eb7, 117-35.
2. Marples, M.J. 'The battle of Winchester, September 1141', *Hatcher R.* 2/19 (1985), 404-10.
3. Walker, S. 'Profit and loss in the Hundred Years War: the subcontracts of Sir John Strother, 1374', *Bull. Inst. Hist. Res.* 58 (1985), 100-6.
4. De Wailly, H. *Crécy 1346: autopsie d'une bataille*. Paris; Lavauzelle; 1985. Pp 93.
5. Bennett, M. *The battle of Bosworth*. Gloucester; Alan Sutton; 1985. Pp xi, 195.
6. Baldwin, D. 'What happened to Lord Lovel?', *The Ricardian* 7/89 (1985), 56-65.
7. Williams, D. '"A place mete for twoo battayles to encountre": the siting of the battle of Bosworth, 1485', *The Ricardian* 7/90 (1985), 86-96.
8. Hampton, W.E. 'Sir Robert Brakenbury of Selaby, County Durham', ibid. 97-114.
9. Harris, O.D. 'The Bosworth commemoration at Dadlington', ibid. 115-31.
10. Southern, Sir Richard. 'Peter of Blois and the third crusade', Bc13, 207-18.
11. Brooks, N. 'The organization and achievements of the peasants of Kent and Essex in 1381', Bc13, 247-70.
12. White, G. 'Were the Midlands "wasted" during Stephen's reign?', *Midland History* 10 (1985), 26-46.
13. Cornford, B., et al. *Studies towards a history of the rising of 1381 in Norfolk*. Norfolk; Norfolk Research Committee; 1984. Pp 60.
14. Taylor, A.J. *Studies in castles and castle-building*. London; Hambledon Press; 1984. Pp 350.
15. Richmond, C. 'The battle of Bosworth, August 1485', *History Today* 35/8 (1985), 17-22.
16. Lewis, N.B. 'The feudal summons of 1385' [with comment by J.J.N. Palmer], *English H R* 100 (1985), 729-46.
17. Tuck, J.A. 'War and society in the medieval North', *Northern History* 21 (1985), 33-52.

18. Gillmor, C.M. 'Naval logistics of the cross-Channel operation, 1066', Bc16, 105-31.

(i) *Intellectual and Cultural*

1. Camilla, M. 'Seeing and reading: some visual implications of medieval literacy and illiteracy', *Art History* 8 (1985), 26-49.
2. Gill, J.S. 'How Hermes Trismegistus was introduced to Renaissance England: the influences of Caxton's and Ficino's "Argumentum" on Baldwin and Palfreyman', *J. of the Warburg & Courtauld Institutes* 47 (1984), 222-5.
3. Pepin, R.E. 'Master John's hilarity [John of Salisbury and satire]', *Hatcher R.* 2/19 (1985), 399-403.
4. Hieatt, C.B.; Butler, S. (eds.). *Curye on Englysch: English culinary manuscripts of the fifteenth century.* London: Oxford UP for Early English Text Society; 1985. Pp vii, 224.
5. Moran, J.A.H. *The growth of English schooling 1340-1548: learning, literacy and laicization in pre-Reformation York diocese.* Princeton UP; 1985. Pp xx, 326.
6. Wright, N. (ed.). *The Historia Regum Britannie of Geoffrey of Monmouth: vol. 1: Bern, Burgerbibliothek ms. 568.* Cambridge; D.S. Brewer; 1985. Pp lxv, 174.
7. K.Y. Wallace (ed.). *La estoire de seint Aedward le Rei, attributed to Matthew Paris.* London; Anglo-Norman Text Soc.; 1983. Pp 1, 181.
8. Fletcher, J.M.; Upton, C.A. 'Expenses at admission and determination in fifteenth-century Oxford: new evidence', *English H R* 100 (1985), 331-7.
9. Harvey, J.H. 'The First English garden book: Mayster Jon Gardener's treatise and its background', *Garden History* 13/2 (1985), 83-101.
10. Ker, N.R. *Books, collectors and libraries.* London; Hambledon; 1984. Pp 510.
11. Oakeshott, W. 'The origin of the "Auct." bible', *Bodleian Library Record* 11 (1985), 401-6.
12. Fletcher, J.M.; Upton, C.A. 'The cost of undergraduate study at Oxford in the fifteenth century: the evidence of the Merton College "founder's kin"', *History of Education* 14 (1985), 1-20.
13. Temple, Elzbieta. 'The calendar of the Douce psalter', *Bodleian Library Record* 12/1 (1985), 13-38.
14. De la Mare, A.C. 'Duke Humfrey's English Palladius', ibid. 39-51.
15. Coss, P.R. 'Aspects of cultural diffusion in medieval England', *Past & Present* 108 (1985), 35-79.
16. Matheson, L.M. 'Printer and scribe: Caxton, the *Polychronicon*, and the *Brut*', *Speculum* 60 (1985), 593-614.

(j) *Visual Arts*

1. McAleer, J.P. 'Romanesque England and the development of the façade harmonique', *Gesta* 23 (1984), 87-105.
2. Fernie, E. 'The use of varied nave supports in Romanesque and early Gothic churches', ibid. 107-17.
3. Woodman, F. 'The vault of the Ely Lady Chapel: fourteenth or fifteenth century?', ibid. 137-44.
4. Thurlby, M. 'The Romanesque elevations of Tewkesbury and Pershore', *J. of the Soc. of Architectural Historians* 44 (1985), 5-17.
5. Bradley, S.A.J. 'The Norman door of St Helen Stillingfleet and the legend of the Holy Rood tree', Bc1, 84-100.
6. Harvey, J.H. 'Henry Yeveley and the nave of Canterbury cathedral', *Canterbury Cathedral Chronicle* 79 (1985), 20-32.
7. Harvey, J.H. 'Somerset Perpendicular: the dating evidence', *T. of the Ancient Monuments Soc.* new ser. 27 (1983), 49-60.
8. Simpson, A. *The connections between English and Bohemian painting during the second half of the fourteenth century.* London; Garland; 1984. Pp 200.
9. Brown, R.A. *The architecture of castles: a visual guide.* London; Batsford; 1984. Pp 120.
10. Routh, P. 'Richard Neville, earl of Salisbury: the Burghfield effigy', *The Ricardian* 6 (1984), 417-23.
11. Henstock, A. 'Late mediaeval building contracts for the Nottingham area', *T. of the Thoroton Soc. of Notts.* 88 (1984), 103-5.
12. Holton-Krayenbuhl, A.P.B. (ed.). *The Three Blackbirds: a medieval house in Ely, Cambridgeshire.* Ely; Ely Preservation Trust; 1984. Pp 38.
13. Cooper, N. 'Burmington manor, Warwickshire: the thirteenth-century building', *Royal Commission on Historical Monuments (England) Annual Review* 1984-5, 27-30.
14. Edwards, John. 'The martyrdom wall-paintings at St Leonard's church, Stowell', *T. of the Bristol & Gloucs. Arch. Soc.* 102 (1985), 133-40.
15. Wilson, D.M. *The Bayeux tapestry.* London; Thames & Hudson; 1985. Pp 234.
16. King, E. 'Medieval wall-paintings in Northamptonshire', *Northants. Past & Present* 7 (1984-5), 69-78.
17. Smith, T.P. 'Three medieval timber-framed church porches in West Kent: Fawkham, Kemsing and Shoreham', *Archaeologia Cantiana* 101 (1985 for 1984), 137-63.
18. Sadler, A.G. *The indents of lost monumental brasses in southern England.* Worthing; the author; 1985. Pp viii, 96.
19. Crook, J. 'The thirteenth-century shrine and screen of St Swithun at Winchester', *J. British Arch. Association* 138 (1985), 125-31.
20. Fernie, E.C. 'The Romanesque church of Waltham Abbey', ibid. 48-78.
21. Turner, B. 'The patronage of John of Northampton: further studies of the wall-paintings in Westminster chapter house', ibid. 89-100.
22. Gibb, J.H.P. 'The fire of 1437 and the rebuilding of Sherborne Abbey', ibid. 101-24.

23. Eames, E. *English Medieval Tiles*. London; British Museum; 1985. Pp 72.

(k) *Topography*

1. Keene, D. *Survey of Medieval Winchester* (Winchester Studies 2). Oxford; Clarendon; 1985. 2 vols; pp xxxviii, 1490.
2. Hayfield, C.; Slater, T. *The Medieval Town of Hedon: Excavations 1975-1976*. Hull; Humberside Leisure Services; 1984. Pp vi, 89.
3. Hayfield, C. 'Wawne, East Riding of Yorkshire: a case study in settlement morphology', *Landscape History* 6 (1984), 41-67.
4. Hayfield, C. 'Excavations on the site of the Mowbray manor house at the Vinegarth, Epworth, Lincolnshire, 1975-1976', *Lincolnshire History & Archaeology* 19 (1984), 5-28.
5. Butler, L. 'The houses of the mendicant orders in Britain: recent archaeological work', Bc1, 123-36.
6. Stocker, D.A. 'The remains of the Franciscan Friary in Lincoln: a reassessment', ibid. 137-44.
7. Poulton, R.; Woods, H. *Excavations on the site of the Dominican Friary at Guildford in 1974 and 1978*. Guildford; Surrey Arch. Soc.; 1984. Pp x, 83.
8. Austin, D. 'The castle and the landscape', *Landscape History* 6 (1984), 69-81.
9. Slater, T.R. 'Medieval new town and port: a plan-analysis of Hedon, East Yorkshire', *Yorkshire Arch. J.* 57 (1985), 23-41.
10. Hurst, H. 'The archaeology of Gloucester castle; an introduction', *T. of the Bristol & Gloucs. Arch. Soc.* 102 (1985), 73-128.
11. Watts, L.; Rahtz, P. 'Upton deserted medieval village, Blockley, Gloucestershire, 1973', ibid. 141-54.
12. Hall, D.N. 'Late Saxon topography and early medieval estates', Bc10, 61-9.
13. Austin, D. 'Dartmoor and the upland village of the south-west of England', Bc10, 71-9.
14. Dyer, C. 'Towns and cottages in eleventh-century England', Bc13, 91-106.
15. Kaye, J.M. (ed.). *A God's House miscellany*. Southampton UP: Southampton records ser. 27; 1984. Pp xxiii, 142.
16. Watts, L.; Rahtz, P. *Mary-le-Port, Bristol: excavations, 1962-1963*. Bristol; City Museum & Art Gallery (Monograph 7); 1985. Pp 224.
17. Goodfellow, P. 'Medieval bridges in Northamptonshire', *Northants. Past & Present* 7/3 (1985), 143-58.
18. Walrond, L.F.J. 'The medieval houses of rural Gloucestershire', Bb61, 304-14.
19. Saunders, A.D. 'The Cow Tower, Norwich: an East Anglian bastille?', *Medieval Archaeology* 29 (1985), 109-19.

Fal

F. ENGLAND 1500-1714

See also Df22; Ea4, 9, c5, 17, e6, 10, 33, 34, 37, 40, f12, 13, g14, h9, i2, 5, j7, k1, 5; Gb39, f27; Ki3.

(a) *General*

1. Mayhew, G.J. 'Rye and the defence of the narrow seas: a 16th-century town', *Sussex Arch. Collections* 122 (1984), 107-26.
2. Farrant, J.H. 'The rise and decline of a south coast seafaring town: Brighton, 1550-1750', *Mariner's Mirror* 71 (1985), 59-76.
3. Brand, P.A. 'New light on the Anstey case', *T. of the Essex Arch. Soc.* 15 (1984 for 1983), 68-83.
4. Graves, M.A.R.; Silcock, R.H. *Revolution, reaction and the triumph of conservatism: English history 1558-1700.* Auckland, N.Z.; Longman Paul; 1984. Pp xi, 525.
5. Erickson, C. *Anne Boleyn.* London; Macmillan; 1984. Pp 288.
6. Johnson, J. *Princely Chandos: James Brydges 1674-1744.* Gloucester; Sutton; 1984. Pp 191.
7. Thorp, J. 'Books on palaeography: sixteenth to eighteenth-century handwriting', *Local Historian* 16 (1985), 327-34.
8. Barker, F. 'Westminster in 1585', *History Today* 35/6 (1985), 8-15.
9. Hill, C. *Collected essays: vol. 1: Society and literature in seventeenth-century England.* Brighton; Harvester; 1985. Pp xi, 340.
10. Gill, C. 'Drake and Plymouth', Fd9, 78-98.
11. Kenyon, J.P. *Stuart England* (2nd edn.). Harmondsworth; Penguin; 1985. Pp 383.
12. Wilson, C.H. 'Aciertos y errores en las decisiones personales en la historia: tres ejemplos: Isabel I de Inglaterra, Cromwell y de Witt', *Las Individualidades en la Historia* (Univ. of Navarra; Conversaciones Internacionales de Historia II, 1985), 195-209.
13. Avery, G. (ed.). *The journal of Emily Pepys.* London; Prospect; 1984. Pp 95.
14. Boyle, J. *In quest of Hasted.* Chichester; Phillimore; 1984. Pp xii, 146.
15. Williams, B. 'A Welsh connection in Stuart Salisbury: John Williams and the Herberts', *Hatcher R.* 2/20 (1985), 480-8.
16. Warnicke, R.M. 'Anne Boleyn's childhood and adolescence', *Historical J.* 28 (1985), 939-52.
17. Brears, P.C.D. *The gentlewoman's kitchen: great food in Yorkshire, 1650-1750.* Wakefield; Wakefield Historical Publications; 1984. Pp 160.
18. Marks, R. 'The Howard tombs at Thetford and Framlingham: new discoveries', *Arch. J.* 141 (1985 for 1984), 252-68.
19. Porter, S. 'The Oxford fire regulations of 1671', *B. Inst. Hist. Res.* 58 (1985), 251-5.

20. Schellinks, W. 'A description of the Epsom well, 1662, transcribed by H.L. Lehmann', *Surrey Arch. Collections* 76 (1985), 77-9.
21. Latham, R. (ed.). *The shorter Pepys.* London; Bell & Hyman; 1985. Pp 1152.
22. Underdown, D. *Revel, riot, and rebellion: popular politics and culture in England 1603-1660.* Oxford; Clarendon; 1985. Pp xii, 324.

(b) *Politics*

1. Butler, M. 'A case study in Caroline political theatre: Brathwaite's "Mercurius Britannicus" (1641)', *Historical J.* 27 (1984), 947-53.
2. Carlin, N. 'Leveller organization in London', ibid. 955-60.
3. Peck, L.L. 'Goodwin *v.* Fortescue: the local context of parliamentary controversy', *Parliamentary History* 3 (1984), 33-56.
4. Thompson, C. *The debate on freedom of speech in the House of Commons in February 1621.* Orsett; Orchard Press; 1985. Pp i, 24.
5. Miller, J. 'The Crown and the borough charters in the reign of Charles II', *English Historical R.* 100 (1985), 53-84.
6. Carter, A. 'The site of Dussindale', *Norfolk Archaeology* (1984), 54-62.
7. Szechi, D. *Jacobitism and Tory politics 1710-14.* Edinburgh; Donald; 1984. Pp ix, 220.
8. Hutton, R. *The Restoration: a political and religious history of England and Wales, 1658-1667.* Oxford; Clarendon; 1985. Pp x, 379.
9. Bernard, G.W. *The power of the early Tudor nobility: a study of the fourth and fifth earls of Shrewsbury.* Brighton; Harvester; 1985. Pp xii, 228.
10. Haley, K.H.D. *Politics in the reign of Charles II.* Oxford; Blackwell; 1985. Pp 87.
11. Dow, F.D. *Radicalism in the English Revolution: 1640-1660.* Oxford; Blackwell; 1985. Pp 96.
12. Durston, C.G. '"Wild as colts untamed": radicalism in the Newbury area during the early modern period', *Southern History* 6 (1984), 36-52.
13. Warnicke, R.M. 'The fall of Anne Boleyn: a reassessment', *History* 70 (1985), 1-15.
14. Seddon, P. 'The East Retford parliamentary election of 1670', *T. of the Thoroton Soc. of Notts.* 88 (1985), 42-6.
15. Edie, C.A. 'News from abroad: advice to the people of England on the eve of the Stuart Restoration', *Bull. of the John Rylands Univ. Library of Manchester* 67 (1985), 382-407.
16. Schwoerer, L.G. 'William, lord Russell: the making of a martyr, 1683-1983', *J. of British Studies* 24 (1985), 41-71.
17. Wormald, J. 'Gunpowder, treason and Scots', ibid. 141-68.
18. Cust, R. 'Charles I, the privy council, and the forced loan', ibid. 208-35.
19. Hughes, A. 'The king, the parliament, and the localities during the English civil war', ibid. 236-63.
20. Tighe, W.J. 'Herbert Croft's repulse', *Bull. Inst. Hist. Res.* 58 (1985), 106-9.

21. Jansson, M. (ed.). *Two diaries of the Long Parliament*. Gloucester; Alan Sutton; 1984. Pp xxvii, 152.
22. Not used.
23. Akrigg, G.P.V. (ed.). *Letters of King James VI and I*. Berkeley; California UP; 1984. Pp xxii, 546.
24. Jones, C. (ed.). *Party and management in parliament, 1660-1784*. Leicester UP; 1984. Pp 205.
25. Woolf, D.R. 'Two Elizabeths? James I and the late queen's famous memory', *Canadian J. of History* 20 (1985), 167-91.
26. Jones, C. 'Introduction', Fb24, xiii-xvi.
27. Davis, R. 'The "Presbyterian" opposition and the emergence of Party in the House of Lords in the reign of Charles II', Fb24, 1-35.
28. Hayton, D. 'The "Country" interest and the party system', Fb24, 37-85.
29. Cruickshanks, E. 'Ashby versus White: the case of the men of Aylesbury 1701-4', Fb24, 87-106.
30. Speck, W.A. 'The most corrupt council in Christendom: decisions in controverted elections 1702-42', Fb24, 107-21.
31. Jones, C. 'The scheme lords, the necessitious lords and the Scots lords, 1711-14'; 'The Earl of Oxford's management and "the party of the Crown" in the House of Lords 1711-14', Fb24, 123-67.
32. Kelly, P. 'Constituents' instructions to members of parliament in the eighteenth century', Fb24, 169-89.
33. Elton, G.R. 'The State: government and politics under Elizabeth and James', Fk45, 1-19.
34. Mullett, M.A. '"Men of knowne loyalty": the politics of the Lancashire borough of Clitheroe, 1660-1689', *Northern History* 21 (1985), 108-36.
35. Hutton, R. 'Rulers and ruled, 1580-1650', *History Today* 35/9 (1985), 16-21.
36. Williams, P. 'English politics after Bosworth' [to 1603], ibid. 30-6.
37. Hoyle, R.W. 'Thomas Master's narrative of the Pilgrimage of Grace', *Northern History* 21 (1985), 53-79.
38. Gunn, S.J. 'The regime of Charles, duke of Suffolk, in North Wales and the reform of Welsh government, 1509-25', *Welsh HR* 12 (1985), 461-94.
39. Thompson, C. *The Holles account of proceedings in the House of Commons in 1624*. Orsett; Orchard Press; 1985. Pp ii, 92.
40. Akrigg, G.P.V. (ed.). *Letters of King James VI & I*. Berkeley & London; U. California P.; 1984. Pp xxii, 546.
41. Henning, B.D. *The House of Commons 1660-1690*. London; Secker & Warburg for History of Parliament Trust; 1983. 3 vols.
42. Miller, J. *Restoration England: the reign of Charles II*. London; Longman; 1985. Pp viii, 118.
43. De Krey, G.S. *A fractured society: the politics of London in the first age of party 1688-1715*. Oxford; Clarendon; 1985. Pp xvi, 304.
44. Starkey, D.R. *The reign of Henry VIII: personalities and politics*. London; George Philip; 1985. Pp 174.
45. Graves, M.A.R. *The Tudor parliaments: Crown, Lords and Commons 1485-1603*. London; Longman; 1985. Pp vii, 173.

46. Patrides, C.A. "'The greatest of the kingly race": the death of Henry Stuart', *The Historian* 47 (1985), 402-8.
47. Bliss, R.M. *Restoration England: politics and government, 1660-1688.* London; Methuen; 1985. Pp vii, 54.
48. Wilson, J. *Fairfax: a life of Thomas, Lord Fairfax ...* London; Murray; 1985. Pp 215.
49. Hutton, R. *The Restoration: a political and religious history of England 1658-1667.* Oxford; Clarendon; 1985. Pp x, 379.
50. Thompson, C. (ed.). *Sir Nathaniel Rich's diary of proceedings in the House of Commons in 1624.* Wivenhoe; Orchard Press; 1985. Pp 46.
51. Gladwish, P. 'The Herefordshire clubmen: a reassessment', *Midland History* 10 (1985), 62-71.
52. Graves, M.A.R. 'Patrons and clients: their role in sixteenth century parliamentary politicking and legislation', *The Turnbull Record* (Wellington, NZ), 18 (1985), 69-85.

(c) *Constitution, Administration and Law*

1. Pawlisch, H.S. *Sir John Davies and the conquest of Ireland: a study in legal imperialism.* Cambridge UP; 1985. Pp x, 244.
2. Quintrell, B.W. 'Towards a "perfect militia": Warwick, Buckingham and the Essex alarum of 1625', *T. of the Essex Arch. Soc.* 15 (1984 for 1983), 96-105.
3. Kennedy, M.E. 'Commissions of sewers for Lincolnshire, 1509-1649: an annotated list', *Lincolnshire History & Archaeology* 19 (1984), 83-8.
4. Dean, D.M. 'Sir Symonds D'Ewes's bills of "no great moment"', *Parliamentary History* 3 (1984), 157-78.
5. Swatland, A. 'Further recorded divisions in the House of Lords 1660-1681', ibid. 179-82.
6. Schwoerer, L.G. 'The transformation of the 1689 Convention into a parliament', ibid. 57-76.
7. Marcus, R.L. 'The Tudor treason trials: some observations of the emergence of forensic themes', *University of Illinois Law R.* (1984), 675-704.
8. Zell, M. 'Fixing the custom of the manor: Slindon, West Sussex, 1568', *Sussex Arch. Collections* 122 (1984), 101-6.
9. Ford, W.K. 'The ordeal of Joan Acton', ibid. 127-37.
10. Guy, J.A. *The court of Star Chamber and its records to the reign of Elizabeth I.* London; Public Record Office (Handbooks No. 21); 1985. Pp x, 112.
11. Slatter, M. 'The Norwich court of requests — a tradition continued', *J. of Legal History* 5/3 (1984), 96-107.
12. Edwards, V.C. 'Criminal equity in Restoration London and Middlesex', ibid. 79-96.
13. Hart, J.S. 'Judicial review in the House of Lords (1640-43)', ibid. 65-78.
14. Sharpe, J.A. '"Last dying speeches": religion, ideology and public execution in seventeenth-century England', *Past & Present* 107 (1985), 144-67.

15. Herrup, C.B. 'Law and morality in seventeenth-century England', ibid. 106 (1985), 102-23.
16. Matthews, N.L. *William Sheppard, Cromwell's law reformer.* Cambridge UP; 1985. Pp xvi, 304.
17. Morgan, V. 'Whose prerogative in late sixteenth and early seventeenth century England?', *Journal of Legal History* 5/3 (1984), 39-64.
18. Post, J.B. 'The admissibility of defence counsel in English criminal procedure', ibid. 23-32.
19. Lidington, D.R. 'Mesne process in penal actions at the Elizabethan exchequer', ibid. 33-8.
20. Gray, M. 'Mr Auditor's man: the career of Richard Budd, estate agent and Exchequer official', *Welsh HR* 12 (1985), 307-23.
21. Baker, J.H. 'English law and the Renaissance', *Cambridge Law J.* 44 (1985), 46-61.
22. Weikel, A. (ed.). *The court rolls of the manor of Wakefield: October 1583 to September 1585.* Leeds; Yorkshire Arch. Soc.; 1984. Pp xv, 189.
23. Bellamy, J. *Criminal law and society in late medieval and Tudor England.* Gloucester; Alan Sutton; 1984. Pp 244.
24. Jack, S.M. 'The conflict of common law and canon law in early sixteenth-century England: Richard Hunne revisited', *Parergon* new ser. 3(1985), 131-45.
25. Holmes, C. 'Drainers and fenmen: the problem of popular political consciousness in the seventeenth century', Fg21, 166-95.
26. Baker, J.H. 'Law and legal institutions', Fk45, 41-54.
27. Brooks, C.W. 'The common lawyers in England, c. 1558-1642', Bc12, 42-64.
28. Prest, W.R. 'The English bar, 1550-1700', Bc12, 65-85.
29. Levack, B.P. 'The English civilians, 1500-1750', Bc12, 108-28.
30. Landau, N. *The justices of the peace, 1679-1760.* Berkeley & London; U. California P.; 1984. Pp xv, 421.
31. Prest, W.R. 'Common lawyers and culture in early modern England', *Law in Context* 1 (1983), 86-106.
32. Guy, J.A. *Christopher St German on chancery and statute.* London; Selden Soc. (Supplementary Ser. 6); 1985. Pp x, 149.
33. Stoate, T.L. (ed.). *Cornwall subsidies in the reign of Henry VIII: 1524 and 1543: and the benevolence of 1545.* Bristol; the author; 1985. Pp xii, 196.
34. Lemmings, D. 'The student body of the inns of court under the later Stuarts', *Bull. Inst. Hist. Res.* 58 (1985), 149-66.
35. Bevan, A.S. 'Justices of the peace, 1509-47; an additional source', ibid. 242-8.

(d) *External Affairs*

1. Green, J.P.; Pole, J.R. (eds.). *Colonial British America: essays in the new history of the early modern era.* Baltimore; London; Johns Hopkins UP; 1984. Pp ix, 508.

2. Quinn, D.B. *Set fair for Roanoke: voyages and colonies 1584-1606*. Chapel Hill; North Carolina UP; 1985. Pp xxiv, 467.

3. Cressy, D. 'The vast and furious ocean: the passage to Puritan New England', *New England Q.* 203 (1984), 511-32.

4. Edwards, F. 'The attempt in 1608 on Hugh Owen, intelligencer for the archdukes in Flanders', *Recusant History* 17 (1984), 140-57.

5. Sutherland, N.M. 'The origins of Queen Elizabeth's relations with the Huguenots', Fe35, 73-96.

6. Sutherland, N.M. 'Queen Elizabeth and the conspiracy of Amboise', Fe35, 97-112.

7. Sutherland, N.M. 'The foreign policy of Queen Elizabeth, the Sea Beggars and the capture of Brill, 1572', Fe35, 183-206.

8. Pollitt, R. 'The defeat of the Northern Rebellion and the shaping of Anglo-Scottish relations', *Scottish HR* 64 (1985), 1-21.

9. Thrower, N.J.W. (ed.). *Sir Francis Drake and the famous voyage, 1577-1580: essays commemorating the quadricentennial of Drake's circumnavigation of the earth*. London; California UP; 1984. Pp xix, 214.

10. Parry, J.H. 'Drake and the world encompassed', Fd9, 1-11.

11. Quinn, D.B. 'Early accounts of the famous voyage', Fd9, 33-48.

12. Andrews, K.R. 'Drake and South America', Fd9, 49-59.

13. Lessa, W.A. 'Drake and the South Seas', Fd9, 60-77.

14. Thrower, N.J.W. 'The aftermath: a summary of British discoveries between Drake and Cook', Fd9, 164-72.

15. Quinn, D.B. 'Travel by sea and land', Fk45, 195-200.

16. Livesay, J.L. 'Shakespeare and foreigners', Fk45, 233-40.

17. De Cossart, M. *This little world: Renaissance Italians' view of English Society*. Liverpool; Janus; 1984. Pp 114.

18. Ives, V.A. (ed.). *The Rich papers: letters from Bermuda 1615-1646: eyewitness accounts sent by the early colonists to Sir Nathaniel Rich*. Toronto UP for Bermuda National Trust; 1984. Pp xxvi, 413.

(e) *Religion*

1. Reay, B. *The Quakers and the English Revolution*. Hounslow; Temple Smith; 1985. Pp xii, 184.

2. Wood-Legh, K.L. (ed.). *Kentish visitations of Archbishop William Warham and his deputies, 1511-1512*. Maidstone; Kent Arch. Soc.; 1984. Pp xxvii, 343.

3. Gwynn, R.D. *Huguenot heritage: the history and contribution of the Huguenots in Britain*. London; Routledge & Kegan Paul; 1985. Pp xii, 220.

4. Cross, C. (ed.). *York clergy wills 1520-1600: 1: Minster clergy*. York; Borthwick Institute of Historical Research; 1984. Pp xii, 179.

5. Bradfield, H. 'Tracking down Puritans', *Local Historian* 16 (1984), 213-16.

6. Ward, J.C. 'The Reformation in Colchester, 1528-1558', *T. of the Essex Arch. Soc.* 15 (1984 for 1983), 84-95.

7. Swaby, J.E. 'Walker, Matthews, and the sufferings of the Lincolnshire clergy', *Lincolnshire History & Archaeology* 19 (1984), 89-92.
8. Guy, J.A. 'Thomas More and Christopher St German: the battle of the books', *Moreana* 21 (1984), 5-25.
9. Thorp, M.R. 'Catholic conspiracy in early Elizabethan foreign policy', *Sixteenth Century J.* 15 (1984), 431-48.
10. Schutte, W.M. 'Thomas Churchyard's "Doleful Discourse" and the death of Lady Katherine Grey', ibid. 471-87.
11. George, T. 'War and peace in the puritan tradition', *Church History* 53 (1984), 492-503.
12. Donagan, B. 'Puritan ministers and laymen: professional claims and constraints in seventeenth century England', *Huntington Library Q.* 47 (1984), 81-112.
13. Klemp, P.J. 'Lancelot Andrewes's "Prayer before sermon": a parallel-text edition', *Bodleian Library Record* 11 (1984), 300-19.
14. McDiarmid, J.F. 'Humanism, Protestantism, and English scripture, 1533-1540', *J. of Medieval & Renaissance Studies* 14 (1984), 121-38.
15. McGrath, P.; Rowe, J. 'The Marian priests under Elizabeth I', *Recusant History* 17 (1984), 103-20.
16. McCoug, T.M. 'The establishment of the English province of the Society of Jesus', ibid. 121-39.
17. Crichton, J.D. 'The *Manual* of 1614', ibid. 158-72.
18. Elliott, B. 'A Leicestershire recusant family: the Nevills of Nevill Holt — I', ibid. 173-80.
19. Yates, N. 'Francis Henry Murray, rector of Chislehurst', *Archaeologia Cantiana* 98 (1983 for 1982), 1-18.
20. Rogers, G.A.J. 'The basis of belief. Philosophy, science and religion in seventeenth-century England', *History of European Ideas* 6 (1985), 19-29.
21. Cross, C. *Urban magistrates and ministers: religion in Hull and Leeds from the Reformation to the Civil War.* York; Borthwick Papers, No. 67; 1985. Pp 29.
22. Rowlands, M.B. 'Recusant women 1560-1640', Fg10, 149-80.
23. Unwin, R. *Charity schools and the defence of Anglicanism: James Talbot, rector of Spofforth 1700-08.* York; Borthwick Papers, no. 65; 1984. Pp 37.
24. Fincham, K.; Lake, P. 'The ecclesiastical policy of King James I', *J. of British Studies* 24 (1985), 169-207.
25. Greaves, R.L. *Saints and rebels; seven nonconformists in Stuart England.* Macon, GA; Mercer UP; 1985. Pp xiv, 223.
26. Owen, T.A. *Lancelot Andrewes.* Boston; Twayne Publishers; 1981. Pp 179.
27. Pleydell-Bouverie, J. 'Laurens des Bouveries (1536-1610), his descendants, and the Huguenot connection', *Harper R.* 2/19 (1985), 411-20.
28. Baker, J.W. 'Sola fide, sola gratia: the battle for Luther in seventeenth-century England', *Sixteenth Century J.* 16 (1985), 115-33.
29. Fincham, K.C. 'Ramifications of the Hampton Court conference in the dioceses, 1603-1609', *J. of Ecclesiastical History* 36 (1985), 208-27.
30. Clark, R. 'Lists of Derbyshire clergymen, 1558-1662', *Derbyshire Arch. J.* 104 (1985), 19-61.

31. Colthorpe, M. 'Edmund Campion's alleged interview with Queen Elizabeth in 1581', *Recusant History* 17 (1985), 197-200.
32. Quintrell, B.W. 'The practice and problems of recusant disarming, 1585-1641', ibid. 208-20.
33. Loomie, A.J. 'Canon Henry Taylor, Spanish Habsburg diplomat', ibid. 223-37.
34. Southgate, B.C. '"That damned booke": *The Grounds of obedience and Government* (1655), and the downfall of Thomas White', ibid. 238-53.
35. Sutherland, N.M. *Princes, politics and religion 1547-1589.* London; Hambledon Press; 1984. Pp ix, 258.
36. Brachlow, S. 'The Elizabethan roots of Henry Jacob's churchmanship: refocusing the historiographical lens', *J. of Ecclesiastical History* 36 (1985), 228-54.
37. Gray, I. 'Records of four Tewkesbury vicars, c. 1685-1769', *T. of the Bristol and Gloucs. Arch. Soc.* 102 (1985), 155-72.
38. Lamont, W. 'The rise of Arminianism reconsidered', *Past & Present* 107 (1985), 227-31.
39. Boulton, J.P. 'The limits of formal religion: the administration of holy communion in late Elizabethan and early Stuart London', *London J.* 10 (1984), 135-54.
40. Thomas, I. 'Fersiwn William Morgan o'r hen Destament Hebraeg', *J. of the National Library of Wales* (1984), 209-91.
41. Cottret, B. 'Glorreiche Revolution, schändliche Revokation? Französische Protestanten und Protestanten Englands', in R. von Thadden, M. Magdelaine (eds.), *Die Hugenotten 1685-1985* (Munich; Beck; 1985), 73-84.
42. Leaver, R.A. *The liturgy of the Frankfurt exiles 1555.* Bramcote; Grove; 1984. Pp 33.
43. Markley, R. 'Robert Boyle on language: some considerations touching the style of the Holy Scriptures [1661]', *Studies in Eighteenth-Century Culture* 14 (1985), 159-71.
44. Lawes, A.H. 'Cosin's post-Restoration correspondence — a re-assessment', *Durham UJ* 77 (1985), 141-7.
45. Beer, B.L. 'John Stow and the English Reformation, 1547-1559', *Sixteenth Century J.* 16 (1985), 257-71.
46. Bond, R.B. '"Dark deeds darkly answered": Thomas Becon's homily against whoredom and adultery ...', ibid. 191-205.
47. Morrill, J.S. 'The attack on the Church of England in the Long Parliament, 1640-1642', Bc3, 105-24.
48. Evans, E.J. 'Tithes', Fc16, pt II, 389-405.
49. Spufford, M. 'Puritanism and social control', Fg21, 41-57.
50. Davies, C.S.L. 'Popular religion and the Pilgrimage of Grace', Fg21, 58-91.
51. Collinson, P. 'The Church: religion and its manifestations', Fk45, 21-40.
52. Dunning, R.W. 'The last days of Cleeve Abbey', Bc15, 58-67.
53. Russel, E. 'Marian Oxford and the Counter-Reformation', Bc15, 212-27.
54. Kitching, C.J. '"Prayers fit for the time": fasting and prayer in response to natural crises in the reign of Elizabeth I', Bc14, 241-50.

55. Williams, M.E. 'The ascetic tradition and the English College at Valladolid', Bc14, 275-83.
56. Hardman, S. 'Puritan asceticism and the type of sacrifice', Bc14, 285-97.
57. Barnard, L.W. 'Joseph Bingham and asceticism', Bc14, 299-306.
58. Seaver, P.S. *Wallington's world: a puritan artisan in seventeenth-century London*. London; Methuen; 1985. Pp ix, 258.
59. Wood-Legh, K.L. *Kentish visitations of Archbishop William Warham and his deputies, 1511-1512*. Maidstone; Kent Arch. Soc. (Kent Records, v. 24); 1984. Pp xxvii, 343.
60. Scott, G. *Sacredness of majesty: the English Benedictines and the cult of King James II*. Huntingdon; Royal Stuart Soc.; 1984. Pp 14.
61. Matthews, V.H. 'Edmund Neville: a Catholic in Elizabethan England', *Hist. Magazine of the Protestant Episcopal Church* 54 (1985), 111-23.
62. Atkinson, D.W. 'The devotionalism of Christopher Sutton: the universal Christianity of a pious Protestant', ibid. 207-17.
63. Senning, C.F. 'Vanini and the diplomats, 1612-1614: religion, politics, and defection in the Counter-Reformation era', ibid. 219-39.
64. Collinson, P. 'England and international Calvinism 1558-1640', in M. Prestwich (ed.), *International Calvinism 1541-1715* (Oxford; Clarendon; 1985), 197-223.
65. Collinson, P. 'Truth and legend: the veracity of John Foxe's Book of Martyrs', in A.C. Duke & C.A. Tamse (eds.), *Clio's Mirror: Historiography in Britain and the Netherlands* (Leyden; De Walburg Pres; 1985), 31-54.
66. Burke, P. 'The politics of Reformation history: Burnet and Brandt', in ibid. 73-86.
67. Paul, R.S. *The assembly of the Lord: politics and religion in the Westminster Assembly and the 'grand debate'*. Edinburgh; T. & T. Clark; 1985. Pp x, 609.
68. Cross, M.C. 'The third earl of Huntingdon's death-bed: a Calvinist example of the "ars moriendi"', *Northern History* 21 (1985), 80-107.
69. Martin, J.W. 'A sidelight on Foxe's account of the Marian martyrs', *Bull. Inst. Hist. Res.* 58 (1985), 248-51.
70. Whitworth, R.H. '1685 — James II, the army and the Huguenots', *J. of the Soc. for Army Hist. Res.* 63 (1985), 130-7.
71. Durston, C. 'Lords of misrule: the Puritan war on Christmas 1642-60', *History Today* 35/12 (1985), 7-14.
72. Guy, J. 'Law, lawyers and the English Reformation', *History Today* 35/11 (1985), 16-22.
73. Grant, A.; Gwynn, R. 'The Huguenots of Devon', *Devonshire Association Report & T.* 117 (1985), 161-94.
74. Goose, N. 'The ecclesiastical returns of 1563: a cautionary note', *Local Population Studies* 34 (1985), 46-7.
75. Hogben, B.M. 'Preaching and the Reformation in Henrician Kent', *Archaeologia Cantiana* 101 (1985 for 1984), 169-85.
76. Finnie, E. 'The house of Hamilton: patronage, politics and the Church in the Reformation period', *Innes R.* 36 (1985), 3-28.

77. Nuttall, G.F. 'The Essex Classes (1648)', *J. of the United Reformed Church History Soc.* 3 (1985), 194-202.
78. Brachlow, S. 'Puritan theology and General Baptist origins', *Baptist Q.* 32 (1985), 179-94.
79. Whiteley, J.B. 'Loughwood Baptists in the seventeenth century', ibid. 148-58.
80. Pailin, D.A. *Attitudes to other religions: comparative religion in seventeenth- and eighteenth-century Britain.* Manchester UP; 1984. Pp ix, 339.

(f) *Economic affairs*

1. Bettey, J.H. 'Livestock trade in the west country in the 17th century', *Somerset Archaeology & Natural History* 127 (1984 for 1983), 123-8.
2. Eddy, M.R.; Ryan, P.M. 'John Ennows: a previously unknown clay-pipe maker of All Saints, Colchester', *T. of the Essex Arch. Soc.* 15 (1984 for 1983), 106-12.
3. Borden, D.G.; Brown, I.D. 'The milled coinage of Elizabeth I', *British Numismatic J.* 53 (1984 for 1983), 108-32.
4. Brandon, P.F. 'Land, technology and water management in the Tilling-bourne valley, Surrey, 1560-1760', *Southern History* 6 (1984), 75-103.
5. Goose, N.R. 'Decay and regeneration in seventeenth century Reading: a study in a changing economy', ibid. 53-74.
6. Prior, M. 'Women and the urban economy: Oxford 1500-1800', Fg10, 93-117.
7. Masters, B.R. (ed.). *Chamber accounts of the sixteenth century.* London; London Record Society vol. 20; 1984. Pp xliv, 164.
8. Keller, A. *Die Getreideversorgung von Paris und London in der zweiten Hälfte des 17. Jahrhunderts* [Grain supply in Paris and London in the second half of the seventeenth century.] Bonn; Röhrscheid; 1983. Pp 162.
9. Holderness, B.A. 'Widows in pre-industrial society: an essay upon their economic functions', Bc2, 423-42.
10. Gwynn, R. 'England's first refugees [Huguenots]', *History Today* 35/5 (1985), 22-8.
11. Beckett, J.V. 'Land tax or excise: the levying of taxation in seventeenth- and eighteenth century England', *English HR* 100 (1985), 285-308.
12. Russell, C. 'Charles I's financial estimates of 1642', *Bull. Inst. Hist. Res.* 58 (1985), 109-20.
13. Woodward, D. '"Swords into ploughshares": recycling in pre-industrial England', *Economic HR* 2nd ser. 38 (1985), 175-91.
14. Wilson, C. *England's apprenticeship 1603-1763.* 2nd edn. London; Longman; 1984. Pp xv, 433.
15. Thirsk, J. *The rural economy of England.* London; Hambledon Press; 1983. Pp 300.
16. Thirsk, J. (ed.). *The agrarian history of England and Wales: vol. 5: 1640-1750.* Cambridge UP; 1984. Pp xv, 941.

17. Wood, N. *John Locke and agrarian capitalism.* London; California UP; 1984. Pp xv, 161.
18. Kenyon, T. 'Labour — natural, property — artificial: the radical insights of Gerrard Winstanley', *History of European Ideas* 6 (1985), 105-27.
19. Evans, E.J.; Beckett, J.V. 'Cumberland, Westmorland and Furness', Ff16, I 1-29.
20. Brassley, P. 'Northumberland and Durham', Ff16, I 30-58.
21. Hey, D. 'Yorkshire and Lancashire', Ff16, I 58-88.
22. Mingay, D. 'Northamptonshire, Leicestershire, Rutland, Nottinghamshire and Lincolnshire', Ff16, I 89-128.
23. Hey, D. 'Derbyshire, Staffordshire, Cheshire and Shropshire', Ff16, I 129-58.
24. Thirsk, J. 'Warwickshire, Worcestershire, Gloucestershire and Herefordshire', Ff16, I 159-96.
25. Holderness, B. 'Norfolk, Suffolk, Cambridgeshire, Ely, Huntingdonshire, Essex, Lincolnshire Fens', Ff16, I 197-238.
26. Richardson, R.C. 'Bedfordshire, Hertfordshire, Middlesex', Ff16, I 239-69.
27. Short, B.M. 'Kent, Surrey, Sussex', Ff16, I 270-316.
28. Wordie, J.R. 'Oxfordshire, Buckinghamshire, Berkshire, Wiltshire and Hampshire', Ff16, I 317-56.
29. Harrison, G.V. 'Dorset, Somerset, Devon and Cornwall', Ff16, I 358-92.
30. Emery, F. 'Wales', Ff16, I 393-428.
31. Bowden, P.J. 'Agricultural prices, wages, farm profits and rents', Ff16, II 1-118.
32. Clay, C. 'Landlords and estate management in England', Ff16, II 119-251.
33. Howell, D.W. 'Landlords and estate management in Wales', Ff16, II 252-97.
34. Thirsk, J. 'Agricultural policy: public debate and legislation', Ff16, II 298-389.
35. Chartres, J.A. 'The marketing of agricultural produce', Ff16, II 406-502.
36. Thick, M. 'Market gardening', Ff16, II 503-32.
37. Thirsk, J. 'Agricultural innovations and their diffusion', Ff16, II 533-89.
38. Harrison, G.V. 'Agricultural weights and measures', Ff16, II 815-27.
39: Coleman, D.C. 'Economic life in Shakespeare's England', Fk45, 67-73.
40. Thirsk, J. 'Forest, field, and garden: landscapes and economies in Shakespeare's England', Fk45, 257-67.
41. Winser, A. *A survey of the manors of Rockbourne and Rockstead in the 17th century.* Fordingbridge; the author; 1984. Pp 79.
42. Clay, C.G.A. *Economic expansion and social change: England 1500-1700: vol. 1: People, land and towns.* Cambridge UP; 1984. Pp xiv, 268.
43. Clay, C.G.A. *Economic expansion and social change: England 1500-1700: vol. 2: Industry, trade and government.* Cambridge UP; 1984. Pp xii, 324.
44. *Up Mill: a Hampshire papermill in 1696.* Winchester; Alembic; 1984. Pp 35.
45. Steckley, G.F. (ed.). *The letters of John Paige, London merchant 1648-1658.* London; London Record Soc.; 1984. Pp xxxix, 172.
46. Thomas, J.H. *The seaborne trade of Portsmouth, 1650-1800.* Portsmouth; Portsmouth City Council; 1984. Pp 28.

47. Woodward, D. (ed.). *The farming and memorandum books of Henry Best of Elmswell, 1642*. London; Oxford Up for British Academy (Records of social & economic history, n.s.8); 1984. Pp lxxiv, 347.
48. Jackson, R.V. 'Growth and deceleration in English agriculture 1660-1790', *Economic HR* 2nd ser. 38 (1985), 333-51.
49. Foister, S. 'Tudor collections and collectors', *History Today* 35/12 (1985), 20-6.
50. Alsop, J.D. 'The development of inland navigation on the River Nene in the early eighteenth century', *Northants. Past & Present* 7 (1985-6), 161-3.
51. Tyson, B. 'Some harbour works in West Cumberland before 1710', *T. Ancient Monuments Soc.*, new ser. 29 (1985), 173-208.

(g) *Social history (general)*

1. Slater, M. *Family life in the seventeenth century: the Verneys of Claydon House*. London; Routledge & Kegan Paul; 1984. Pp x, 209.
2. Wilkinson, B. 'The poore of the parish' [Coney Weston, Suffolk], *Local Historian* 16 (1984), 21-3.
3. Herrup, C. 'New shoes and mutton pies: investigative responses to theft in seventeenth-century East Sussex', *Historical J.* 27 (1984), 811-30.
4. Snell, K.D.M. 'Parish registration and the study of labour mobility', *Local Population Studies* 33 (1984), 29-43.
5. Outhwaite, R.B. 'Dearth, the English crown, and the "crisis of the 1590s"', in *The European Crisis of the 1590s*, ed. P. Clark (London; Allen & Unwin; 1985), 23-43.
6. Clark, P. 'A crisis contained? The condition of English towns in the 1590s', ibid. 44-66.
7. Schwoerer, L.G. 'Seventeenth-century English women engraved in stone?', *Albion* 16 (1984), 389-403.
8. Walter, J. 'A "rising of the people"? The Oxfordshire rising of 1596', *Past & Present* 106 (1985), 90-143.
9. Tittler, R. 'The building of civic halls in Dorset, c. 1560-1640', *Bull. Inst. Hist. Res.* 58 (1985), 37-45.
10. Prior, M. (ed.) *Women in English Society 1500-1800*. London; Methuen; 1985. Pp xvi, 294.
11. Thirsk, J. 'Foreword', Fg10, 1-21.
12. Prior, M. 'Reviled and crucified marriages: the position of Tudor bishops' wives', Fg10, 118-48.
13. Horwitz, H. 'Testamentary practice, family strategies and the last phases of the custom of London, 1660-1725', *Law & History R.* 2 (1984), 223-39.
14. Macfarlane, A. 'The myth of the peasantry; family and economy in a northern parish', Bc2, 333-49.
15. Wales, T. Poverty, poor relief and the life-cycle: some evidence from seventeenth-century Norfolk', Bc2, 351-404.

16. Newman-Brown, W. 'The receipt of poor relief and family situation: Aldenham, Hertfordshire 1630-90', Bc2, 405-22.
17. Howells, J. 'Haverfordwest and the plague', *Welsh History R* 12 (1985) 411-19.
18. Sharpe, J.A. *Crime in early modern England 1550-1750*. London; Longman; 1984. Pp 256.
19. Larner, C. *Witchcraft and religion*. Oxford; Blackwell; 1984. Pp 192.
20. Rappaport, S. 'Social structure and mobility in sixteenth-century London', *London J.* 10 (1984), 107-34.
21. Fletcher, A.; Stevenson J. (eds.). *Order and disorder in early modern England*. Cambridge UP; 1985. Pp xiii, 248.
22. Fletcher, A.; Stevenson, J. 'Introduction', Fg21, 1-40.
23. Morrill, J.S.; Walter, J.D. 'Order and disorder in the English Revolution', Fg21, 137-65.
24. Stevenson, J. 'The "moral economy" of the English crowd: myth and reality', Fg21, 218-38.
25. Garrett, G.P. 'Daily life in city, town and country', Fk45, 215-32.
26. Slack, P. *The impact of plague in Tudor and Stuart England*. London; Routledge; 1985. Pp 416.
27. Not used.
28. Jones, F. 'Lloyd of Hendre and Cwmgloyn', *National Library of Wales J.* 23 (1984), 334-56.
29. Barratt, D.M. *Probate records of the courts of the bishop and archdeacon of Oxford 1516-1732: vol. 2: L-Z*. Keele; British Record Soc.; 1985. Pp 313.
30. Tronrud, T.J. 'Dispelling the gloom: the extent of poverty in Tudor and early Stuart towns: some Kentish evidence', *Canadian J. of History* 20 (1985), 1-21.
31. Edwards, P.R. 'Disputes in the Weald Moors in the late 16th and early 17th centuries', *Shropshire Arch. Soc. T.* 63 (1985 for 1981-2), 1-10.

(h) *Social structure and population*

1. Chess Valley Archaeological and Historical Society (ed.). *The people of Chesham: their births, marriages and deaths 1637-1730: transcribed from the registers of baptisms, marriages and burials of St Mary's parish church, Chesham*. Buckingham; Barracuda; 1984. Pp xvi, 488.
2. Webster, W.F. (ed.). *Protestation returns 1641/2 - Lincolnshire*. Nottingham; Technical Print Services; ca. 1984. Pp x, 142.
3. Zell, M. 'Families and households in Staplehurst, 1563-64', *Local Population Studies* 33 (1984), 54-8.
4. Taylor, J. 'Plague in the towns of Hampshire: the epidemic of 1665-6', *Southern History* 6 (1984), 104-22.
5. McLaren, D. 'Marital fertility and lactation 1570-1720', Fg10, 22-53.
6. Todd, B.J. 'The remarrying widow: a stereotype reconsidered', Fg10, 54-92.

7. Hidden, N. and J. (eds.). *Hungerford, Berks. & Wilts. parish register: C-M-B 1559-1619*. London; 2 Gulham Court N44JB; 1984. Pp 154.

8. Wrightson, K. 'Kinship in an English village: Terling, Essex 1500-1700', Bc2, 313-32.

9. Not used.

10. Fletcher, A.J. 'Honour, reputation and local officeholding in Elizabethan and Stuart England', Fg21, 92-115.

11. Underdown, D.E. 'The taming of the scold: the enforcement of patriarchal authority in early modern England', Fg21, 116-36.

12. Amussen, S.D. 'Gender, family and the social order, 1560-1725', Fg21, 196-215.

13. Spring, E.; Spring, D. 'The English landed elite: 1540-1879' [review of L. Stone, *An Open Elite?*]; Stone, L. 'Spring back' [reply], *Albion* 17 (1985), 149-80.

14. Beach, J. (ed.). *Registers of the church of St Mary, Kingswinford, Staffordshire: baptisms, marriages, burials, 1603-1704*. Kingswinford; Birmingham & Midland Soc. for Genealogy & Heraldry; 1984. Pp ii, 179.

15. Dyer, A. 'Epidemics of measles in a seventeenth-century English town' [Bolton], *Local Population Studies* 34 (1985), 35-45.

16. Knowling, E. 'A list of the inhabitants of Buckfastleigh, Devon, in 1698', ibid. 48-50.

17. Taylor, H. & J. (eds.). *The parish register of Almondbury: Vol. 2: 1653-1682*. Leeds; Yorks. Arch. Soc. (Parish register ser. 148); 1984. Pp 146.

18. Hoyle, R.W. (ed.). *The parish register of Giggleswick: Vol. 1: 1558-1669*. Leeds; Yorks. Arch. Soc. (Parish reg. ser. 147); 1984. Pp xii, 265.

19. Scouloudi, I. *Returns of strangers in the metropolis 1593, 1627, 1635, 1639: a study of an active minority*. London; Huguenot Soc. of London (Quarto ser. 1vii); 1985. Pp iii, 368.

(i) *Naval and military*

1. Dore, R.N. (ed.) *The letter books of Sir William Brereton: vol. 1: January 31st - May 29th 1645*. Chester; Record Soc. of Lancashire and Cheshire; 1984. Pp xvii, 534.

2. Roy, I. 'The British army, 1500-1715; recent writing reviewed', *J. of the Soc. for Army Hist. Res.* 62 (1984), 194-200.

3. Hale, J.R. 'Shakespeare and warfare', Fk45, 85-98.

4. Young, P. *Naseby 1645: the campaign and the battle*. London; Century; 1985. Pp 400.

5. Chandler, D.G. 'Some thoughts on the battle of Sedgemoor, 1685', *J. of the Soc. for Army Hist. Res.* 63 (1985), 138-43.

6. Bennett, M. ' Leicester's royalist officers and the war effort in the county, 1642-1646', *Leicestershire Arch. & Hist. Soc. T.* 59 (1984-5), 44-51.

7. Taylor, A. 'The dismantling of Conwy castle', *T. Ancient Monuments Soc.* new ser. 29 (1985), 81-9.
8. Redknap, M. *The Cattewater wreck: the investigation of an armed vessel of the early sixteenth century.* Oxford; B.A.R. (British ser. 131); 1984. Pp xiii, 145.

(j) *Political thought and history of ideas*

1. Clark, J.K. *Goodwin Wharton.* Oxford UP; 1984. Pp xii, 391.
2. Nutton, V. 'Conrad Gesner and the English naturalists', *Medical History* 29 (1985), 93-7.
3. Bowler, G. '"An axe or an acte": the parliament of 1572 and resistance theory in early Elizabethan England', *Canadian J. of History* 19 (1984), 349-59.
4. Sargent, L.T. 'More's *Utopia*: an interpretation of its social theory', *History of Political Thought* 5 (1984), 195-210.
5. Metz, K.H. '"Providence" und politisches Handeln in den englischen Revolution (1640-60). Eine Studie zu einer Wurzel moderner Politik, dargestellt am politischen Denken Oliver Cromwells ['Providence' and political action in the English Revolution: a study of one root of modern politics, illustrated by means of Oliver Cromwell's political thought]', *Zeitschrift für historische Forschung* 12 (1985), 43-84.
6. State, S.A. 'Text and context: Skinner, Hobbes and theistic natural law', *Historical J.* 28 (1985), 27-50.
7. Mayer, T.F. 'Faction and ideology: Thomas Starkey's *Dialogue*', ibid. 1-25.
8. Taft, B. 'The Council of Officers' *Agreement of the People*, 1648/9', ibid. 169-85.
9. Worden, B. 'The commonwealth kidney of Algernon Sidney', *J. of British Studies* 24 (1985), 1-40.
10. Timmins, W.T. & D.B. 'Hobbes and Locke: the antipodal conflict between authority and personal liberty', in D.H. Nelson & R.L. Sklar (eds.), *Towards a humanistic science of politics* (Lanham; UP of America; 1983), 385-97.
11. Grace, D. 'Thomas More's *Epigrammata*: political theory in a poetic ideom', *Parergon* new ser. 3 (1985), 115-29.
12. Sanderson, J.B. 'Michael Hudson and the implications of "order"', *Durham UJ* 77 (1985), 179-85.
13. Nippel, W. '"Klassischer Republikanismus" in der Zeit der englischen Revolution', *Xenia* (Univ. of Constance) 15 (1985), 211-24.
14. Goldie, M. 'Absolutismus, Parlamentarismus und Revolution in England', *Pipers Handbuch der politischen Ideen* vol. 3 (ed. I. Fetscher & H. Münkler, Munich, 1985), 275-352.

(k) *Cultural and history of science*

1. Durant, D.N.; Riden, P. (eds.). *The Building of Hardwick Hall: Pt. 2: the New Hall, 1591-98*. Chesterfield; Derbyshire Record Society; 1984. Pp xxxii, 136.
2. Powell, J. *Restoration theatre production*. London; Routledge & Kegan Paul; 1984. Pp xiv, 226.
3. Bentley, G.E. *The profession of player in Shakespeare's time, 1590-1642*. Princeton UP; ca. 1984. Pp xiv, 315.
4. Orrell, J. *The theatres of Inigo Jones and John Webb*. Cambridge UP; 1985. Pp xiii, 218.
5. Parry, G.J.R. 'William Harrison and Holinshed's chronicles', *Historical J.* 27 (1984), 789-810.
6. Roberts, D.L. 'John Thorpe's drawings for Thornton College, the house of Sir Vincent Skinner', *Lincolnshire History & Archaeology* 19 (1984), 57-63.
7. Louw, H.J. 'Some royal and other great houses in England: extracts from the journal of Abram Booth', *Architectural History* 27 (1984), 503-9.
8. Airs, M. 'Laurence Shipway, freemason', ibid. 368-75.
9. Beard, G. 'William Winche and interior design', ibid. 150-62.
10. Baggs, A.P. 'Two designs by Simon Basil', ibid. 104-10.
11. Johnson, G.D. 'John Busby and the stationers' trade, 1590-1612', *The Library* 6th ser. 7 (1985), 1-15.
12. Barber, P.M. 'Marlborough, art and diplomacy: the background to Peter Strudel's drawing of Time revealing Truth and confounding Fraudulence', *J. of the Warburg & Courtauld Institutes* 47 (1984), 119-35.
13. Whittingham, A.B. 'The White Swan Inn, St Peter's Street, Norwich', *Norfolk Archaeology* (1984), 38-50.
14. Anglin, J.P. 'The schools of defense in Elizabethan London', *Renaissance Q.* 37 (1984), 393-410.
15. Orme, N. 'Alexander Barclay at Ottery St. Mary', *Devon & Cornwall Notes & Queries*, 35 (1984), 184-9.
16. Jennings, S.; Atkin, A. 'A 17th-century well group from St Stephen's Street, Norwich', *Norfolk Archaeology* (1984), 13-37.
17. Kear, D.C. 'Bede Cottage and Monkton Farm, Monkton', *Archaeologia Aeliana* 5th ser. 12 (1984), 181-207.
18. Ribhegge, W. 'Thomas More: *Utopia* (1516) — Geschichte als Gespräch [Thomas More: *Utopia* (1516) — History as discussion], *Die alte Stadt* 10 (1983), 327-47.
19. Mendelson, S.H. 'Stuart women's diaries and occasional memoirs', Fg10, 181-210.
20. Crawford, P.; Bell, R. 'Women's published writings 1600-1700', Fg10, 211-82.
21. Holtgen, K.J. 'Sir Robert Dallington (1561-1637): author, traveller, and pioneer of taste', *Huntington Library Q.* (1985), 147-77.
22. Pelling, M. 'Healing the sick poor: social policy and disability in Norwich

1550-1640', *Medical History* 29 (1985), 115-37.
23. Tyacke, S. 'Samuel Pepys as map collector', Bc7, 1-29.
24. Skempton, A.W. 'Engineering in the English river navigations to 1760', Bc6, 23-44.
25. Shepherd, S. (ed.). *The women's sharp revenge: five women's pamphlets from the Renaissance.* London; Fourth Estate; 1985. Pp 208.
26. Galloway, D. (ed.). *Records of early English drama: Norwich 1540-1642.* London; Toronto UP; 1984.
27. North, J.J.; Preston-Morley, P.J. *Sylloge of coins of the British Isles: 33: The John G. Brooker collection: coins of Charles I.* London; Spink; 1984. Pp 1xix, 260.
28. Adlard, J. *In sweet St James's Clerkenwell: the muscial coal-man and his friends and neighbours in the golden age of a London suburb.* London; Islington Libraries; 1984. Pp vi, 37.
29. Hampshire, G. (ed.). *The Bodleian Library account book 1613-1646.* Oxford; Oxford Bibliographical Soc.; 1983. Pp xiv, 199.
30. Murdin, L. *Under Newton's shadow: astronomical practices in the seventeenth century.* Bristol; Hilger; 1985. Pp viii, 152.
31. Wheeler, H. 'Science out of law: Francis Bacon's invention of scientific empiricism', in D.H. Nelson & R.L. Sklar (eds.), *Towards a humanistic science of politics* (Lanham; UP of America; 1983), 101-44.
32. Foakes, R.A. *Illustrations of the English stage 1580-1642.* London; Scolar; 1984. Pp 256.
33. Walch, G. 'Shakespeares Dramen als geschichtliche Aktivität ...' [Shakespeare's plays as a historical performance ...], *Shakespeare Jahrbuch* 121 (1985), 9-29.
34. Myers, M. 'Domesticating Minerva: Bathsua Makin's "curious" argument for women's education', *Studies in Eighteenth-Century Culture* 14 (1985), 173-92.
35. Murphy, M.; Barrett, E. 'Abraham Wheelock, arabist and saxonist', *Biography* 8 (1985), 163-85.
36. Pearlman, E. 'Typological autobiography in seventeenth-century England', ibid. 95-118.
37. Worden, B. 'Oliver Cromwell and the sin of Achan', Bc3, 125-45.
38. Waters, D.W. 'Elizabethan navigation', Fd9, 12-32.
39. Allan, M.J.B. 'Charles Fitzgeffrey's commendatory lamentation on the death of Drake', Fd9, 99-111.
40. Jowkes, W.T. 'Sir Francis Drake revived: from letters to legend', Fd9, 112-20.
41. Wallis, H. 'The cartography of Drake's voyages', Fd9, 121-60.
42. May, P. *The changing face of Newmarket: a history from 1600 to 1760.* Newmarket; Peter May; 1984. Pp viii, 81.
43. Barley, M.W. 'Rural building in England', Ff16, II. 590-685.
44. Smith, P. 'Rural building in Wales', Ff16, II. 687-814.
45. Andrews, J.F. (ed.). *William Shakespeare: his world, his work, his influence* (3 vols.). New York; Scribner's; 1985. Pp xix, 954.
46. Grafton, A. 'Education and apprenticeship', Fk45, 55-65.

47. Pelling, M. 'Medicine and sanitation', Fk45, 75-84.
48. Levy, F.J. 'Patronage and the arts', Fk45, 99-105.
49. Gurr, A. 'Theaters and the dramatic profession', Fk45, 107-28.
50. Slavin, A.J. 'Printing and publishing in the Tudor age', Fk45, 129-42.
51. Pocock, J.G.A. 'The sense of history in Renaissance England', Fk45, 143-57.
52. Heninger, S.K. 'The literate culture of Shakespeare's audience', Fk45, 159-74.
53. MacDonald, M. 'Science, magic, and folklore', Fk45, 175-94.
54. Smith, L.B. '"Style is the man": manners, dress and decorum', Fk45, 201-14.
55. Sypher, W. 'Painting and other fine arts', Fk45, 241-56.
56. Pringle, R. 'Sports and recreations', Fk45, 269-80.
57. Gatch, M.McC. 'John Bagford as a collector and disseminator of manuscript fragments', *The Library* 6th ser. 7 (1985), 95-114.
58. Kuin, R.J.P. 'The purloined *Letter*: evidence and probability regarding Robert Langham's authorship', ibid. 115-25.
59. Orrell, J. *The theatres of Inigo Jones and John Webb*. Cambridge UP; 1985. Pp xiii, 318.
60. Crone, R.W.A. *Covenanters' monuments of Scotland*. London; Regency; 1984. Pp 80.
61. Roncaglia, A. *Petty: the origins of political economy*. Cardiff UP; 1985. Pp xi, 118.
62. Eisenthal, E. 'John Webb's reconstruction of the ancient house', *Architectural History* 28 (1985), 7-31.
63. Harris, F. 'Holywell House, St Albans: an early work by William Talman?' ibid. 32-9.
64. Hodgetts, M. 'Secret hiding places: a narrative of tradition and trunk from the Restoration to the Regency', *Eighteenth Century Life* 9/2 (1985), 36-50.
65. Limon, J. *Gentlemen of a company: English players in central and eastern Europe, 1590-1660*. Cambridge UP; 1985. Pp xii, 191.
66. Weller, R.B. 'Some aspects of the life of Richard Haydocke, physician, engraver, painter & translator', *Hatcher R.* 2/20 (1985), 456-77.
67. Whitby, C.L. 'John Dee and Renaissance scrying', *B. of the Soc. for Renaissance Studies* 3/2 (1985), 25-36.
68. Sessions, W.K. *The first printers at Ipswich in 1547-1548 and Worcester in 1549-1553*. York; Sessions; 1984. Pp 190.
69. Crook, J. *The wainscot book: the houses of Winchester cathedral close and their interior decoration, 1660-1800*. Winchester; Hampshire Record Office; 1984. Pp xxxvii, 184.
70. Woodger, A. 'Post-Reformation Mixed Gothic in Huntingdonshire church towers and its campanological associations', *Arch. J.* 141 (1985 for 1984), 269-308.
71. Ravenhill, W. 'Mapping a united kingdom', *History Today* 35/10 (1985), 27-33.

72. Warnicke, R.M. 'The harpy in More's household; was it Lady Alice?', *Moreana* 22 (1985), 5-13.
73. Harrison, C. 'The Paget tomb', *T. Ancient Monuments Soc.* new ser. 29 (1985), 124-36.

G. BRITAIN 1714-1815

See also Fa2, 6, 7, e29, 30, f46, h13, k42, 69; Hb44, f23, 92, 96, i2; Ka8, f2, i3

(a) *General*

1. Bantock, A. *The later Smyths of Ashton Court: from their letters, 1741-1802.* Bristol; Malago Soc.; ca. 1984. Pp 237.
2. Wagner, P. 'Researching the taboo: sexuality and eighteenth-century English erotica' [review article], *Eighteenth-Century Life* 8 (1983), 108-14.
3. Kramnick, I. 'Labour and leisure in eighteenth-century England' [review essay], ibid. 99-107.
4. Osborne, J.W. 'William Cobbett's anti-semitism' [review essay], *The Historian* 47 (1984-5), 86-92.
5. Sprott, D. *1784.* London; Allen & Unwin; 1984. Pp xiii, 336.
6. Simpson, J. 'Arresting a diplomat, 1717', *History Today* 35/1 (1985), 32-7.
7. Vaisey, D. (ed.). *The diary of Thomas Turner 1754-1765.* Oxford UP; 1984. Pp xxxix, 386.
8. Garland, C.; Klein, H.S. 'The allotment of space for slaves aboard eighteenth-century British slave ships', *William & Mary Q.* 3rd ser. 42 (1985), 238-48.
9. Harris, M. 'London guidebooks before 1800', Bc7, 31-66.
10. McCallum, N. *A small country: Scotland 1700-1830.* Edinburgh; James Thin; 1983. Pp x, 224.
11. Rain, J. *An eye plan of Sunderland and Bishopwearmouth 1785-1790*, repr. & ed. by M. Clay, G. Milburn & S. Miller. Newcastle upon Tyne; Graham; 1984. Pp 67.
12. Mathias, P. 'Concepts of revolution in England and France in the eighteenth century', *Studies in Eighteenth-Century Culture* 14 (1985), 29-45.
13. Gassman, B.W. 'Smollett's *Briton* and the art of political cartooning', ibid. 243-58.
14. Hunt, P.J. (ed.). *Devon's age of elegance described by the diaries of the Reverend John Swete, Lady Paterson, and Miss Mary Cornish.* Exeter; Devon Books; 1984. Pp 160.
15. Ayres, J. (ed.). *Paupers and pig killers: the diary of William Holland, a Somerset parson 1799-1818.* Gloucester; Alan Sutton; 1984. Pp 160.
16. Ritchie-Noakes, N. *Liverpool's historic waterfront: the world's first mercantile dock system.* London; HMSO; 1984. Pp xii, 192.

56

17. Jenkins, P. 'Tory industrialism and town politics: Swansea in the eighteenth century', *Historical J.* 28 (1985), 103-23.
18. Winch, D. 'The Burke-Smith problem and late eighteenth-century political and economic thought', ibid. 231-49.
19. MacDougall, J. *Highland postbag: the correspondence of four MacDougall chiefs 1715-1865.* London; Shepheard-Walwyn; 1984. Pp ix, 294.
20. Wickham, H. *Worsley in the eighteenth century: a study of a Lancashire landscape.* Manchester; Neil Richardson; 1984. Pp 35.
21. Gibbs, G.C. 'The contribution of Abel Boyer to contemporary history in England in the early eighteenth century', in Duke, A.C.; Tamse, C.A. (eds.), *Clio's Mirror: Historiography in Britain and the Netherlands* (Zutphen; De Walburg Pres; 1985), 87-108.
22. Clare, T. 'The perils of a West Indian heiress: case studies of the heiresses of Nathaniel Phillips of Slebech', *Welsh HR* 12 (1985), 495-513.
23. McGarvie, M. 'An Irishman in Wales: Daniel Beaufort's journals for 1766 and 1779', *T. Ancient Monuments Soc.* new ser. 29 (1985), 90-100.

(b) *Politics*

1. Donnelly, F.K. 'The Levellers and early nineteenth century radicalism', *Soc. for the Study of Labour History B.* 49 (1984), 24-8.
2. Schweitzer, D.R. 'The failure of William Pitt's Irish trade propositions 1785', *Parliamentary History 3* (1984), 129-45.
3. Peters, M. '"Names and cant": party labels in English political propaganda *c.* 1755-1765', ibid. 103-27.
4. Black, J. 'Parliament and the political and diplomatic crisis of 1717-1718', ibid. 77-101.
5. Not used.
6. Osborne, J.W. 'The politics of resentment: political, economic, and social interaction in eighteenth-century England', *Eighteenth Century Life* 8 (1983), 49-64.
7. Belchem, J. '"Orator" Hunt, 1773-1835: a British radical reassessed', *History Today* 35/3 (1985), 21-7.
8. Money, J. 'Constituencies and communities: voters, rioters and politics in Georgian England', *Canadian J. of History* 19 (1984), 387-98.
9. O'Gorman, F. 'Electoral deference in "unreformed" England: 1760-1832', *J. of Modern History* 56 (1984), 391-429.
10. Black, J. 'Flying a kite: the political impact of the eighteenth-century British press', *J. of Newspaper & Periodical History* 1/2 (1985), 12-19.
11. Bohstedt, J. *Riots and community politics in England and Wales 1790-1810.* Cambridge, Mass.; Harvard UP; 1983. Pp ix, 310.
12. Dickinson, H.T. *British radicalism and the French Revolution, 1789-1815.* Oxford; Blackwell; 1985. Pp vii, 88.
13. Liesenfeld, V.J. *The Licensing Act of 1737.* Madison; London: University of Wisconsin Press; 1984. Pp xiv, 259.

14. Nokes, D. 'The radical conservatism of Swift's Irish pamphlets', *British J. for Eighteenth-Century Studies* 7 (1984), 169-76.

15. Frearson, A. 'The identity of Junius', ibid. 211-27.

16. McLynn, F.J. 'The ideology of Jacobitism on the eve of the rising of 1745 — part 1', *History of European Ideas* 6 (1985), 1-18.

17. Godwin, J. *Some notable 18th century Staffordshire M.Ps.* Stafford; Staffs. County Library; 1984. Pp 30.

18. Jupp, P. *Lord Grenville 1759-1834.* Oxford; Clarendon; 1985. Pp xiv, 480.

19. Hempton, D. *Methodism and politics in British society 1750-1850.* London; Hutchinson; 1984. Pp 256.

20. McLynn, F.J. 'The ideology of Jacobitism — part II', *History of European Ideas* 6 (1985), 173-88.

21. Knox, T.R. '"Bowes and liberty": the Newcastle by-election of 1777', *Durham Univ. J.* 77 (1985), 149-64.

22. Thomas, P.G.D. 'George III and the American revolution', *History* 70 (1985), 16-31.

23. Cannon, J. *Aristocratic century: the peerage of eighteenth-century England.* Cambridge UP; 1984. Pp x, 193.

24. Black, J. (ed.). *Britain in the age of Walpole.* London; Macmillan; 1984. Pp 260.

25. Cruickshanks, E. 'The political management of Sir Robert Walpole', ibid. 23-43.

26. Dickinson, H.T. 'Popular politics in the age of Walpole', ibid. 45-68.

27. Lenman, B.P. 'A client society: Scotland between the '15 and the '45', ibid. 69-94.

28. Hayton, D. 'Walpole and Ireland', ibid. 95-120.

29. Black, J. 'Foreign policy in the age of Walpole', ibid. 145-170.

30. Downie, J.A. 'Walpole, "the poet's foe"', ibid. 171-88.

31. Harris, M. 'Print and politics in the age of Walpole', ibid. 189-210.

32. Black, J. *British foreign policy in the age of Walpole.* Edinburgh; Donald; 1985. Pp ix, 202.

33. Kelly, G. 'Revolution, crime, and madness: Edmund Burke and the defense of the gentry', *Eighteenth Century Life* 9/1 (1985), 16-32.

34. Middleton, R. *The bells of victory: the Pitt-Newcastle ministry and the conduct of the Seven Years War, 1757-1762.* Cambridge UP; 1985. Pp xiii, 251.

35. Nicholls, D. 'The English middle class and the ideological significance of radicalism, 1760-1886', *J. of British Studies* 24 (1985), 415-33.

36. Rogers, N. 'The City Elections Act (1725) reconsidered', *English HR* 100 (1985), 604-17.

37. Quinn, J.F. 'Yorkshiremen go to the polls: county contests in the early eighteenth century', *Northern History* 21 (1985), 137-74.

38. Paton, D. 'National politics and the local community in the 18th century: the Northampton election of 1734', *Northants. Past & Present* 7 (1985-6), 164-72.

39. Devine, T.M. 'The Union of 1707 and Scottish development', *Scottish Economic & Social History* 5 (1985), 23-40.

(c) *Constitution, Administration and Law*

1. Butel, P. 'Le fonds des prises de la haute Cour d'Amiraute au Public Record Office de Londres', *Bulletin du Centre d'Histoire des Espaces Atlantiques* 1 (1983), 81-95.
2. Nippel, W. '"Reading the Riot Act": the discourse of law-enforcement in 18th century England', *History & Anthropology* 1 (1985), 401-26.
3. Baer, J.H. '"The complicated plot of piracy": aspects of English criminal law and the image of the pirate in Defoe', *Studies in Eighteenth-Century Culture* 14 (1985), 3-28.
4. Simpson, A.W.B. *Cannibalism and the common law: the story of the tragic last voyage of the Mignonette and the strange legal proceedings to which it gave rise.* Chicago & London; Chicago UP; 1984. Pp xiv, 353.
5. Randall, A.J. 'The Gloucestershire food riots of 1766', *Midland History* 10 (1985), 72-93.
6. Duman, D. 'The English bar in the Georgian era', Bc12, 86-107.
7. East Yorks. Family History Soc. *Transportation: from Hull and the East Riding to America and Australia taken from quarter sessions records.* Hull; the society; 1984. Pp 19.
8. Emsley, C. 'Repression, "terror" and the rule of law in England during the decade of the French Revolution', *English HR* 100 (1985), 801-25.

(d) *External Affairs*

1. Ware, R. 'The case of Antonio Rivero and sovereignty over the Falkland Islands', *Historical J.* 27 (1984), 961-7.
2. Steven, M. *Trade, tactics and territory: Britain in the Pacific 1783-1823.* Carlton, Vic.; Melbourne UP; 1983. Pp xi, 155.
3. Marshall, P.J.; Mukherjee, R. 'Debate: early British imperialism in India', *Past & Present* 106 (1985), 164-73.
4. Morgan, K. 'The organization of the convict trade to Maryland: Stevenson, Randolph & Cheston, 1768-1775', *William & Mary Quarterly*, 3rd ser. 42 (1985), 201-27.
5. Ekinch, A.R. 'Bound for America: a profile of British convicts transported to the colonies, 1718-1775', ibid. 184-200.
6. Hobson, C.F. 'The recovery of British debts in the Federal circuit Court of Virginia, 1790 to 1797', *Virginia Magazine of History & Biography* 92 (1984), 176-200.
7. Frost, A.; Gillen, M. 'Botany Bay: an imperial venture of the 1780s', *English HR* 100 (1985), 309-30.
8. Bryant, G.J. 'Scots in India in the eighteenth century', *Scottish HR* 64 (1985), 22-41.

Ge1

(e) *Religion*

1. Lee, E.A.M. 'Bankers and Evangelicals: Thorntons and Wilberforces', *Three Banks Review* 145 (1985), 54-62.
2. Holt, T.G. 'An eighteenth century chaplain: John Champion at Sawston Hall', *Recusant History* 17 (1984), 181-7.
3. Donovan, R.K. 'Sir John Dalrymple and the origins of Roman Catholic relief, 1775-1778', ibid. 188-96.
4. Ruston, A. 'Unitarian trust funds: the Hibbert and the Rawdon', *Trans. Unitarian Historical Soc.* 18 (1985), 138-51.
5. Nicholson, H.M.; McLachlan, J. (eds.). 'Correspondence of Theophilus Lindsey with William Turner of Wakefield and his son (1771-1803), ibid. 152-64.
6. Connell, J. *The Roman Catholic Church in England 1780-1850: a study in internal politics.* Philadelphia: American Philosophical Soc.; 1984. Pp x, 218.
7. Mullett, M. 'From sect to denomination? Social developments in eighteenth-century English Quakerism', *J. of Religious History* 13 (1984), 168-91.
8. Turnbull, P. 'Edward Gibbon: a new letter of 1789', ibid. 213-25.
9. Champion, L.G. 'The Chesham and Berkhemsted church book', *Baptist Quarterly* 31 (1985) 74-82.
10. Brown, R. 'Baptist preaching in early 18th century England', ibid. 4-23.
11. Welch, C. 'Samuel Taylor Coleridge', in N. Smart et al. (eds.), *Nineteenth Century Religious Thought in the West*, 2 (Cambridge UP; 1985), 1-28.
12. Cheyne, A.C. (ed.). *The practical and the pious: essays on Thomas Chalmers (1780-1847).* Edinburgh: St Andrew: 1985. Pp 211.
13. Sell, A.P.F. 'John Chater: from independent minister to Sandemanian author', *Baptist Q.* 31 (1985) 100-17.
14. Not used.
15. Not used.
16. Taylor, S. 'Sir Robert Walpole, the Church of England, and the Quakers' tithe bill of 1736', *Historical J.* 28 (1985), 51-77.
17. Donovan, R.K. 'The military origins of the Roman Catholic relief programmes of 1778', ibid. 79-102.
18. Mather, F.C. 'Georgian churchmanship reconsidered: some variations of Anglican public worship 1714-1830', *J. of Ecclesiastical Hist.* 36 (1985), 255-83.
19. Olsen, D.M. 'Richard Champion and the Society of Friends', *T. of the Bristol & Gloucs. Arch. Soc.* 102 (1985), 173-95.
20. Hall, D.J. 'Plainness of speech, behaviour and apparel in eighteenth-century English Quakerism', Bc14, 307-18.
21. Bellenger, D.A. '"A standing miracle": La Trappe at Lulworth 1794-1817', Bc14, 343-50.
22. Köster, P. 'Baptist Noel Turner's "Intelligence of John Bull": an

allegorical satire on the subscription controversy', *Church History*
54 (1985), 338-52.
23. Pemberton, W.A. 'The parochial visitation of James Bickham D.D.,
archdeacon of Leicester ... 1773 to 1779', *Leics. Arch. & Hist. Soc. T.*
59 (1984-5), 52-72.
24. Martin, R.H. 'The Bible Society and the French connection', *J. of the
United Reformed Church Hist. Soc.* 3. (1985), 278-90.
25. Thompson, D.M. 'The Irish background to Thomas Campbell's
Declaration and Address', ibid. 215-25.
26. Everitt, A. 'Springs of sensibility: Philip Doddridge of Northampton
and the evangelical tradition', Ba34, 201-45.

(f) *Economic Affairs*

1. Hawkins, R.N.P. 'Supplement III to catalogue of the advertisement
imitations of "spade" guineas and their halves', *British Numismatic J.*
53 (1984 for 1983), 160-75.
2. Thomson, G. *The Monkland Canal: a sketch of the early history.*
Monklands; Library Services Department; ca. 1984. Pp 64.
3. Cage, R.A. (ed.). *The Scots abroad: labour, capital, enterprise, 1750-1914.*
London: Croom Helm, 1985. Pp 287.
4. Campbell, R.H. 'Scotland', Gf3, 1-28.
5. Cage, R.A. 'The Scots in England', Gf3, 29-45.
6. Macmillan, D.S. 'Scottish enterprise and influences in Canada, 1620-1900',
Gf3, 46-79.
7. Aspinwall, B. 'The Scots in the United States', Gf3, 80-110.
8. Richards, E. 'Australia and the Scottish connection, 1788-1914', Gf3,
111-55.
9. Brooking, T. '"Tom McCanny and Kitty Clydeside"' — the Scots in New
Zealand', Gf3, 156-90.
10. Parker, J.G. 'Scottish enterprise in India, 1750-1914', Gf3, 191-219.
11. Fernandez, M.A. 'The Scots in Latin America: a survey', Gf3, 220-50.
12. Checkland, O. 'The Scots in Meiji Japan, 1868-1912', Gf12, 251-71.
13. McCusker, J.J. 'Bulletins de trafic et listes des navires: sources pour
l'histoire économique du monde atlantique', *Bulletin du Centre d'Histoire
des Espaces Atlantiques* 1 (1983), 21-26.
14. White, L.H. *Free banking in Britain: theory, experience and debate,
1800-1845.* Cambridge UP; 1984. Pp xv, 171.
15. Lythe, S.G.E. *Thomas Garnett (1766-1802).* Glasgow; Polpress; 1984.
Pp vi, 58.
16. Berg, M. *The age of manufactures: industry, innovation and work in Britain
1700-1820.* Oxford; Blackwell & Fontana; 1985. Pp 368.
17. Crafts, N.F.R. *British economic growth during the Industrial Revolution.*
Oxford; Clarendon; 1985. Pp 193.
18. Alsop, J.D. 'The politics of Whig economics: the National Debt on the
eve of the South Sea Bubble', *Durham Univ. J.* 77 (1985), 211-18.

19. Reitan, E.A. 'Edmund Burke and economic reform 1779-83', *Studies in Eighteenth-Century Culture* 14 (1985), 129-58.
20. Rider, B. *A more expeditious conveyance: the story of the Royal Mail coaches*. London; J.A. Allen; 1984. Pp 159.
21. Miller, M.G.; Fletcher, S. *The Melton Mowbray Navigation*. Oakham; Railway & Canal Hist. Soc.; 1984. Pp 48.
22. Reedman, K.; Sissons, M. 'Unstone coke ovens', *Derbyshire Arch. J.* 104 (1985), 10-18.
23. Riden, P. 'Joseph Butler, coal and iron master, 1763-1837', ibid. 87-95.
24. 'Longyester Farm and the agricultural revolution in East Lothian', *T. of the E. Lothian Antiquarian & Field Naturalists' Soc.* 18 (1984), 61-67.
25. Fontana, B. *Rethinking the politics of a commercial society: the Edinburgh Review 1802-1832*. Cambridge UP; 1985. Pp viii, 256.
26. Devine, T.M. (ed.). *A Scottish Firm in Virginia: 1767-1777: W. Cuninghame & Co.* Edinburgh; Scottish Hist. Soc. 4th ser. 20; 1984. Pp xix, 255, 32.
27. Jones, H. *Accounting, costing, and cost estimation: Welsh industry, 1700-1830*. Cardiff; U Wales P.; 1985. Pp ix, 285.
28. Hansman, W.J. 'The tax on London coal: aspects of fiscal policy and economic development in the eighteenth century', *Eighteenth Century Life* 9/2 (1985), 21-34.
29. Turnbull, G. 'State regulation in the 18th-century English economy: another look at carriers' rates', *J. of Transport History* 3rd ser. 6 (1985), 18-36.
30. Chapman, S.D. 'Quantity versus quality in the British industrial revolution: the case of printed textiles', *Northern History* 21 (1985), 175-92.
31. Thwaites, W. 'Dearth and the marketing of agricultural produce: Oxfordshire c. 1750-1800', *Agricultural HR* 33 (1985), 119-31.
32. Devine, T.M. (ed.). *Farm servants and labour in lowland Scotland, 1770-1914*. Edinburgh; Donald; 1984. Pp ix, 262.
33. Viner, D. 'Industrial archaeology in Gloucestershire', Bb61, 317-42.
34. Malmgreen, G. *Silk town: industry and culture in Macclesfield 1750-1835*. Hull UP; 1985. Pp xii, 259.

(g) *Social Structure and Population*

1. Hall, W.G. 'The meaning of poverty — a Somerset example', *Local Historian* 16 (1984), 15-20.
2. Whipp, R. '"Plenty of excuses, no money": the social bases of trade unionism, as illustrated by the potters', *Soc. for the Study of Labour History B.* 49 (1984), 29-37.
3. Pain, A.J.; Smith, M.T. 'Do marriage horizons accurately measure migration? A test case from Stanhope parish, County Durham', *Local Population Studies* 33 (1984), 44-8.
4. Schofield, R. 'Traffic in corpses: some evidence from Barming, Kent (1788-1812)', ibid. 49-53.

5. Barham, C.; Schofield, R. 'Extracts from the parish registers of Barming, Kent' (1788-1812), ibid. 59-63.
6. Freeman, M. 'The industrial revolution and the regional geography of England: a comment', *T. Institute of British Geographers*. N.S.9 (1984), 507-12.
7. Lawson, P.; Phillips, J. '"Our execrable banditti": perceptions of nabobs in mid-eighteenth century Britain', *Albion* 16 (1984), 225-41.
8. Short, B. 'The decline of living-in-servants in the transition to capitalist farming: a critique of the Sussex evidence', *Sussex Arch. Collections* 122 (1984), 147-64.
9. Ekirch, A.R. 'Great Britain's secret convict trade to America, 1783-1784', *American HR* 89 (1984), 1285-98.
10. Wall, R. 'Real property, marriage and children: the evidence from four pre-industrial communities', Bc2 443-79.
11. Staffordshire Parish Registers Society, *Bloxwich Parish Register, Deanery of Tamworth: baptisms 1721-91, burials 1733-91*. Sedgley; Birmingham & Midlands Soc. for Genealogy & Heraldry; 1984. Pp ii, 86, 7.
12. Staves, S. 'Pin money' [married women's property rights], *Studies in Eighteenth-Century Culture* 14 (1985), 47-77.
13. Hanson, H. *The canal boatmen 1760-1914*. Gloucester; Alan Sutton; 1984. Pp 244.
14. Brown, R.L. *The Lewis' of Greenmeadow*. Cardiff; the author; 1984. Pp 40.
15. Whatley, C.A. 'A saltwork and the community: the case of Winton, 1716-1719', *T. of the E. Lothian Antiquarian & Field Naturalists' Soc.* 18 (1984), 45-60.
16. Newton, R. *Eighteenth century Exeter*. Exeter UP; 1984. Pp xiii, 182.
17. Teitelbaum, M.S. *The British fertility decline: demographic transition in the crucible of the Industrial Revolution*. Princeton UP; 1984. Pp xv, 269.
18. White, E. *The ladies of Gregynog*. Newtown, Powys; Gwasg Gregynog; 1984. Pp 53.
19. Dugaw, D. 'Balladry's female warriors: women, warfare, and disguise in the eighteenth century', *Eighteenth Century Life* 9/2 (1985), 1-20.
20. Stapleton, B. 'Age structure in the early eighteenth century', *Local Population Studies* 34 (1985), 27-34.

(h) *Naval and Military*

1. Boyden, P.B. 'Fire beacons, volunteers, and local militia in Napoleonic Essex — 1803-1811', *T. of the Essex Arch. Soc.* 15 (1984 for 1983), 113-18.
2. Carman, W.Y. 'Banastre Tarleton and the British Legion', *J. of the Soc. for Army Historical Research* 62 (1984), 127-31.
3. Hyden, J.S. 'The sources, organisation and uses of intelligence in the Anglo-Portuguese army, 1808-1814', (ctd.), ibid. 169-75.
4. Guy, A.J. *Oeconomy and discipline: officership and administration in the British army, 1714-63*. Manchester UP; 1985. Pp xi, 188.
5. Hudson, A. 'Volunteer soldiers in Sussex during the revolutionary and

Napoleonic wars, 1793-1815', *Sussex Arch. Collections* 122 (1984), 165-81.

6. Scouller, R.E. 'Purchase of commissions and promotions', *J. of the Soc. for Army Historical Research* 62 (1984), 217-26.

7. Not used.

8. Livingstone, A.; Aikman, C.W.H.; Hart, B.S. (eds.). *Muster roll of Prince Charles Edward Stuart's army 1745-46.* Aberdeen; Aberdeen UP; 1984. Pp xii, 219.

9. Conway, S.R. 'The recruitment of criminals into the British army, 1775-81', *Bull. Inst. Hist. Res.* 58 (1985), 46-58.

10. Murdoch, A. 'More "reluctant heroes": new light on military recruiting in north-east Scotland, 1759-1760', *Northern Scotland* 6 (1985), 157-68.

11. Hayter, T. 'The British army 1713-1793: recent research work', *J. of the Soc. for Army Historical Research* 63 (1985), 11-19.

12. Khanna, D.D.; Tandon, R.K. (eds.). 'Siege of the Fort of Deeg, 9th December to 26th December 1804', ibid. 31-52.

13. Carman, W.Y. 'The Lancers of the British Auxiliary Legion in Spain', ibid. 63-7.

14. Bennell, A.S. 'The Anglo-Maratha war of 1803-5', ibid. 144-61.

15. Strach, S.G. 'A memoir of the exploits of Captain Alexander Fraser and his company of British marksmen 1776-1777', ibid. 91-8, 164-79.

16. Harrington, P. 'Images of Culloden', ibid. 208-19.

17. Ashby, T. 'Fédon's rebellion, part 2', ibid. 220-35.

18. Williams, J.R. 'The 91st (Shropshire Volunteers) Regiment of Foot', *Shropshire Arch. Soc. T.* 63 (1985 for 1981-2), 21-3.

(i) *Intellectual and Cultural*

1. Rosenfeld, S. *The Georgian theatre of Richmond, Yorkshire, and its circuit: Beverley, Harrogate, Kendal, Northallerton, Ulverston and Whitby.* London; Soc. for Theatre Research in association with William Sessions; 1984. Pp vi, 114.

2. Stainton, T. 'John Milton, medallist, 1759-1805', *British Numismatic J.* 53 (1984 for 1983), 133-59.

3. Tyack, G. 'Thomas Ward and the Warwickshire country house', *Architectural History* 27 (1984), 534-42.

4. Girouard, M. 'Early drawings of Bolsover Castle', ibid. 510-18.

5. Leach, P. 'James Paine junior: an unbuilt architect', ibid. 392-405.

6. Cruft, K. 'The enigma of Woodhall House', ibid. 210-13.

7. Rowen, A. 'The building of Hopetoun', ibid. 183-209.

8. Gomme, A. 'Badminton revisited', ibid. 163-82.

9. Connor, T.P. '"Bubo's" house', ibid. 111-17.

10. Farrant, J.H. 'The Brighton charity school in the early 18th century', *Sussex Arch. Collections* 122 (1984), 139-46.

11. McGuinness, R. 'Newspapers and musical life in 18th century London: a systematic analysis', *J. of Newspaper & Periodical History* 1/1 (1984), 29-36.

12. Burrow, J.W. *Gibbon.* Oxford UP; 1985. Pp vii, 117.

13. Raphael, D.D. *Adam Smith*. Oxford UP; 1985. Pp viii, 120.
14. Leatherbarrow, D. 'Architecture and situation: a study of the architectural writings of Robert Morris [c.1701-54], *J. of the Soc. of Architectural Historians* 44 (1985), 48-59.
15. Smith, O. *The politics of language: 1791-1819*. Oxford; Clarendon; 1985. Pp xvi, 269.
16. Rogers, P. *Literature and popular culture in eighteenth-century England*. Brighton; Harvester; 1985. Pp xiv, 215.
17. Haakonssen, K. 'The science of a legislator in James Mackintosh's moral philosophy', *History of Political Thought* 5 (1984), 245-80.
18. Proby, C.T. 'James Harris: Salisbury philosophe 1709-1780, *Hatcher R.* 2/19 (1985), 421-35.
19. Symmons, S. *Flaxman and Europe: the outline illustrations and their influence*. New York; London: Garland; 1984. Pp 303, 107.
20. Cave, K. (ed.). *The diary of Joseph Farington: vol. 13: January 1814-December 1815; vol. 14: January 1816-December 1817*. New Haven & London; Yale UP; 1984. Pp 687.
21. Fleeman, J.D. *A preliminary handlist of copies of books associated with Dr. Samuel Johnson*. Oxford; Oxford Bibliographical Soc.; 1984. Pp vii, 101.
22. Field, M. *The lamplit stage: the Fisher Theatre Circuit, 1792-1844*. Norwich; Running Angel; 1985. Pp 57.
23. Copley, S. *Literature and the social order in 18th century England*. London; Croom Helm; 1984. Pp 272.
24. Flavell, M.K. 'The Enlightenment reader and the new industrial towns: a study of the Liverpool library 1758-1790', *British J. for Eighteenth-Century Studies* 8 (1985), 17-35.
25. Friedman, T. *James Gibbs*. London; Yale UP; 1984. Pp vi, 362.
26. Gross, G.S. 'Dr. Johnson's practice: the medical context for *Rasselas*', *Studies in Eighteenth-Century Culture* 14 (1985), 275-88.
27. Hope, V. (ed.). *Philosophers of the Scottish Enlightenment*, Edinburgh UP; 1984. Pp xii, 261.
28. Amies, M. 'Amusing and instructive conversations: the literary genre and its relevance to home education', *Hist. of Education* 14 (1985), 87-99.
29. Landon, H.C.R. *Handel and his World*. London; Weidenfeld; 1984. Pp 256.
30. Porter, R. 'Man, animals and nature' [rev. art.], *Historical J.* 28 (1985), 225-9.
31. Evans, R. 'Theatre music in Nottingham, 1760-1800', *T. of the Thoroton Soc. of Notts.* 88 (1985), 47-53.
32. Bradshaw, J. 'Occupation and literacy in the Erewash valley coalfield, 1760-1880', Bc11, 7-19.
33. Campbell, J. 'Occupation and literacy in Bristol and Gloucestershire, 1755-1870', Bc11, 20-36.
34. Harrop, S.A. 'Literacy and educational attitudes as factors in the industrialization of north-east Cheshire, 1760-1830', Bc11, 37-53.

35. Grayson, J. 'Literacy, schooling and industrialization: Worcestershire, 1760-1850', Bc11, 54-67.
36. Unwin, R. 'Literacy patterns in rural communities in the Vale of York, 1660-1840', Bc11, 68-81.
37. Joppien, R.; Smith, B. *The art of Captain Cook's voyages*. New Haven & London; Yale UP; 2 vols.; 1985. Pp xv, 247; xiii, 286.
38. Ribeiro, A. *The dress worn at masquerades in England, 1730 to 1790, and its relation to fancy dress in portraiture.* London; Garland; 1984. Pp xlvi, 476, 293 p of plates.
39. Dinwiddy, J.R. (ed.). *The correspondence of Jeremy Bentham: vol. 6: Jan. 1798 to Dec. 1801.* Oxford; Clarendon; 1984. Pp 440.
40. Hall, I. *Georgian Buxton.* Buxton; Derbyshire Museum Service; 1984. Pp 48.
41. Rock, J. *Thomas Hamilton: architect 1784-1858.* Edinburgh; J. Rock; 1984. Pp iii, 73.
42. Jeffery, S. 'John James and George London at Herriand', *Architectural History* 28 (1985), 40-70.
43. Kelly, A. 'Coade stone in Georgian architecture', ibid. 71-101.
44. Bennett, S. 'Anthony Pasquin and the function of art journalism in late 18th-century England', *British J. for Eighteenth-Century Studies* 8 (1985), 197-207.
45. Crompton, L. *Byron and Greek love: homophobia in 19th century England.* London; Faber; 1985. Pp 400.
46. Feather, J. *The provincial book trade in eighteenth-century England.* Cambridge UP; 1985. Pp xvi, 176.
47. Levine, J.M. 'The battle of the books and the shield of Achilles', *Eighteenth Century Life* 9 (1984), 33-61.
48. Levine, J.M. 'Edward Gibbon and the quarrel between the Ancients and the Moderns', *The Eighteenth Century* 26 (1985), 47-62.
49. Robertson, J. *The Scottish Enlightenment and the militia issue.* Edinburgh; Donald; 1985. Pp viii, 272.
50. Horn, P. (ed.). *Life in a country town: Reading and Mary Russell Mitford (1787-1855).* Abingdon; Beacon Publications; 1984. Pp ii, 81.
51. Porritt, A. 'The Society of Antiquaries and the Rev. John Watson, M.A., F.S.A.', *Halifax Antiquarian Soc. T.* (1985 for 1984), 36-40.
52. Porter, R. '"Under the influence": Mesmerism in England', *History Today* 35/9 (1985), 22-9.
53. Smith, T.P. 'Brick-tiles (mathematical tiles) in 18th- and 19th-century England', *J. of the British Arch. Association* 138 (1985), 132-64.
54. Ellis, F.H. (ed.). *Swift vs. Mainwaring: the Examiner and the Medley.* Oxford; Clarendon; 1985. Pp lxx, 514.

(j) *Science*

1. Skempton, A.W. 'The engineering works of John Grundy (1719-1783)', *Lincolnshire History and Archaeology* 19 (1984), 65-82.

2. Stansfield, D.A. *Thomas Beddoes M.D., 1760-1808: chemist, physician, democrat.* Dordrecht; Lancaster; Reidel; 1984. Pp xix, 306.
3. Loudon, I. 'The nature of provincial medical practice in eighteenth-century England', *Medical History* 29 (1985), 1-32.
4. Stewart, L. 'The edge of utility: slaves and smallpox in the early eighteenth century', ibid. 54-70.
5. Richards, S. 'Agricultural science in higher education: problems of identity in Britain's first chair of agriculture, Edinburgh, 1790-c.1831', *Agricultural HR* 33 (1985), 59-65.
6. Reid, J.S. 'Patrick Copeland 1748-1822: aspects of life and times at Marischal College', *Aberdeen Univ. Review* 172 (1984), 359-79.
7. Cumming, D.A. 'John MacCulloch's "Millstone survey" and its consequences', *Annals of Science* 41 (1984), 567-91.
8. Porter, R. 'Lay medical knowledge in the eighteenth century: the evidence of the *Gentleman's Magazine*', *Medical Hist.* 29 (1985), 138-68.
9. Baxby, D. 'The genesis of Edward Jenner's *Inquiry* of 1798: a comparison of the two unpublished manuscripts and the published version', ibid. 193-9.
10. Morrison-Low, A.D.; Christie, J.J.R. (eds.). *'Martyr of science': Sir David Brewster 1781-1863.* Edinburgh; Royal Scottish Museum; 1984. Pp 138.
11. Whittle, E.S. *The inventor of the marine chronometer: John Harrison of Foulby (1693-1776).* Wakefield; Wakefield Historical Publications; 1984. Pp vi, 32.
12. Waddington, I. *The medical profession in the industrial revolution.* Dublin; Gill & Macmillan; 1984. Pp xi, 236.
13. Millburn, J.R. 'James Ferguson's lecture tour of the English Midlands in 1771', *Annals of Science* 42 (1985), 397-415.
14. Withers, C.W.J. 'A neglected Scottish agriculturalist: the "Georgical Lectures" and agricultural writings of the Rev. Dr. John Walker (1731-1803)', *Agricultural HR* 33 (1985), 132-46.

H. BRITAIN 1815-1914

See also Fh13; Ga10, 19, b1, 7, 9, 35, d2, e6, f3-12, 14, 25, 27, 32; 34, g2, 10, h13, 32-36, i3, 15, 20, 41, 45, j5, 6, 10; Ib15, 17, f10-12, 14, 22, 27, 39; Ka8, f2.

(a) *General*

1. Cowan, Sir Z. 'Protecting Press and public', Hg6, 8-11.
2. Newman, Sir K. 'The media and public order', Hg6, 12-17.
3. Bainbridge, C. 'One hundred years of journalism – part II', Hg6, 33-150.
4. Phillips, K.C. *Language and class in Victorian England.* Oxford; Blackwell & Deutsch; 1984. Pp viii, 190.

Ha5

5. Briggs, A. *The collected essays of Asa Briggs: vol. 2: Images, problems, standpoints, forecasts.* Brighton; Harvester; 1985. Pp xviii, 324.
6. Cunningham, H. 'Leisure', Hf60, 133-64.
7. Nord, D.E. *The apprenticeship of Beatrice Webb.* London; Macmillan; 1984. Pp 320.
8. Carter, T. *The Victorian garden.* London; Bell & Hyman; 1984. Pp 192.
9. Trinder, B. (ed.). *Victorian Shrewsbury: studies in the history of a county town.* Shrewsbury; Shropshire Libraries; 1984. Pp 159.
10. Kelly, A.; Wilson, C. *Jack the Ripper: a bibliography and review of the literature* (2nd edn.). London; Association of Assistant Librarians S.E.D.; 1984. Pp 83.
11. Clarke, P. *The governesses: letters from the colonies 1862-1882.* London; Hutchinson; 1985. Pp xii, 236.
12. Drower, M.S. *Flinders Petrie: a life in archaeology.* London; Gollancz; 1985. Pp 512.
13. Fraser, F. (ed.). *Maud: the diaries of Maud Berkeley.* London; Secker & Warburg; 1985. Pp 192.
14. Honri, P. *John Wilton's music hall: the handsomest room in town.* Hornchurch; Ian Henry; 1985. Pp 161.
15. Owen, J. et al. *Change at Crewe: original photographs and copies by Bernard Owen.* Chester; Cheshire Libraries; 1984. Pp 56.
16. Leeves, E. *Leaves from a Victorian diary.* London; Alison Press/Secker & Warburg; 1985. Pp xviii, 126.
17. Bottomley, A.F. (ed.). *The Southwold diary of James Maggs 1818-1876: Vol. II: 1848-1876.* Woodbridge; Boydell (Suffolk Records Soc. 26); 1984. Pp vii, 183.
18. Moore, D. (ed.). *Barry: the centenary book.* Barry; Barry Centenary Book Committee; 1984. Pp xxi, 496.
19. Clarke, F.G. *Will-o'-the-Wisp: Peter the Painter and the anti-tsarist tourists in Britain and Australia.* Melbourne; Oxford UP; 1983. Pp 131.

(b) *Politics*

1. Pugh, P. *Educate, agitate, organize: 100 years of Fabian socialism.* London; Methuen; 1984. Pp xiii, 330.
2. Smith, D. 'Sir George Grey at the mid-Victorian Home Office', *Canadian J. of History* 19 (1984), 361-86.
3. Kennedy, T.C. 'The Quaker renaissance and the origins of the British peace movement, 1895-1920', *Albion* 16 (1984), 243-72.
4. Adelman, P. 'The peers *versus* the people: the Reform crisis of 1884-85', History Today 35 (1985), 24-34.
5. Carter, P. *Islington at Westminster: the story of members of parliament for Islington and Finsbury, 1884-1983.* London; Islington Fabian Society; 1984. Pp 48.
6. Max, S.M. 'Tory reaction to the Public Libraries bill, 1850', *J. of Library History* 19 (1984), 504-24.

7. Offer, A. 'The working classes, British naval plans and the coming of the Great War', *Past & Present* 107 (1985), 204-26.
8. Feuchtwanger, E.J. *Democracy and empire: Britain, 1865-1914.* London; Edward Arnold; 1985. Pp vii, 408.
9. Swartz, M. *The politics of British foreign policy in the era of Disraeli and Gladstone.* London; Macmillan; 1985. Pp xiii, 221.
10. Vogeler, M.S. *Frederic Harrison: the vocations of a positivist.* Oxford; Clarendon; 1984. Pp xvii, 493.
11. Rose, K. *Curzon: a most superior person.* London; Macmillan; 1985. Pp 496.
12. Waters, M. 'Dockyards and parliament: a study of the unskilled workers in Chatham yard, 1860-1900', *Southern History* 6 (1984), 123-38.
13. Jones, D.J.V. *The last rising: the Newport insurrection of 1839.* Oxford; Clarendon; 1985. Pp xii, 290.
14. Blake, R. *The Conservative party from Peel to Thatcher.* London; Methuen; 1985. Pp xi, 320.
15. Bentley, M. *Politics without democracy, 1815-1914: perception and preoccupation in British government.* London; Fontana; 1984. Pp 446.
16. Mendilow, J. 'Past, future and present perfect: three tenses of the British idea of empire', *Australian J. of Politics & History* 30 (1984), 209-23.
17. Brooks, D. 'Gladstone and Midlothian: the background to the first campaign', *Scottish HR* 64 (1985), 42-67.
18. Lubenow, W.C. 'Irish home rule and the social basis of the great separation in the Liberal party in 1886', *Historical J.* 28 (1985), 125-42.
19. Lieberman, D. 'From Bentham to Benthamism', ibid. 199-224.
20. Coogan, J.W. & P.F. 'The British cabinet and the Anglo-French staff talks, 1905-1914 ...', *J. of British Studies* 24 (1985), 110-31.
21. Briggs, A. *The collected essays and reviews of Asa Briggs: vol. 1: words, numbers, places, people.* Brighton; Harvester; 1985. Pp xix, 245.
22. Jagger, P.J. (ed.). *Gladstone, politics and religion: a collection of Founder's Day Lectures delivered at St Deiniol's Library, Hawarden, 1967-83.* London; Macmillan; 1985. Pp xxiv, 183.
23. Blake, Lord. 'Disraeli and Gladstone', Hb22, 1-20.
24. Home, Lord. 'Mr Gladstone', Hb22, 21-27.
25. Foot, M.R.D. 'The Gladstone diaries', Hb22, 28-39.
26. Checkland, S. 'Mr Gladstone, his parents and his siblings', Hb22, 40-48.
27. Ratcliffe, F.W. 'Mr Gladstone, the librarian and St Deiniol's Library, Hawarden', Hb22, 49-67.
28. Chadwick, O. 'Young Gladstone and Italy', Hb22, 68-87.
29. Shannon, R.T. 'Midlothian: 100 years after', Hb22, 88-103.
30. Ramm, A. 'Gladstone as politician', Hb22, 104-116.
31. Steele, D. 'Gladstone and Palmerston 1855-65', Hb22, 117-47.
32. Golant, W. *Image of empire: the early history of the Imperial Institute, 1887-1925.* Exeter; the university; 1984. Pp 52.
33. Cleaver, D. 'Labour and Liberals in the Fower constituency, 1885-1910', *Welsh Hist. Rev.* 12 (1985), 388-410.

34. Jones, R.A. *The British diplomatic service, 1815-1914*. Gerrards Cross; Smythe; 1983. Pp xiii, 258.
35. Mileham, P.J.R. 'The Stirlingshire Yeomanry cavalry and the Scottish Radical disturbances of April 1820', *J. of the Soc. for Army Hist. Res.* 63 (1985), 20-30, 104-12.
36. Gavin, M. 'The Guildford Guy riots (1842-1865)', *Surrey Arch. Collections* 76 (1985), 61-8.
37. Morris, D. '"Merched y screch a'r twrw": yr WSPU yn Llanystumdwy 1912' [reaction to suffragettes], *Caernarvonshire Hist. Soc. T.* 46 (1985), 115-32.
38. Hughes, D.G.L1. 'Pwllheli: llywodraeth leol yn y crochan berw 1847-56' [A crisis in local government at Pwllheli], ibid. 51-84.
39. Young, J.D. 'Militancy, English socialism and *The Ragged Trousered Philanthropists*', *J. of Contemporary History* 20 (1985), 283-303.
40. Mullins, E.L.C. 'The making of the "Return of Members"', *Bull. Inst. Hist. Res.* 58 (1985), 189-209.
41. Alexander, A. *Borough government and politics: Reading 1835-1985*. London; Allen & Unwin; 1985. Pp xi, 235.
42. Pollock, J. *Shaftesbury: the poor man's earl*. London; Hodder & Stoughton; 1985. Pp 192.
43. Dilks, D. *Neville Chamberlain: Vol. 1: Pioneering and reform, 1869-1929*. Cambridge UP; 1984. Pp xv, 645.
44. Belchem, J. *'Orator' Hunt: Henry Hunt and English working-class radicalism*. Oxford; Clarendon; 1985. Pp xiv, 304.
45. Mackay, R.F. *Balfour: intellectual statesman*. Oxford UP; 1985. Pp vi, 388.
46. Howkins, A. *Poor labouring men: rural radicalism in Norfolk, 1872-1923*. London; Routledge; 1985. Pp xiv, 225.
47. Electoral Reform Society of Great Britain and Ireland. *The best system: 1884-1984: an account of its first hundred years*. Dartford; Arthur McDougall Fund; 1984. Pp 28.
48. Daunton, M.J. 'Rowland Hill and the penny post', *History Today* 35/8 (1985), 31-7.

(c) *Constitution, Administration and Law*

1. Read J. *Ellis, Wood, Bickersteth & Hazel, 1883-1983*. London; Ellis, Wood, Bickersteth & Hazel; 1983. Pp 54.
2. Scarman, Lord. 'Some observations on the law and freedom of the Press', Hg6, 3-7.
3. Hoeflich, M.H. 'John Austin and Joseph Story: two nineteenth century perspectives on the utility of the civil law for the common lawyer', *American J. of Legal History* 29 (1985), 36-77.
4. Jackson, C. *A history of the Pontefract borough police*. Wakefield; S.M. Jackson; 1984. Pp viii, 42.
5. Cantwell, J. 'The making of the first deputy keeper of the records', *Archives* 17 (1985), 22-37.

6. Edwards, O.D. *Burke & Hare*. Newton Grange; Lang Syne Publications; 1980. Pp ix, 300.
7. Woods, D. 'Community violence', Hf60, 165-205.
8. Swift, R. 'Sources and methods for the study of urban crime in the early nineteenth century [Exeter]', *Local Historian* 16/5 (1985), 289-97.
9. Gordon, P. '"A county parliament": the first Northamptonshire County Council', *Northamptonshire Past & Present* 7 (1985-6), 188-95.
10. Coltman. P. (ed.). *The diary of a prison governor: James William Newham, 1825-1890*. Maidstone; Kent County Library; 1984. Pp x, 196.
11. Foster, D. 'The East Riding constabulary in the nineteenth century', *Northern History* 21 (1985), 193-211.
12. Wasson, E.A. 'The great Whigs and parliamentary reform, 1809-30', *J. of British Studies* 23 (1985), 434-64.

(d) *External Affairs*

1. Barthorp, M. *War on the Nile: Britain, Egypt and the Sudan, 1882-1898*. Poole; Blandford; 1984. Pp 190.
2. Emery, F.V. 'Geography and imperialism: the role of Sir Bartle Frere', *Geographical J.* 150 (1984), 342-50.
3. Jenkins, B. 'Anglo-American relations before the First World War', *Canadian J. of History* 19 (1984), 407-9.
4. Judd, D. 'Gordon of Khartoum: the making of an imperial martyr;, *History Today* 35 (1985), 19-25.
5. Wilson, K.M. *The policy of the entente: essays on the determinants of British foreign policy, 1904-1914*. Cambridge UP; 1985. Pp viii, 199.
6. King, P. (ed.). *A viceroy's India: leaves from Lord Curzon's notebook, by the Marquess Curzon of Kedleston*. London; Sidgwick & Jackson; 1984. Pp 192.
7. Knee, S.E. 'Anglo-American understanding and the Boer War', *Australian J. of Politics & History* 30 (1984), 196-208.
8. Neilson, K. *Strategy and supply: the Anglo-Russian alliance, 1914-17*. London; Allen & Unwin; 1984. Pp xiv, 338.
9. Eldridge, C.C. (ed.). *British imperialism in the 19th century*. London; Macmillan; 1984. Pp 256.
10. Kennedy, P, 'Continuity and discontinuity in British imperialism 1815-1914', Hd9, 20-38.
11. Burroughs, P. 'Colonial self-government', Hd9, 39-63.
12. Moore, R.J. 'India and the British Empire', Hd9, 64-84.
13. Sturgis, J. 'Britain and the New Imperialism', Hd9, 85-105.
14. Atmore, A.E. 'The extra-European foundations of British imperialism: towards a reassessment', Hd9, 106-25.
15. Eldridge, C.C. 'Sinews of empire: changing perspectives', Hd9, 168-89.
16. Gilbert, B.B. 'Pacifist interventionist: Lloyd George in 1911 and 1914. Was Belgium an issue?', *Historical J.* 28 (1985), 863-85.

17. Pakenham, V. *The noonday sun: Edwardians in the tropics.* London; Methuen; 1985. Pp 255.
18. Nish, I. *The Anglo-Japanese alliance: the diplomacy of two island empires, 1894-1907* (2nd edn.). London; Athlone; 1985. Pp xxi, 420.
19. Chamberlain, M.E. 'New light on British foreign policy', *History Today* 35/7 (1985), 43-8.
20. Thorne, R. 'Tom's letters to his kinsfolk', *National Library of Wales J.* 23 (1984), 357-65.
21. Reynolds, J. 'Politics vs. persuasion: the attempt to establish Anglo-Roman diplomatic relations in 1848', *Catholic HR* 71 (1985), 372-93.

(e) *Religion*

1. Carrick, J. *Evangelicals and the Oxford Movement.* Bridgend; Evangelical Press of Wales on behalf of the Evangelical Library, London; 1984. Pp 52.
2. Westwood, W.J. 'The Press and the Church', Hg6, 27-30.
3. Lipman, V.D.; Lipman, S. (eds.). *The century of Moses Montefiore.* Oxford UP; 1985. Pp x, 385.
4. McClelland, V.A. 'Gladstone and Manning: a question of authority', Hb22, 148-70.
5. Rogers, T.D. 'A memoir of a Sussex parson — Charles Townsend (1789-1870) — by William Twopeny', *Bodleian Library Record* 11 (1985), 408-16.
6. McIntyre, M.L. 'Deliverance: notes on a sermon ... delivered by F.D. Maurice ... 1848', *Historical Magazine of the Protestant Episcopal Church* 54 (1985), 51-66.
7. Kollar, R.M. 'The Caldey monks and the Catholic Press, 1905-1913', *Recusant History* 17 (1985), 287-98.
8. Supple, J.F. 'Ultramontanism in Yorkshire, 1850-1900', ibid. 274-86.
9. Murphy, M. 'Blanco White's evidence', ibid. 254-73.
10. Hilton, B. 'The role of Providence in evangelical social thought', Bc3, 215-33.
11. Norman, E.R. 'Cardinal Manning and the temporal power'. Bc3, 235-56.
12. Williams, H. (ed.). *Bulwark and bridge: essays in memory of Elsie Pritchard of Brecon.* Merthyr Tydfil; the editor; 1984. Pp 58.
13. Cameron, J.M. 'John Henry Newman and the Tractarian movement', *Nineteenth Century Religious Thought in the West,* ed. N. Smart et al., 2 (Cambridge UP; 1985), 69-111.
14. Livingston, J.C. 'British agnosticism', ibid. 231-70.
15. Lewis, H.D. 'The British idealists', ibid. 271-314.
16. Endelman, T.M. 'Communal solidarity among the Jewish elite of Victorian London', *Victorian Studies* 28 (1985), 491-526.
17. Ireson, T. 'A Victorian rector and his village: J.H. Holdich at Bulwick', *Northamptonshire Past & Present* 7 (1984-5), 106-13.
18. Cowling, M. *Religion and public doctrine in modern England, vol. II: Assaults.* Cambridge UP; 1985. Pp xxvii, 403.

19. Supple, J.F., 'The Catholic clergy of Yorkshire, 1850-1900: a profile', *Northern History* 21 (1985), 212-35.
20. Gowler, S. 'No second-hand religion: Thomas Erskine's critique of religious authorities', *Church History* 54 (1985), 202-14.
21. Aspinwall, B. 'Changing images of Roman Catholic orders in the nineteenth century', Bc14, 351-63.
22. Frances, A. 'William John Butler and the revival of the ascetic tradition', Bc14, 365-76.
23. Kollar, R.M. 'Archbishop Davidson, Bishop Gore and Abbot Carlyle: Benedictine monks in the Anglican Church', Bc14, 377-96.
24. Keep, D.J. 'Self-denial and the Free Churches: some literary responses', Bc14, 397-404.
25. Binfield, C. 'Freedom through discipline: the concept of the Little Church', Bc14, 405-50.
26. Gilley, S.W. 'Newman and prophecy, evangelical and catholic', *J. of the United Reformed Church Hist. Soc.* 3 (1985), 160-88.
27. Cornick, D. '"Catch a Scotchman becoming an Englishman!" Nationalism, theology and ecumenism in the Presbyterian Church in England 1845-76', ibid. 202-15.
28. Binfield, C. 'In search of Mrs A: a transpennine quest', ibid. 234-51.
29. Peake, F.A. 'Studies in a Derbyshire parish — religion in nineteenth-century Heanor', *Derbyshire Arch J.* 104 (1985), 71-86.

(f) *Economic Affairs*

1. Bullen, A. *The Lancashire Weavers' Union: a commemorative history.* Manchester; Amalgamated Textile Workers' Union; 1984. Pp 75.
2. Hewer, C. *A problem shared: a history of the Institute of London Underwriters, 1884-1984.* London; Witherby; 1984. Pp xiii, 136.
3. Thompson, N.W. *The people's science: the popular political economy of exploitation and crisis 1816-34.* Cambridge UP; 1984. Pp 252.
4. Buchanan, R.A. 'Institutional proliferation in the British engineering profession, 1847-1914', *Economic HR* 38 (1985), 42-60.
5. Michie, R.C. 'The London Stock Exchange and the British securities market, 1850-1914', ibid. 61-82.
6. Godden, S. *At the sign of the fourposter: a history of Heal's.* London; Heal & Son; 1984. Pp 127.
7. Pearce, S.A. 'The impact of the railway on Uckfield in the 19th century', *Sussex Arch. Collections* 122 (1984), 193-206.
8. Parton, A.G. 'Parliamentary enclosure in nineteenth-century Surrey — some perspectives on the evaluation of land potential' *Agricultural HR* 33 (1985), 51-8.
9. Hobsbawm, E.J. *Worlds of labour: further studies in the history of labour.* London; Weidenfeld & Nicholson; 1984. Pp x, 369.
10. Harrison, R.; Zeitlin, J. (eds.). *Divisions of labour: skilled workers*

and technological change in nineteenth-century Britain. Brighton: Harvester; 1985. Pp ix. 254.

11. Blankenhorn, D. '"Our class of workmen": the cabinet-makers revisited', Hf10, 19-47.

12. Mackay, I. 'Bondage in the bakehouse? The strange case of the journeymen bakers, 1840-1880', Hf10, 47-86.

13. Hirsch, M. 'Sailmakers: the maintenance of craft tradition in the age of steam', Hf10, 87-113.

14. Whipp, R. 'The stamp of futility: the Staffordshire potters, 1880-1905', Hf10, 114-50.

15. McClelland, K.; Reid, A. 'Wood, iron and steel: technology, labour and trade union organization in the shipbuilding industry, 1840-1914', Hf10, 151-84.

16. Zeitlin, J. 'Engineers and compositors: a comparison', Hf10, 185-250.

17. Vale, V. *The American peril: challenge to Britain on the North Atlantic, 1901-04.* Manchester UP; 1984. Pp viii, 256.

18. Everitt, A. *Transformation and tradition: aspects of the Victorian countryside.* Norwich; Centre of East Anglian Studies: 1984. Pp 33.

19. Beckett, Sir T. 'The Press and industry', Hg6, 18-23.

20. Lea, R. *Steaming up to Sutton: how the Birmingham to Sutton Coldfield railway line was built in 1862.* Sutton Coldfield; Westwood; 1984. Pp 48.

21. Maloney, J. *Marshall, orthodoxy and the professionalisation of Economics.* Cambridge UP; 1985. Pp x, 278.

22. Thorpe, D. *The railways of the Manchester Ship Canal.* Poole; Oxford Publishing; 1984. Pp 185.

23. *Farming in Gloucestershire 1800-1914.* Gloucester; Gloucester Folk Museum: 1984. Pp 75.

24. Fox, A. *History and heritage: the social origins of the British industrial relations system.* London; Allen & Unwin; 1985. Pp xiii, 481.

25. Newman, R. 'The "Swing" riots: agricultural revolt in 1830', *Hatcher R.* 2/19 (1985), 436-47.

26. Mommsen, W.J.; Husung, H.-G. *The development of trade unionism in Great Britain and Germany, 1880-1914.* London; Allen & Unwin for German Historical Institute; 1985. Pp 336.

28. Semmens, P.W.B. *A history of the Great Western Railway: vol. 1: Consolidation, 1923-29.* London; Allen & Unwin; 1985. Pp 102.

28. Semmens, P.W.B. *A history of the Great Western Railway: vol. 2: The Thirties, 1930-39.* London; Allen & Unwin; 1985. Pp 96.

29. Gough, J. *The Northampton and Harborough line.* Oakham; Railway & Canal Historical Society; 1984. Pp 112.

30. Semmens, P.W.B. *A history of the Great Western Railway: vol. 3: Wartime and the final years, 1939-48.* London; Allen & Unwin; 1985. Pp 102.

31. Capie, F. *A monetary history of the United Kingdom, 1870-1982: vol. 1: Data, sources, methods.* London; Allen & Unwin; 1985. Pp 480.

32. Martin, J.M. 'The social and economic origins of the Vale of Evesham market gardening industry', *Agriculture HR* 33 (1985), 41-50.

33. Miller, C. 'The hidden workforce: female field workers in Gloucestershire, 1870-1901', *Southern History* 6 (1984), 139-55.
34. Harper, R.H. *Victorian building regulations: summary tables of the principal English building acts and model by-laws 1840-1914.* London; Mansell; 1985. Pp xxxv, 137.
35. Hobsbawm, E.J. 'The "New Unionism" reconsidered', Hf26, 13-31.
36. Pollard, S. 'The New Unionism in Britain: its economic background', Hf26, 32-52.
37. Cronin, J.E. 'Strikes and the struggle for union organisation: Britain and Europe', Hf26, 55-77.
38. Boll, F. 'International strike waves: a critical assessment', Hf26, 78-99.
39. Lovell, J. 'The significance of the Great Dock Strike of 1889 in British labour history', Hf26, 100-113.
40. Price, R. 'The New Unionism and the labour process', Hf26, 133-49.
41. Reid, A. 'The division of labour and politics in Britain, 1880-1920', Hf26, 150-65.
42. Burgess, K. 'New Unionism for old? The Amalgamated Society of Engineers in Britain', Hf26, 166-84.
43. Bagnell, P.S. 'The New Unionism in Britain: the railway industry', Hf26, 185-200.
44. Hyman, R. 'Mass organisation and militancy in Britain: contrasts and continuities', Hf26, 250-65.
45. Holton, R.J. 'Revolutionary syndicalism and the British labour movement', Hf26, 266-82.
46. Alderman, G. 'The National Free Labour Association: working class opposition to New Unionism in Britain', Hf26, 302-11.
47. Saville, J. 'The British state, the business community and the trade unions', Hf26, 315-24.
48. Zeitlin, J. 'Industrial structure, employer strategy and the diffusion of job control in Britain 1880-1920', Hf26, 325-37.
49. Winter, J.M. 'Trade unions and the Labour Party in Britain', Hf26, 359-70.
50. Jones, D. 'Did Friendly Societies matter? A study of Friendly Societies in Glamorgan, 1794-1910, *Welsh HR* 12 (1985), 324-49.
51. Slinn, J. *A history of May & Baker [1834-1984].* Cambridge; Hobsons; 1984. Pp 196.
52. Cassis, Y. 'Bankers in English society in the late nineteenth century', *Economic HR* 2nd Ser. 38 (1985), 210-29.
53. Chapman, S.D. 'British-based investment groups before 1914', ibid. 230-51.
54. Winch, D. 'Economic liberalism as ideology: the Appleby version', ibid. 287-97.
55. Michie, R.C. 'Income, expenditure and investment of a Victorian millionaire: Lord Overstone, 1823-83', *Bull. Inst. Hist. Res.* 58 (1985), 59-77.
56. Britton, R. 'Wealthy Scots, 1876-1913', ibid. 78-94.
57. Howe, M. *The Commissioners of Rhyl: the men who built the town.* Rhyl; the author; 1984. Pp 95.

Hf58

58. Mappen, E. *Helping women at work: the Women's Industrial Council 1889-1914.* London; Hutchinson; 1985. Pp 135.

59. Matsumara, T. *The labour aristocracy revisited: the Victorian flint glass makers, 1850-80.* Manchester; 1983. Pp x, 196.

60. Benson, J. (ed.). *The working class in England 1875-1914.* London; Croom Helm; 1985. Pp 214.

61. Benson, J. 'Work', Hf60. 63-88.

62. Haynes, M.J. 'Strikes', Hf60, 89-132.

63. Elvin, L. *Bishop and Son, organ builders: the story of J.C. Bishop and his successors.* Lincoln; the author; 1984. Pp 356.

64. Williams-Davies, J. *Cider making in Wales.* Cardiff; National Museum of Wales; 1984. Pp 53.

65. Bartrip, P. 'Food for the body and food for the mind: the regulation of freshwater fisheries in the 1870s', *Victorian Studies* 28 (1985), 285-304.

66. Lampard, K. 'The promotion and performance of the London Chatham and Dover Railway', *J. of Transport History* 3rd ser. 6 (1985), 148-63.

67. Simmons, J. 'Suburban traffic at King's Cross 1852-1914', ibid. 71-8.

68. Harrison, A.E. 'The origins and growth of the UK cycle industry to 1900', ibid. 41-70.

69. Jones, S. 'George Benjamin Dodwell: a shipping agent in the Far East, 1872-1908', ibid 23-40.

70. Yuzawa, T. 'The introduction of electric railways in Britain and Japan', ibid. 1-22.

71. Horn, P. 'Child workers in the Victorian countryside: the case of Northamptonshire', *Northamptonshire Past & Present* 7 (1985-6), 173-85.

72. Greeves, T.A.P. 'Steeperton Tor tin mine, Dartmoor, Devon', *Devonshire Association Report & T.* 117 (1985), 101-27.

73. Smith, D.J. *New Street remembered: the story of Birmingham's New Street Railway Station 1854-1967.* Birmingham; Barbryn: 1984. Pp 124.

74. Peacock, A.E. 'Factory Act prosecutions: a hidden consensus?', *Economic HR* 2nd ser. 38 (1985), 431-6.

75. Nardinelli, C. 'The successful prosecution of the Factory Acts: a suggested explanation', ibid. 428-30.

76. Bartrip, P. 'Success or failure? The prosecution of the early Factory Acts', ibid. 423-7.

77. Hassan, J.A. 'The growth and impact of the British water industry in the nineteenth century', ibid. 531-47.

78. Pollard, S. 'Capital exports, 1870-1914: harmful or beneficial?', ibid. 489-514.

79. Haas, J.M. 'Trouble at the workplace: industrial relations in the royal dockyards, 1889-1914', *Bull. Inst. Hist. Res.* 58 (1985), 210-25.

80. Zimmeck, M. 'Gladstone holds his own: the origins of income tax relief for life insurance policies', ibid. 167-88.

81. Crouzet, F. *The first industrialists: the problem of origins.* Cambridge UP; 1985. Pp 229.

82. Mellor, R.E.H. (ed.). *The railways of Scotland: papers of Andrew C. O'Dell.* Aberdeen; Centre for Scottish Studies; 1984. Pp 53.

83. Daunton, M.J. *Royal Mail: the Post Office since 1840.* London; Athlone; 1985. Pp xviii, 388.
84. Levy, C. *Ardrossan shipyards: struggle for survival: 1825-1983.* Glasgow; W.E.A.; 1984. Pp ii, 44.
85. Lummis, T. *Occupation and society: the East Anglian fishermen 1880-1914.* Cambridge UP; 1985. Pp xiii, 212.
86. Phillips, G.; Whiteside, N. *Casual labour: the unemployment question in the port transport industry, 1880-1970.* Oxford; Clarendon; 1985. Pp ix, 324.
87. Williams, C. *Driving the Clay Cross tunnel: navvies on the Derby/Leeds railway.* Cromford; Scarthin; 1984. Pp 88.
88. Tomlinson, M. *Three generations in the Honiton lace trade: a family history.* Exeter; the author; c. 1983. Pp 94.
89. Burt, R.; Waite, P.; Burnley, R. *Devon and Somerset mines: metaliferous and associated minerals 1845-1913.* Exeter; the university; 1984. Pp xxviii, 136.
90. Tordoff, M. *The servant of colour: a history of the Society of Dyers and Colourists: 1884-1984.* Bradford; the society; 1984. Pp vi, 481.
91. Briggs, A. *Wine for sale: Victoria Wine and the liquor trade 1860-1984.* London; Batsford; 1985. Pp ix, 199.
92. Ryan, R. 'The early expansion of the Norwich Union Life Insurance Society, 1808-37', *Business History* 27 (1985), 166-96.
93. Sanderson, M. 'Adam Smith, Sir Herbert Tree and the wages of actors 1890-1914', ibid, 197-206.
94. Chapman, S. *The rise of merchant banking.* London; Allen & Unwin; 1984. Px xi, 235.
95. Kutolowski, J.F. 'Victorian provincial businessmen and foreign affairs: the case of the Polish insurrection, 1863-1864', *Northern History* 21 (1985), 236-58.
96. Howat, J.N.T. *South American packets: the British packet service to Brazil, the River Plate, the West Coast ... and the Falkland Islands, 1808-80.* York; Postal Hist. Soc./Sessions; 1984. Pp xi, 283.
97. Duncan, R. *Textiles and toil: the factory system and the industrial working class in early 19th century Aberdeen.* Aberdeen City Libraries; 1984. Pp viii, 56.
98. Carnegie, H. *Harnessing the wind: Captain Thomas Mitchell of the Aberdeen White Star Line.* Aberdeen; Centre for Scottish Studies; c. 1984. Pp 68.
99. Saunders, D. 'Tyneside and the making of the Russian Revolution', *Northern History* 21 (1985), 259-84.
100. Boyns, T. 'Work and death in the South Wales Coalfield, 1874-1914', *Welsh HR* 12 (1985), 514-37.
101. Munting, R. 'Agricultural engineering and European exports before 1914', *Business History* 27 (1985), 125-45.
102. Rodger, R.G. 'Business failure in Scotland, 1839-1913', ibid. 75-99.
103. Wilson, J. 'A strategy of expansion and combination: Dick, Kerr & Co., 1897-1914', ibid. 26-41.

104. Gourvish, T.R.; Wilson, R.G. 'Profitability in the brewing industry 1885-1914', ibid. 146-65.

105. Williamson, J.G. *Did British capitalism breed inequality?* London; Allen & Unwin; 1985. Pp ix, 270.

106. Wilson, C. *First with the news: the history of W.H.Smith 1792-1972.* London; Cape; 1985. Pp 416.

107. Connor, J.E. *Stepney's own railway: a history of the London & Blackwall system.* Colchester; Connor & Butler; 1984. Pp 116.

108. Jackson-Stevens, E. *100 years of British electric tramways.* Newton Abbot; David & Charles; 1985. Pp 96.

109. *The West Drayton enclosure: copies from documents relating to the enclosure of land in the parish of West Drayton under the Act of 1824.* West Drayton; West Drayton & District Local History Society; 1984. Pp 28.

110. Lloyd, L. *The brig 'Susannah' of Aberdyfi: the story of a coasting brig (1815-1843).* Meirionnydd; the author; 1984. Pp 59.

111. Hatton, T.J. *The British labour market in different economic eras, 1857-1938.* London; Centre for Economic Policy Research; 1984. Pp 32.

112. Treble, J.H. 'The performance of the Standard Life Assurance Company in the ordinary market for life insurance, 1825-1850', *Scottish Economic & Social History* 5 (1985), 57-77.

113. Cohen, I. 'American management and British labor: Lancashire immigrant spinners in industrial New England', *Comparative Studies in Society and History* 27 (1985), 608-50.

114. Boot, H.M. *The commercial crisis of 1847.* Hull UP (Occasional Papers in Economic & Social History 11); 1984. Pp 101.

(g) *Social Structure and Population*

1. Foster, B. *Living and dying: a picture of Hull in the nineteenth century.* Hull; 58 de Grey St., HU5 2SA; 1984. Pp 272.

2. Gaskell, S.M. 'The making of a model village' [Oving, W. Sussex], *Local Historian* 16 (1984), 4-14.

3. Chiswell, A. 'The nature of urban overcrowding', ibid. 156-60.

4. Bailey, V. '"In darkest England and the way out". The Salvation Army, social reform and the Labour movement, 1885-1910', *International R. of Social History* 29 (1984), 133-71.

5. Barker, K. 'The early development of music hall in Brighton', *Sussex Arch. Collections* 122 (1984), 183-91.

6. Bainbridge, C. (ed.). *One hundred years of journalism: social aspects of the Press.* Basingstoke; Macmillan; 1984. Pp xvii, 166.

7. Lambertz, J. 'Sexual harrassment in the nineteenth century English cotton industry', *History Workshop* 19 (1985), 29-61.

8. Eattell, M. *The people of the parish of Seal 1820-1880.* Sevenoaks; Seal & Kemsing History Publications; 1984. Pp 30.

9. Thomson, D. '"I am not my father's keeper": families and the elderly in nineteenth century England', *Law & History Review* 2 (1984), 265-86.

10. Goodbody, J. 'The *Star*: its role in the rise of popular newspapers, 1888-1914', *J. of Newspaper & Periodical History* 1/2 (1985), 20-9.
11. Roberts, E. 'The Family', Hf60, 1-35.
12. Harper, M. 'Emigration from north east Scotland in the nineteenth century', *Northern Scotland* 6 (1985), 169-81.
13. Erickson, C. *English women immigrants in America in the nineteenth century: expectations and reality.* London; LLRS Publications; 1983. Pp 175.
14. Cooper, W.G. *The Ancient Order of Foresters Friendly Society: 150 years: 1834-1984*, ed. K. Anthony. Southampton; The Society; 1984. Pp 40.
15. Not used.
16. Behlmer, G.K. 'The gypsy problem in Victorian England', *Victorian Studies* 28 (1985), 231-53.
17. Evand, N. 'The Welsh Victorian city: the middle class and civic and national consciousness in Cardiff 1850-1914', *Welsh HR* 12 (1985), 350-87.
18. Lewis, J. *Women in England 1870-1950: sexual divisions and social change.* Brighton; Wheatsheaf; 1984. Pp xv, 240.
19. Burnett, J.; Vincent, D.; Mayall, D. (eds.). *The autobiography of the working class.* Brighton; Harvester; 1984. Pp 463.
20. Jones, O.V. 'Bangor: the growth of a city during the first half of the nineteenth century', *Caernarvonshire Hist. Soc. T.* 46 (1985), 23-43.
21. Bristow, B.R. 'Population and housing in nineteenth-century urban Lancashire: a framework for investigation', *Local Population Studies* 34 (1985), 12-26.
22. Gill, C. 'The Western Morning News, 1860-1985', *Devonshire Association Report & T.* 117 (1985), 195-226.
23. Mayall, D. 'Palaces for entertainment and instruction: a study of the early cinema in Birmingham, 1908-18', *Midland History* 10 (1985), 94-109.
24. Pollins, H. 'Immigration into Britain: the Jews', *History Today* 35/7 (1985), 8-14.
25. Rodgers, M. 'Immigration into Britain: the Lithuanians', ibid. 15-20.
26. Morgan, P.B. 'Bronwydd and Sir Thomas Lloyd', *National Library of Wales J.* 23 (1984), 377-405.
27. Lunn, K. 'Immigration into Britain: immigrants and British labour's response, 1870-1950', *History Today* 35/11 (1985), 48-52.

(h) *Social policy*

1. Gutchen, R.M. 'Masters of workhouses under the New Poor Law', *Local Historian* 16 (1984), 93-9.
2. Bailey, V. 'Churchill as Home Secretary: reforming the prison service', *History Today* 35/3 (1985), 10-13.
3. Selleck, R.J.W. 'Mary Carpenter: a confident and contradictory reformer', *History of Education* 14 (1985), 101-15.
4. Chamberlain, M.E. 'Imperialism and social reform', Hd9, 148-67.

5. Forsythe, W.J. 'Paupers and policy makers in Exeter 1830-1860', *Devonshire Association Report & T.* 117 (1985), 151-60.
6. Levine, D. 'The Danish connection: a note on the making of British old age pensions', *Albion* 17 (1985), 181-5.
7. Cooney, A. *The sources of poverty: the causes of poverty in general and Toxteth in particular during the decade 1900-1910* ... Liverpool; Gild of St George; 1984. Pp 79.
8. Rice, F.J. 'The origins of an Organisation of Insanity in Scotland', *Scottish Economic & Social History* 5 (1985), 41-56.
9. Collinge, J.M. *Officials of royal commissions of inquiry 1815-1870.* London; Inst. Hist. Res.; 1984. Pp ix, 108.
10. Best, W.C.F. *'C' or St James's: a history of policing in the West End of London 1829 to 1984.* Kingston-upon-Thames; the author; 1985. Pp 71.

(i) *Education*

1. Stubbs, J. *A history of Cutthorpe village, 1860-1933.* Cutthorpe; the Dower House, Cutthorpe, Chesterfield S42 7AR; 1983. Pp 72.
2. Bantock, G.H. *Studies in the history of educational theory, vol. 2: The minds and the masses, 1760-1980.* London; Allen & Unwin; 1984. Pp ix, 374.
3. Anderson, R. 'In search of the "lad of parts": the mythical history of Scottish education', *History Workshop* 19 (1985), 82-104.
4. Pollins, H. *The History of Ruskin College.* Oxford; Ruskin College Library; 1984. Pp 71.
5. Morley, C.W. *John Ruskin: late work 1870-1890: the Museum and Guild of St George: an educational experiment.* New York; London; Garland; 1984. Pp 650 in various paginations.
6. Sondheimer, J. *Castle Adamant in Hampstead: a history of Westfield College 1882-1982.* London; Westfield College; 1983. Pp 189.
7. Lynch, J.; Lock, J.A. 'Early childhood education in Sunderland in the nineteenth century', *Historia Infantiae* 1 (1984), 91-8.
8. Mason, D.M.; Anderson, R.D. 'School attendance in nineteenth-century Scotland', *Economic HR* 2nd ser. 38 (1985), 276-86.
9. Gardner, P. *The people's schools in Victorian England.* London; Croom Helm; 1984. Pp 256.
10. Lawn, M. 'Teachers in dispute: the Portsmouth and West Ham strikes', History of Education 14 (1985), 35-47.
11. Williams, J.G. 'Arguments on behalf of Bangor as the site of the University College of North Wales', *Caernarvonshire Hist. Soc. T.* 46 (1985), 85-114.
12. Paz, D.G. 'Sir James Kay-Shuttleworth: the man behind the myth', History of Education 14 (1985), 185-98.
13. De Cogan, D. 'More light on John James Graves of Lamport', *Northants. Past & Present* 7 (1984-5), 101-5.
14. Cooper, P. et al. *'For present comfort and for future good'*: the story of

Queen Alexandra's House, 1884-1984. London; Friends of Queen
Alexandra's House; 1984. Pp 56.

15. Leinster-Mackay, D. *The rise of the English prep school.* London; Falmer;
1984. Pp xvi, 398.

16. Ellis, A. *Educating our masters: influences on the growth of literacy in
Victorian working class children.* Aldershot; Gower; 1985. Pp vii, 209.

17. Carter, P.C. *A history of elementary schooling in Trowbridge before the 1870
Education Act.* Trowbridge; Wilts. Library & Museum Service; 1984.
Pp 53.

18. Wright, C. *The Kent College centenary book.* London; Batsford; 1985.
Pp 160.

19. Miller, J. *The York Place-Varndean story: 1884-1984.* Brighton; the
author; 1984. Pp 67.

(j) *Naval and Military*

1. Bramall, Sir E. 'Reporting conflict: the media and the armed services',
Hg6, 24-26.

2. Barthrop, M. 'Anatomy of a troop and squadron 10th Royal Hussars
1859-1872', *J. of the Soc. for Army Hist. Res.* 62 (1984), 201-16.

3. Trench, C.C. *The frontier scouts.* London; Cape; 1985. Pp 256.

4. Strachan, H. 'The British Army, 1815-1856: recent writing reviewed', *J. of
the Soc. for Army Hist. Res.* 63 (1985), 68-79.

5. Not used.

6. Barthorp, M. 'The battle of Tofrek [Sudan], 1885', ibid. 1-10.

7. Downe, D. 'The Mutiny diary and sketches of John North Crealock, 95th
Regiment', ibid. 80-90.

8. Spiers, E.M. 'The British Army 1856-1914: recent writing reviewed', ibid.
194-207.

9. Macfie, A.L. 'The boatmen of Dover and Deal: the report of the House of
Commons Select Committee on the Cinque-Port pilots, 1833',
Archaeologia Cantiana 101 (1985 for 1984), 131-6.

10. Hiley, N. 'The failure of British counter-espionage against Germany,
1907-1914', *Historical J.* 28 (1985), 835-62.

11. Warner, P. *Kitchener.* London; H. Hamilton; 1985. Pp 247.

12. Royle, T. *The Kitchener enigma.* London; Joseph; 1985. Pp 448.

13. Gray, E.A. *The trumpet of glory: the military career of John Shipp, first
veterinary surgeon to join the British Army.* London; Hale; 1985. Pp 127.

14. Maxwell, L. *The Ashanti Ring: Sir Garnet Wolseley's campaigns 1870-1882.*
London; Leo Cooper/Secker & Warburg; 1985. Pp 248.

15. Vines, S. 'How the Army came to Salisbury Plain', *Hatcher R.* 2/20 (1985),
492-9.

16. Burroughs, P. 'Crime and punishment in the British Army, 1815-1870',
English HR 100 (1985), 545-71.

17. Trousdale, W. (ed.). *The Gordon Creeds in Afghanistan, 1839 and
1878-79.* London; BACSA; 1984. Pp x, 189.

Hk1

(k) *Science and Medicine*

1. Metz, K.H. 'Social thought and social statistics in the early nineteenth century: the case of sanitary statistics in England', *International R. of Social History* 29 (1984), 254-73.
2. Brown, P.S. 'The vicissitudes of herbalism in late nineteenth- and early twentieth-century Britain', *Medical History* 29 (1985), 71-92.
3. Gollin, A. *No longer an island: Britain and the Wright brothers: 1902-1909.* London; Heinemann; 1984. Pp x, 478.
4. Harry, O.G. 'The Hon. Mrs Ward and "A windfall for the microscope" of 1856 and 1864', *Annals of Science* 41 (1984), 471-82.
5. Forbes, H.G. 'The professionalization of dentistry in the United Kingdom', *Medical History* 29 (1985), 169-81.
6. Dale, G.; Miller, F.J.W. *Newcastle School of Medicine, 1834-1984: sesquicentennial scrapbook.* Newcastle-upon-Tyne; Faculty of Medicine, the University; 1984. Pp 152.
7. Smith, F.B. 'Health', Hf60, 36-62.
8. Di Gregorio, M.A. *T.H. Huxley's place in natural science.* London; Yale UP; 1984. Pp 288.
9. Richards, R.L. *Dr John Rae.* Whitby; Caedmon; 1984. Pp xii, 231.
10. Not used.
11. Bud, R.; Roberts, G.K. *Science versus practice: chemistry in Victorian Britain.* Manchester UP; 1984. Pp 236.
12. Penfold, J.B. *The history of the Essex County Hospital, Colchester ... 1820-1948.* Colchester; the author; 1984. Pp ix, 279.
13. Rupke, N. 'Richard Owen's Hunterian lecturer on comparative anatomy and physiology, 1837-55', *Medical History* 29 (1985), 237-58.
14. Cholmeley, J.A. *History of the Royal National Orthopaedic Hospital.* London; Chapman & Hall; 1985. Pp 150.
15. Lansbury, C. 'Gynaecology, pornography, and the antivivisection movement', *Victorian Studies* 28 (1985), 413-37.
16. Hamlin, C. 'Providence and putrefaction: Victorian sanitarians and the natural theology of health and disease', ibid. 381-411.
17. Oswald, N.C. 'The Budds of North Tawton: a medical family of the 19th century', *Devonshire Association Report & T.* 117 (1985), 139-50.
18. Hughes, R.E. '"Corvinus" a "Llewelyn Conwy"; juvenilia Cymraeg dau Naturiaethwr', *National Library of Wales J.* 23 (1984), 366-76.
19. Corbett, H.V. *A royal catastrophe: a modern account of the death in childbirth of the Royal Highness Princess Charlotte Augusta ...* Broadway; the author; 1985. Pp xviii, 70.
20. Burkhardt, F.; Smith, S. (eds.). *A calendar of the correspondence of Charles Darwin, 1821-1882.* New York & London; Garland; 1985. Pp 690.
21. Soloway, R.A. 'Feminism, fertility, and eugenics in Victorian and Edwardian England', in S. Drescher et al. (eds.), *Political Symbolism in Modern Europe: Essays in honour of G.L. Mosse* (London; Transaction Books; 1982), 121-45.
22. Jones, O.V. *The progress of medicine: a history of the Caernarfon and*

82

Anglesey Infirmary 1809-1948. Llandysul; Gomer; 1984. Pp xiii, 317.
23. Hall, M.B. *All scientists now: the Royal Society in the nineteenth century*. Cambridge UP; 1984. Pp xii, 261.

(l) *Intellectual and cultural*

1. Henderson, I.T.; Crook, J. *The Winchester diver: the saving of a great cathedral*. Crawley; Henderson & Stirk; 1984. Pp 128.
2. Spurrell, M. (ed.). *Stow church restored 1846-1866*. Woodbridge; Boydell; Lincoln Record Soc. 75; 1984. Pp xxxii, 220.
3. Curr, G.G. 'Who saved York walls?', *York Historian* 5 (1984), 25-38.
4. White, A.J. 'The Revd John Skinner's tour to Lincolnshire, 1825', *Lincolnshire History & Archaeology* 19 (1984), 93-8.
5. Gow, I. 'Sir Rowand Anderson's national art survey of Scotland', *Architectural History* 27 (1984), 543-54.
6. Howell, P. 'The Jubilee tower of Moel Famau', ibid. 331-43.
7. Coren, M. *Theatre Royal: 100 years of Stratford East*. London; Quartet; 1984. Pp xi, 112.
8. Roberts, M.J.D. 'Making Victorian morals? The Society for the Suppression of Vice and its critics, 1802-1886', *Historical Studies* 21(1984), 157-73.
9. Banham, J.; Harris, J. (eds.). *William Morris and the middle ages: a collection of essays: together with a catalogue of works exhibited at the Whitworth Art Gallery, 28 September - 8 December 1984*. Manchester UP; 1984. Pp xii, 225.
10. Haward, B. *Nineteenth century Norfolk stained glass; gazetteer, directory: an account of Norfolk stained glass painters*. Norwich; Geo; 1984. Pp xxxiii, 302.
11. Stokes, R. *Henry Bradshaw 1831-1886*. London; Scarecrow; 1984. Pp v, 272.
12. Mendilow, J. 'Merrie England and the Brave New World: two myths of the idea of empire', *History of European Ideas* 6 (1985), 41-58.
13. Hilton, T. *John Ruskin: vol. 1: the early years*. New Haven & London; Yale UP; 1985. Pp 320.
14. Feldman, J. 'Population and ideology', *History of Political Thought* 5 (1984), 361-75.
15. Coover, J. (ed.). *Music publishing, copyright and piracy in Victorian England ... 1881-1906*. London; Mansell; 1985. Pp xvi, 169.
16. Woodfield, J. *English theatre in transition, 1881-1914*. London; Croom Helm; 1984. Pp 213.
17. Yeldham, C. *Women artists in nineteenth-century France and England*. London; Garland; 1984. 4 vols. in 2; pp 1165.
18. Lutyens, Sir E. *The letters of Edwin Lutyens*. London; Collins; 1984. Pp 320.
19. Haley, B. 'Wilde's "decadence" and the positivist tradition', *Victorian Studies* 28 (1985), 215-29.

20. Kass, A.M. & E.H. 'The Thomas Hodgkin portraits: a case of mistaken identity', *Medical History* 29 (1985), 259-63.
21. Bolt, C. 'Race and the Victorians', Hd9, 126-47.
22. Bledsoe, R. 'Henry Fothergill Chorley and the reception of Verdi's early operas in England', *Victorian Studies* 28 (1985), 631-55.
23. Roberts, M.J.D. 'Morals, art, and the law: the passing of the Obscene Publications Act, 1857', ibid. 609-29.
24. Bennett, J.D. 'Illustrations in the architectural press of Victorian and Edwardian buildings in Leicestershire', *Leics. Arch. & Hist. Soc. T.* 59 (1984-5), 73-85.
25. Linnard, W. 'Rodenberg's autumn in Wales: a German visit to Caernarfonshire in 1856', *Caernarvonshire Hist. Soc. T.* 46 (1985), 45-50.
26. Cusack, P. 'Lion Chambers: a Glasgow experiment', *Architectural History* 28 (1985), 198-211.
27. Taylor, A. 'Francis Goodwin's "Domestic Architecture" and two Cockermouth villas', ibid. 125-35.
28. Sharples, J. 'A.W. Pugin and the patronage of Bishop James Gillis', ibid. 136-58.
29. Brownlee, D.B. 'That "regular-mongrel" affair: G.G. Scott's design for the government offices', ibid. 159-97.
30. Johnson, B.C. *Lost in the Alps: a portrait of Robert Proctor the "great bibliographer" and of his career in the British Museum.* London; the author; 1985. Pp 49.
31. Franks, D. *Printing and publishing in Stokesley.* Middlesbrough; Stokesley & District Local History Study Group; 1984. Pp 63.
32. Smith, H. *Decorative painting in the domestic interior in England and Wales c. 1850-1890.* New York & London; Garland; 1984. Pp 396.
33. Thomson, A. *Ferrier of St Andrews: an academic tragedy.* Edinburgh; Scottish Academic; 1985. Pp xv, 133.
34. Wilson, D.M. *The forgotten collector; Augustus Wollaston Franks of the British Museum.* London; Thames & Hudson; 1984. Pp 63.
35. Sudworth, G. *The great little Tilley: Vesta Tilley and her times: a biography.* Luton; Cortney; 1984. Pp ii, 159.
36. Not used.
37. Errington, L. *Social and religious themes in English art 1840-1860.* New York & London; Garland; 1984. Pp 493.
38. Stansley, P. *Redesigning the world: William Morris, the 1880s, and the Arts and Crafts.* Guildford; Princeton UP; 1985. Pp xvi, 293.
39. Woodfield, J. *English theatre in transition 1881-1914.* London; Croom Helm; 1984. Pp 192.
40. Marsh, J. *Pre-Raphaelite sisterhood.* London; Quartet; 1985. Pp 408.
41. Cross, N. *The common writer: life in nineteenth-century Grub Street.* Cambridge UP; 1985. Pp vi, 265.
42. Vance, N. *The sinews of the Spirit: the ideal of Christian manliness in Victorian literature and religious thought.* Cambridge UP; 1985. Pp 256.
43. Rosenberg, J.D. *Carlyle and the burden of history.* Oxford; Clarendon; 1985. Pp viii, 209.

44. Crawford, A. *C.R.Ashbee*. London; Yale UP; 1985. Pp 416.
45. Deacon, R. *The Cambridge Apostles: a history of Cambridge University's elite intellectual secret society*. London; Royce; 1985. Pp 224.

I. BRITAIN SINCE 1914

See *also* Ha15, 18, b3, 11, 14, 43, 45, c1, 4, d8, f6, 27, 28, 30, 31, 82-84, 86, 90, 91, 106-8, 111, g6, 22-5, 27, h10, i1, 2, 6, 14, 18, 19, k2, 5, 6, 22, 145.

(a) *General*

1. Vansittart, P. (ed.). *John Masefield's letters from the Front 1915-1917*. London; Constable; 1984. Pp 307.
2. Howarth, T. *Prospect and reality: Great Britain 1945-1955*. London; Collins; 1985. Pp 256.
3. Cronin, J.E. *Labour and society in Britain, 1918-1979*. London; Batsford; 1984. Pp x, 248.
4. Marwick, A. *Britain in our century: images and controversies*. London; Thames & Hudson; 1984. Pp 224.
5. Ware, G. '*A rose in Picardy': the diaries of Gwen Ware 1916-1918*. Farnham; Farnham & District Museum Society; 1984. Pp 43.
6. Mitchison, N. *Among you taking notes: the wartime diary of Naomi Mitchison 1939-1945*, ed. D. Sheridan. London; Gollancz; 1985. Pp 352.
7. Duff, D. *Queen Mary*. London; Collins; 1985. Pp 262.
8. Kee, R. *1945: the world we fought for*. London; Hamish Hamilton; 1985. Pp xxviii, 371.
9. Blake, R. *The decline of power, 1915-1964*. London; Paladin (Paladin History of England); 1985. Pp x, 462.
10. Addison, P. *Now the war is over: a social history of Britain 1945-51*. London; B.B.C./Cape; 1985. Pp viii, 223.
11. Havighurst, A.F. *Britain in transition: the twentieth century* (revised edn.). Chicago UP; 1985.
12. Berry, P.; Bishop, A. (eds.). *Testament of a generation: the journalism of Vera Brittain and Winifred Holtby*. London; Virago; 1985. Pp 352.
13. Bishop, A. (ed.). *Chronicle of friendship: Vera Brittain's diary of the Thirties, 1932-1939*. London; Gollancz; Pp 448.

(b) *Politics*

1. Langley, H.M. 'The Woolton papers', *Bodleian Library Record* 11 (1984), 320-37.
2. Grigg, J. *Lloyd George: from peace to war 1912-1916*. London; Methuen; 1985. Pp 527.

3. Trory, E. *Churchill and the Bomb: a study in pragmatism.* Hove; Crabtree; 1984. Pp 128.
4. Durbin, E. *New Jerusalems: the Labour Party and the economics of democratic socialism.* London; Routledge; 1985. Pp xvii, 341.
5. Ayerst, D. *Garvin of the Observer.* London; Croom Helm; 1985. Pp 314.
6. Radice, L. *Beatrice and Sidney Webb: Fabian socialists.* London; Macmillan; 1984. Pp x, 342.
7. Pelling, H. *The Labour governments, 1945-51.* London; Macmillan; 1984. Pp vii, 313.
8. Wrigley, C. 'The General Strike, 1926, in local history'. *Local Historian* 16 (1984), 36-48, 83-9.
9. Haydn, J. 'Factory politics in Britain and the United States: engineers and machinists, 1914-1919', *Comparative Studies in Society and History* 27 (1985), 57-85.
10. Peacock, A. J. 'Conscience and politics in York 1914-18', *York Historian* 5 (1984), 39-50.
11. Smith, H. 'Sex vs. class: British feminists and the Labour movement, 1919-1929', *The Historian* 47 (1984-5), 19-37.
12. Dutton, D. *Austen Chamberlain: gentleman in politics.* Bolton; Ross Anderson; 1985. Pp viii, 373.
13. Higgins, S. *The Benn inheritance: the story of a radical family.* London; Weidenfeld & Nicolson; 1984. Pp ix, 228.
14. Ramsden, J. (ed.) *Real old Tory politics: the political diaries of Sir Robert Sanders, Lord Bayford, 1910-35.* London; Historians' Press; 1984. Pp vii, 260.
15. Terrins, D.; Whitehead, P. (eds.). *100 years of Fabian socialism: 1884-1984.* London; Fabian Society; 1984. Pp 34.
16. Bush, J. *Behind the lines: East London Labour, 1914-1919.* London; Merlin; 1984. Pp xxiii, 254.
17. Walter, D. *The Oxford Union: playground of power.* London; Macdonald; 1984. Pp 240.
18. MacKenzie, N. & J. (eds.). *The diary of Beatrice Webb: Vol. 4: 1924-1943, 'The wheel of life'.* London; Virago & London School of Economics; 1985. Pp xvi, 519.
19. Colville, J. *The fringes of power: Downing Street diaries 1939-1955.* Sevenoaks; Hodder & Stoughton; 1985. Pp 796.
20. Burridge, T. *Clement Attlee: a political biography.* London; Cape; 1985. Pp xiii, 401.
21. Grigg, J. 'Lloyd George and ministerial leadership in the Great War', Ii27, 1-8.
22. Street, D. 'The domestic scene: parliament and people', Ii27, 9-20.
23. Cecil, H. 'Lord Robert Cecil and the League of Nations during the First World War', Ii27, 69-82.
24. Craig, F.W.S. *City and Royal Burgh of Glasgow municipal election results 1949-73.* Chichester; the author; 1984. Pp 86.
25. Heren, L. *The power of the press?* London; Orbis; 1985. Pp 208.
26. Stafford, P. 'Political autobiography and the art of the possible: R.A. Butler

at the Foreign Office, 1938-1939', *Historical J.* 28 (1985), 901-22.

27. Walker, G. '"Protestantism before Party!": the Ulster Protestant League in the 1930s', ibid. 961-7.

28. McCulloch, G. 'Labour, the Left, and the British general election of 1945', *J. of British Studies* 24 (1985), 465-89.

29. Mór-O'Brien, A. 'The Merthyr boroughs election, November 1915', *Welsh HR* 12 (1985), 538-66.

30. Rintala, M. 'Renamed roses: Lloyd George, Churchill, and the House of Lords', *Biography* 8 (1985), 248-64.

31. Sainty, J.C. 'Assistant Whips 1922-1964', *Parliamentary History* 4 (1985), 201-04.

32. Thomas, G. *Mr. Speaker: the memoirs of Viscount Tonypandy.* London; Century; 1985. Pp 242.

33. Clegg, H.A. *A history of British trade unions since 1889: Vol. II: 1911-1933.* Oxford UP; 1985. Pp xi, 619.

34. Gallagher, T. 'Protestant extremism in urban Scotland, 1930-1939: its growth and contraction', *Scottish HR* 64 (1985), 143-67.

35. Weller, K. 'Don't be a soldier!': the radical anti-war movement in North London, 1914-1918. London; Journeyman Press; 1985. Pp 96.

36. Branson, N. *History of the Communist Party of Great Britain, 1927-1941.* London; Laurence & Wishart; 1985. Pp ix, 350.

37. Moore, B. *All out: the dramatic story of the Sheffield demonstration against dole cuts on February 6th 1935.* Sheffield; Sheffield City Libraries; 1985. Pp ii, 60.

(c) *Constitution, Administration and Law*

1. Deacon, R. *'C': a biography of Sir Maurice Oldfield.* London; Macdonald; 1985. Pp vii, 279.

2. Cockerell, M.; Hennessy, P.; Walker, D. *Sources close to the prime minister: inside the hidden world of the news manipulators.* London; Macmillan; 1984. Pp 261.

3. Boadle, D. 'Vansittart's administration of the Foreign Office in the 1930s', Id9, 68-84.

4. Tomlinson, J.D. 'Women as "anomalies": the anomalies regulations of 1931, their background and implications', *Public Administration* 62 (1984), 422-37.

5. Rubin, G.R. 'Labour courts and the proposals of 1917-19', *Industrial Law J.* 14 (1985), 33-9.

6. Seyfert, M. 'His Majesty's most loyal internees', Id22, 163-93.

7. Loughlin, M.; Gelfand, M.D.; Young, K. *Half a century of municipal decline, 1935-1985.* London; Allen & Unwin; 1985. Pp xiii, 270.

8. Young, K. 'Re-reading the municipal progress: a crisis revisited', Ic7, 1-25.

9. Dawson, D.A. 'Economic change and the changing role of local government', Ic7, 26-49.

10. Alexander, A. 'Structure, centralization and the position of local government', Ic7, 51-76.

11. Gyford, J. 'The politicization of local government', Ic7, 77-97.
12. Stewart, J.D. 'The functioning and management of local authorities', Ic7, 98-120.
13. Loughlin, M. 'Administrative law, local government and the courts', Ic7, 121-43.
14. Jackman, R. 'Local government finance', Ic7, 144-68.
15. Grant, M.; Healey, P. 'The rise and fall of planning', Ic7, 169-86.
16. Geary, R. *Policing industrial disputes, 1893 to 1985.* Cambridge UP; 1985. Pp vii, 171.
17. Pattison, M. 'Scientists, government and invention: the experience of the Invention Board, 1915-1918', Ii27, 83-101.
18. Barnett, L.M. *British food policy in the First World War.* London; Allen & Unwin; 1985. Pp xix, 241.
19. West, W.T. *The trial of Lord de Clifford, 1935: the last trial of a British peer by his fellow peers.* York; Sessions; 1984. Pp viii, 62.
20. Fraser, P. 'Cabinet secrecy and war memoirs', *History* 70 (1985), 397-409.

(d) *External Affairs*

1. Kent, M. 'Great Britain and the end of the Ottoman Empire, 1900-1923', in Kent, M. (ed.), *The Great Powers and the End of the Ottoman Empire* (London; Allen & Unwin; 1984), 172-205.
2. Burk, K. *Britain, America and the sinews of war, 1914-1918.* London; Allen & Unwin; 1985. Pp x, 286.
3. Jaffe, L.S. *The decision to disarm Germany: British policy towards postwar German disarmament, 1914-1919.* London; Allen & Unwin; 1985. Pp 286.
4. Macmillan, H. *War diaries: politics and war in the Mediterranean: January 1943-May 1945.* London; Macmillan; 1984. Pp xxiv, 804.
5. Cohen, M.J. *Churchill and the Jews.* London; Cass; 1985. Pp xii, 388.
6. Lentin, A. *Lloyd George, Woodrow Wilson and the guilt of Germany: an essay in the pre-history of appeasement.* Leicester UP; 1984. Pp 192.
7. Keyserlingk, R.M. 'Die deutsche Komponente in Churchills strategie der nationalen Erhebungen: der Fall Otto Strasser', *Vierteljahrshefte für Zeitgeschichte* 31 (1983), 614-45.
8. Kahler, M. *Decolonization in Britain and France: the domestic consequences of international relations.* Princeton UP; 1984. Pp xiv, 426.
9. Langhorne, R. (ed.). *Diplomacy and intelligence during the Second World War: essays in honour of F.H. Hinsley.* Cambridge UP; 1985. Pp vii, 329.
10. Andrew, C. 'F.H. Hinsley and the Cambridge moles: two patterns of intelligence recruitment', Id9, 22-40.
11. Zweig, R. 'The political uses of military intelligence: evaluating the threat of a Jewish revolt against Britain during the second world war', Id9, 109-25.
12. Smyth, D. 'The politics of asylum: Juan Negrín and the British government in 1940', Id9, 126-46.
13. Reynolds, D. 'Churchill and the British "decision" to fight on in 1940: right policy, wrong reasons', Id9, 147-67.
14. Lawlor, S. 'Britain and the Russian entry into the war', Id9, 168-83.

15. Wheeler, M. 'Crowning the revolution: the British, King Peter, and the path to Tito's cave', Id9, 184-218.
16. Salmon, P. 'Crimes against peace: the case of the invasion of Norway at the Nuremberg trials', Id9, 245-69.
17. Papastratis, P. *British policy towards Greece during the Second World War, 1941-1944*. Cambridge UP; 1984. Pp viii, 274.
18. Callahan, R.A. *Churchill: retreat from Empire*. Tunbridge Wells; Costello; 1984. Pp xiii, 293.
19. Kimball, W.F. (ed.). *Churchill & Roosevelt: the complete correspondence.* Guildford; Princeton UP; 1984. 3 vols; pp clxiv, 674, 742, 773.
20. Hauser, O. *England und das Dritte Reich, zweiter Band: 1936 bis 1938.* Göttingen; Muster-Schmidt; 1982. Pp 415.
21. Fleay, C.; Saunders, M.L. 'The Labour Spain Committee: Labour party policy and the Spanish civil war', *Historical J*. 28 (1985), 187-97.
22. Hirschfeld, G. (ed.). *Exile in Great Britain: refugees from Hitler's Germany.* Leamington Spa; Berg; 1984. Pp 314.
23. Carsten, F.L. 'German refugees in Great Britain, 1933-1945', Id22, 11-28.
24. Fox, J.P. 'Nazi Germany and German emigration to Great Britain', Id22, 29-62.
25. Wasserstein, B. 'The British government and the German immigration, 1933-1945', Id22, 63-81.
26. Glees, A. 'The German political exile in London, 1939-1945', Id22, 83-99.
27. Kettenacker, L. 'The influence of German refugees on British war aims', Id22, 101-28.
28. Pütter, C. 'German refugees and British propaganda', Id22, 129-61.
29. Tinker, H. (ed.). *Burma: the struggle for independence 1944-1948: documents from official and private sources: Vol. 2: From general strike to independence, 31 Aug. 1946 to 4 Jan. 1948.* London; H.M.S.O.; 1984. Pp cxi, 947.
30. Butler, R.; Pelly, M.E. (eds.). *Documents on British policy overseas: ser. 1, vol. 1: The conference at Potsdam, July-August 1945.* London; H.M.S.O.; 1984. Pp cvii, 1278.
31. Bullen, R.; Pelly, M.E. (eds.). *Documents on British policy overseas: ser. 1, vol. 2: conferences and conversations 1945: London, Washington and Moscow.* London; H.M.S.O.; 1985. Pp 951.
32. Porter, B. 'Britain and the Middle East in the Great War', Ii27, 159-74.
33. Young, J.W. 'Churchill's "no" to Europe ... 1951-1952', *Historical J*. 28 (1985), 923-37.
34. Polonsky, A.B. 'Polish failure in wartime London: attempts to forge a European alliance, 1940-44', *International HR* 7 (1985), 576-91.
35. Kimball, W.F. 'Naked versus right: Roosevelt, Churchill, and eastern Europe from TOLSTOY to Yalta — and a little beyond', *Diplomatic History* 9 (1985), 1-24.
36. Dilks, D. *Three visitors to Canada: Stanley Baldwin, Neville Chamberlain and Winston Churchill.* London; Canada House Lecture Ser. 28; 1985. Pp 31.
37. Richter, H. *British intervention in Greece: from Varkiza to civil war,*

Feb. 1945 to Aug. 1946. London; Merlin; 1985. Pp xii, 573.

38. Durham, M. 'British revolutionaries and the suppression of the Left in Lenin's Russia, 1918-1924', *J. of Contemporary History* 20 (1985), 203-19.

39. Deli, P. 'The image of the Russian purges in the Daily Herald and the New Statesman', ibid. 261-82.

40. Ben-Israel, H. 'Cross purposes: British reactions to the German Anti-Nazi opposition', ibid. 423-38.

41. Merrick, R. 'The Russia committee of the British Foreign Office and the Cold War, 1946-47', ibid. 453-68.

42. Singh, A.I. 'Keeping India in the Commonwealth: British political and military aims, 1947-49', ibid. 469-81.

43. Fyrth, J. (ed.). *Britain, Fascism and the Popular Front.* London; Laurence & Wishart; 1985. Pp 261.

44. Fyrth, J. 'Introduction: in the Thirties', Id43, 9-29.

45. Atienza, T. 'What the papers said', Id43, 55-73.

46. Branson, N. 'Myths from Right and Left', Id43, 115-30.

47. Bruley, S. 'Women against war: Communism, Fascism and the People's Front', Id43, 131-56.

48. Prazmowska, A.J. 'The Eastern front and the British guarantee to Poland of March 1939', *European History Quarterly* 14 (1984), 183-209.

49. Greenwood, S. 'Ernest Bevin, France and "Western Union": August 1945-February 1946', ibid. 319-37.

50. Alpert, M. 'Humanitarianism and politics in the British response to the Spanish Civil War, 1936-9', ibid. 423-40.

51. Tomlinson, B.R. 'Indo-British relations in the post-colonial era: the sterling balances negotiations, 1947-49', *J. of Imperial & Commonwealth History* 13 (1985), 142-62.

52. Newton, S. 'Britain, the Sterling area and European integration, 1945-50', ibid. 163-82.

53. Smyth, R. 'Britain's African colonies and British propaganda during the Second World War', *J. of Imperial & Commonwealth Studies* 14 (1985), 65-82.

54. Henderson, N. *The Private Office: a personal view of five foreign secretaries.* London; Weidenfeld; 1985. Pp xiv, 138.

55. Lamb, R. *Whitehall madness: the failures to stop the Second World War 1935-45.* London; Buchan & Enright; 1985. Pp 448.

56. Andrew, C. *Secret Service: the making of the British intelligence community.* London; Heinemann; 1985. Pp 516.

57. Wark, W. *The ultimate enemy: British intelligence and Nazi Germany 1933-39.* London; Tauris; 1985. Pp 462.

58. Jones, M. *Failure in Palestine: Britain and United States policy after the Second World War.* London; Mansell; 1985. Pp 350.

59. Lapping, B. *End of Empire.* London; Granada; 1985.

(e) *Religion*

1. Stacpoole, A. 'Anglican/Roman Catholic relations after the Council, 1965-70', *The Month* 267 (1985), 55-62, 91-8.

2. Henry, S.D. 'Scottish Baptists and the First World War', *Baptist Quarterly* 31 (1985), 52-65.
3. Robbins, K. 'Britain, 1940 and "Christian civilization"', Bc3, 279-99.
4. Marson, P.N.; Burcham, W.E. *St. Mary's church, Selly Oak: a history 1933-1983.* Birmingham; the church; 1984. Pp xiv, 106.
5. Manwaring, R. *From controversy to co-existence: evangelicals in the Church of England 1914-1980.* Cambridge UP; 1985. Pp xii, 227.

(f) *Economic Affairs*

1. Garside, W.R.; Hatton, T.J. 'Keynesian policy and British unemployment in the 1930s', *Economic HR* 38 (1985), 83-8.
2. Glynn, S.; Booth, A. 'Building counterfactual pyramids', ibid. 89-94.
3. Rollings, N. 'The "Keynesian revolution" and economic policy-making: a comment', ibid. 95-100.
4. Booth, A. 'The "Keynesian revolution" and economic policy-making: a reply', ibid. 101-06.
5. Negus, G.; Staddon, T. *Aviation in Birmingham.* Leicester; Midland Counties; 1984. Pp 128.
6. Taylor, A.J. '"The pulse of one fraternity": non-unionism in the Yorkshire coalfield, 1931-8', *Soc. for the Study of Labour History* 49 (1984), 46-56.
7. Hession, C.H. *John Maynard Keynes.* London; Collier Macmillan; 1984. Pp xv, 400.
8. Thomas, A. *Leyland heritage.* Feltham; Temple; 1984. Pp 144.
9. Somner, G. *From 70 North to 70 South: a history of the Christian Salvesen fleet.* Edinburgh; Christian Salvesen Ltd; 1984. Pp 142.
10. Brock, W.H.; Meadows, A.J. *The lamp of learning: Taylor & Francis and the development of science publishing.* Basingstoke; Taylor & Francis; n.d. Pp xv, 240.
11. Pope, R.; Hoyle, B. (eds.). *British economic performance, 1880-1980.* London; Croom Helm; 1984. Pp xi, 214.
12. Scott, J.; Griff, C. *Directors of industry: the British corporate network, 1904-1976.* Cambridge; Polity; 1984. Pp 226.
13. Loebl, H. 'Refugee industries in the Special Areas of Britain', Id22, 219-49.
14. Jones, A.E. *Roads & rails of West Yorkshire, 1890-1950.* London; Ian Allan; 1984. Pp 176.
15. Pettigrew, A.M. *The awakening giant: continuity and change in Imperial Chemical Industries.* Oxford; Blackwell; 1985. Pp xxi, 542.
16. Holderness, B.A. *British agriculture since 1945.* Manchester UP; 1985. Pp 185.
17. Davenport-Hines, R.P.T. *Dudley Docker: the life and times of a trade warrier.* Cambridge UP; 1984. Pp xii, 295.
18. Cairncross, A. *Years of recovery: British economic policy, 1945-51.* London; Methuen; 1985. Pp xiv, 527.
19. Jones, M.E.F. 'The regional impact of an overvalued pound in the 1920s', *Economic HR* 2nd ser. 38 (1985), 393-401.
20. Foreman-Peck, J.S. 'Seedcorn or chaff? New firm formation and the performance of the interwar economy', ibid. 402-22.

21. Smithies, E. *The black economy in England since 1914*. Dublin; Gill & Macmillan; 1984. Pp 165.
22. Lewchuk, W. 'The return to capital in the British motor vehicle industry 1896-1939', *Business History* 27 (1985), 3-25.
23. Crompton, G.W. '"Efficient and economical working"? The performance of the railway companies 1923-33', ibid. 222-37.
24. Teichova, A.; Ratcliffe, P. 'British interests in Danube navigation after 1918', ibid. 283 ff.
25. Segreto, L. '"More trouble than profit": Vickers' investments in Italy, 1905-39', ibid. 316-37.
26. Rooth, T. 'Trade agreements and the evolution of British agricultural policy in the 1930s', *Agricultural HR* 33 (1985), 173-90.
27. *Johnsen and Jorgensen 1884-1984*. London; Johnsen & Jorgensen Packaging; 1984. Pp 81.
28. Atterbury, P.; Mackenzie, J. *A golden adventure: the first 50 years of Ultramar*. London; Hurtwood; 1985. Pp 287.
29. Hatton, T.J. *Vacancies and unemployment in the 1920s*. London; Centre for Economic Policy; 1984. Pp ii, 20.
30. Harvey-Bailey, A.; Evans, M. *Rolls-Royce: the pursuit of excellence*. Paulerspury; Royce Memorial Foundation; 1984. Pp 124.
31. Dickinson, M. *Cinema and state: the film industry and the government 1927-84*. London; BFI Publishing; 1985. Pp 280.
32. Fearon, P. 'The growth of aviation in Britain', *J. of Contemporary History* 20 (1985), 21-40.
33. Myerscough, J. 'Airport provision in the inter-war years', ibid. 41-70.
34. *The development of atomic energy 1939-1984: chronology of events*. (2nd edn.). London; UKAEA: 1984. Pp 66.
35. Booth, A.; Pack, M. *Employment, capital and economic policy: Great Britain 1918-1939*. Oxford; Blackwell; 1985. Pp 205.
36. Booth, A. 'Economists and points rationing in the Second World War', *J. of European Economic History* 14 (1985), 299-317.
37. Hatton, T.J. 'The British labour market in the 1920s: a test of the Search-Turnover approach', *Explorations in Economic History* 22 (1985), 257-70.
38. Jones, M.E.F. 'Regional employment multipliers, regional policy, and structural change in interwar Britain', ibid. 417-39.
39. Fuller, K. *Radical aristocrats: London busworkers from the 1880s to the 1980s*. London; Laurence & Wishart; 1985. Pp 256.
40. McBeth, J.S. *British oil policy 1919-1939*. London; Cass; 1985. Pp xvii, 171.
41. Capie, F.; Webber, A. *A survey of estimates of UK money supply and components: 1870-1982*. London; City University; 1984. Pp 52.
42. Pagnamenta, P. *All our working lives*. London; B.B.C.; 1984.

(g) *Social Structure and Population*

1. Berghahn, M. *German-Jewish refugees in England: the ambiguities of assimilation*. London; Macmillan; 1984. Pp ix, 294.
2. Weightman, G.; Humphries, S. *The making of modern London 1914-1939*.

London; Sidgwick & Jackson; 1984. Pp 175.

3. Lane, T. 'Neither officers nor gentlemen' [merchant navy officers], *History Workshop* 19 (1985), 128-43.

4. Mitchell, M. 'The effects of unemployment on the social condition of women and children in the 1930s', ibid. 105-27.

5. Penn, R. *Skilled workers in the class structure.* Cambridge UP; 1985. Pp x, 259.

6. Kölmel, R. 'Problems of settlement: German-Jewish refugees in Scotland', Id22, 251-83.

7. Berghahn, M. 'German Jews in England', Id22, 285-306.

8. Winter, J. 'Army and society: the demographic context', Ii15, 193-210.

9. Marx, R. *La vie quotidienne en Angleterre au temps de l'expérience socialiste (1945-1951).* Paris; Hachette; 1983. Pp 323.

10. Horn, P. *Rural life in England in the First World War.* Dublin; Gill & Macmillan; 1984. Pp 300.

11. Waites, B. 'The government of the home front and the "moral economy of the working-class"', Ii27, 175-94.

12. Deakin, D. (ed.). *Wythenshawe: the story of a garden city: Vol. 2: 1926 to 1984.* Manchester; Northenden Civic Soc.; 1984. Pp xii, 229.

13. *Mortimer between the wars.* Mortimer (Berks.); Mortimer Local History Group; 1984. Pp 72.

14. Thane, P. *Ageing and the economy: historical issues.* London; Centre for Economic Policy and Research; 1984. Pp ii, 22.

15. Summerfield, P. 'Mass-observation: social research or social movement', *J. of Contemporary History* 20 (1985), 439-52.

16. Edgington, M.A. *Bournemouth and the First World War.* Bournemouth; Bournemouth Local Studies; 1985. Pp 90.

17. Munson, J. (ed.). *Echoes of the Great War: the diary of the Reverend Andrew Clark, 1914-1919.* Oxford UP; 1985. Pp xxiii, 304.

18. Costello, J. *Love, sex and war: changing values, 1939-45.* London; Collins; 1985. Pp 384.

19. Waterson, M. *The country house remembered: recollections of life between the wars.* London; Routledge; 1985. Pp 256.

20. Jackson, C. *Who will take our children? The story of the evacuation in Britain 1939-1945.* London; Methuen; 1985. Pp xxi, 217.

21. Aronsfeld, C.C. 'Immigration into Britain: the Germans', *History Today* 35/8 (1985), 8-15.

22. Holmes, C. 'Immigration into Britain: the myth of fairness: racial violence in Britain, 1911-19', *History Today* 35/10 (1985), 41-5.

23. Layton-Henry, Z. 'Immigration into Britain: the New Commonwealth migrants 1945-62', *History Today* 35/12 (1985), 27-32.

24. *York memories: nine first-hand accounts of life in York 1900-1939.* York; York Oral History Project; 1984. Pp 48.

(h) *Social Policy*

1. Whitehead, F. 'The Government Social Survey', Ij4, 83-100.

2. Willmott, P. 'The Institute of Community Studies', Ij4, 137-50.
3. Barlow, K. 'The Peckham experiment', *Medical History* 29 (1985), 264-71.
4. Murie, A. 'The nationalization of housing policy', Ic7, 187-201.
5. Deakin, N. 'Local government and social policy', Ic7, 202-31.
6. Jones, K. *Eileen Younghusband: a biography.* London; Bedford Square Press/NCVO; 1984. Pp iv, 122.
7. Swenarton, M.; Taylor, S. 'The scale and nature of the growth of owner-occupation in Britain between the wars', *Economic HR* 2nd ser. 38 (1985), 373-92.
8. Hall, L.A. '"Somehow very distasteful": doctors, men and social problems between the wars', *J. of Contemporary History* 20 (1985), 553-74.
9. Zamoyska, B. *The Burston rebellion.* London; Ariel/BBC; 1985. Pp 118.
10. Lowe, R. *Conflict and consensus in British industrial relations 1916-1948.* Brighton; Harvester Press Microform; 1985. Pp xiv, 47.

(i) *Naval and Military*

1. Mackesy, P. 'Churchill as chronicler: the Narvik episode 1940', *History Today* 35/3 (1985), 14-20.
2. Jeffery, K. *The British army and the crisis of empire 1918-22.* Manchester UP; 1984. Pp viii, 200.
3. Bowyer, C. *Fighter pilots of the RAF, 1939-1945.* London; Kimber; 1984. Pp 223.
4. Nesbit, R.C. *The strike wings: special anti-shipping squadrons, 1942-1945.* London; Kimber; 1984. Pp 288.
5. Montgomery, B. *Shenton of Singapore: governor and prisoner of war.* London; Leo Cooper with Secker & Warburg; 1984. Pp xviii, 218.
6. Fletcher, D. *Vanguard of victory: the 79th armoured division.* London; H.M.S.O.; 1984. Pp 86.
7. Fletcher, D. *Landships: British tanks in the First World War.* London; H.M.S.O.; 1984. Pp 60.
8. Liddle, P. *The sailors' war 1914-18.* Poole; Blandford; 1985. Pp 224.
9. Barker, R. *Goodnight, sorry for sinking you: the story of the S.S. City of Cairo.* London; Collins; 1984. Pp 251.
10. Jeffery, K. (ed.). *The military correspondence of Field Marshal Sir Henry Wilson 1918-1922.* London; Bodley Head for Army Records Soc.; 1985. Pp xiv, 438.
11. Beckett, I.F.W. 'The Singapore mutiny of February, 1915', *J. of the Soc. for Army Hist. Research* 62 (1984), 132-53.
12. Molony, C.J.C.; Jackson, W.G.F. *The Mediterranean and the Middle East: vol. 4: Victory in the Mediterranean: pt. 1: 1st April to 4th June 1944.* London; H.M.S.O.; 1984. Pp xi, 520.
13. Dewar, M. *Brush fire wars: minor campaigns of the British army since 1945.* London; Hale; 1984. Pp 208.
14. Chamberlain, G. *Airships – Cardington: a history of Cardington airship station and its role in world airship development.* Lavenham; Dalton; 1984. Pp xv, 223.

15. Beckett, I.F.W.; Simpson, K. (eds.). *A nation in arms: a social history of the British army in the first World War*. Manchester UP; 1985. Pp x, 276.
16. Beckett, I. 'The nation in arms, 1914-18', Ii15, 1-36.
17. Spiers, E.M. 'The regular army in 1914', Ii15, 37-62.
18. Simpson, K. 'The officers', Ii15, 63-98.
19. Hughes, C. 'The New Armies', Ii15, 99-126.
20. Beckett, I. 'The Territorial Force', Ii15, 127-64.
21. Simkins, P. 'Soldiers and civilians: billeting in Britain and France', Ii15, 165-92.
22. Jeffery, K. 'The post-war army', Ii15, 211-34.
23. Hackman, W. *Seek and strike: sonar, anti-submarine warfare and the Royal Navy 1914-54*. London; H.M.S.O.; 1984. Pp xxxv, 487.
24. Crawley, A. *Escape from Germany: the methods of escape used by R.A.F. airmen during the Second World War* (2nd edn.). London; H.M.S.O.; 1985. Pp xi, 351.
25. Terraine, J. *The right of the line: the Royal Air Force in the European War, 1939-1945*. London; Hodder & Stoughton; 1985. Pp xix, 841.
26. Warner, P. *Horrocks: the general who led from the front*. London; H. Hamilton; 1984. Pp xi, 195.
27. Liddle, P.H. (ed.). *Home fires and foreign fields: British social and military experience in the First World War*. London; Brassey's Defence; 1985. Pp xiii, 233.
28. Beckett, I. 'The Territorial Force in the Great War', Ii27, 21-38.
29. Terraine, J. 'British military leadership in the First World War', Ii27, 39-52.
30. Smith, M. 'The tactical and strategic application of air power on the Western Front', Ii27, 53-68.
31. Liddle, P. 'The Dardanelles-Gallipoli campaign: concept and execution', Ii27, 101-14.
32. White, C. 'The navy and naval war considered', Ii27, 115-34.
33. Simpson, K. 'The British soldier on the Western Front', Ii27, 135-59.
34. Trythall, T. 'Fuller and the tanks', Ii27, 195-204.
35. Glover, M. *The fight for the Channel ports: Calais to Brest 1940: a study in confusion*. London; Leo Cooper; 1985. Pp xv, 269.
36. Popham, H. *F.A.N.Y.: the story of the Women's Transport Service 1907-1984*. London; Leo Cooper/Secker & Warburg; 1984. Pp xiii, 146.
37. Harfield, A. *Blandford and the military: including the history of Blandford Camp*. Sherborne; Dorest Publishing; 1984. Pp vii, 100.
38. Middlebrook, M.; Everitt, C. *The Bomber Command war diaries: an operational reference book, 1939-1945*. Harmondsworth; Viking; 1985. Pp 804.
39. Longmate, N. *Hitler's rockets: the story of the V-2s*. London; Hutchinson; 1985. Pp 423.
40. Kinsey, G. *Aviation: flight over the Eastern counties since 1937* (2nd edn.). Lavenham; Terence Dalton; 1984. Pp 278.
41. French, D. 'Sir Douglas Haig's reputation, 1918-1928: a note', *Historical J.* 28 (1985), 953-60.

42. Harrison, R.A. 'Testing the water: a secret probe towards Anglo-American military co-operation in 1936', *International HR 7* (1985), 214-34.
43. Englander, D.; Mason, T. *The British soldier in World War II*. Coventry; Univ. of Warwick; 1984. Pp 18.
44. Middleton, D.H. *Test pilots: the story of British test flying 1903-1984*. London; Willow; 1985. Pp 272.
45. Davis, J. 'ATFERO: the Atlantic Ferry organization', *J. of Contemporary History* 20 (1985), 71-97.
46. Reid, B.H. 'T.E. Lawrence and Liddell Hart', *History* 70 (1985), 218-31.
47. Middlebrook, M. *Operation Corporate: the Falklands War 1982*. London; Viking; 1985. Pp 400.

(j) Intellectual and Cultural

1. Kaye, H.J. *The British Marxist historians: an introductory analysis*. Cambridge; Polity; 1984. Pp xii, 316.
2. Vadgama, K. *India in Britain: the Indian contribution to the British way of life*. London; Royce; 1984. Pp 256.
3. Briggs, A. *The BBC: a short history of the first fifty years*. Oxford UP; 1985. Pp xvi, 439.
4. Bulmer, M. (ed.). *Essays on the history of British sociological research*. Cambridge UP; 1985. Pp xiv, 257.
5. Bulmer, M. 'The development of sociology and of empirical sociological research in Britain', Ij4, 3-36.
6. Kent, R. 'The emergence of the sociological survey, 1887-1939', Ij4, 52-69.
7. Selvin, H.C.; Bernert, Z. 'Durkheim, Booth and Yule: the non-diffusion of an intellectual innovation', Ij4, 70-82.
8. Hoinville, G. 'Methodological research on sample surveys: a review of developments in Britain', Ij4, 101-20.
9. Calder, A. 'Mass-observation, 1937-1949', Ij4, 121-36.
10. Halsey, A.H. 'Provincials and professionals: the British post-war sociologists', Ij4, 151-64.
11. Abrams, P. 'The uses of British sociology, 1841-1981', Ij4, 181-205.
12. Keith, S.T. 'Scientists as entrepreneurs: Arthur Tyndall and the rise of Bristol physics', *Annals of Science* 41 (1984), 335-57.
13. Tapsell, M. *Memoirs of Buckinghamshire's picture palaces*. Birmingham; Mercia Cinema Society; 1984. Pp 76.
14. Leventhal, F.M. *The last dissenter: H.N. Brailsford and his world*. Oxford; Clarendon; 1985. Pp x, 326.
15. Willett, J. 'The emigration and the arts', Id22, 195-217.
16. McCulloch, G. '"Teachers and missionaries": the Left Book Club as an educational agency', *History of Education* 14 (1985), 137-53.
17. Rowell, G.; Jackson, A. *The repertory movement: a history of regional theatre in Britain*. Cambridge UP; 1984. Pp ix, 230.
18. Cecil, H. 'The literary legacy of the war: the post-war British war novel: a select bibliography', Ii27, 205-30.

19. Low, R. *The history of the British film 1929-1939*. London; Allen & Unwin; 1985. Pp xv, 452.
20. Quinlan, D. *British sound films: the studio years 1928-1959*. London; Batsford; 1984. Pp 407.
21. Calnon, J. *The Hammersmith 1935-1985: the first 50 years of the Royal Postgraduate Medical School at Hammersmith Hospital*. Lancaster; MTP; 1985. Pp vii, 184.
22. Barlen, M.E.; Stambach, M.P.; Stileman, D.P.C. *Bedford School: and the great fire*. London; Quiller; 1984. Pp 168.
23. Ranger, D. *The Middlesex Hospital Medical School: centenary to sesquicentenary 1935-1985*. London; Hutchinson Benham; 1985. Pp 274.
24. Dickson, T. 'Marxism, nationalism and Scottish history', *J. of Contemporary History* 20 (1985), 323-36.
25. Young, J.D. [Reply to Ij24], ibid. 337-55.
26. Veitch, C. '"Play up! play up! and win the war!" Football, the nation, and the First World War 1914-15', ibid. 363-78.
27. Alban, J.R. (ed.). *The Guildhall, Swansea: essays to commemorate the fiftieth anniversary of its opening*. Swansea; the city; 1985. Pp xi, 114.
28. Heinemann, M. 'The People's Front and the intellectuals', Id43, 157-86.
29. Seymour-Ure, C.; Schoff, J. *David Low*. London; Secker & Warburg; 1985. Pp xii, 180.
30. Hart-Davis, R. (ed.). *Siegfried Sasson: Diaries, 1923-1925*. London; Faber; 1985. Pp 320.
31. Hoch, P.K. 'Immigration into Britain: No Utopia: refugee scholars in Britain', *History Today* 35/11 (1985), 53-6.
32. Carleton, D. *A university for Bristol: an informal history in text and pictures*. Bristol UP; 1984. Pp vii, 152.

J. MEDIEVAL WALES

See also Li3, 10.

(a) *General*

1. Vaughan-Thomas, W. *The history of Wales*. London; Joseph; 1984. Pp 256.
2. Williams, G.A. *When was Wales?* London; Black Raven; 1984. Pp 336.
3. Davies, R.R. 'Henry I and Wales', Bc13, 133-47.

(b) *Politics*

1. Rees, D. *The son of prophecy: Henry Tudor's road to Bosworth*. London; Black Raven Press; 1985. Pp viii, 168.
2. Jones, E.W. *Bosworth Field and its preliminaries: a Welsh retrospect*. Liverpool; Modern Welsh Publications; 1984. Pp 80.

3. Griffiths, R.A.; Thomas, R.S. *The making of the Tudor dynasty.*
Gloucester; Alan Sutton; 1985. Pp xiii, 210.
4. Waters, G. 'Richard III, Wales and the charter to Llandovery', *The
Ricardian* 7/89 (1985), 46-55.

(c) *Constitution, Administration and Law*

1. Siddons, M.P. 'Welsh equestrian seals', *J. of the National Library of Wales*
23/3 (1984), 292-318.

(d) *External Affairs*

1. Davies, A. 'Prince Madoc and the discovery of America in 1477',
Geographical J. 150 (1984), 363-72.

(e) *Religion*

1. Pryce, H. 'Ecclesiastical sanctuary in thirteenth-century Welsh law', *J. of
Legal History* 5/3 (1984), 1-13.
2. Jack, R.I. 'Religious life in a Welsh marcher lordship: the lordship of
Dyffryn Clwyd in the later middle ages', Bc15, 143-57.

(f) *Economic Affairs*

1. Lewis, J.M. 'A medieval brass mortar from South Wales and its affinities',
Antiquaries J. 64 (1984), 326-36.
2. Jones, G.R.J. 'The multiple estate: a model for tracing the interrelation-
ships of society, economy, and habitat', Bc4, 9-41.
3. Jack, R.I. 'The fulling mills of Chirk', *National Library of Wales J.* 23
(1984), 321-8.

(g) *Social Structure and Population*

1. Barrow, J.S. 'Gerald of Wales's great-nephews', *Cambridge Medieval Celtic
Studies* 8 (1984), 101-6.
2. Bartrum, P.C. *Welsh Genealogies: AD 1400-1500.* Aberystwyth; National
Library of Wales; 1983. 18 volumes: vols. 1-10, pp vi, 1776; index vols.
11-18, pp 1842.
3. Jones, G.R.J. 'Forms and patterns of medieval settlement in Welsh Wales',
Bc10, 155-69.
4. Jones, M.L. *Society and settlement in Wales and the Marches, 500 B.C. to
A.D. 1100.* Oxford; B.A.R.; 1984. 2 vols: pp xiii, 475.
5. Aris, M.A. *Settlement history for geographers: the towns and villages of
Gwynedd.* Caernarfon; Gwynedd Archives Service; 1983. Pp 92.
6. Butler, L. 'Planned Anglo-Norman towns in Wales, 950-1250', Lg2,
469-504.

K. SCOTLAND BEFORE THE UNION

See also Fe76; Lg11

(a) *General*

1. Holmes, N.M. McQ. 'A fifteenth-century coin hoard from Leith', *British Numismatic J.* 53 (1984 for 1983), 78-107.
2. Grant, A. *Independence and Nationhood: Scotland 1306-1469*. London; Edward Arnold; 1984. Pp viii, 248.
3. Murray, J.C. 'The Scottish Burgh Survey — a review', *P. of the Soc. of Antiquaries of Scotland* 113 (1984 for 1983), 1-10.
4. Not used.
5. Fenton, A. 'Wheelless transport in northern Scotland', Bc8, 105-23.
6. Ruddock, T. 'Bridges and roads in Scotland, 1400-1750', Bc8, 67-91.
7. Barrow, G.W.S. 'Land routes: the medieval evidence', Bc8, 49-66.
8. Moore, J.N. 'The early printed maps of East Lothian, 1630-1848', *Trans. East Lothian Antiquarian & Field Naturalists' Soc.* 18 (1984), 23-44.
9. Burns, J.H. 'Stands Scotland where it did?' [Review art.], *History* 70 (1985), 46-59.
10. Fenton, A.; Palsson, H. (eds.). *The Northern and Western Isles in the Viking world: survival, continuity and change*. Edinburgh; Donald; 1984. Pp x, 347.
11. *Argyll: an inventory of the monuments: Vol. 5: Islay, Jura, Colonsay and Oronsay*. Edinburgh; Royal Commission on the Ancient and Historical Monuments of Scotland; 1984. Pp xxiv, 373.
12. Friell, J.G.P.; Watson, W.G. (eds.). *Pictish studies: settlement, burial and art in Dark Age Northern Britain*. Oxford; B.A.R. (B.A.R. British ser. 125); 1984. Pp x, 216.
13. Miket, R.; Burgess, C. (eds.). *Between and beyond the walls: essays on the prehistory and history of North Britain in honour of George Jobey*. Edinburgh; Donald; 1984. Pp xii, 424.
14. Truckell, A. 'Some lowland native sites in western Dumfriesshire and Galloway', Ka13, 199-205.
15. Harding, D. 'The function and classification of brochs and duns', Ka13, 206-23.
16. Welfare, H. 'The southern souterrains', Ka13, 305-23.
17. Thomas, C. 'Abercorn and the provincia Pictorum', Ka13, 324-37.
18. Nieke, M.R. 'Settlement patterns in the first millennium A.D.: a case-study of the island of Islay', Ba40, 299-325.
19. Shepherd, I.A.G. 'Pictish settlement problems in north-east Scotland', Ba40, 327-56.

(b) *Politics*

1. Stevenson, D. 'Scotland revisited: the century of the three kingdoms: Scotland 1567-1625', *History Today* 35/3 (1985), 28-33.
2. Watt, W.S. 'George Hay's *Oration* at the purging of King's College, Aberdeen, in 1569: translation', *Northern Scotland* 6 (1985), 91-6.
3. Durkan, J. 'George Hay's Oration ... commentary', ibid. 97-112.
4. Stringer, K.J. *Earl David of Huntingdon 1152-1219: a study in Anglo-Scottish history.* Edinburgh UP; 1985. Pp xi, 347.

(c) *Constitution, Administration and Law*

1. Forte, A.D.M. 'Some aspects of the law of marriage in Scotland: 1500-1700', Bc5, 104-18.
2. Cowan, I.B.; Mackay, P.H.R.; Macquarrie, A. (eds.). *The Knights of St John of Jerusalem in Scotland.* Edinburgh; Clark Constable; 1983. Pp lxxxix, 277.
3. Murdoch, A. 'The advocates, the law and the nation in early modern Scotland', Bc12, 147-63.
4. Barrow, G.W.S. 'The Scots charter', Bc13, 149-64.

(d) *External affairs*

1. Donaldson, G. *The Auld Alliance: the Franco-Scottish connection.* Edinburgh; Saltire Soc. & L'Institut Francais d'Ecosse; 1985. Pp 36.
2. Grant, J.S. *The Gaelic Vikings.* Edinburgh; James Thin; 1984. Pp 172.
3. Goodman, A. 'A letter from an earl of Douglas to a king of Castile', *Scottish Hr* 64 (1985), 68-75.
4. Fellows-Jensen, G. 'Viking settlement in the Northern and Western Isles', Ka10, 148-68.

(e) *Religion*

1. Kyle, R. 'John Knox and apocalyptic thought', *Sixteenth Century Journal* 15 (1984), 449-69.
2. Kyle, R. 'The nature of the church in the thought of John Knox', *Scottish J. of Theology* 37 (1984), 485-501.
3. Bourke, C. 'The hand-bells of the early Scottish church', *P. of the Soc. of Antiquaries of Scotland* 113 (1984 for 1983), 464-68.
4. Dunlop, A.I.; MacLauchlan, D. (eds.) *Calendar of Scottish supplications to Rome: vol. 4: 1433-1447.* Glasgow U.P.; 1983. Pp 394.
5. Edwards, G.P. 'William Elphinston, his college chapel and the second of April', *Aberdeen Univ. Review* 51 (1985), 1-17.

6. Kirk, J. (ed.). *Visitation of the diocese of Dunblane: and other churches 1586-1589*. Edinburgh; Scottish Record Soc. (new ser. 11); 1984. Pp lviii, 115.

7. Adams, D.G. *Celtic and mediaeval religious houses in Angus*. Brechin; Chononry Press; 1984. Pp36.

8. Eldjárn, K. 'Graves and grave goods: survey and evaluation', Ka10, 2-11.

9. Close-Brooks, J. 'Pictish and other burials', Ka12, 87-114.

10. Bigelow, G.F. 'Two kerbed cairns from Sandwick, Unst, Shetland', Ka12, 115-30.

11. Morris, C.D.; Pearson, N.F. 'Burials in Birsay, Orkney', Ka12, 135-44.

12. Stevenson, J.B. 'Garbeg and Whitebridge: two square-barrow cemeteries in Inverness-shire', Ka12, 145-50.

13. Maclagan-Wedderburn, L.M.; Grime, D.M. 'The cairn cemetery at Garbeg, Drumnadrochit', Ka12, 151-68.

14. Fairless, K.J. 'Three religious cults from the northern frontier region', Ka13, 224-42.

(f) *Economic affairs*

1. Pryce-Jones, J.; Parker, R.H. *Accounting in Scotland: a historical bibliography*. (2nd edn.). London; Garland; 1984. Pp x, 107.

2. Whatley, C.A. *That important and necessary article: the salt industry and its trade in Fife and Tayside c. 1570-1850*. Dundee; Abertay Hist. Soc.; 1984. Pp 68.

3. Spence, D. 'Documents illustrative of the long history of coal mining in East Lothian', *Trans. East Lothian Antiquarian & Field Naturalists' Soc.* 18 (1984), 1-4.

4. Scott, W.W. 'Sterling and usual money of Scotland, 1370-1415', *Scottish Economic & Social History* 5 (1985), 4-22.

5. Ritchie, P.R. 'Soapstone quarrying in Viking lands', Ka10, 59-84.

6. Breeze, D.J. 'Demand and supply on the northern frontier', Ka13, 264-86.

7. Casey, J. 'Roman coinage of the fourth century in Scotland', Ka13, 295-304.

(g) *Social Structure and Population*

1. Lynch, M. 'Scotland revisited: the Scottish early modern burgh', *History Today* 35/2 (1985), 10-15.

2. *Links in the chain: Scottish family history resources in Aberdeen City Libraries*. Aberdeen; Aberdeen City Libraries; 1984. Pp 38.

3. Mitchell, A. (ed.) *Pre-1855 gravestone inscriptions in Angus: Vol. 4: Dundee & Broughty Ferry*. Edinburgh; Scottish Genealogy Soc.; 1984. Pp iii, 300.

4. Tyson, E. 'The population of Aberdeenshire, 1695-1755: a new approach', *Northern Scotland* 6 (1985), 113-31.

5. Withers, C.W.J. '"The shifting frontier": the Gaelic-English boundary in the Black Isle, 1698-1881', ibid. 133-55.
6. Houston, R. 'Births and baptisms: Haddington in the mid-seventeenth century', *Trans. East Lothian Antiquarian & Field Naturalists' Soc.* 18 (1984), 43-44.
7. Ralston, I.; Inglis, J. *Foul hordes: the Picts in the north-east and their background*. Aberdeen; University Anthropological Museum; 1984. Pp 64.
8. Anderson, M.A. *Anderson families of Westertown and the north east of Scotland*. Chichester; Phillimore; 1984. Pp xiii, 176.
9. Gelling, P.S. 'The Norse buildings at Skaill, Deerness, Orkney, and their immediate predecessors', Ka10, 12-39.
10. Cant, R.G. 'Settlement, society and church organisation in the Northern Isles', Ka10, 169-79.
11. Ritchie, A. 'An archaeology of the Picts: some current problems', Ka12, 1-6.
12. Alcock, L. 'A survey of Pictish settlement archaeology', Ka12, 7-42.
13. Lane, A. 'Some Pictish problems at Dunadd', Ka12, 43-62.
14. Watkins, T. 'Where were the Picts? An essay in settlement archaeology', Ka12, 63-86.
15. Gillam, J. 'A note on the Numeri Brittonum', Ka13, 238-94.

(h) *Naval and Military*

1. Fojut, N.; Love, P. 'The defences of Dundarg Castle, Aberdeenshire', *P. of the Soc. of Antiquaries of Scotland* 113 (1984 for 1983), 449-56.
2. Furgol, E.M. 'The diary of the Rev. John Lauder of Tynninghame', *Scottish H.R.* 64 (1985), 75-8.
3. Christenson, A.E. 'Boats and boatbuilding in western Norway and the Islands', Ka10, 85-95.

(i) *Intellectual and Cultural*

1. Mason, R.A. 'Scotland revisited: "Scotching the Brut"', *History Today* 35/1 (1985), 26-31.
2. Lyall, R.J. (ed.). *William Lamb: Ane resonyng of ane Scottis and Inglis merchand betuix Rowand and Lionis.* Aberdeen UP; 1985. Ppxxxviii, 196.
3. Houston, R.A. *Scottish literacy and the Scottish identity: illiteracy and society in Scotland and northern England 1600-1800.* Cambridge UP; 1986. Pp xi, 600.
4. Brown, I.G. *Poet and painter: Allen Ramsey father and son 1684-1784.* Edinburgh; National Library of Scotland; 1984. Pp 51.
5. Stokland, B. 'Building traditions in the northern world', Ka10, 96-115.
6. Fenton, A. 'Northern links: continuity and change', Ka10, 129-46.
7. Simpson, J. 'Icelandic-Scottish contacts: Sir William Craigie, Séra Einar Guomandsson and Skotlands Rimur', Ka10, 180-96.

8. Cheape, H. 'Recounting tradition: a critical view of medieval reportage', Ka10, 197-222.
9. Liestol,. A. 'Runes', Ka10, 224-38.
10. Fidjestøl, B. 'Arnórr Joórdarson, skald of the Orkney jarls', Ka10, 239-57.
11. Pálsson, H. 'A florilegium in Norse from medieval Orkney', Ka10, 258-64.
12. MacDonald, D.A. 'The Vikings in oral tradition', Ka10, 265-79.
13. Sigmundsson, S. 'A critical review of the work of Jakob Jakobson and Hugh Marwick', Ka10, 280-91.
14. Nyman, A. 'Faroese folktale traditions', Ka10, 292-336.
15. Gourlay, R. 'A symbol stone and cairn at Watenan, Caithness', Ka12, 131-4.
16. Thomas, C. 'The Pictish Class I symbol stones', Ka12, 169-88.
17. Solly, M.C. 'Zoomorphic design: a new look at Pictish art?', Ka12, 189-210.
18. Ross, A.; Feachem, R. 'Heads baleful and benign', Ka13, 338-52.

(j) *Local History*

1. Callender, R.M.; Macaulay, J. *The ancient metal mines of the Isle of Islay, Argyll*. Sheffield; Northern Mine Research Soc. 1984. Pp 46.
2. Walker, B.; Gauldie, W.S. *Architects and architecture on Tayside*. Dundee; Dundee Institute of Architects; 1984. Pp iii, 206.
3. Spiers, S.M. (ed.) *Monumental inscriptions for Millbrex and Woodhead of Fyvie churchyards*. Aberdeen; Aberdeen & N.E. Scotland Family Hist. Soc.; 1984. Pp 30.
4. Hay, G.; Stell, G. 'Old Bridge, Bridge of Earn, Perthshire: a posthumous account', Bc8, 92-104.
5. Watson, A.; Allan, E. *The place names of Upper Deeside*. Aberdeen UP; 1984. Pp xxvii, 192.
6. Simpson, J.H. 'The origins of Gifford', *Trans. East Lothian Antiquarian & Field Naturalists' Soc.* 18 (1984), 5-22.
7. Martin, A. *Kintyre: the hidden past*. Edinburgh; Donald; 1984. Pp xi, 232.
8. Spiers, S.M. *Monumental inscriptions for Peathill old churchyard*. Aberdeen; Aberdeen & N.E. Scotland Family History Soc.; 1984. Pp 44.
9. Knox, S.A. *The making of the Shetland landscape*. Edinburgh; Donald; 1985. Pp x, 255.
10. Kerr, A.J.C. *Ferniehirst Castle: Scotland's frontier stronghold*. Jedburgh; the author; 1985. Pp 87.
11. Pirie, R.W. *Monumental inscriptions for Strachan churchyard*. Aberdeen; Aberdeen & N.E. Scotland Family History Soc.; 1984. Pp 32.
12. Spiers, S.M. *Monumental inscriptions for Belhelvie churchyard*. Aberdeen; Aberdeen & N.E. Scotland Family History Soc.; 1984. Pp 39.
13. Crawford, B.E. 'Papa Stour: survival, continuity and change in one Shetland island', Ka10, 40-58.
14. Kolsrud, K. 'Fishermen and boats', Ka10, 116-28.

L. IRELAND TO ca. 1640

(a) *General*

1. Nicholls, K. 'The land of the Leinstermen', *Peritia* 3 (1984), 535-58.
2. Connolly, P. 'List of Irish material in the class of Chancery Files (Recorda) (C.260) Public Record Office, London', *Analecta Hibernica* 31 (1984), 3-18.
3. Ellis, S.G. *Tudor Ireland: Crown, community and the conflict of cultures, 1470-1603.* London; Longman; 1985. Pp x, 388.
4. Nicholls, K.W. 'Abstract of Mandeville deeds', *Analecta Hibernica* 32 (1985), 3-26.
5. Nolan, W.; McGrath, T.G. (eds.) *Tipperary: history and society.* Dublin; 1985. Pp xvi, 493.
6. Richter, M. 'The interpretation of medieval Irish history', *Irish Historical Studies* 24 (1985), 289-98.

(b) *Politics*

1. Cunningham, B. 'The Composition of Connacht in the lordships of Clanricarde and Thomond, 1577-1641', *Irish Historical Studies* 24 no. 93 (1984), 1-14.
2. Duffy, P.J. 'The nature of the medieval frontier in Ireland', *Studia Hibernica* 22/23 (1983), 21-38.
3. Empey, C.A. 'The Norman period: 1150-1500', La5, 71-91.
4. Gorman, V. 'Richard, duke of York and the development of an Irish faction', *P. Royal Irish Academy* C 85 (1985), 169-79.
5. Mac Niocaill, G. 'Die politische Szene Irlands im 8. Jahrhundert: Königtum und Herrschaft', Le9, 38-44.
6. Simms, K. *From kings to warlords: the changing political structures of Gaelic Ireland in the later Middle Ages.* (Studies in Celtic history, 7). Woodbridge; Boydell; 1985. Pp 192.
7. Waters, G. 'Richard III and Ireland'. *The Ricardian* 6 (1984), 398-409.

(c) *Constitution, Administration and Law*

1. Brand, P. 'King, church and property: mortmain in the lordship of Ireland', *Peritia* 3 (1984), 481-502.
2. Breatnach, L. 'Canon law and secular law in early Ireland: the significance of *Bretha Nemed*', ibid. 439-59.
3. Ó Corráin, D.; Breatnach, L.; Breen, A. 'The laws of the Irish', ibid. 382-438.
4. Ellis, S.G. 'The Common Bench plea roll of 19 Edward IV (1479-80)', *Analecta Hibernica* 31 (1984), 21-60.

5. McCone, K. 'Notes on the text and authorship of the early Irish bee-laws', Cambridge Medieval Celtic Studies 8 (1984), 45-56.

(d) *External Affairs*

1. Hillgarth, J.N. 'Ireland and Spain in the seventh century', *Peritia* 3 (1984), 1-16.
2. Canny, N. 'Migration and opportunity: Britain, Ireland and the New World', *Irish Economic & Social History* 12 (1985), 7-32.
3. Moisl, H. 'Das Kloster Iona und seine Verbindungen mit dem Kontinent im 7. und 8. Jahrhundert', Le9, 27-37.
4. Ó Cathasaigh, T. 'The Déisi and Dyfed', *Éigse* 20 (1984), 1-33.
5. Schieffer, R. 'Die Iren und Europa im frühen Mittelalter', *Deutsches Archiv für Erforschung des Mittelalters* 40 (1984), 591-605.

(e) *Religion*

1. Doherty, C. 'The basilica in early Ireland', *Peritia* 3 (1984), 303-15.
2. Empey, C.A. 'The sacred and the secular: the Augustinian priory of Kells in Ossory, 1193-1541', *Irish Historical Studies* 24: 94 (1984), 131-51.
3. Manning, C. 'The excavation of the early Christian enclosure of Killederdadrum in Lackenavorna, Co. Tipperary', *P. Royal Irish Academy* (C) 84 (1984), 237-68.
4. MacDonald, A. 'Aspects of the monastery and monastic life in Adomnan's Life of Columba', *Peritia* 3 (1984), 271-302.
5. Sharpe, R. 'Some problems concerning the organization of the Church in early medieval Ireland', ibid. 230-70.
6. Bottigheimer, K. 'The failure of the Reformation in Ireland: une question bien posée', *J. of Ecclesiastical History* 36 (1985), 196-207.
7. Breatnach, P.A. 'Über Beginn und Eigenart der irischen Mission auf dem Kontinent einschliesslich der irischen Missionare in Bayern', Le9, 84-91.
8. Corish, P.J. 'A contemporary account of the martyrdom of Conor O'Devany, OFM, bishop of Down and Connor, and Patrick O'Loughran', *Collectanea Hibernica* 26 (1984), 13-19.
9. Dopsch, H.; Juffinger, R. (eds.). *Virgil von Salzburg, Missionar und Gelehrter.* Salzburg; 1985. Pp 416.
10. Ford, A. *The Protestant Reformation in Ireland, 1590-1641.* (Studies in the intercultural history of Christianity, 34). Frankfurt; Peter Lang; 1985. Pp 316.
11. Haren, M.J. 'Vatican archives *Minutae brevium in forma gratiosa* relating to Clogher diocese', *Clogher Record* 12/1 (1985), 55-77.
12. Hennessey, M. 'Parochial organisation in medieval Tipperary', La5, 60-70.
13. Irwin, L. 'The historiography of the twelfth-century reform', *North Munster Antiquarian J*. 25 (1985 for 1983), 19-29.

14. McGuckin, J.H. 'Aodh Mac Doimhín: clerical advancement in fourteenth century Armagh', *Seanchas Ardmhacha* 11/1 (1983-4), 32-47.
15. Ó Cróinín, D. '"New heresy for old": Pelagianism in Ireland and the papal letter of 640', *Speculum* 60 (1985), 505-16.
16. Ó Raifeartaigh, T. 'St Patrick and the *Defensio*', *Seanchas Ardmhacha* 11/1 (1983-4), 22-31.
17. Ó Fiaich, T. 'Virgils Werdegang in Irland und sein Weg auf dem Kontinent', Le9, 17-26.
18. Ó Riain-Raedel, D. 'Spuren irischer Gebetsverbrüderungen zur Zeit Virgils', Le9, 141-6.
19. Sheehan, A.J. 'An interrogation carried out in Cork in 1600 by the Ecclesiastical High Commission for Recusancy: a document from Laud ms. 612', *Analecta Hibernica* 31 (1984), 61-68.
20. Silke, J.J. 'Some aspects of the Reformation in Armagh province', *Clogher Record* 11/3 (1984), 342-62.
21. Walsh, K. 'The Roman career of John Swayne, archbishop of Armagh 1418-1439: plans for an Irish hospice in Rome', *Seanchas Ardmhacha* 11/1 (1983-4), 1-21.

(f) *Economic Affairs*

1. Gillespie, R. 'Harvest crises in 17th-century Ireland'. *Irish Economic and Social History* 11 (1984), 5-18.
2. Ryan, M.; Ó Floinn, R.; et al. 'Six silver finds of the Viking period from the vicinity of Lough Ennell, Co. Westmeath', *Peritia* 3 (1984), 334-81.
3. Barnard, T.C. 'An Anglo-Irish industrial enterprise: iron-making at Enniscorthy, Co. Wexford, 1657-92', *P. Royal Irish Academy* C 85 (1985), 101-44.
4. Bradley, J. 'The medieval towns of Tipperary', La5, 34-59.
5. Gillespie, R. 'The origins and development of an Ulster urban network, 1600-1641', *Irish Historical Studies* 24 no. 93 (1984), 15-29.
6. Ellis, S.G. 'Ioncam na hÉireann [Irish revenue], 1384-1534', *Studia Hibernica* 22/23 (1983), 39-49.
7. Johnston, J. 'Settlement on a plantation estate: the Balfour rentals of 1632 and 1636', *Clogher Record* 12/1 (1985), 92-109.
8. Lucas, A.T. 'Toghers or causeways: some evidence from archaeological, literary, historical and place-name sources', *P. Royal Irish Academy* C 85 (1985), 37-60.
9. Nicholls, K. 'Gaelic landownership in Tipperary from the surviving Irish deeds', La5, 92-103.

(g) *Social structure and population*

1. Bradley, J. 'Planned Anglo-Norman towns in Ireland', Lg2, 411-67.
2. Clarke, H.B.; Simms, A. (eds.). *The comparative history of urban origins*

in non-Roman Europe: Ireland, Wales, Denmark, Germany, Poland and Russia from the ninth to the thirteenth century. Oxford; B.A.R. (B.A.R. International ser. 255, 2 vols.); 1985. Pp xxxii, 748.

3. Clarke, H. 'The mapping of medieval Dublin: a case-study in thematic cartography', Lg2, 617-43.
4. Cunningham, B.; Gillespie, R. 'The East Ulster bardic family of Ó Gnímh', *Eigse* 20 (1984), 106-14.
5. Doherty, C. 'The monastic town in early medieval Ireland', Lg2, 45-75.
6. Gillespie, R. *Colonial Ulster: the settlement of East Ulster 1600-1641.* Cork UP (for Irish Committee of Historical Sciences); 1985. Pp xiv, 270.
7. Graham, B. 'Anglo-Norman colonization and the size and spread of the colonial town in medieval Ireland', Lg2, 355-71.
8. McCone, K. 'Clones and her neighbours in the early period: hints from some Airgialla saints' lives', *Clogher Record* 11/3 (1984), 305-25.
9. MacNiocaill, G. 'The colonial town in Irish documents', Lg2, 373-8.
10. O'Connor, P.J. 'The Munster plantation era: rebellion, survey and land transfer in north county Kerry', *J. Kerry Arch. Soc.* 15-16 (1982-3), 15-36.
11. Ó Cuív, B. 'The family of Ó Gnímh in Ireland and Scotland: a look at the sources', *Nomina* 8 (1984), 57-71.
12. O'Dowd, M. 'Irish concealed lands papers in the Hastings manuscripts in the Huntington Library, San Marino, California', *Analecta Hibernica* 31 (1984), 69-176.
13. Priestly, E.J. 'An early seventeenth-century map of Baltimore', *J. Cork Hist. & Arch. Soc.* 89 no. 248 (1984), 33-54.
14. Smyth, W. 'Property, patronage and population — reconstructing the human geography of mid-seventeenth century Tipperary', La5, 104-38.
15. Swan, L. 'Monastic proto-towns in early medieval Ireland: the evidence of aerial photography, plan analysis and survey', Lg2, 77-102.
16. Wallace, P. 'The archaeology of Viking Dublin', Lg2, 103-45.
17. Wallace, P. 'The archaeology of Anglo-Norman Dublin', Lg2, 379-410.
18. Briggs, C.S. 'A neglected Viking burial with beads from Kilmainham, Dublin, discovered in 1847', *Medieval Archaeology* 29 (1985), 94-108.

(h) *Naval and Military*

1. Lynch, A. 'Excavations of the medieval town defences at Charlotte's Quay, Limerick', *P. of the Royal Irish Academy* C 84 (1984), 281-331.
2. Appleby, J.C.; O'Dowd, M. 'The Irish admiralty: its organisation and development, c. 1570-1640', *Irish Historical Studies* 24 (1985), 299-326.
3. Frame, R. (ed.). 'Select documents 37: The campaign against the Scots in Munster, 1317', ibid. 361-72.

(i) *Intellectual and Cultural*

1. Breen, A. 'Some seventh-century Hiberno-Latin texts and their relation-ships', *Peritia* 3 (1984), 204-14.

2. De Pontfarcy, Y. 'Le *Tractatus de Purgatorio Sancti Patricii* de H. de Saltrey: sa date et ses sources', ibid. 460-80.

3. Grabowski, K.; Dumville, D. *Chronicles and annals of mediaeval Ireland and Wales: the Clonmacnoise-group texts*. Woodbridge; Boydell Press (Studies in Celtic history, 4); 1984. Pp x, 242.

4. Harrison, K. 'A letter from Rome to the Irish clergy, AD 640', *Peritia* 3 (1984), 222-9.

5. Ní Chatháin, P. 'Bede's Ecclesiastical History in Irish', ibid. 115-30.

6. Ó Cróinín, D. 'Rath Melsigi, Willibrord and the earliest Echternach manuscripts', ibid. 17-49.

7. Picard, J.M. 'Bede, Adomnán and the writing of history', ibid. 50-70.

8. Breatnach, P.A. 'Irish narrative poetry after 1200 A.D.', *Studia Hibernica* 22/23 (1983), 7-20.

9. Byrne, F.J. 'Irland in der europäischen Geisteswelt des 8. Jahrhunderts', Le9, 45-51.

10. Not used.

11. Hamlin, A. 'Die irische Kirche des 8. Jarhhunderts in der Archäologie', Le9, 265-85.

12. Haren, M.J. 'A description of Clogher cathedral in the early sixteenth century', *Clogher Record* 12/1 (1985), 48-54.

13. Leerssen, J. Th. 'Archbishop Ussher and Gaelic culture', *Studia Hibernica* 22/23 (1983), 50-58.

14. Mersmann, W. 'Orientalische Einflüsse auf die insulare Kunst im Zeitalter des hl. Vergil', Le9, 216-28.

15. Murray, H. *Viking and early medieval buildings in Dublin: a study of the buildings excavated under the direction of A.B. Ó Ríordáin in High Street, Winetavern Street and Christchurch Place, Dublin, 1962-63, 1967-76*. Oxford; B.A.R. (British ser. 119); 1983. Pp xv, 215.

16. Ní Chatháin, P. 'Beobachtungen zur irischen und lateinischen Literatur des 8. Jahrhunderts in Irland', Le9, 130-34.

17. Ó Buachalla, B. '*Annála Ríoghachta Éireann* is *Foras Feasa ar Éirinn*: An comhthéacs comhaimseartha' [The *Annals of the Kingdom of Ireland* and (Keating's) *History of Ireland*: the contemporary context], *Studia Hibernica* 22/23 (1983), 59-105.

18. Ó Caithnia, L.P. Apalóga na bhFilí 1200-1650. [*The poets' apologues 1200-1650*]. Dublin; 1984. Pp 239.

19. O'Shea, K. 'A Castleisland inventory, 1590', *J. Kerry Arch. & Hist. Soc.* 15-16 (1982-3), 37-46.

20. Richardson, H. 'Die Kunst in Irland im 8. Jahrhundert', Le9, 185-215.

21. Walsh, K. 'Preaching, pastoral care, and sola scriptura in later medieval Ireland: Richard Fitzralph and the use of the Bible', Bc9, 251-68.

22. Walsh, K. 'Die Naturwissenschaften in Irland zur Zeit des hl. Virgil', Le9, 154-61.

M. IRELAND SINCE ca. 1640

See also Bb137; Ga23, b2, 28, e25.

(a) *General*

1. O'Brien, E. *The Royal College of Surgeons in Ireland: 1784-1984.* Dublin; Eason; 1983. Pp 28.
2. Winstanley, M. *Ireland and the land question 1800-1922.* London; Methuen; 1984. Pp xii, 47.
3. Not used.
4. Keatinge, P. *A singular stance: Irish neutrality in the 1980s.* Dublin; Institute of Public Administration; 1984. Pp x, 162.
5. Colgan, M. 'Prophecy against reason: Ireland and the Apocalypse', *British J. of Eighteenth-Century Studies* 8 (1985), 209-15.
6. Dickel, H. *Die deutsche Aussenpolitik und die irische Frage von 1932 bis 1944* [*German foreign policy and the Irish question 1932-44*]. Wiesbaden: Steiner (Frankfurter historische Abhandlungen 26); 1983. Pp x, 254.
7. Kluge, H.D. *Irland in der deutschen Geschichtswissenschaft, Politik und Propaganda vor 1914 und im ersten Weltkrieg* [*Ireland in German historiography, politics and propaganda before 1914 and during World War I*]. Frankfurt; Paul Lang; 1985. Pp 454.
8. Canning, P. *British policy towards Ireland 1921-1941.* Oxford; Clarendon; 1985. Pp xiii, 360.

(b) *Politics*

1. Knight, D. (ed.). *Cobbett in Ireland: a warning to England.* London; Lawrence & Wishart; 1984. Pp 302.
2. Lowe, J. (ed.). *Letter-book of the earl of Clanricarde: 1643-47.* Dublin; Stationery Office for the Irish Manuscripts Commission; 1983. Pp xlix, 504.
3. Milotte, M. *Communism in modern Ireland: the pursuit of the workers' republic since 1916.* Dublin; Gill & Macmillan; 1984. Pp 326.
4. Belchem, J. 'English working-class radicalism and the Irish, 1815-1850', *Éire-Ireland* 19 (1984), 78-93.
5. Gallagher, T. 'Fianna Fáil and partition 1926-1984', *Éire-Ireland* 20 (1985), 28-57.
6. Trench, C.C. *The great Dan: a biography of Daniel O'Connell.* London; Cape; 1984. Pp xvii, 345.
7. Nowlan, K.B.; O'Connell, M.R. (eds.). *Daniel O'Connell: portrait of a radical.* Belfast; Appletree Press; 1984. Pp 120.
8. Owens, R.C. *Smashing times: a history of the Irish Women's Suffrage Movement 1889-1922.* Dublin; Attic; 1984. Pp 159.

9. O'Flaherty, E. 'The Catholic Convention and Anglo-Irish politics, 1791-3', *Archivium Hibernicum* 40 (1985), 14-34.
10. Newsinger, J. '"In the hunger-cry of the nation's poor is heard the voice of Ireland": Sean O'Casey and politics 1908-1916', *J. of Contemporary History* 20 (1985), 221-40.
11. Thompson, F. 'Attitudes to reform: political parties in Ulster and the Irish land bill of 1881', *Irish Historical Studies* 24 (1985), 327-40.
12. Loughlin, J. 'The Irish Protestant Home Rule Association and nationalist politics, 1886-93', ibid. 341-60.
13. Bartlett, T. 'Select documents 38: Defenders and Defenderism in 1795', ibid. 373-94.
14. Berbig, H.J. 'Oliver Cromwell's Irlandpolitik [Irish policy]', *Archiv für Kulturgeschichte* 66 (1984), 159-73.
15. Farren, S. 'Unionist-protestant reaction to educational reform in Northern Ireland 1923-1930', *History of Education* 14 (1985), 227-36.
16. Ó Cathaoir, B. 'Terence Bellew McManus: Fenian precursor', *Irish Sword* 16/63 (1985), 105-09.

(c) *Constitution, Administration and Law*

1. O'Brien, G. 'The new Poor Law in pre-famine Ireland: a case study', *Irish Economic & Social History* 12 (1985), 33-49.

(d) *External Affairs*

1. Mulloy, S. (ed.). *Franco-Irish correspondence: December 1688 - February 1692. Vol. 1.* Dublin; Stationery Office for the Irish Manuscripts Commission; 1983. Pp xlv, 457.
2. Kiernan, C. (ed.). *Ireland and Australia.* Dublin; Mercier and Radio Telefis Eireann; 1984. Pp 85.
3. Raymond, R.J. 'David Gray, the Aiken mission, and Irish neutrality, 1940-41', *Diplomatic History* 9 (1985), 55-71.

(e) *Religion*

1. Lysaght, M. *Theobald Matthew, OFM (Cap.).* Blackrock; Four Courts Press; 1984. Pp 48.
2. Parkes, S.M. *Kildare Place: the history of the Church of Ireland Training College 1811-1969.* Dublin; CICE; ca 1984. Pp viii, 224.
3. *The notebooks of George Berkeley, Bishop of Cloyne* (tercentenary facsimile B.L. Add. MS. 39305, with postscript by D. Park). Oxford; Alden; 1984. Pp 180 (i.e. 360).
4. [Anon.] *A History of congregations in the Presbyterian church in Ireland 1610-1982.* Belfast; Presbyterian Hist. Soc. of Ireland; 1982. Pp vi, 808.

5. Newman, J. *Maynooth and Victorian Ireland*. Galway; Kenny's; 1983. Pp ii, 268.
6. Clarke, B. 'Joseph Stock and Killala', *Éire-Ireland* 20 (1985), 58-72.
7. Purcell, M. 'Dublin diocesan archives: Murray papers, 5', *Archivium Hibernicum* 40 (1985), 35-114.
8. Munck, R. 'Class and religion in Belfast – a historical perspective', *J. of Contemporary History* 20 (1985), 241-59.

(f) *Economic Affairs*

1. Murphy, A.E. (ed.). *Economists and the Irish economy: from the eighteenth century to the present day*. Blackrock; Irish Academic Press and Hermathena; 1984. Pp 174.
2. Nash, R.C. 'Irish Atlantic trade in the seventeenth and eighteenth centuries', *William and Mary Q.* 42 (1985), 329-56.
3. Vaughan, W.E. *Landlords and tenants in Ireland 1848-1904*. Dublin; Economic & Social History Society of Ireland; 1984. Pp 48.
4. O'Connor, E. 'Active sabotage in industrial conflict, 1917-23', *Irish Economic & Social History* 12 (1985), 50-62.
5. O'Connor, R.; Guiomard, C. 'Agricultural output in the Irish Free State area before and after independence', ibid. 89-97.
6. Solar, P. 'The reconstruction of Irish external trade statistics for the nineteenth century', ibid. 63-78.
7. Smyth, H.P. *The B & I line: a history of the British and Irish Steam Packet Company*. Dublin; Gill & Macmillan; 1984. Pp 246.

(g) *Social Structure and Population*

1. Ellis, P.B. *A history of the Irish working class* (new edn.). London; Pluto; 1985. Pp 372.
2. Gillespie, R. *Colonial Ulster: the settlement of East Ulster 1600-1641*. Cork U.P. for Irish Committee of Hist. Sciences; 1985. Pp xiv, 270.
3. Ó Gráda, C. *Did the Catholics always have larger families?: religion, wealth and fertility in rural Ulster before 1911*. London; Centre for Economic Policy Research; 1984. Pp 25.
4. Ó Gráda, C. 'Did Ulster Catholics always have larger families?' *Irish Economic & Social History* 12 (1985), 79-88.
5. Fitzpatrick, D. *Irish emigration 1801-1921*. Dublin; Economic & Social History Society of Ireland; 1984. Pp 51.
6. Taylor, L.J. 'The priest and the agent: social drama and class consciousness in the west of Ireland', *Comparative Studies in Society & History* 27 (1985), 696-712.
7. Drudy, P.J. (ed.). *The Irish in America: emigration, assimilation and impact*. Cambridge UP (Irish Studies, 4); 1985. Pp ix, 359.

Mh1

(h) *Naval and Military*

1. Browne, J.P. 'Wonderful knowledge: the Ordnance Survey of Ireland', *Eire-Ireland* 20 (1985), 15-27.
2. McDonnell, H. 'Irishmen in the Stuart navy, 1660-90', *Irish Sword* 16/63 (1985), 87-104.
3. Davison, R.S. 'The Belfast Blitz', ibid. 65-83.

(i) *Intellectual and Cultural*

1. O'Donnell, S. *William Rowan Hamilton: portrait of a prodigy.* Dun Laoghaire; Boole Press; 1983. Pp xvi, 224.
2. Campbell, J. *The Irish Impressionists: Irish artists in France and Belgium 1850-1914.* Dublin; National Gallery of Ireland; 1984. Pp 288.
3. Herries Davies, G.L. *Sheets of many colours: the mapping of Ireland's rocks, 1750-1890.* Dublin; Royal Dublin Society; 1983. Pp xiv, 242.
4. Kohfeldt, M.L. *Lady Gregory: the woman behind the Irish renaissance.* London; Deutsch; 1985. Pp xiii, 366.
5. Logan, P. *Medical Dublin.* Belfast; Appletree; 1984. Pp 151.
6. De Courcy, C. *The foundation of the National Gallery of Ireland.* Dublin; The Gallery, 1985. Pp xii, 108.
7. Crookshank, A.O. *Irish sculpture from 1660 to the present day.* Dublin; Department of Foreign Affairs; 1984. Pp 72.
8. Olbricht, K.-H.; Wegener, H.M. *Irish houses; history, architecture, furnishing.* London; Macmillan; 1984. Pp 274.
9. Fraser, M. 'Public building and colonial policy in Dublin, 1760-1800', *Architectural History* 28 (1985), 102-23.
10. Ó Raifeartaigh, T. (ed.). *The Royal Irish Academy: a bicentennial history 1785-1985.* Dublin; The Academy; 1985. Pp ix, 351.
11. McParland, E. *James Gandon – Vitruvius Hibernicus.* London; Zwemmer; 1985. Pp xvi, 224.

(j) *Local History*

1. Roberts, O.T.P. 'The cots of Rosslare Harbour and of Wexford', *Mariner's Mirror* 71 (1985), 13-34.
2. Ferguson, K. *The Irish Driver-Harris Company and electric cable making at New Ross 1934-1984.* Dublin; the Company; 1984. Pp ix, 38.
3. Dunlop, E. *Ballymena Town Hall, 1928: and other aspects of the civic history.* Ballymena; Braid; 1984. Pp vi, 64.
4. Stewart, A.T.Q. *Belfast Royal Academy. The first century, 1785-1885.* Belfast; the Academy; 1985. Pp xii, 132.
5. Clarkson, L.A.; Crawford, E.M. *Ways to wealth: the Cust Family of*

eighteenth-century Armagh. Belfast; Ulster Society for Irish Historical Studies; 1985.

6. Conlon, L. *The heritage of Collon: an outline history of Collon parish 1764-1984.* Ardee; the author; 1984. Pp 87.

INDEXES

AUTHOR INDEX

Abels, R., Db7
Abrams, P., Ij11
Abulafia, A.S., Ee28
Adams, D.G., Ke7
Addison, P., Ia10
Addyman, P.V., Bb3, c1
Adelman, P., Hb4
Adkins, R.A., Df20
Adlard, J., Fk28
Aikman, C.W.M., Gh8
Ainsley, H., Ec12
Airs, M., Fk8
Akrigg, G.P.V., Fb23, 40
Alexander, A., Hb41
Alban, J.R., Ij27
Alcock, L., Kg12
Aldcroft, Derek, Ab20
Alderman, G., Hf46
Alsworth, F.G., Ca25
Alexander, A., Ic10
Alexander, J.W., Ea6
Allan, E., Kj5
Allan, J.P., Bb12
Allan, M.J.B., Fk39
Allason-Jones, L., Ca8, 39
Allen, M., Ca24
Allen, P., Bb104
Allison, K.J. Bb2
Allmand, C.T., Eh1
Alpert, M., Id50
Alsop, J.D., Ff50; Gf18
Amies, M., Gi28
Amussen, S.D., Ba44; Fh12
Anderson, M.A., Kg8
Anderson, R.D., Hi3, 8
Andrew, C., Id10, 56
Andrews, G., Bb6
Andrews, J.F., Fk45
Andrews, K.R., Fd12
Andrus, F.S., Bd14
Anglin, J.P., Fk14

Anthony, K., Hg14
Appleby, J.C., Lk2
Aris, M.A. Jg5
Arnold, M.S., Ec32
Aronsfeld, C.C., Ig21
Arthur, J., Bb124
Ashby, T., Gh17
Ashton, E.T., Ba19
Aslet, Clive, Bb30
Aspinwall, B., Aa7; Gf7; He21
Aston, Margaret, Ee10
Aston, Michael A., Ba39, b54; Df25
Atienza, T., Id45
Atkin, A., Fk16
Atkin, M.A., Bb57
Atkinson, D.W., Fe62
Atmore, A.E., Hd14
Atterbury, P., If28
Austin, David, Ek8, 13
Avery, G., Fa13
Ayerst, D., Ib5
Ayres, J., Ga15

Baer, J.H., Gc3
Baggs, A.P., Fk10
Bagley, J.J., Bb120, d20
Bagnell, P.S., Hf43
Bailey, B., Ab41
Bailey, V., Hg4, h2
Bainbridge, C., Ha3, g6
Baker, J.H., Ec17; Fc21, 26
Baker, J.W., Fe28
Baker, T.F.T., Bb67
Baldwin, D., Eh6
Baldwin, Mark, Aa10; Bc6
Banham, J., Hl9
Banks, Olive, Ab3
Bann, Stephen, Ac2
Bantock, A., Ga1
Bantock, G.H., Hi2
Barber, P.M., Fk12

117

Author Index

Mate, M., Ef10
Mather, F.C., Ge18
Matheson, L.M., Ei16
Mathias, P., Ga12
Matsumura, T., Hf59
Matthews, M.H., Ac10
Matthews, N.L., Fc16
Matthews, V.H., Fe61
Maule, J.P., Bd27
Max, S.M., Hb6
Maxwell, G.S., Ca58, b6, 21
Maxwell, L., Hj14
May, P., Fk42
Mayall, D., Hg19, 23
Mayer, T.F., Fj7
Mayhew, G.J., Fa1
Mayhew, N.J., Ef7
Mayr-Harting, H., Bc13; Ee20
Meadows, A.J., If10
Meaney, A.L., Dc3, 5
Meekings, C.A.F., Ec28
Melrose, E.A., Ac11
Melrose, M., Ab13
Mendelson, S.H., Fk19
Mendilow, J., Hb16, l12
Merrick, R., Id41
Mersmann, W., Li14
Metcalf, D.M., Dd2
Metz, K.H., Fj5; Hk1
Michel, P., Ef5
Michie, R.C., Hf5, 55
Middlebrook, M., Ii38, 47
Middleton, D.H., Ii44
Middleton, R., Gb34
Miket, R., Ca39
Mileham, P.J.R., Hb35
Miles, D., Ca54
Millburn, J.R., Gj13
Miller, C., Hf33
Miller, F.J.W., Hk6
Miller, Joan, Hi19
Miller, John, Fb5, 42
Miller, M.G., Gf21
Millett, B., Aa21
Millett, M., Df21
Millon, D., Ec8
Milotte, M., Mb3

Mingay, K., Ff22
Mitchell, A., Kg3
Mitchell, M., Ig4
Mitchiner, M., Ef8
Mitchison, N., Ia6
Mizon, L., Bb35
Moisl, H., Ld3
Molony, C.J.C., Ii12
Mommsen, W.J., Ac1; Ba10; Hf26
Money, J., Gb8
Montgomery, B., Ii5
Moore, B., Ib37
Moore, D., Ha18
Moore, J.N., Ka8
Moore, R.I., Bc13
Moore, R.J., Hd12
Moran, J.A.H., Ei5
Morgan, D., Ed2
Morgan, G., Hb36
Morgan, K., Gd4
Morgan, P.B., Hg26
Morgan, V., Fc17
Morley, C.W., Hi5
Mor-O'Brien, A., Ib29
Morrill, J.S., Aa1; Fe47, g23
Morris, C.D., Ke11
Morris, D., Hb37
Morris, J., Ea2
Morris, R.K., Ba31
Morrison-Low, A.D., Gj10
Morton, A., Aa24
Moss, M., Ac6
Muir, R., Da11
Mukherjee, R., Gd3
Mullett, M.A., Fb34
Mullett, Michael, Ge7
Mullins, E.L.C., Hb40
Mulloy, S. (ed.), Md1
Munck, R., Me8
Munson, J., Ig17
Munting, R., Hf101
Murdin, L., Fk30
Murdoch, A., Gh10; Kc3
Murie, A., Ih4
Murphy, A.E., Mf1
Murphy, Martin, He9
Murphy, Michael, Fk35

133

Author Index

Author Index

Author Index

SUBJECT INDEX

Subject Index

Bermuda, Fd18
Best, Henry, Ff47
Beverley, (Yorks.), Gi1
Bevin, Ernest, Id31, 49, 54
Bible, Ac20, Bc9; Ei11; Fe14, 40, 43;
    Li21; Society, Ge24; Welsh, Fe40
Bibliography, Ha10, l11, 30
Bickham, James, Ge23
Bielby (Yorks.), Cb9
Bignold, Samuel, Hf92; Thomas, Hf92
Billeting, Ii21
Bill of Rights, Fc6
Bingham, Joseph, Fe57
Biography, Ha12, j11, l13; Lg8
Birmingham (Warw.), Bb44, d3; Hb43,
    f20, 73, g23; ie4, f5, 17; bishop of,
    see Gore
Bishops, Bb139; Fb21, e74, g12;
    registers of, Ee4, 49
Bishops Stortford, Bb88
Bishopwearmouth, (Co. Durham),
    Ga11
'Black Death', Eg1; and see Plague
Black Isle, Kg5
Blackloist, Fe34
'Black market', If21
Blandford (Dorset), Fg9; Ii37
Blenheim (Oxon.), Bd16; Fk12
Blitz, The, Mh3
Bloxwich, (Staffs.), Gg11
Boarstall (Bucks.), Bb53
Boatmen, boats, Bb111; Gg13; Hj9;
    Kh3
Bohemia, Ej8
Boleyn, Anne, Fa5, 16, b13, 44
Bolingbroke, earl of, see St. John
Bolsover Castle, (Derbs.), Gi4
Bolton (Lancs.), Fh15
Bone, animal, Bb8; artefacts of, Ca30,
    39, 51
Bookland, Db7
Books, book trade, Aa11; Bc7; De12,
    15; Ei10, 15, 16; Fk50; Gi46; licensing
    of, Fk50
Booth, Abram, Fk7; Charles, Ij7
Bordars, Ek14
Borders, Kj10

Bordesley Abbey (Worcs.), Eb17
Boroughs, Ea25; charters of, Ec11; Fb5;
    and see Burghs; Towns
Boston (Lincs.), Ec14, f18
Bosworth Field (Leics.), battle of, Eb16,
    h5-9, 15; Jb1-3
Botanical evidence, Ca20
Botany, Ha8; and see Herbal,
    Horticulture
Botany Bay (Australia), Gd7
Boundaries, Df3
Bourgchier, Thomas, archbishop of
    Canterbury, Ee41
Bournemouth, Id29
Bouveries, Laurens des, Fe27
Bovium Cb15
Boyer, Abel, Ga21
Boyle, Robert, Fe43
Bracton, treatise known as
    Ec25
Bradford, (Yorks), Hf90
Bradley, F.H., He15
Bradshaw, Henry, Hl11
Brailsford, Henry Noel, Ij14
Braintree (Essex), Ca15
Brakenbury, Sir Robert, Eh8
Brampton (Norfolk), Ca35
Brandon, Charles, duke of Suffolk,
    Fb38
Brasses, memorial, Ej18
Brassington (Derbs.), Bb40
Brathwaite, Richard, Fb1
Braunstone (Leics.), Bd2
Breamore (Hampshire), Df4
Brecon, He12
Brereton, Sir William, Fi1
Bretha Nemed, Lc2
Brewing industry, Ab22; Hf104
Brewster, Sir David, Gj10
Brick-making industry, Ef22
Brick-tiles, Bb126; Gi53
Bridge of Earn (Perthshire), Kj4
Bridges, Ek17; Ka6, 7, j4
Bridport, (Dorset), Fg9
Brigantes, Cb1
Brighton (Sussex), Fa2; Gi10; He5, g5,
    i19

144

Subject Index

Subject Index

Factory: Acts, Hf74-76; inspectorate, Aa26

Fairfax, Sir Thomas, Fb48, i4

Fairies, Fj1

Fairs, Ff16, 35

Falernian wine, Cb13

Falkland Islands, Gd1; Hf96; Ii47

Family, Ba21, 28, 35; Ea11, g12; Fe58, f15, g7, 14, 28, h3; Gg10, 14; Hg9, 11, 18; Ib8; Jgl, 2; Kg2; income, Hf71; proletarian, Ba28; *and see* Households

Famine, *see* Dearth

Far East, Hd13, f69

Farington, Joseph, Gi20

Farming, Ff15, 16, 42; Gf24, g8; If16; books, Ff47

Farms, Fk17, 43, 44

Farningham Hill (Kent), Bb13

Faroes, Ki14

Fascism, Id43-47

Fasting, Fe54

Faversham (Kent), Bb126

Fawkham (Kent), Ej17

Fédon's Rebellion, Gh17

Felley Priory (Notts.), Ee15

Feminism, Ab3; Hf58, g13, k21; Ib11

Fenianism, Mb16

Fenlands, Bb124; Eg19; Fc25, f15, 25, 34, 40

Ferguson, James, Gj13

Ferniehirst Castle, Kj10

Ferrier, James Frederick, Hl33

Fertility, Fh5, 14, 17, 18; Gg17; Hg21; Kg4; Mg3, 4; *and see* Illegitimacy, Pregnancy

Feudalism, Eg22

Fianna Fáil, Mb5

Ficino, Marsilio, Ei2

Field systems, Bb51; Ef16; Ff15; Jg3

Fife, Kf2

Fifth Monarchy Men, Fe25, g23

Figurines, Roman, Ca51, b42

Film: industry, If31; films, Ig19, 20; *and see* Cinema

Finance, Hf31, 66, 103; If12; international, Hf94; local government, Ic14; royal, Ec4, 6; Fc33, f12

Financial policy (in wartime), Id2, 51, 52, f19; *see also* Economic policy

Fire beacons, Gh1

Fires, Fa19; urban, Ba51

First Aid Nursing Yeomanry (FANY), Ii36

Firth, Sir Charles, Ac24

Fisher Theatre Circuit, Gi22

Fisheries, Ef4; inland, Hf65

Fishing industry, Bb9, 134; Fa2; Hf85; If9; Kj14

Fitzgeffrey, Charles, Fk39

Fitzralph, Richard, archbishop of Armagh, Li21

Flanders, Fd4; *see also* Flemings, Fd4

Fleming, Richard (bishop of Lincoln), Ee4

Flaxman, John, Gi19

Fleetwood, Sir William, Fb3

Flemings, Ja3; *and see* Flanders

Foley, B.C., bishop of Lancaster, Bb74

Folklore, Fk53

Folksong, Ba68

Food, Ee37, f12, i4; Fg5; resources, Hf65; riots, Gc5; supply, Ic18, f36

Football, Ij26

Forced Loans, Fb18

Ford, Roman, Ca45

Foreign Office, Hb34; Ib26, c3, d41, 54

Foreign Policy, Gb32; Hb9

Foresters, Ancient Order of, Hg14

Forests, Ff34, 40

Formularies, Ec28

Fortescue, Sir John, Ec26; Fb3

Fortifications, Kh1; Lh1

Fortresses, Roman, Ca34, 37, 44, b29, 30, 34

Forts, Roman, Ca2, b41; *see also* Hillforts

Fox, George, Fe1

Foxe, John, Fe65, 69

Framlingham (Norfolk), Fa18

France, Ac2; Ea7; Fd5, 6, e35, 41;

167